Praise

"Intriguing danger, sharp humor, and plenty of simmering sexual chemistry."

—*Booklist*

"Sweeps readers along at a lively pace in a lusciously spicy romp."

—*Library Journal*

"Amelia Grey's writing style is fresh and expressive, bringing you right into the minds of the characters she so obviously built with love."

—Blog Critics

"Deliciously sensual… storyteller extraordinaire Amelia Grey grabs you by the heart, draws you in and does not let go."

—Romance Junkies

"Bewitching, beguiling and unbelievably funny… Amelia Grey starts off her new trilogy, The Rogues' Dynasty, with an absolutely enchanting and addictive tale."

—Fresh Fiction

Praise for *A Marquis to Marry*

"The second in Grey's elegantly written Rogues' Dynasty Regency trilogy delivers a captivating mix of discreet intrigue and potent passion."

—*Booklist*

"The combination of a gripping plot, scorching love scenes and well drawn characters make this book impossible to put down."

—The Romance Studio

"Grey's latest Rogues' Dynasty story mixes romance with a touch of mystery. Add in lively characters and a strong hero and heroine, and the result is one delightful novel."

—*Romantic Times, 4 Stars*

"*A Marquis to Marry* exemplifies the very essence of what a romance novel should be. It was superbly written and I've added Amelia Grey to my list of top authors. I recommend this book to every romance lover, regardless of their favorite sub-genre…. A happy, witty, feel-good romantic tale."

—Love Romance Passion

"Full of intrigue, suspense and a wonderful romance. Ms. Grey is a wonderful storyteller."

—Anna's Book Blog

Praise for *An Earl to Enchant*

"What a sinfully delicious read... Completely beguiling and never misses a beat."

—Book Junkie

"Another divinely funny and spicy sensual adventure by Ms. Grey... most highly recommended."

—CK2's Kwips and Kritiques

"One of my top pick books of 2010... Unforgettable characters that will leave you speechless."

—Renee's Reads

"A vivid and unforgettable story... The writing is fantastic, and the characters are absolutely wonderful."

—The Long and Short of It

Never a Bride

Amelia Grey

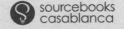
sourcebooks
casablanca

Published by Sourcebooks Casablanca, an imprint of Sourcebooks, Inc.
P.O. Box 4410, Naperville, Illinois 60567-4410
(630) 961-3900
FAX: (630) 961-2168
www.sourcebooks.com

Originally published in 2001 by The Berkley Publishing Group, a
division of Penguin Putnam Inc., New York

Printed and bound in Canada
WC 10 9 8 7 6 5 4 3 2 1

One

WILL THIS BE THE YEAR?

Another Season opens and the patient Miss Mirabella Whittingham begins one more year waiting for her long-absent fiancé to return. One would hope that Viscount Stonehurst would appear this year to claim his bride. Hmm. Lord Stonehurst certainly knows how to keep everyone in the *ton* guessing.

—Lord Truefitt, *Society's Daily Column*

"MIRABELLA, WHAT'S THIS I HEAR ABOUT YOU BEING free with your affections?"

Mirabella Whittingham froze at the sound of her uncle's voice. Heaven have mercy, she was caught. And she'd bet the amethyst earrings she wore that Sir Patrick Stephenson was the young gentleman who'd given her away.

She forced herself to remain calm and formulated a plan to pretend she had no idea what Uncle Archer was talking about. But as sure as she knew her name, she knew what he intended to say.

She wrinkled her nose and tried to come up with an

expedient prevarication to explain her recent actions. Nothing coming to mind, she decided on the truth— at least part of it.

"Now, Uncle. I haven't been free with my affections." In fact, what she was doing would end up costing some young man a great deal when she was through with these London dandies. But her uncle didn't need to know that. "I've only kissed one or two."

As soon as the words were out of her mouth, she realized *truth* hadn't been the way to go. Archer Hornbeck's round face flamed red, and a telltale vein popped out on his wide forehead.

"Blue heavens, Mirabella. I can't have your father or anyone else hear you say something like that, even in jest."

Guilt pricked her. The last thing she wanted was her ill father to know what she was doing. At all costs, she wanted to keep her plans from him. If he found out, she'd never accomplish her goal.

Her uncle's pale blue gaze darted across the empty dance floor, around the perimeter of the great hall and back to Mirabella. He touched her elbow and ushered her to a secluded corner of the brightly lit room. There was no dancing or music at the moment, but it was far from quiet at the party. Dowagers chattering, men chuckling and young ladies laughing behind fluttering fans filled the air around them.

Mirabella had to strain to hear her uncle's whispered voice.

"I'm happy to be your escort while your father is ill, but I cannot allow this sort of behavior."

Indeed Archer Hornbeck was her chaperone for the

Season, but he wasn't her true uncle. He had been her father's friend since Mirabella was a little girl, and had insisted she call him uncle ever since.

He was looking to make a match for himself and often found reasons to excuse himself from her during parties so that he could dance with an eligible young lady or wealthy widow. No doubt her father would be furious to know Uncle Archer had not remained faithful to his duty, but right now it worked to her advantage that he was neglectful.

"I won't have gossip about you making the rounds while you are in my care." Pallor washed his face. "If your father should get wind of this, he would look to me for answers."

"You are a sweet, dear man to worry so about me." She reached out and gingerly patted his forearm.

Archer's expression softened, and he sighed. He took her gloved hand and squeezed her fingers affectionately. Looking down into her eyes, he said, "I'll do anything for you, my lovely Mirabella. That includes stopping scandalous talk. But you must do your part and stop this... this kissing."

Mirabella hated putting him through such an ordeal, but she'd made her choice. She couldn't stop now. Certainly not for fear of scandal. She had been an enigma in Society since she'd made her debut. She attended the parties and balls each Season, but she wasn't eligible to make a match. She had been betrothed for six years to a man she had never met. A man who had made no attempt to marry her despite his promise.

"There's no fear, Uncle. I'm sure the gossip will

pass. It always does. Next week someone else will be on the tips of all the loose tongues."

His thin lips widened into a forced smile. "I must insist that you don't put yourself in a position to catch the attention of the gossipmongers. They can be fierce and unforgiving when given a reason. If any hint of this should hit the Society papers, you'll be ruined. Not even marrying a duke would save you from their scorn."

Mirabella kept a strained smile on her face, too, as she searched for the right thing to say this time. She hadn't made her decision lightly, and she couldn't make any promises. There were only five weeks left of the Season— five weeks in which to carry out her plan.

"You have no cause to fret about me, Uncle." She slipped her hand from his. "This is my fourth and final London Season. By now, I know how these things work."

"If that were the case, you wouldn't allow yourself to be alone with a gentleman."

"I have nothing in common with the young girls making their debuts each year, which is where all the attention will be. All of my friends have married and have babies to occupy their time." She swallowed a sigh. "Given my unfortunate betrothal situation, I've come to accept my fate, so what does a little gossip matter?"

Uncle Archer opened his mouth to speak, but a bevy of young ladies suddenly rushed by them in a flurry of satin skirts. Mirabella noticed that a short, pretty blonde deliberately knocked his arm. When he looked at the young woman, the blonde smiled at him and winked before rushing away with the others. Archer watched her all the way down the corridor until she moved out of sight.

He cleared his throat and said, "There is no such thing as a little gossip. And of course you'll marry someday."

She was thoughtful a moment while she considered his words. "Perhaps when I'm old and gray," she answered, stating almost verbatim what she'd overheard her fiancé say that day so long ago when she was listening outside her father's library. She never saw Viscount Stonehurst's face, but she would never forget the words he spoke.

"Nonsense. Your father told me he sent word to Earl Lockshaven stating that if his errant son doesn't show his face by the last party of this Season he'll consider the engagement broken, and the dowry will have to be repaid. You'll be free to make a match with another young man."

"Oh, Uncle, I am not a fanciful debutante anymore. Who will want me if the man I'm betrothed to won't return to London and marry me? Everyone already looks at me as having been put on the shelf."

"Pure rubbish, my dear girl. With your beauty and your father's wealth any man would want to marry you."

His words reminded her of Sarah and the reason she was having this conversation with her uncle. Her dear friend had had only a very small dowry, no beauty and no offers of marriage. Gentlemen had always confounded Mirabella. Why would they seek beauty and money when looking for a wife and ignore the kind of love and attention Sarah could have given? She would have been a devoted wife and loving mother.

Mirabella turned away from her uncle and looked at the crowd of people gaily dressed in their finest clothes milling about the great hall. Her fiancé perplexed her more than most. She could understand him rejecting her had they met and he had found her unsuitable. But he hadn't broken the engagement, and he hadn't come for her. She had not heard one word from him since he left London six years earlier.

"Should Lord Stonehurst ever return to London, I shall be forced to marry him to please my father, but if he continues to stay away as he pledged he would, I shall be happy to remain an old maid."

"Blue heavens, girl. Your father would never allow you to remain unwed and neither would I. Not marry indeed." Uncle Archer took hold of her upper arm, and she turned to look at him. "I am your father's closest friend. I would marry you before I'd let you be an old spinster." He smiled. "I would consider it an honor."

"An obligation would be more like it. Even if I didn't consider you family, I couldn't take you away from the ladies who are fighting for your attention at all the parties we attend."

"I would be foolish to contemplate a match with another woman if there were any chance I could have you."

There was something too serious about his tone. She stepped away from him and said, "Enough of this talk, Uncle. I need a moment to collect my thoughts before the next dance. Would you please excuse me?"

His thick, gray eyebrows shot up, wrinkling his brow into a deep frown that settled his features in a questioning glare.

"Don't worry. I shall behave," Mirabella quickly said before he had the chance to protest further.

She didn't tell him that she intended to collect her thoughts outside. She wanted to get away from the party, away from the people and the merriment that crackled in the ballroom. She wanted to feel the night air against her skin.

It was well past midnight when she slipped out the side door, having been stopped twice by young men who wanted to remind her that they were on her dance card. She took in a deep breath of air heavy with moisture. A full moon shone down on her from a velvet sky. Scattered mist lingered and wafted across the garden in front of her.

Mirabella gathered up the hem of her skirt and stepped onto the dew-covered lawn. She stayed on the stone walkway that split a lush garden. Her mind swirled with thoughts as she passed through a wooden gate and followed the footpath that led away from the house. Between patches of openings in the tall shrubs and blooming bushes that lined the edge of the road she could see horses and carriages. She heard snatches of muted conversations from the drivers who waited on nearby streets for their employers to call for them.

The smell of tobacco smoke and wet horse hair mingled with the fragrant scent of dampened foliage. Mirabella stayed well away from the wide hedgerow and, not wanting to be seen, stepped noiselessly onto the pebbled path.

Sarah should have been with her tonight. They should have been sharing whispered conversations about the cut of the young gentlemen's hair, or the styles and colors of the young ladies' dresses. Mirabella missed her.

Despite what her uncle had said, she was determined to find the man who had seduced Sarah and caused her death. And if kissing the dandies was the only way to get it done, so be it. As far as Mirabella was concerned, kissing was far overrated anyway. The pressing of dry lips upon hers left her cold and uninspired. She certainly hadn't felt any of the warm, tingling feelings or breathless sensations she'd heard other young ladies whisper about in the retiring rooms.

Taking her time, Mirabella had carefully and accurately made a list of all the young bachelors Sarah had danced with more than once last Season who fit the description Mirabella had read in Sarah's diary. That had been a wearisome task, which would have been impossible had Sarah not kept her dance cards that listed each gentleman. At any given party there were never more than two or three names written down.

One by one, Mirabella was allowing each young gentleman to take her into the garden for short interludes. While he kissed her, she would carefully brush her hand along his neck, letting her little finger quickly slip beneath his neckcloth in search of a wide, raised scar. That was the main clue she had to the despicable man's identity. When she didn't find the scar, she would just as quickly disentangle herself from the man and make her way back inside. The men rarely knew what had hit them since it happened so fast.

Perfunctory kissing had proven to be the only foolproof way Mirabella had come up with to get close enough to determine if a man had the scar. She had tried searching their necks while dancing, but it was impossible with the high collars and wide, fancy cravats and neckcloths covering the very area she needed to inspect.

Her plan had been progressing very well until tonight. All the young gentlemen she'd encouraged throughout the Season had been easy to manage. Some had even been polite and apologetic, but earlier in the evening Sir Patrick Stephenson had lived up to his brash reputation. After she determined he didn't have a scar, he had refused to let go of her. She shuddered remembering how tightly he held her, laughing and forcing her to remain in his arms while he kissed her cheeks, her neck and behind her ear. She was sure she'd still be fighting off his advances if they hadn't heard someone approaching the secluded garden nook where they stood.

She hadn't decided on this course lightly. When the idea first came to her, she had rejected it completely. But she hadn't been able to keep the possibility of it from drifting back into her mind. It had consumed her for more than two weeks before she'd made her decision to proceed. She'd labored over all the possible consequences. The price for success would be high.

Mirabella knew she would be talked about and possibly shunned if word got out, but she hadn't expected the gossip to start so early in the Season. The truth was, she had never been known for agreeing with what Society thought was of the utmost importance:

parties, beauty, the latest fashions and whom to marry. Not to mention one's reputation. She grimaced at the thought. Her main concern was to keep her father from finding out what she was doing. She didn't want to cause him undue distress in his weak condition.

But no matter, she had gone too far to turn back now. She had made it through the easy part of her list. The rest of the gentlemen would be more difficult if Sir Patrick Stephenson was any indication of how the older bachelors behaved. In future encounters she would be more careful.

The distant sound of carriage wheels clanking over rough ground caused Mirabella to stop and look around. With a start, she realized she'd been so deep in thought that she had made her way past the back garden and had ended up on the street behind the house. Rows of high town houses and tall shrubs lined each side of the road.

She was without her velvet pelisse and the damp nighttime air penetrated the thin layer of lavender skirt and shift she wore, making her shiver. Her satin party slippers were wet from the dew-soaked grass. Thankfully, her gloves covered her arms all the way up to the capped sleeves of her gown.

Just as she turned to head back the way she came, a voice out of the darkness stopped her.

"Miss? Are you all right?"

Mirabella spun and looked up into eyes the color of shiny chestnuts sparkling from a handsome face. She hadn't heard the man approach. Quickly she looked him over from head to toe to assess whether she was in immediate danger. He was tall and expensively dressed in a gray suit of lightweight wool. His starched neckcloth was simply but expertly tied. His unfashionably long, brown hair was brushed away from his face exposing a broad brow. A well-defined jaw-line accentuated a square chin. She guessed his age to be near thirty.

"I didn't mean to startle you," he said, when she didn't answer. "Are you out here alone?"

From all she could gather, it appeared he was a gentleman, not a marauder.

"No. I mean, yes." Merciful heavens! She was sounding like she had an affliction.

"Which is it?" he asked.

There was an expression of concern on his features. She had never been any good at lying, and obviously tonight was no exception. "That is, I meant to say, I'm alone right now but I won't be shortly." *As soon as I can get back to the party.*

Mirabella quickly glanced back, but the house was concealed by a tall yew hedge. The street was lighted by moonlight, and there wasn't a carriage or another person in sight. She was alone—with this persistent stranger. She should have been frightened, but she only felt a shiver of awareness.

His shapely dark eyebrows formed a curious expression. "I see. Are you waiting for someone to join you?"

In the bright moonlight she saw that his face was a golden shade of tan. Sun lines creased the corners of his eyes. His mouth was boldly masculine with full, well-defined lips. He was broadly built with wide shoulders and chest, yet his waist and hips were attractively trim.

Feeling more at ease, she met his gaze comfortably and said, "No. The truth is I was attending a soiree not far from here and decided to get away by myself for a few minutes. I walked farther than I intended and I certainly didn't expect to meet anyone out here at this hour."

"I should think not."

He regarded her a moment longer and nodded his head in understanding, though Mirabella knew he was thinking that no properly brought up young lady should ever wander away from anywhere without a chaperone. And he was right. But being *proper* had become less of a concern for her recently.

Mirabella realized he was carefully looking her over to decide if she was a lady from polite Society or merely a well-dressed lady of the evening. Heat rose up her neck at his blatant appraisal.

She tilted her nose back a fraction. "I assure you, sir, that this is *not* something I do often."

"In that case, you shouldn't be left alone without a chaperone."

She liked the sound of his voice. It was soothing, comforting in its richness of tone and a bit authoritative. There was no doubt he was British and a member of Polite Society, but she detected a faint American flavor to some of his words. She'd seen that same golden brown color to his skin on some of the visiting Americans she'd encountered in London.

"I'll escort you back to the party," he said.

She blinked. Although she had been doling out kisses like they were sweets, even she recognized that returning to the Talbots' party escorted by a stranger was beyond the pale. She'd have to slip back into the formal garden the way she had stolen out of it, and the sooner the better.

"No, I couldn't let you do that. I arrived here safely and have no doubt I shall return the same. No cause to worry. A short stroll, and I'll be there."

She started to turn away, but he touched her upper arm and she stopped. It was only a feather-light brush of his hand, and it didn't linger, but the contact was enough to send sizzling tingles across her breasts. For reasons she didn't understand, there was something strangely compelling about him, and somehow she knew she was not in any danger from him.

"What kind of gentleman would I be if I allowed you to walk back to the party alone?"

"A perfectly fine one," she insisted.

He smiled. "You're right. I am, which is why I want to make sure you come to no harm. If it will make you more comfortable, I'll flag the next cab that comes along and have you driven there."

Drive her there? Then she realized that he couldn't tell that a party was going on in the house beyond the hedge and gardens. Thank goodness he didn't know where she had come from. The less he knew about her the better. The last thing she needed was another man talking about her impropriety.

"Yes, that's a good idea. I will wait here for a carriage. It's not necessary for you to stay with me." She made a point of looking up one side of the quiet street and down the other before settling her green gaze on his eyes. "I don't see danger lurking around the corner, and I'm not afraid."

He chuckled softly. "I'm sure you're not. But I'm not going to leave you out here alone."

Merciful heavens, why did she have to meet such a gentleman now of all times? What was she to do? He was deliberately not taking her word that she didn't need his help.

"That is kind of you, sir, and I'm most grateful," she said, forcing a smile while trying to keep her tone calm and level. "But I truly don't want to keep you from your plans."

His gaze didn't leave her face. "I've only just returned to London from a long absence, so I don't have anything for you to intrude upon."

A vagrant cloud sailed past the moon and white light from the sphere seemed to wrap around them, making her forget that she didn't know this man, and that she didn't want to know him. Why was she suddenly having these unsettling, womanly feelings?

"In that case, sir, welcome home," she whispered.

The sparkle in his eyes darkened and the corners of his mouth tightened just enough for her to see that something was wrong. Conflicting emotions that flashed across his face made her wonder if he was indeed happy to be back in London. And if not, she couldn't help but wonder why.

"You've been in America," she stated without thinking.

"Yes." He sounded surprised, and his eyes brightened again. His gaze continued to hold softly on her face.

"Each year we have more and more Americans visiting London, and I've become acquainted with some of them. I heard a trace of their accent in your voice. I see their sun in your face." She lowered her gaze to his hands. "The color of your skin. Not many Englishmen have such a golden hue."

"You're very perceptive."

She tilted her chin a little higher. She was intensely aware of everything about him. From his slow, even breaths to the shine on his boots. She didn't know why, but she wanted to drink in every detail of this man.

"It's not a difficult thing to detect when you've spent time with Americans," she offered.

"And you?" His expression took on a thoughtful quality. "It would be my guess that you spend the Season in London and the rest of the year in Kent or some other home, as do most Londoners. Am I right?"

"Yes. We have a home in Kent, but we've spent more than the spring and summer at our town house here in London the past couple of years."

"Why is that? Most people can't wait to retire to their country estates and begin their house parties."

Mirabella looked past him to the rows of streetlamps fading in the thickening mist. She could have easily told this stranger they stayed to be near her father's physician, but she restrained herself from being so intimate with him. It was scandalous that she was talking to him.

Instead she said, "I love London, especially in the winter when the wind has a bite. The commercial district is always so alive with shoppers and businessmen hurrying about their daily duties. The shops are warm and toasty. In the evenings, lamplight glistens off the snow and makes everything so white."

The last trace of concern left his face. "That tells me you like to take walks and tonight was no unusual occurrence."

His smile was so genuine, so charming, that she was enchanted. She returned his smile, liking him more with each passing moment. The warmth she saw in his brown eyes and his caring attitude captivated her.

The clop of hooves on cobblestones and clank of carriage wheels caught her attention and forced her to glance away from his gaze. "Here comes a cab. That didn't take long."

"No, not long enough," he said, his voice a rugged breath of sound.

His words brushed over her, and she was foolishly pleased that he felt the same way she did.

The gentleman stepped forward and held up his hand, signaling the two-wheeled carriage. The driver pulled the horse to a stop in front of them.

He turned back for her. Their gazes held for a long moment, as if neither wanted to break away first. Finally he said, "The address?"

His eyes inspired trust. She wanted to give him her address and her name as well. She wanted to add that she could be free for a ride in Hyde Park tomorrow afternoon, but she couldn't say any of those things to him.

A light breathy feeling fluttered deep in her throat and she softly, reluctantly said, "I can't tell you that."

The corners of his wide mouth lifted in an amused smile. Her heart tripped. For the first time in her life she was attracted to a man. That he was handsome had nothing to do with it. She'd been kissed by handsome men and never felt this way. This man was kind, clever and cared about her welfare.

His smile turned into a devilish grin. "Then how am I to give the driver instructions as to how to get you back to the party?"

Heat flamed in her cheeks for the second time. What a besotted ninny she was to think he wanted to know about her and where she lived. For a moment, the warmth of his smile had her believing he was feeling the same wondrous attraction she felt.

"Yes, of course. Number one hundred and three Ferrington Place."

The gentleman repeated the address for the driver, then opened the door of the cab and turned back to her. "Are you sure you don't want me to accompany you?"

No, I'm not sure. Come with me.

"Quite." She hesitated. "Though, if you'd like to give me an address or your name, my father will see to it that the fare is repaid."

"You wound me. I wouldn't dream of accepting money for helping a lady in distress."

He held out his hand palm up. She paused only for a second before she placed her gloved hand in his. She immediately felt warmth as he closed his fingers around hers. Heat shimmied up her arms, across her chest to flood her neck and face. Her pulse tapped erratically in her ears. For one untamed moment, she felt giddy, and that made Mirabella feel wonderful.

She wanted to toss aside caution and ask this gentleman to ride with her. She wanted to step into the carriage and be cocooned with him in the darkness. She wanted to smile at him, laugh with him, and flirt with him. She didn't want this to be the last time she saw him.

He lightly squeezed her fingers. An exhilarating flame of desire awakened inside her. This was her fourth Season of London's parties and balls. She'd met gentlemen of all ages, all heights and with many different personalities. This was the first man who made her want to dance under the stars and steal kisses in the moonlight.

She gathered her skirt with her free hand and, with his help, stepped into the carriage. She quickly turned back to face him, but slowly let her fingers slide through his as she said softly, "Thank you. I wish I could repay your kindness."

A rakish smile lifted one corner of his mouth. "You can."

An expectant breath caught in her throat. Her heart tripped for the second time. Would he ask for a kiss? No, she couldn't allow it even if he asked. He was a stranger. But kissing gentlemen was exactly what she'd been doing since she devised the scheme to find the man responsible for Sarah's death. Why not kiss one more? She longed to feel his lips on hers and erase all the trite intimacies she'd endured this past week.

"Yes," she managed to say, feeling herself lean forward wanting, needing, already offering her lips.

"Promise me the next time you are at a boring party and want fresh air that you'll ask someone to escort you properly."

Her lashes fluttered. A flush surged in her cheeks once again as she drew back from him. She swallowed a shallow breath. "Of course. You can be sure I'll do that."

A dancing light played in his eyes and twitched the corners of his desirable mouth. "You look, somehow, disappointed."

Now he was the one flirting with her, but she didn't mind. She had always been circumspect when with a gentleman until this year. Now it seemed as if she were casting away all her inhibitions.

Her embarrassment faded and before she could think better of it, she boldly said, "I thought you were going to ask for a kiss as payment for your help."

His eyes flashed with surprise. "As a gentleman, I couldn't." Then his eyes darkened with desire. "But as a man, if I had thought there was any possibility I'd receive one, I would have asked."

Mirabella smiled, confidence filling her. All week she had been kissing gentlemen for whom she had no feelings whatsoever. Now she was going to kiss a man because she wanted to. She bent down and briefly touched her lips to the side of his mouth, lingering only a moment but long enough to catch the masculine scent of him, capture the taste of him. She heard his breath lodge in his throat. It pleased her that she had surprised him.

He reached for her, but she deftly leaned back into the carriage and escaped his grasp. "Thank you again for your help," she said softly and pulled the door shut behind her.

❧

"She allowed me to kiss her."

"Truly? I kissed her, too."

"All I can add is that she is a delicious morsel, and I plan to have a go at walking with her in the garden."

Camden Thurston Brackley, Viscount Stonehurst, sat back in his chair at Jack's Tavern. He couldn't help overhearing the conversation at the next table, but gave it little thought. He had his own kiss on his mind. After walking back to the gentlemen's club and settling into the first chair he found, he had ordered a brandy.

He could still feel the young lady's invitingly tempting lips on the side of his mouth. He had been with his share of women and couldn't understand why this one had affected him more than most. But she had. And he didn't even know her name. Maybe that was part of her allure.

Forcing her from his mind, he turned his attention back to the conversation of three young bucks sitting at a nearby table.

"With our first kiss she was slipping her fingers down my neckcloth, trying to get under my shirt."

"Mine, too!"

"I've not yet had an opportunity to ask her to dance."

"You'll have to get in line. Every chap in Town is trying to get on her dance card in hopes of slipping out into the garden with her."

Camden listened, slightly amused by the boasting. From their conversation it was clear that London Society hadn't changed in the six years he'd been gone. Well, maybe some things. The bachelors seemed younger to him now that he was nearing his thirtieth birthday.

The dim lighting and masculine decor of the taproom hadn't changed over the years. Neither had the heavy smells of liquor and cooked food or the constant drone of hushed conversations and muted laughter coming from the gaming tables in the next room. Many were the times years ago when he would sit in this very club with his friends and discuss the latest debutantes. The ones bold enough to allow kisses were always a favorite topic of conversations.

Camden didn't pity the young lady they were discussing. No doubt she was enjoying the attention and assumed she could still make an acceptable match. He knew from experience that for some women one man just wasn't enough, but only the most desperate of men would offer for a young lady who was so free with her affection.

His thoughts drifted back to the young lady he'd met earlier in the evening. He'd known immediately that she was from quality and money. Although, he had wondered why she was alone on the street. He found it difficult to believe she had wandered so far away from the party simply because she was in need of fresh air.

The invitingly scooped neckline of her silk evening gown showed the pale skin of her chest and the swell of her breasts. He'd had the urge to reach out and glide his fingertips down her cheeks and outline her lips with his thumb. He wanted to reach over and place a kiss in the hollow of her throat.

At first it had struck him that she was running from someone, but he discounted that when he looked into her eyes and saw no fear. They were such a clear shade of green. The color reminded him of the fresh appeal of spring's first leaf. Wispy strands of her dark auburn hair had fallen from the confines of the carefully placed bows and flowers pinned on the top of her head. She was slightly built but taller than most young women—and certainly more daring.

He liked what he saw when he looked at her and what he heard when he spoke to her. She was intelligent, friendly and bold to the point of being careless with her reputation. He liked the way the moonlight shone on her hair and glistened off her beautiful skin. He liked the way she teased him with the brief kiss that had just missed his lips. Had she kissed the corner of his mouth by mistake or design? Did she know that it would intrigue him until he discovered the answer?

He remembered how the limp silk of her dress had molded softly to her rounded breasts. Their fullness barely peeked from beneath the flimsy material. She held herself well with a slight tilt to her chin so she could look into his eyes. At times, he had felt she hadn't wanted to look away—and neither had he.

When she'd reached down and pressed her lips to the side of his mouth, he'd caught a whisper of the scent of a spice. Cinnamon or clove? He wasn't sure, though he was sure that he wanted to see her again and find out. But that was impossible. He was destined for another.

The clink of glasses and good-natured laughter caught Camden's attention. The chaps at the table next to him were on their second round. He had to stop thinking of the young lady who had intrigued him. He couldn't allow himself to continue to dwell on her dreamy eyes, her heart-shaped face or her softly pale skin.

Camden sipped his aged brandy and looked around the dimly lit room, searching for a face he recognized among the members. Surely conversation with an old acquaintance would get his mind off her. If he didn't know better, he'd think he'd been thunderstruck by a woman again, after all these years. And there was no way in hell he would allow that.

He had arrived in Town late in the evening and hadn't wanted to disturb his father's household in the middle of the night, so he had taken a carriage directly to the club his family had been members of since it opened fifty years ago. He knew he would find food, drink and a bed. After securing a room, he decided to go for a brisk walk to purge his senses of the salty sea air that clung to him from the long sea voyage.

His father, Wilson Thurston Brackley, Earl of Lockshaven, had finally gotten his attention by having his mother write a letter and plead with him to come home immediately. She insisted that he had neglected his responsibilities to his family and that as a man of honor he must come home. He hadn't wanted to return. Not yet. He'd needed another year in America to solidify his investments.

But while it had been easy to ignore his father's many appeals for him to claim his bride, he hadn't been able to disregard his mother's pleas that he marry the young lady he'd been betrothed to for six years.

Two

"OH, CAMDEN, THANK GOD YOU'RE HOME." His mother's lips trembled with happiness as he walked into the parlor of his parents' town home. "We've worried so about you, and wondered if you'd ever return." Her pale brown eyes turned misty with tears of relief as he reached her.

"You don't look a day older than when I left, Mama," Camden said. Though he was surprised at how her classic features had aged in the half dozen years he'd been gone. He reached down and kissed her soft, blushing cheek, and gave her a gentle hug before turning to his father.

"It's good to see you, sir." He shook his father's hand and gripped his upper arm affectionately. Camden didn't remember being taller than his father when he left home, but now he saw that he stood at least an inch or two higher than the master of the house. He also noticed his father had streaks of gray in his hair and in the beard he'd grown since Camden last saw him. Maybe he was a little thinner through the shoulders, too.

"It's been a long time, son. Too long. I'd almost given up hope. Welcome home."

"Thank you, sir. Hudson, how are you?" Camden shook hands and briefly hugged his younger brother. "You've grown up."

Shorter than Camden and his father, Hudson was no longer a boy now that he was twenty-one. There was strength in the grip of his hand and hardness in the muscles of his upper arm, but his face was still full of youth and inexperience.

"I've been well, Brother, but I have to agree with Mama. I was beginning to think you had decided not to return to England at all."

"I don't know why you would have worried. London is home, and I promised to return one day."

Camden let his gaze sweep all three family members. Yes, it was relief he read in each face. Had they missed him that much? He watched his mama dab the corners of her eyes and then her nose with an embroidered handkerchief. The ends of the square of cloth were raveling and showing age. His gaze skimmed down her dress. The fabric was faded and stained and hung loosely on her thin frame.

An uneasy feeling stole over Camden. He quickly scanned his father's attire and found it old and worn like his mama's, but that wasn't the case for Hudson. His dark coat, trousers and white shirt looked crisp and new. His parents might be scrimping on their own clothing but they were seeing to it that Hudson was dashing.

"You're here now, dear," his mama said, coming to stand beside him. She wrapped a thin hand around his upper arm. "That's all that matters. And see how you've filled out. But what has happened to your face? It's so dark now. And your skin has so much color to it." She picked up his hands and looked them over.

Camden gave her fingers a gentle squeeze and smiled at her. "It's from working outside in the shipyard, under the hot sun."

She pursed her full lips in a studious way. "Working in the sun?" She waved her hand. "I'm sure I don't want to hear about it."

"Hard work doesn't hurt a man, Mama."

"Well, you don't look natural. I'll ask the apothecary if he has a cream that will help lighten your skin."

Camden chuckled under his breath. He saw no reason to tell his mother that he was the same color all the way down to his waist from working shirtless on the shipyard, or that most of the men who worked beside him looked just like him.

"Don't worry, Mama, I think time will take care of the coloring."

"He even sounds different," Hudson said, looking at their father. "He's picked up more than a different color of skin from his years in America."

"I noticed," his father said, handing a drink to Hudson. "It's clear that the young man who went away is not the one who's returned to us."

"Enough about me," Camden said and accepted the glass of wine his father had poured for him. "Let's sit down. I want to hear about all of you. Letters have been far too infrequent between us."

No one spoke or moved even though he'd invited them to. All eyes were latched on Camden. The quietness stretched and grew. Instinctively he knew something wasn't right, and he suddenly felt uncomfortable.

"You all look well and healthy." He would have liked to say happy but that was one thing he didn't see any trace of on their faces. They looked tense and on edge. "Why don't we sit down," he said again.

His mama quietly headed for her favorite chair by the small Hepplewhite side table. His father took the worn brocade armchair on the other side. Hudson chose to stand behind their mother.

Camden looked around the parlor of the two-story town house as he walked to the thin-striped settee which faced his parents' chairs. All was not right. He immediately noticed the silver tea service was missing from the rosewood pedestal table by the window. The marble-and-gilt clock was gone from the mantel, the seventeenth-century tapestry no longer hung on the wall over the settee and the expensive rug his mother had been so fond of wasn't on the floor.

Suddenly Camden felt a chill in the room even though it was warm for a late spring afternoon. It was clear they had not been living well and were afraid to come right out and tell him. He didn't want to bring up the subject and ask embarrassing questions when he'd been home for less than five minutes.

He placed his untouched drink on the round butler's table in front of him and calmly said, "All right, we'll skip the chitchat. Why doesn't someone tell me why Mama wrote me that I was neglecting my family and my fiancée by not coming home sooner? What dire circumstance has happened to this family that required me to return home immediately?"

"Oh, nothing out of the ordinary, dear," his mother said, leaning forward. "We wanted you to come home because we love you, and we've missed you."

Her tone was sincere. He believed she truly wanted him home because she loved him, but from the chilling atmosphere in the room he knew there had to be something more. Everyone was tense.

"And?" he finally said.

"You belong here," his father said. "It was time for you to come home and marry the lady you promised to wed. Past time."

His father's clipped tone did nothing to ease the tension. "Why?" He looked pointedly at his mother before turning his gaze toward his father. "I allowed you to make the marriage contract for the benefit of this family. There was no time limit put on the date of my return that I'm aware of."

"No." The earl's tone was brusque suddenly. "Surely Miss Whittingham's father didn't expect you to stay away so long. Nor, I assume, did your future bride."

Camden didn't like the sound of the word "bride." When he first left England, he told himself that if he stayed away long enough the young lady would get tired of waiting, find a husband of her choosing and force her father to break the engagement. That never happened. Which led him to believe that his fiancée was not a young lady he needed to rush home to. If she was beautiful or intelligent surely some other man would have been clamoring for her hand long before now.

"I'm quite willing to bow out of this engagement without any consequence if that's what the young lady and her father would like."

"No!" The word echoed throughout the room.

It surprised Camden that his mother, father, and Hudson, who'd just perched on the arm of the small sofa, said "No" at the same time.

"What's going on?" he asked again. "All of you are acting like I'm about to sit on a cushion filled with needles."

"Nothing is wrong," his father said.

"Nothing that your return doesn't take care of," his mother added with a bright smile as she tucked her handkerchief under the sleeve at her wrist.

Camden couldn't let it go. His father had needed money when the marriage contract was arranged, and an uneasy feeling in his stomach had Camden believing that was the case now.

"Sir, just tell me what is going on here," Camden said.

"All right," his father said in an exasperated tone. "Mr. Whittingham threatened terminating the engagement if you didn't return by this Season's end and start making plans for a wedding."

"I've already stated I'm agreeable to letting the young lady out of the engagement."

"We're not," the earl said.

"We need that money from—"

"Norine." Wilson cut off his wife's soft voice, and he gave her a stern warning with his eyes before returning his attention to Camden.

But his mother had already taken the bloom off the rose. He now understood the circumstances and the dire need for him to hurry home. They needed money. His parents wanted to make sure the engagement *wasn't* broken.

"Quite frankly," his father continued, "I had to agree with Whittingham that a wedding was long overdue. I'll send a message to him right away that you are home, and we can start making arrangements immediately."

Camden felt a tightening in his chest. For six years, he'd been his own man. It wasn't going to be easy to walk back into the life his father had laid out for him. His natural inclination was to revolt even though he'd known from childhood that he'd be the ninth Earl of Lockshaven one day.

There was only one good reason for continuing with this arranged marriage, and it was the same reason he'd agreed to the engagement when his father asked him years ago. He didn't know this lady who was to be his bride. They had never met. Therefore, he didn't have an emotional attachment to her. He had no intention of falling in love so why not let his father pick his bride?

He'd given his heart to one lady, and she had betrayed him. He would never be foolish enough to love again. All he needed was someone to share his bed when he so desired, and to give him sons. No doubt one woman could do that as well as another as long as she was respectable.

"Wait," Hudson said with a good-natured smile on his young face. "I have a better idea than simply sending word to her father. Your fiancée has been attending every ball this Season, Camden. She'll surely be at the Worsters' tonight. Come with me. You can observe her from a distance, and when you're ready I will present you to Miss Mirabella Whittingham."

"You've met her?" Camden asked.

"Yes, last Season. I think you are the only one who hasn't met her."

Camden picked up his drink and took a long sip. In his youth such an escapade might have intrigued him. "I'm too old for games."

"Not that old, brother dear." Hudson chuckled. "You can't tell me that the idea of watching your fiancée when she has no idea you are even in the country doesn't hit your fancy."

Hudson was wrong. His idea held no appeal to Camden. The betrothal had been set. In fact, he'd be quite happy if his bride held no attraction to him whatsoever. All of a sudden, sparkling green eyes, strands of auburn hair gently fluttering in the night breeze, moisture-kissed skin and silk molded to breasts that were the perfect size flashed across his mind. He wanted to see *her* again.

"I believe I vowed to never attend another party. My sentiments haven't changed."

"That's ridiculous," Hudson said. "You've come back from America a new man. The past is behind you. Leave it there. Everyone else has forgotten what happened, and so should you. Besides, this will be the perfect time for you to meet Miss Paulette Pemberton."

"Aha, your true reason for wanting me to go with you to the Worsters'."

"I'm afraid I have to agree with Camden," his father said. "I should just send word to Whittingham."

"Surely Camden hasn't lost his sense of adventure. I truly want you to meet your Miss Whittingham. But I would also like for you to meet Miss Pemberton, the beautiful young lady who is trying to steal my heart."

"Hold to it tightly, Brother. You've only one."

Hudson smiled. "A heart was made to give away."

Camden thought that once, too, when he was Hudson's age. "Then why do only the foolish fall in love?"

"No, not the foolish, Camden, the brave. So, will you come with me and surprise your fiancée with an unexpected appearance?"

He looked over at his younger sibling. Camden supposed it would show some amount of courage if he attended a ball or two. Maybe it would be best for the *ton* to know that he was not hiding away from Society the rest of his life because of what happened six years ago. And he had to admit that some part of him wanted the chance to see the sprite he'd met last evening.

"All right. I'll go."

Hudson lifted his glass in salute to Camden. "Good. I knew that sneaking a peek at your fiancée before she knows you have arrived in Town would be too much of a temptation to resist. Do we have your permission, sir?"

"I will agree."

For once Camden thanked God he had a fiancée. If not, he'd be tempted to find out the identity of that intriguing young lady from the previous evening.

❧

Good heavens! Even at three parties a night, Mirabella wasn't sure she could possibly manage to put her finger down the neckcloths of every eligible gentleman Sarah had danced with last Season. Thank goodness Mirabella had narrowed the field by eliminating the tallest men, and she had discounted those who had spent the entire winter away from London.

The task she'd set for herself was enormous. Sarah had left her so little to go on. The second week of the Season would begin tonight and already Mirabella knew she had to come up with some other plan if she was going to succeed in finding the man who had seduced Sarah. She wouldn't rest until she found him and had him branded an outcast by all of Society.

Forcing herself to push all that to the back of her thoughts for the time being, Mirabella knocked lightly on the door frame. "Papa, are you sleeping?"

"No, Mirabella. Come in."

She pushed open the door and walked into the second-story bedroom of their large town house. Bertram Whittingham lay propped up on fluffy pillows, a heavy velvet robe closed snugly around his chest.

Mirabella was always impressed at how her father managed to look distinguished even though he was pale and gaunt. Although he seldom left his room, she insisted that Newton keep his gray hair and beard neatly trimmed and his clothing and bedding changed each day.

She wished she could confide in her father about Sarah's secret, but she couldn't. She knew he wouldn't feel the same way she did about finding out who was responsible for Sarah taking her own life. He would be outraged should he ever find out what Mirabella was doing. It was early evening. Dusk lay on the air outside the window. It was that time of day Mirabella disliked most. Too light for lamps and too late for sunshine.

Mirabella did everything possible to keep her father's bedroom from looking and feeling like a sickroom. She brought in fresh flowers every other day, and she insisted the windows be opened each morning. She wouldn't allow his medicine bottles to be left on the night table by his bed.

"I'm trying to get through the *Times,* but I don't know why I bother. There's seldom anything worth reading in here except the reviews of the latest plays. I always get a chuckle out of those clever writings. When I get better, we're going back to Drury Lane to see another play."

Her spirits lifted. If he was talking of going out, maybe it meant that all the medication he was ingesting was making him better. "That sounds wonderful, Papa. As soon as you're feeling up to it, we'll make plans. Everyone is talking about a new satire that is playing now."

Bertram folded the paper and laid it on top of a stack of other London newspapers. "There's a scandal about the Lord Mayor, and everyone's complaining about the heat when summer is not even upon us yet. I'd much rather read the poetry you write."

She smiled. "But it's not nearly as clever or interesting as what's written in the newsprint. Would you like for me to bring you a book from the library? You've only read that new book of poetry by Lord Byron one time."

He placed his index finger on his closed lips for a moment. "Actually I read it twice before I sent it down to the library."

"You're a sly one," she said, pulling and tugging on the bedcovers, smoothing out every wrinkle. "Shall I bring it up anyway—or something else?"

"No, no. I'll get Newton to bring up something for me later tonight. No need for you to worry with it or with the blankets." He gently pulled the end of the covers out of her grasp.

Mirabella put a mock expression of surprise in her face and placed her hands on her hips. "When would it be a worry for me to do things for you?" She bent and kissed his forehead, then plopped on the edge of his bed and smiled at him. "I do believe you look better today, Papa. You have more color to your cheeks and there is a sparkle in your eyes."

Her father chuckled. "Dear girl, you've said the same thing every evening for the past two months, and I'm still not strong enough to walk down the stairs by myself. Do you ever give up?"

"Never." She smiled at him. "And I say it today and every day because it's true," she insisted, knowing she was fibbing, but it was the only way she knew to keep up his spirits. She was sure he'd be doomed if he ever gave up hope of getting better.

His green eyes glinted mischievously. "Then I must be the healthiest looking sick man in all of London."

Mirabella laughed. "Oh, Papa, I'm so happy when you feel good enough to tease me. You know, I still think one of the things that keeps you so weak is all the medication the doctor gives you."

"Hmm." He fingered his gray beard as he thought about what she'd said. "It is a lot, but I'm sure the man knows what he's doing. He's up on the latest medications. Now, tell me how many parties you attended last night, who you saw and who you danced with."

He always changed the subject whenever she mentioned his illness. She knew he didn't want her to be upset by his declining health, but how could she not be? She loved him. He was all she had now that Sarah was gone and Aunt Helen had left for their country home in Kent.

"Uncle Archer and I attended three parties. We stayed so long I felt quite distressed that I kept him out late." She didn't want to talk about anyone in particular that she'd danced with. The less she told her father about the parties, the better. She didn't want him suspicious of anything.

She would have loved to tell him about the gentleman she met on the street, but she couldn't share that meeting with anyone, not even her trusted maid, Lily. That man had intrigued her so that she hadn't been able to sleep last night for remembering everything they said to each other. Maybe she would have shared it with Sarah were she still here, but no one else.

Mirabella didn't understand the thrilling sensations that had washed over her when the gentleman had smiled at her, when he had touched her hand and when he had looked deeply into her eyes while questioning her about why she was out alone. She would keep those memories for herself and remember how he talked, how he looked, how he smelled, and how he tasted when her lips touched his skin.

"I'm sure the lateness of the hour didn't bother Archer. He's always been something of a night owl."

He placed one finger under her chin. "Tell me. Are you doing all right without Helen in the house?"

"Oh, yes, Papa. I miss her, of course, but I understand why she needed to get away to the country during the Season. I miss Sarah most of all."

"It was absolutely wretched what happened to the poor girl. Dying in her sleep like that while still so young." Her father paused and cupped Mirabella's cheek. "I know how desperately Helen wanted to make a match for her ward and see her happily wed. But with her being so plain, and that problem with her eye, it was almost an impossible task from the beginning."

Mirabella's heart grew heavy. Sarah's appearance belied the sweet, devoted person she was inside. Anger and frustration coiled tightly inside Mirabella, remembering how helpless she'd felt when she'd been told of Sarah's death. If only Sarah had come and talked to her and told her what had happened. Mirabella could have helped her.

In her diary, Sarah had written she was afraid Mirabella's father would throw her out on the street, so she couldn't bring shame to his house if he learned she was with child. Mirabella would have never let her father do that to Sarah. She could have gone to their home in Kent to have her baby, and lived there with her child.

Mirabella's thoughts drifted to the past, to when she was ten and heartbroken because her mother had died of consumption. Her father had asked his maiden sister, Helen, and her ward, Sarah, to come live with them. Sarah was older than Mirabella and had a problem with one of her eyes. The lid drooped to the point of covering her eye. But that didn't keep Sarah from being a wonderful person. Mirabella loved her and always treated her like a sister.

Sarah made her debut two years before Mirabella, but after five London Seasons not one young man had shown an interest in making a match with her. Sarah was doomed to spinsterhood. They both knew it was because of her eye and the fact that she had only a meager dowry.

A month before the Season started, Sarah took a dose of laudanum and went to sleep. She never woke up. Mirabella was horrified and saddened. The physician agreed that Sarah died from a weak heart, so there would be no hint of scandal on the family.

A few days later, Mirabella discovered the truth. While putting away Sarah's things, Mirabella found a diary and discovered that Sarah had been meeting a gentleman late at night whom she called Prince Charming. They became lovers and soon Sarah discovered she was pregnant. When the man refused to marry her, Sarah became despondent and took her life.

The pages in the diary held few clues to the despicable man's identity. Mirabella knew only that he was a well-known, eligible gentleman, shorter than the average man—and he had a wide, raised scar on the right side of his neck just above his collarbone. Sarah had also written that she had danced with him more than once last Season. That information had allowed Mirabella to make a list of possible suspects from Sarah's dance cards.

Mirabella couldn't bear the thought of such an unscrupulous man passing himself off as a gentleman and living the rest of his life without consequences. Keeping this knowledge to herself for fear he'd leave Town should he know anyone was looking for him, she devised a way to find him and discreetly expose him to Society as an unconscionable man. A few chosen words passed around Town would see to it that he would be shunned by every respectable household. Pushy mamas of the *ton* wouldn't allow their innocent daughters near a man who might violate them.

If Sarah hadn't been so desperate for a man's love, Prince Charming would never have succeeded in seducing her. Mirabella never wanted to be in that position. If her fiancé never returned to claim her, so be it. Love couldn't be that important. She was content to live as a spinster in her father's house.

Bertram touched Mirabella's cheek with a cupped hand. "Let's not talk about that anymore. It's too upsetting for you. We have something else to discuss. I've heard nothing from Lord Lockshaven since sending him an ultimatum more than two months ago. I want you to know I'm committed to breaking the engagement if his son hasn't returned by the end of the Season."

Mirabella turned her thoughts from Sarah. "I think our engagement was over before it started, Papa. I never told you, but that day years ago when the earl and his son were here, I was eavesdropping outside the library."

He smiled. "I suspected as much. You were always a bright child, always wanting to know everything that was going on. I never had the heart to reprimand you."

"I heard him say he'd be an old man with gray hair before he returned to claim his bride. I know he meant it, Papa. I never saw his face, but I heard conviction in his voice."

He nodded. "I've come to the same conclusion. That is why we won't wait any longer. I can't wait any longer."

Mirabella's chest tightened with alarm. She knew her father believed his time to be short, but she wouldn't allow herself to agree with him. "Papa, I'm happy here with you. I'm content to be alone. You know I don't want to marry and leave you."

"Poppycock. It's what daughters do."

"Not all young ladies marry."

"All daughters as beautiful as you do. Now, I want to hear no more foolish talk about remaining unwed."

At the sound of a knock, Mirabella turned. Lily stood in the open doorway clutching the hem of her damp apron. Her pristine appearance and chipmunk cheeks always made Mirabella feel like smiling.

"Pardon me, sir."

"Yes, Lily?"

"Miss Bella's wash water is poured." She turned her attention to Mirabella. "I know how you hate for the water to get cold."

"Thank you, Lily."

"You run along and pamper yourself. We've had enough talk for one day. Be sure to come and let me see how lovely you look before you leave."

"I will, Papa." She kissed his cheek, and then left the room.

The last thing Mirabella wanted to do tonight was go to more parties with her uncle. She would much rather have dinner upstairs with her father and later read to him, or play a game of whist, cribbage or speculation unless—unless she could see the handsome man with the shiny brown eyes. She wondered if they would ever meet again.

Mirabella walked into her room and closed the door. She loved her private chamber with its floral-printed walls and luxurious bedcovers. The yellow velvet draperies reminded her of a day filled with sunshine. Her dark wood furniture added a measure of distinction to the feminine decor. She slipped her lace fichu off her shoulders and turned her back to Lily so her maid could unbutton the bodice of her muslin morning gown.

Mirabella chided herself. What did it matter about the stranger? She would never see him again or her phantom fiancé. Sarah had to be her only concern.

"Lily, what are you doing on your day off?" Mirabella asked.

The maid stopped her task and looked around her mistress's shoulder at her. "I don't get in trouble, Miss Bella. You know I'm a good girl."

"Of course I do." Mirabella tried to sound casual. "I wasn't scolding. I was just wondering if you still helped your sister at that *place* down on Fortenberry Street."

Lily went back to work on the buttons. "Hannah Jack's Tavern? Every week. And if my mama, God bless her soul, doesn't quit having babies to feed, I'm likely to be there the rest of my life."

Mirabella slipped her arms out of the long-sleeved bodice and turned for Lily to unlace her corset. "What exactly do you do there?"

"Whatever they tell me to do. I scrub floors, wash dishes, whatever I'm told to do."

"Do you ever see any of the men who go there?"

"Of course I do. It's a place for gentlemen," Lily said, sounding a bit perturbed as she pulled on the strings of the corset, but suddenly stopped. Her hands jerked to her portly hips and her brows drew together in a frown. "Why are you asking me these questions? Are you going to ask me to put on a man's shirt and neckcloth again so you can practice slipping your finger down the collar of the shirt?"

Mirabella felt color rise to her cheeks. Lily had grumbled for days about that; but without practice, how else was Mirabella to learn to check the neck area just above the collarbone quickly? Due to practicing on Lily, Mirabella was quite adept at the task, which saved her valuable time.

"No, of course not."

"You shouldn't be doing things like that, Miss Bella. It's not natural."

"Oh, Lily, don't fret so. I'm merely curious about what happens at a tavern or a gentleman's club, or at a bathhouse."

"Bathhouses? Where did you hear about such?"

"I read everything that comes into this house, and I also listen to the servants talk."

"Proper ladies like you shouldn't be curious about such places. And you shouldn't be wondering how to get your finger down a man's tight neckcloth, either. Are you planning something improper?"

"It wouldn't concern you if I was, but I'm not." *Not right away.* "Now, tell me about when men play billiards and cards at their clubs and in taverns. Do they take off their cravats and collars and get more relaxed?"

Lily didn't take her gaze off Mirabella's face. "Sometimes, but not often."

"Do they look at you when you are there?"

"No. I don't look at them, and they don't look at me."

"How do you know they don't look at you if you don't look at them to see them not looking at you?"

"One, because those are places for gentlemen to act like gentlemen. Two, there are other places for a man to go if he wants to look at servants. Three, the way my upper lip is twisted out of shape no man wants to look at me."

Mirabella smiled affectionately at her portly maid. "I think any man should want to look at you. I think you have a pretty face with lovely eyes."

"Well, you are the only one who thinks that, Miss Bella. And why are you asking me all these questions about clubs and taverns?"

"Merciful heavens, Lily, you have no reason to worry so much about me doing something wrong. I am only trying to learn a few things that you already know. Now, what exactly happens at a bathhouse?"

"I don't know. I can't tell you because I haven't been to one and most women haven't. Now, Miss Bella, we have to stop this kind of talk. It's not proper."

Mirabella stepped out of her shift and drawers and into the warm water, a plan forming in her mind. Maybe going to a bathhouse was beyond the pale even for a female servant, but what about being a male servant in a tavern or a gentleman's club where men felt relaxed and at ease. It seemed to her that it would be a perfect way to see a man's neck and to search for a scar. It would be risky, but certainly not any more risky than allowing gentlemen to take her into the garden for a kiss. She had to consider the idea of posing as a servant and give it careful thought.

This kissing business was getting her nowhere fast.

Three

CANDLELIGHT THREW MILLIONS OF SPARKLES AND glimmers across the crowded room. Camden scanned the faces of women dressed in colorful gowns and skirts that swept across the dance floor. He'd had a moment's hesitation when he first walked through the entrance, but he'd managed to shake free of the past before it had grabbed hold of him. He was going to be all right.

He wasn't really here to let the *ton* know that he was over what had happened six years ago, or to catch his fiancée unaware as Hudson thought. He was searching for the young lady who'd been brave enough to leave a party without a chaperone, talk to a stranger in the dark of night, and kiss the side of his mouth.

Every time she crossed his mind, his heart beat a little faster than normal. She had been so appealing that he hadn't been able to get her out of his thoughts for more than a few minutes at a time.

Camden smiled to himself. He wouldn't have thought it possible, but it was true. He had been seduced.

She was the real reason he was here tonight. No other.

He had always considered himself a man of honor, and duty called. His father was right. It was past time he should have respected the engagement and made his fiancée his bride, but right now he couldn't muster any enthusiasm to wed that young lady. He had wanted to wait until he made enough money in America so that he could be free of his father and the title, if he so chose.

It had been his choice to allow his father to bind him to a woman he'd never met. Having his father pick a bride for him seemed the best way to avoid falling in love, a trap he never wanted to be caught in again. He didn't have a problem with the earl picking his bride, but Camden had wanted to set the time for the marriage. And he'd wanted to wait another year.

Few men fell in love with their wives if they didn't love them before marriage. He was confident he'd never fall in love again. He'd come to know many beautiful women in America, and he hadn't even come close to thinking he was in love with any of them.

But the intriguing lady he'd met last night had certainly caught his attention. He didn't mind being amazed or infatuated with the fairer sex. In fact, the thought of enjoying a woman that much again intrigued him. But once love entered a man's heart, he was committed and bound to drop his guard or act foolishly.

Light from the chandeliers glinted off jewels wrapped around necks, hanging from ears, and adorning the hair of the ladies on the dance floor and those who stood along the perimeter of the ballroom.

"You keep searching the dance floor, Brother. Do you think you'll recognize her?" Hudson asked.

Of course.

He couldn't tell his brother that he wasn't looking for his fiancée.

"No. I'm sure I've never met Miss Whittingham. I was just thinking how much some people have changed while I've been away. I've seen friends and acquaintances who have gained weight, lost hair, married and had sons."

"Dear Camden, are you surprised London didn't stand still waiting for you to return?"

"I had no fear of that, but the debutantes do look younger than they did a few years ago."

"It's you who has gotten older."

Camden let Hudson's comment pass. "What I'm surprised about is that you haven't yet managed to present me to Miss Paulette Pemberton."

Hudson carefully scanned the room before turning back to Camden. "We've only been here five minutes. Miss Pemberton will be here soon, I'm sure. Don't look so intense, Camden. No one but family knows you made a vow not to attend another soiree. And I'm sure everyone is looking at you because you have been gone a long time."

"Knowing that you also think that everyone is staring at me as if I'm a ghost returned from the dead does not help, Brother."

Hudson chuckled. "It's only natural that you will be the center of attention. But hear me well. You won't be disappointed when you see your fiancée. Father did an excellent job in selecting your bride. Miss Mirabella Whittingham is a beautiful lady."

"How lucky for me," he said with no conviction in his voice. He continued to look at the face of every young lady who passed.

"America has changed you, Camden."

"I would think so. They are far less formal than we are, especially when you travel out of the East."

"Dreadful, I'm sure. I hear that outside of Boston, Philadelphia and Baltimore, they are really quite uncivilized."

"I wouldn't go so far as to say that, Hudson. Besides, I rather liked the people in the new country. You should visit there."

"No doubt I will eventually. But something or someone kept you there six years."

'True. One feels freer to plan his own destiny and make his own choices."

"You almost sound wistful, Camden. Tell me, did a young lady catch your eye in America?"

"Several."

Hudson laughed. "You know we all suspected it was a mistress who kept you there so long."

Camden pondered his brother's words. "A mistress to be sure, but not a woman."

If all went well this winter with the shipyard company he worked for in America, by next spring he should be independently wealthy. He had been smart to stay away from indulging in a lavish lifestyle, choosing to live frugally while in America. The money he invested should reward him tenfold with the completion of the new steam engine for ships.

Hudson gave him a queer look. "That sounds intriguing. What do you mean? A mistress but not a woman?"

"Stonehurst, it *is* you. I was told you were back in London, and I didn't believe it. When did you return?"

The familiar voice and the clap on the back of his shoulder brought Camden up short. He turned and faced a man who had been a close friend since boyhood.

Camden grinned. "Albert Farebrother. It's good to see you."

The slim built, sandy-haired man beamed as he pumped Camden's arm and clapped him on the shoulder again. "Have you been back long? Why haven't you come around to see me? You should have let me know."

"Just returned last evening. You remember my younger brother Hudson, don't you?"

"Of course, I remember him." Albert and Hudson greeted each other. Then Albert said to Camden, "Didn't waste any time getting back into the swing of things I see, attending a party your first full day back. Bravo for you. No doubt you want to catch up on everything that has happened."

Camden ignored Albert's comments. "You're looking well, Albert. You haven't changed a dram while I've been away."

"Oh, but I have. My father passed on, and I'm now Earl of Glenbrighton. I married last year and have a son born just months ago—with another babe on the way."

"I'm sorry to say I didn't know about the earl. My condolences, and congratulations on your son. You've been a busy man."

Albert grinned. "I've a legacy to uphold, you know."

"Sounds as if you are well on your way."

"To be sure." Albert hesitated, looked around the room. He leaned in close to Camden and almost whispered, "I hope it wasn't bad news that brought you home after all this time?"

"Not at all."

"Well, I mean, there have been rumors that you wouldn't return, not even to claim your bride."

"Really? With all the *ton* has to talk about, why would I cross anyone's mind? Surely something of magnitude has happened since I've been away. Someone far more worthy of gossip than I am."

Albert straightened and looked from Camden to Hudson. "Well, I'm sure it's—well you've been gone so long. It's the gossip columnists. They never forget anything." He cleared his throat. "Glad to have you back, old chap. Maybe we can meet at White's or one of the other clubs later in the week for a drink and talk over old times."

"We'll do it," Camden answered and watched the new Earl of Glenbrighton walk away. His old friend had seemed uncomfortable and on edge. Intuitively Camden knew Albert was hinting at something he didn't want to come out and say. No doubt it had to do with Camden's past.

He looked beyond the swirling colors of dresses and dinner jackets and focused on the flickering flames of a candle on a gilt wall sconce across the ballroom. Unbidden, the years rolled back to Hortense, his first fiancée, and the last party they had attended in London.

He had been captivated by Hortense the moment he saw her. It was her first Season and every young bachelor sought her attention, plying her with sweets, flowers, and calling on her for rides in the park. But from all appearances she was enchanted only by Camden. They danced at every ball for four weeks before his father agreed he could offer for her hand. She accepted. The engagement was announced and the arrangements were being made by their fathers.

It happened at the last big party of the Season and most everyone who was anyone in the *ton* was in attendance. At half past one there was to be a presentation of a copy of the statue Diana the Huntress in the formal garden. Everyone gathered in the great hall for the exhibition. The draperies were pulled back from the windows, but instead of revealing the statue of the goddess, everyone saw Hortense in the arms of another man—kissing madly.

Someone passing by knocked Camden's arm and brought him out of his reverie. A cold chill of anger shook him. He realized he was standing stiffly and relaxed his shoulders, thankful for whoever had seen fit to walk into him. Blast it! He was over all that. Forgotten! He vowed to never think of it again. Not Hortense or the man who had been with her.

Hudson was having a whispered conversation with a sweet-looking petite blonde standing beside him. They were so engrossed in each other Camden could have sworn that they didn't realize anyone else was in the room. This had to be Miss Pemberton, the young lady who had caught Hudson's heart and wouldn't let go. And from the way she was looking at him, she felt the same way about him.

Clearing his throat, Camden interrupted and said, "I don't believe I've had the pleasure."

"Oh, yes. Camden, may I present Miss Paulette Pemberton. Miss Pemberton, I'd like you to meet my brother, Viscount Stonehurst, who just returned from America."

"It's a pleasure, Miss Pemberton."

"For me, too, Lord Stonehurst. Welcome home."

Camden nodded. "You are as lovely as my brother said you were."

"Thank you. Hudson has often mentioned you, but I was beginning to think you were but a hopeful figment of his imagination. But here you are in the flesh, and almost as dashing as your brother."

She barely glanced his way before returning her gaze back to Hudson and giving him a smile. It was clear the two were smitten with each other. Right now, anyway. Camden knew that could change without a moment's notice.

"Oh, Camden," Hudson said quickly. "Here comes the man who can help us. Mr. Archer Hornbeck is over by the buffet table. He is Miss Whittingham's chaperone for the Season. We have to catch him before he gets away. Miss Pemberton, I hate to rush off when you've only just arrived, but would you please excuse us?"

"I will, although I'm loath to do so." She smiled up at him, her blue eyes sparkling with young love. "You won't miss our dance, will you? Promise?"

He smiled down at her. "Not a chance of it, I assure you. I'll meet you by the punch table as always."

Camden and Hudson strode through the crowd, knocking elbows, brushing against shoulders and rushing greetings and introductions with the people who stopped them along the way.

"You have a special place to meet Miss Pemberton?" Camden asked when they were once again walking side by side.

"If we don't, the dance can be half over before we find each other." Hudson smiled. "I love her, Camden. I want to marry her."

Camden didn't want to see his brother make the mistakes he'd made when he was Hudson's age. No one knew better than Camden the pitfalls of being blinded by love.

"You're too young to know what you want."

"Just because things didn't work out for you when you were younger doesn't mean they won't for me. I know that Miss Pemberton is true to me."

Camden stiffened. "I wasn't aware you knew that much about what happened with Hortense. You were away at school."

"Some stories linger longer than others, as you well know. Lord Glenbrighton was right about the scandal sheets."

"So it was still the talk of the town when you returned home?"

"Maybe it was only because everyone wanted to make sure I knew what had happened to my brother."

"And do you?"

"I know enough to imagine how you felt. Thank God you were in America for so long or the talk might have never died away."

"Gossip seldom tells the truth, Brother."

Hudson stepped in front of Camden and smiled. "Correction. Gossip seldom tells the *whole* truth."

Camden returned the smile. "Perhaps you are wiser than your years."

"Perhaps I am," Hudson said and turned away from Camden and approached a short, balding gentleman. "Mr. Hornbeck, excuse me for interrupting."

"Yes," the sturdily built man turned from the group of men he was talking to and looked squarely at Hudson, then Camden.

It was clear he didn't immediately recognize either man, so Hudson stepped forward and made the introductions.

Camden watched surprise light the man's pale blue eyes. Camden was certain he saw sweat pop out on his balding head while they exchanged polite greetings.

"Ah—I'm afraid I didn't know that you had returned to London, Lord Stonehurst. Does Miss Whittingham and her father know you're here?"

"No, I only arrived late last evening. I spent most of the day catching up with my family."

Mr. Hornbeck blinked rapidly. "I'm sure."

"I've been watching for Miss Whittingham, but haven't seen her," Hudson explained. "Is she here tonight?"

The man looked nervously around the dance floor. "Oh, yes. Indeed she is."

"How fortunate for Camden," Hudson said. "We had hoped she would be, but there was always a chance she had attended another party. Perhaps you could present her to my brother. I was going to do the honors, but so far she has eluded us this evening."

"Yes, yes, she's here, but we haven't been here that long. I'm not sure this is the time or place to... er..." His eyes brightened like blue fire as his gaze continued to scan the dance floor. "Maybe a private meeting between the two of you would be better. Or perhaps her father and the earl would like to be in attendance at the momentous occasion."

"I can't see any reason to stand on ceremony, Mr. Hornbeck," Camden replied. "Since we're both in here, I'd like to meet her."

Archer Hornbeck was stumbling over his words and wringing his hands like a worried mama. Camden wanted to know why his wanting to meet Miss Whittingham had put her uncle on edge. Had everyone assumed he wouldn't return to claim his bride?

"Very well, Lord Stonehurst. I can see you won't be swayed. I will go find her and bring her to you. Shall we meet on the south patio?"

"I'll wait for you there."

Mr. Hornbeck turned away and Camden looked to his brother. "Are you coming with me, Hudson?"

"No. That is, if you don't mind. It's very close to time for the next dance, and I don't want to miss it."

"I understand." Camden gave his brother a knowing smile. "I'll catch up with you later in the evening."

Camden was stopped by two friends and several acquaintances as well as being presented to two debutantes before he was able to break away and make his way to the south patio. His return was fast making its way around the large ballroom. He opened the door that led to the stone patio and walked out. Three couples were there talking quietly. He looked at each of them, hoping to find his mystery lady.

He turned to walk closer to a side door and a flash of something pale in the distance caught his eye. It was a young lady in a white dress wrapped in the arms of a man. His senses heightened. Something about her seemed familiar. Was that the lady he met last night? He had to know.

He strode down the steps of the patio and into the floral-scented garden. He heard Mr. Hornbeck call to him, but Camden kept walking. The couple sat on a garden bench kissing rather awkwardly, the young lady's hand seeming to caress the man's neck.

"Mirabella!" Hornbeck called from behind Camden. "What in blue heavens is going on here? By all the saints! What are you doing to her, sir? Unhand her this instant."

The couple broke apart and both jumped up. The young man's face was ashen and the young lady's cheeks flamed red.

Mirabella? Whittingham?

Camden's heart went cold. This young lady kissing, embraced in the arms of another man, was the enchantress he'd met on the street last night.

She was the woman who had stirred his blood like no other woman had in years, and she was his fiancée.

Four

MIRABELLA WAS MORTIFIED. LIGHT-HEADED. ANGRY with herself for getting caught. She should have known her uncle would be keeping a closer eye on her after their discussion last night. This humiliation was her fault.

She should have waited a day or two while her uncle's suspicions receded, before resuming her search for the man with the scar. But Mr. Farthingdale had been so eager to dance with her, and he was on her list. She couldn't pass up the opportunity to check for the blemish that marked Sarah's seducer.

Thank God she had managed to discover Mr. Farthingdale had no scar before her uncle showed up and she could strike one more man off her list.

But what was the dashing gentleman she'd met last night doing standing there with her uncle, looking so very handsome in his formal evening coat? Mirabella never expected to see the stranger again. Her heart fluttered when she glanced at him and that had nothing to do with the fact that she'd been caught in a compromising position.

There was nothing to do but gather her wits and accept the consequences. Whatever they might be.

"Would you please excuse us, Mr. Farthingdale?" she said to the gentleman who, looking frightened, was already showing signs of backing away from them.

"Ah—well, I—"

It was clear he was being a gentleman in not wanting to leave her facing her uncle and the glaring stranger alone, but he was also eager to be gone. She appreciated him for that, but it would only make matters worse if she let him stay. She could handle her uncle.

Under her breath she whispered to Mr. Farthingdale. "This is not the time to be chivalrous. I'd like for you to leave."

"Surely you don't want me abandoning you?"

"Yes, I do. You will end up looking like a nincompoop. You don't want my uncle calling you out, do you?"

He barely shook his head. His gaze seemed frozen on her uncle.

"Go immediately."

"Yes, yes, Miss Whittingham," Mr. Farthingdale managed in a trembling voice. "I believe I will take my leave. If you'll excuse me. Gentlemen." He turned his back on them and started walking away.

"Not so fast, young man."

"Uncle Archer, please. Let him go. It's better that we handle this between you and I."

"If only we could, Mirabella," her uncle said. He blew out a loud breath and wiped the top of his head with his handkerchief.

Mr. Farthingdale glanced from Mirabella to her uncle. She nodded to him, and he hurried away.

Her uncle approached with faltering steps. "Mirabella, I'm speechless. Tell me that young blade accosted you, and you were trying to cry out for help. I'll have him apprehended at once."

Uncle Archer's knitted brows and red face said it all. He was horrified, and had every reason to be. Why did the moon have to be so bright? She didn't want to see the anger and disappointment in his eyes. Nor did she want to know what was written on the stranger's face. This was not how she envisioned seeing him again.

Summoning courage she wasn't sure she had, Mirabella admitted, "I'm afraid that's not true, Uncle."

"Blue heavens!"

Mirabella was hot with embarrassment and only wanted to sink into the ground. But she wouldn't let either of the two men staring at her know how distraught she was over being caught during such an indiscretion.

"We can discuss this at a more appropriate time, Uncle. Perhaps you'd like to introduce me to the gentleman with you."

Reluctantly she took a long look at the man who'd captured her dreams last night and her thoughts all day. She saw brooding anger and condemnation in the depths of his eyes and the way a small muscle worked at the corner of his mouth. His expression crushed her. Why did it bother her so to see how her inappropriate behavior affected him? It hadn't bothered him like this last night when she was forward with him.

"No, Mirabella, I wouldn't." Uncle Archer shook his head so hard the loose skin under his chin trembled. "I can assure you *this* is the last man I want to present to you."

She held her head high, trying to calm her breathing. Any other night there would be a breeze to cool her heated cheeks, but all she felt was moist, warm air. She desperately wanted to reach up and wipe Mr. Farthingdale's kiss from her lips, but instead she held her hands at her sides and gently crushed the soft tulle of her gown in her fists.

"And why is that?" she somehow managed to say with as much calm as if she were pouring afternoon tea.

The man took a step toward her and very coldly said, "Perhaps because I am Camden Thurston Brackley, Viscount Stonehurst and your fiancé."

For a moment she couldn't breathe. "Oh my, no. That's impossible." Mirabella's whispered words were a protest. She stared at the viscount, trying to make sense of his words. "Surely you can't be. He's abroad. Gone."

She backed away from him until her legs hit the garden bench she'd just vacated. This couldn't be true. Fate wouldn't be that cruel. This intriguing man who'd been so charming last night couldn't be her fiancé?

"I was. I just returned from America *last night*."

Mirabella cringed with shame. He had to emphasize the words "last night." Reminding her they had met. She had been alone. She had kissed him. Oh, merciful heavens, what must he think of her? And all of it was true! What rotten, rotten luck.

She looked up at him and realized she had been prepared for *everything* but this. She wanted to run home and bury her face in her father's shoulder and sob. But she couldn't do that. She had to stay calm and dig deep inside herself and find the strength to face Lord Stonehurst.

Mirabella forced herself to look into his eyes and say, "I'm sorry you chose this awkward moment to seek me out."

"I'm sure you are." His words were clipped.

"I'm afraid you've caught me off guard."

"Obviously."

"I don't know what to say."

"You could start with an apology," her uncle barked in a barely controlled tone of anger, "but I doubt it will do any good."

"I'm sure it wouldn't," the viscount answered.

"What to do? What to do?" Archer mumbled under his breath along with a few other incoherent words as he mopped his face with his handkerchief. He turned to Lord Stonehurst and said, "You're not going to call Mr. Farthingdale out for this, are you?"

"No," he said coldly. "You have my word on that. Once was enough. I don't need anyone else seeking asylum in France because of me."

"Yes, very well. Good. No doubt Mr. Farthingdale will be pleased to hear that, too."

Lord Stonehurst's piercing gaze didn't waver from Mirabella's as he talked to her uncle or when he said to her, "I think it would be appropriate to conclude you haven't been pining away with loneliness during my absence."

Mirabella winced. His cutting words hit their mark, but instead of being cowed by them, she lifted her chin and shoulders and answered as strongly as she had a moment ago. "Pining away? Over a man who left me on the shelf for six years. I think not, my lord."

"Mirabella, it's best you don't say anything else," her uncle said and motioned for her to come to him. "I'm not responsible for this—this is a situation for your father to handle. No doubt he'll blame me, but I'm not responsible for what you have done. Come. We'll get your wrap and go home immediately."

Ignoring her uncle, she stared into Lord Stonehurst's fathomless dark brown eyes and a part of her wanted to cry. God help her, she was angry with *him* for being her fiancé, angry with *him* for being here tonight, and angry with herself for getting caught doing something she had to do. She knew as far as he was concerned she was without excuse. She had no defense. She had no way to explain her unacceptable behavior. Mirabella would tell no one of Sarah's shame.

This was far worse than she could have ever imagined. She had convinced herself that Viscount Stonehurst would never return for her. That her fiancé could have shown up and caught her in the arms of another man was bad enough, but for her fiancé to be the same man who had filled her heart with a longing to be kissed made the hurt almost unbearable.

If only they had exchanged names last night. If only she'd waited a few days after Uncle Archer had spoken to her about her behavior. If only fate hadn't decided to be so cruel. And worst of all, her father would have to know what she had been up to and that she had deliberately ruined her reputation and the possibility of marriage.

"Mr. Hornbeck, would you leave us alone for a few moments?"

Mirabella's gaze flew to Lord Stonehurst's again.

Her uncle shook his head, clearly distressed. "I'm sure I can't do that under the circumstances, Lord Stonehurst. I think you should talk to her father, not to me and not to her."

"It's all right, Uncle Archer," Mirabella said, walking closer. Her legs were shaky, and her body was stiff with pain, but she had to push all that aside. "I think we do need a moment alone."

He uncle sighed heavily. "If you insist, I guess it's all right. The harm is already done. I'll stand over there on the patio and wait for you because I'm not letting you out of my sight again."

Lord Stonehurst looked at her, allowing his gaze to sweep up and down her face as if seeing her for the first time. His outrage was to be expected. But she was committed to Sarah, and she couldn't have changed her course of action.

Tension clogged in her throat. She sensed that he was holding the brunt of his anger in check by a mere breath. The air around them seemed to crackle like lightning during a summer thunderstorm.

Refusing to buckle under the strain, softly she asked, "Why didn't you tell me who you were last night?"

"You didn't tell me your name."

"You were a stranger to me."

He raised an eyebrow.

Mirabella instantly wanted to take back her words. Naturally he would remind her that she had kissed *that* stranger. "I didn't know you, but it's clear now that you knew who I was. That was unfair."

"No." His eyes darkened with anger. "I didn't know your identity. How could I? We had never met. I had just arrived in London, and I hadn't even been to see my family because it was so late when the ship docked."

She believed him. That he hadn't deceived her about that made her feel a little better, but there was no graceful way out of this very uncomfortable situation. "The only thing I can do is apologize."

"Under the circumstances that's little comfort."

The condemning tone of his truthful words rattled her for a moment, but only for a moment. Who did he think he was to sound so righteous? What encouragement had she received from him these past years?

She shook off her shame and embarrassment and suddenly bristled with anger. "I understand you feel betrayed, but at least I've offered you an apology. I haven't heard one from you."

He folded his arms across his chest and glared at her. "An apology from me? Whatever for?"

"For being gone six years."

"You jest, Miss Whittingham. There's nothing to apologize for. I'm certain there wasn't a time limit on our families' arrangement."

"A properly brought up gentleman would have been aware of the passing time and not have kept his fiancée waiting so long."

The muscle at the corner of his mouth twitched with tension again. "So in my absence, you decided to seek solace in the arms of another man?"

Solace was not the word she would have used, and Mirabella wasn't about to admit to anything. "I'm sure you never sought the comfort of a woman's arms these years you've been gone." She took a step closer to him and lowered her voice even more. "If you haven't, then I will confess to being a weaker person than you, Lord Stonehurst."

A slight flare of what she thought to be admiration glinted in his eyes for a few seconds, but all too quickly the anger returned. "You give me too much credit, Miss Whittingham."

"Accept only what's deserved."

"Are you in love with him?"

"Who? Mr. Farthingdale?" She lifted her chin. "Certainly not."

"You were kissing him. If you don't love him, then obviously I am to assume you make a habit of kissing men you don't love?"

Oh, why had she been so enchanted by him last night that she kissed him? She was trapped. "It would appear to you that is the case, for it is true I have no affectionate feelings for Mr. Farthingdale."

He unfolded his arms and advanced one step toward her. "You puzzle me, Miss Whittingham. Last night I found you walking the streets alone. You kissed me when we parted."

"It was only a little buss on the cheek." *A powerful kiss.*

His dark eyes stayed steady on her face. "A kiss nonetheless. And tonight I find you wrapped in the arms of a man. What am I to think?"

"It is your fault, Lord Stonehurst."

He frowned deeply and tensed again. "Mine?" he asked ruefully.

She wouldn't back down. "Yes."

"This is because I've been gone longer than what you deemed proper? Longer than you'd hoped?"

"I dared not hope you would return," she said, her own anger rising again. "I overheard you tell my father you would not return until you were old and gray. Congratulations, sir, you almost made it."

"You were eavesdropping?"

She ignored his accusation and allowed him to add it to his ever growing list of her faults. She was guilty of far worse.

"After my first Season passed and you didn't return, I assumed I'd been put on the shelf. If you'd been here three years ago, or two months ago or even last week, I wouldn't have been kissed by another man. Therefore it is your fault."

"Your courage is extraordinary."

Mirabella's voice grew softer. "I speak the truth. I resigned myself to never being a bride, Lord Stonehurst. Must I go through life without a kiss, too?"

His eyes narrowed. His expression softened, but only for a flash.

"A kiss is all you wanted?" His voice lowered. His eyes grew fierce. Fury radiated from him. "Very well, Miss Whittingham."

Camden grasped her upper arms and pulled her to him. His lips covered hers quickly, hard and hungry, completely scorching her with his strength, his heat, and his desire. Blood rushed to her ears. Her breasts pressed against his chest. Breath swooshed out of her lungs. She felt his power, his anger, his punishment in the way his hands held her arms and his lips moved over hers.

As suddenly as he had grabbed her, he let her go and stepped away unapologetically.

Gooseflesh rose on her skin.

Mirabella was astonished, frightened, exhilarated. Lord Stonehurst's kiss was nothing like the flat pressing together of dry lips that she had endured from fumbling gentlemen all week. There was nothing awkward or hesitating in the viscount's kiss. It was hot, searing, and passionate.

"You should have waited until I returned." His words spilled from a ragged breath.

Behind an unexpected broken gasp she whispered, "If only I had known you would. Right now, I feel as if I haven't ever been kissed before you."

He looked stunned, caught off guard by her honesty, but quickly recovered and said, "What's done can't be undone. I will not be made a fool of twice. The engagement must be broken."

Mirabella felt as if a knife had pierced her heart. His rejection of her was complete. "Of course, I understand that."

She kept her composure, if not her dignity. For reasons she couldn't fathom, she was wounded down to her inner soul by this intriguing man.

"I'll call on your father tomorrow and settle the final arrangements with him."

"All right, but I would like the opportunity to speak with him first, if you don't mind. He hasn't been well recently, and I think this will be easier for him to accept coming from me. Would you please not come until early in the evening, or perhaps even the day after tomorrow?"

He nodded and looked away from her and she wondered if it was that he could no longer tolerate the sight of her.

Mirabella managed to walk past him toward her uncle with her head held high. She wouldn't think about Lord Stonehurst or what might have been.

She had begun her search for Sarah's seducer knowing it would ruin her reputation. She had set a course that now she couldn't stop, but she had never dreamed her fiancé would return and catch her in the arms of another man.

What a cruel hand fate had dealt her. Her fiancé was the only man she had kissed because she wanted to, and the only man whose kiss she had enjoyed. And the only man she couldn't have.

Five

VISCOUNT STONEHURST RETURNS

If you missed the ball at the Worsters' last evening you missed the party of the Season. Viscount Stonehurst has returned, and all the debutantes' heads are turning toward him. There's already talk that his engagement to Miss Mirabella Whittingham, which has lasted over six years, will not last the Season. Hmm. One has to wonder why he stayed away so long. Could the reason be the long-standing rumor of a jealous mistress was true? And if so, will he go back to America for her? Word has it that no one actually saw him last evening with his patient, dutiful bride-to-be, but there is no doubt he was looking for her. I'm told he carelessly brushed off everyone who tried to speak to him when he departed, and Miss Whittingham left by way of the back garden. Hmm. If anyone has any details of what appears to be an unhappy reunion please let this one know and all will be told right here.

—Lord Truefitt, *Society's Daily Column*

CAMDEN THREW THE PAPER ON THE BED. HE DIDN'T know why his mother had slipped it under his door. Surely she, of all people, knew he had no desire to read about himself in the "Society Column." Their heavy-inked gossip was one of the reasons he went abroad. And that's where he should have stayed. Responsibility be damned.

He was a man with a purpose as he strode down the stairs of his parents' town home the next morning. He needed to tell them immediately that the wedding was off, and that there would be no further talk of it. He didn't care how the scandal sheets handled this broken betrothal.

He'd been through it before. All those angry feelings stirred up from the past had knotted his stomach all night. Thank God he wasn't in love with Miss Mirabella Whittingham as he had been with Hortense. Miss Whittingham had intrigued him with her freshness, her boldness, and her intelligence. That was all. Surely in all of London, he could find another lady as provoking and as invigorating as Miss Whittingham, who had not been as free with her affections.

The thing that bothered him most about her was that even after he had seen her in the arms of another man, still she haunted his dreams. She had such an innocent appearance about her to be so strikingly bold.

Two unfaithful fiancées. What were the odds that would happen to any man? Could no woman be faithful? Maybe he was destined to seek his pleasure in the arms of a paid mistress who was not interested in marriage or in the fact that he'd bear the title of earl one day. Perhaps he should leave it to Hudson to marry and produce a son and one day assume his father's legacy.

Imagine Miss Whittingham trying to lay the blame on him and make him feel like a schoolboy who needed his knuckles rapped for misbehaving, simply because he failed to notify her when he would be home to wed her. The chit had nerve.

He strode into the dining room, but it was empty. He went through the doorway into the kitchen and found the maid. She told him his parents were in the garden. His parents' lifestyle was another surprise to him. Something wasn't right in their household. Their servants had been reduced to an old footman who could hardly get around on his own and two maids who took care of the cleaning, caring for the clothes and the cooking. Camden didn't know how the two of them kept up with everything.

He walked through the kitchen and into the cupboard room and stopped to look out the window at the small garden. His father sat in a chair reading the *Times*. His mother stood beside him arranging flowers in a vase that was placed in the center of the table. They were the perfect picture of a titled couple, when he didn't look too closely.

His father was dressed in a brown striped suit, a shirt that was no longer white and a faded, brown cravat. His mother wore a faded puce-colored morning dress that should have been discarded long ago. Her wide brimmed hat was pulled low over her eyes. The rice straw hat had crimped edges from years of use.

Camden realized he had missed them. He was glad to be home. He didn't know what had happened to his father's income and holdings. He wanted to help restore the life they were used to, but marrying Miss Whittingham wasn't the answer. His gaze drifted upward to the sky. He hadn't missed the gray days of London when he'd been in America. Baltimore had plenty of days filled with sunshine. That was one thing he'd miss about that land across the sea.

He opened the door and stepped outside onto the slate patio.

"Good morning, Camden." His mother's face brightened with a smile. "It fills my heart with cheer to have you home."

He walked over to the table and kissed her cheek.

"Did you find the newsprint I put under your door? I do want to hear all about what happened at the Worsters'."

Camden nodded.

His father laid down the paper. "No sooner will we get used to having him home again than it will be time for him to move into his own place with his new bride."

"I know. The time will pass too quickly," his mama said in a sighing voice. "Earlier, I was making a list of all the things we need to do: the guest list for the wedding, looking at houses to lease, and of course hiring servants. You'll need your own carriage and footman. Cabs are just too expensive these days, and no one walks the streets anymore." She stuck the last flower into the vase and said, "I'll pour you some tea."

"Wait, Mama. I don't care for tea right now." A mild breeze blew his hair across his forehead and he brushed it aside. "I need to tell you something. There won't be a marriage between me and Miss Whittingham."

"What?" His father rose from his chair.

His mother went rigid beside him. "Don't tease about this, Camden. Of course there will be a wedding. That's why you came home."

"We settled this yesterday, Camden," his father said, picking up the newsprint again and immediately slamming it back down on the table. The wind picked it up, sailed it across the lawn where it caught on a flowering shrub. "You came back home to fulfill your vow and marry her. Why are you fighting this so hard?"

His father's words angered him, but he held his tone in check. "It's true I returned knowing it was your intention for me to marry Miss Whittingham. Even though I preferred to wait a year longer, I was willing to consider the possibility of doing that. Unfortunately things have changed."

He refused to go into details about what happened last night. He didn't want his father to know he'd caught Miss Whittingham in the arms of another man. It wasn't just the fact that he didn't want his father to know that he'd been taken by another dishonorable woman.

For some reason he didn't understand, Camden was reluctant to further besmirch Miss Whittingham's reputation. He didn't know why he cared whether or not her name was ruined. It was obvious she had no thought for her own character. She admitted she didn't even love the man she was kissing.

"Your plans can't change." His mother whimpered, her bottom lip trembling. She pulled a handkerchief from under the cuff of her sleeve.

"We don't have the money for them to change. I thought you understood that." His father's voice softened from anger to a tone that sounded like defeat. Suddenly he looked older than his fifty-four years.

Camden was uncomfortable with the way the conversation was going. He didn't like the way he was feeling, and he didn't like having to defend himself. "This doesn't have anything to do with money. I have enough, and I'll repay the dowry."

"It has everything to do with money. You have to forget whatever has happened and marry that girl. There is no need to plan for a long engagement. We have all waited long enough."

Camden gritted his teeth.

"I wish everyone would stop telling me how long I've been gone. You act as if I've been away thirty years. Miss Whittingham wasn't even of marriageable age when I left."

"We don't need you to repay the first half of the dowry. We need to secure the other half of it as soon as possible. All my investments have gone sour. We have enough money to get by from the entitled lands but there is no extra money for other things, Camden."

His father was acting as if he hadn't protested at all and Camden knew why. His had always been short of cash as long as Camden could remember. That was one of the reasons he'd allowed his father to make this match. Twice was one time too many.

"I'm sorry if you were counting on that, sir."

"Son," his father said, "let me see if I can make this clear. You have to marry Miss Whittingham. There is not enough time to work out details on a new match for you or Hudson. Creditors are knocking at our door. If they suspect the betrothal is off, there's no telling what they will do."

Exasperation quickly rose in Camden that his father had somehow managed to get himself in such dire financial straits again. And for the second time he expected Camden to rescue him.

"Last night I caught my fiancée in the arms of another man. Does that bring back memories for anyone other than me?" His gaze jerked from one parent to the other.

His father looked away from him and blinked slowly. "Are you sure?"

"Of course I'm sure."

"Perhaps they were dancing," his mother offered nervously. "Surely if she was in a man's arms they were dancing."

"No, Mama, they were not dancing. They were in the garden embracing, kissing."

"Oh, dear, I've never heard a breath of scandal about her. Wilson?"

"No."

His father didn't look at him. His voice was less than convincing. Camden's stomach knotted. He knew his father must have heard rumors about Mirabella. Damnation! Those young bachelors he overheard talking the first night he arrived in Town must have been talking about *his* fiancée. It was probably only a matter of time until her indiscretions showed up in the gossip columns.

"Neither had we heard anything years ago, as I recall, when we saw Hortense in the arms of another man.

I've no idea how many other men Miss Whittingham has been with. I don't care to find out. And I have no desire to wed or bed her."

"I can't believe this, Camden." His mother sank into a chair. "Wilson, what are we to do? If the engagement is broken, and Camden pays back the dowry, where will we get the money to pay back all that money we borrowed?"

"Yes, paying back the dowry is the least of our worries," his father muttered weakly. For the first time he looked Camden in the eyes. "It's creditors we have to concern ourselves with. You must marry her."

Camden had a feeling that by creditors his father really meant gambling debts. "You would have me marry a woman I found in the arms of another man?"

"For the good of the family," his father said.

"You don't know how bad things are. Tell him, Wilson."

Anger flared in his father's eyes and tears pooled in his mother's. Camden took a settling breath. "It doesn't matter. I told you I have money. I'll help you pay your debts."

"You couldn't have enough." His father sighed. "All the land we have outside the entailed lands are mortgaged and will be lost by the end of the month."

Camden took a step forward. "All your land? That can't be true."

"It's true," Wilson admitted, shaking his head in frustration. "I've been very foolish over the years and not a very good keeper of what my father left to me. Our income is down to a meager amount and most of that is obligated to debts."

Camden swore under his breath. "Father, how did you let yourself get in this situation?"

"Gambling," his mama said, confirming what Camden suspected.

"Not entirely," his father remarked abruptly.

Camden made a fist of desperation at his side. "Why didn't you stop after the trouble you had years ago."

"He did," his mother admitted. "For a while."

His father looked abashed. "I got in too deep when I put everything but Lockshaven up as collateral on an investment that was supposed to return my money threefold. I was going to get us on solid ground again, but it was a scam. The man absconded with the money, and I can't locate him."

"The Pembertons will never agree to let Hudson marry Miss Pemberton if they find out what a financial state we're in. And Hudson loves her so."

Yes, Camden saw how much in love the two were last night. They couldn't keep their eyes off each other. Just like he and Hortense had been. No, he thought. He had looked at Hortense that way, but she had never looked at him with such love in her eyes. How could she? She had loved another man. Camden was young and had missed all the signs that what Hortense had wanted from him was the comfortable life his title would afford her.

Camden looked at his mother, at her sad eyes and worrying lips. No wonder his father had aged and their clothing was worn. They were probably spending every extra shilling they had to keep up Hudson's appearance.

His heart constricted. "I knew the minute I walked in yesterday there was a problem, but I had no idea your finances were this bad. You're asking me to marry a completely unsuitable woman—for money."

His father pleaded, "We have no choice. I can cope with going to jail, if it ever came to that, but I don't think your mother could bear it."

Damnation! What was he to do? He had enough money to attend to his family's everyday needs for a while and pay off some debts, too. He'd actually saved a little money, choosing to spend most of his extra pounds on stock in the Maryland Ship Building Company where he'd worked in America. He thought he'd be set for life. He hadn't planned to be paying off his father's gambling debts.

Camden had to think, and he couldn't do it rationally while he watched the tears roll down his mother's pale cheeks.

"I'll get back with you on what I intend to do." Camden turned and walked back into the town house.

~~

Mirabella wanted to see Lord Stonehurst again, yet she didn't. One moment she was telling herself she was happy the engagement was off and in the next she was distressed by the thought of never seeing him again. There was no reason to suspect she could ever be happy with a man such as he, but she kept remembering how he'd taken care of her that first night they met. How he'd made her breath quicken with anticipation. How his brief kiss in the Worsters' garden had seared her with so many powerful sensations at once.

She took her time in changing from her morning dress to a fancier afternoon gown of pale yellow muslin that was banded at the sleeves and waist with pink satin. The last thing she'd expected today was for Viscount Stonehurst to show up and ask to see her. She assumed Lily had made a mistake and sent her down to speak to him again. He assured her maid that he wanted to see Mirabella and not her father. He asked specifically that her father not be notified of his visit.

His anger had not been as violent as she would have thought, given the circumstances. Perhaps after a night to think on it he had more to say to her.

Throughout last night and all morning, Mirabella had been functioning in a dismal cloud of apprehension, knowing she had to confess to her father what had happened. She had alerted Lily last night to grab the Society columns of all the papers her father received.

She had no idea what, if anything, about Camden's return would be in those columns, but she couldn't let her father see them until she had spoken with him first. Thank God the attention to Camden's return had been minimal because of a scandal concerning the Duke of Highbury. But the author of the "Society's Daily Column" made it clear he was going to dig for details on their meeting. She knew her uncle would not breathe a word, nor Camden. But she was not certain that Mr. Farthingdale would be a gentleman and remain quiet about what happened.

Uncle Archer had wanted to come in with her last night and tell her father immediately everything that had happened. She wouldn't let him and insisted it was her place to tell her father. Losing her spotless reputation didn't bother her nearly so much as disappointing her father. That made her feel absolutely wretched. She had planned to tell him during her afternoon visit with him. Dreading the task had caused her to postpone it as long as possible. She had practiced in her bedroom all day on just how to tell him with the fewest details possible.

Why did Lord Stonehurst want to talk to her again? She would have to admit to Lord Stonehurst's charges and face whatever consequences her father desired. She didn't regret what she had done. Neither did she regret that she had to continue.

Her soft kid shoes were soundless on the carpeted floor as she walked to the parlor doorway. Her breath caught in her throat. She was stunned by how the sight of Camden affected her. He stood before the front window. He had brushed aside the gold velvet window dressing and stared out onto the street below. He seemed so deep in thought she hated to disturb him.

A slice of rare sunshine fell across his face and glinted off his dark hair, dappling him with an attractive glow. Once again she noticed the breadth of his chest, his height, the arrogant tilt of his chin and the proud lift to his shoulders. The stripe in his fitted trousers and the dark brown shade of his coat made a handsome combination. Seeing him like this, she felt that without a doubt she could have been happy with this man had things been different between them. Still there was no way to change what she'd done, and there was no one to avenge Sarah, if not Mirabella.

"Lord Stonehurst."

He dropped the velvet panel and stared at her, taking in every detail of her face just as he had last night, and the night before. Mirabella realized what she remembered most about the evening was not their unpleasant conversation but his powerful kiss. It had been brief, demanding and seductive. That was how she expected a kiss to feel, not the cold uninspiring lips she had heretofore felt on hers.

"You are earlier than we agreed on," she said, walking farther into the drawing room.

"My apologies."

"It's just that I need more time. Because of my father's illness, I haven't had the opportunity to speak with him about our engagement."

"I'm glad you haven't. I wanted to talk with you about that. Thank you for agreeing to see me on such short notice."

"I must admit I was quite sure after last evening you wouldn't want to ever see me again. I thought you would just say the betrothal is off and be done with it."

"I have to admit that did cross my mind more than once."

Why wasn't she calm? She had accepted that Lord Stonehurst had caught her in Mr. Farthingdale's arms. By now he would have heard rumors there were other gentlemen she had allowed to kiss her. The engagement had been broken, and she knew she must tell her father the truth. Nothing worse could happen, so why was her heart pounding in her chest like a meaty fist against a solid wood door?

"I've sent my maid to ask the cook to make tea. It should be here shortly. Would you like to sit down?"

"No, I'll stand if you don't mind." He walked closer to her and stood facing her.

Lord Stonehurst was a fearless, powerful-looking man and her pulse reacted aggressively to his nearness. She wanted to deny her attraction to him but couldn't.

"Very well."

"I came here today to make you a proposition."

Mirabella tensed. How dare he? Just when she thought things could not get worse. "That would not be appropriate even under our unusual circumstances, Lord Stonehurst."

He looked disconcerted for a moment. "No, you misunderstand me."

Her ire was piqued that he should be so brash. "I think not. I'll ask Lily to show you the door." She whirled and headed to the door.

"Wait, Miss Whittingham, I mean no offense. Let me explain. I assure you my proposition is not out of line."

Something in his tone made her stop. His voice had no accusatory quality. She faced him again but not without disapproval set in her expression. "All right. I'll hear what you have to say."

His brows drew together in frustration. "I'll get right to the point."

"Please do," she said, ready to flee the parlor at any moment.

"I've had time to think over everything you said last evening, and something you remarked upon has stuck with me."

She eyed him cautiously. "What was that?"

"That I've been away a long time with no word to you on my intentions to honor our betrothal."

"It is some comfort that you have come around to understand my way of thinking, but I believe we said all that needed to be said on the subject last night."

"Not quite. My honor dictates that I accept part of the blame for your indiscretion."

Suddenly she was wary. His turnabout stunned her. What was he getting at? He looked so sincere, yet something didn't feel right. "Your generosity surprises me, but yes, it would have been appropriate to hear from you from time to time. If you had even let me know what year you expected to return."

He let her dig at him slide and said, "My lack of any communication is inexcusable."

How could she remain angry with him when he looked and sounded sincere in what he was saying? He was forcing her to back off from her bold statement of claiming her actions were his fault. If this was a clever way to get her to admit she was to blame, it was working.

She relented and said, "I agree that we both made mistakes," she said.

"Perhaps some more damaging than others."

"True."

He looked away from her for a moment before gazing back into her eyes. "I've thought about how we should go about breaking the engagement so we both save face."

He stunned her again.

"You won't lose face for something of which only I am guilty."

"Miss Whittingham, take my word for it that no man likes to acknowledge to the world that his fiancée has been untrue to him with another man."

Mirabella winced. His gaze zeroed in on her eyes so tightly, she flushed. She had heard the scandalous story about what had happened with his first fiancée, but she truly had never expected him to return and be hurt by what she had been doing.

He spoke with such conviction that she felt compelled to say, "I'm sure that's true. And I'm not unaware of your past."

"Yes, unfortunately, it seems everyone is aware of my past. However, I propose that we don't break our engagement right away."

She smiled nervously. "Surely you are teasing me, Lord Stonehurst."

"I have thought about doing many things to you, Miss Whittingham, but teasing you was not one of them."

"Does that mean you thought of kissing me again, or that you want to throttle me for what I have done to you?"

"Both, I assure you."

"Thank you for your honesty."

A light glinted in his eyes but Mirabella didn't know if it was a teasing spark or one of anger. "You are never at a loss for words, are you, Miss Whittingham?"

"Oh, yes. More times than I care to remember. I'm sure many things have crossed your mind in the past twenty-four hours."

"Too many, and we'll leave it at that. My proposition to you is that I would like for us to appear around Town as a properly engaged couple. We'll attend the parties together and even make a few wedding plans. When everyone sees that I'm not deserting you, they'll accept anything that has been said about you as vicious gossip set to ruin our reunion and my return. After winter, sometime in the spring before the new Season begins, we'll announce that the engagement is off and go our separate ways. In time you should be able to find a suitable husband."

Something didn't fit, but Mirabella didn't know what. He was saying all the right things, but his proposal didn't feel legitimate. "This is noble of you to be sure, Lord Stonehurst, but what is in this for you?"

"Me?" He cleared his throat. "Surely I've already explained that I feel somewhat obliged to save your reputation from further damage since you think my delay in returning brought on your indiscretion."

"Did I say that?"

"You indicated it by words something like you would never be a bride, but you didn't want to go through life having never been kissed."

She felt a pang of guilt. That was not exactly the truth. "Is that all?"

"You do try my patience, Miss Whittingham. Isn't it enough that I want to help you keep your good name?"

"No, I believe there's more."

Mirabella didn't know what was wrong with her. Why was she questioning him? He was right. This would help her. She should be grateful he wanted to do this for her, but she wasn't. How could she pretend to be this man's fiancée day after day, knowing he considered her an unfaithful woman rather than a devoted fiancée? What would that do to her? Even now, she couldn't look at him without thinking about how warm, moist and delicious his lips felt upon hers.

She'd rather be done with it all now. It would be torture to prolong their engagement only to break it in the end. Her position in Society had never been an issue in what she was doing for Sarah. If she agreed to play the part of his dutiful betrothed she wouldn't be able to continue the hunt for Sarah's seducer. As much as she would like to take him up on his offer and save her father the stress of hearing what she'd done, she couldn't. She must continue her quest to avenge Sarah.

"What you are offering is generous after what I have done to embarrass you. Thank you, but I must decline."

Six

CAMDEN BLINKED—HAD HE HEARD HER RIGHT? DID she refuse him? This lovely lady standing so demurely in front of him in her pale yellow dress was damned full of surprises. He had half expected her to be crying when he arrived and was delighted to find she wasn't. He'd convinced himself she'd be begging him to forgive her and save her reputation by marrying her as Hortense had years ago. At the very least she should be grateful to him for wanting to help her.

Damnation. He certainly hadn't expected her to refuse his chivalrous offer, which was made at great cost to him. He had pushed aside the fact that her agreeing would actually save him and his family because he had convinced himself that she would eagerly agree to his suggestion.

He had even taken the time to go to a jeweler and pick out a lovely necklace and earrings as his first gift to her as his betrothed. Now the weight of the box seemed unusually heavy in his pocket.

Mirabella Whittingham was a true enigma.

From his conversations with her he knew her to

be an intelligent young lady. But perhaps she didn't understand him. "I'm offering you a way to save your reputation, Miss Whittingham, so that you can marry a suitable gentleman some day in the future."

He watched her face, and he thought he saw signs of hesitation. She wasn't sure of her stand. That's all she would give him, but enough to work on.

"While I would rather have had an unblemished reputation, sir, I can certainly live happily without one. I will disappoint my father greatly, and I do hate to do that, but I have no fear of losing his love."

It wasn't that she didn't understand Lord Stonehurst. He didn't understand her. Outwardly she seemed brave and capable, but instinct told him inside she was different. She was softer, more vulnerable than she appeared. Something troubled her, and she wasn't saying what.

"Because of the circumstances I don't see how you can refuse me."

"Oh, my lord, I thought I had made it clear that I gave up all hope of marrying long ago."

She knew how to hit him hard with her accusations. He had already admitted that maybe he should have written to her, but their families had an agreement and she should have had faith that he would live up to it one day.

He wouldn't apologize again. If her father hadn't approved, he should have notified the earl that the agreement had to be canceled. Camden remembered hoping that would happen.

"You make six years sound like an eternity, Miss Whittingham."

"Obviously time passes faster in the Americas than it does in London, sir—with all of Society watching every move I made and whispering about everything I did, time went especially slowly for me."

Considering what he'd been through with her and Hortense, he was finding it hard to feel sorry for her distress at the moment.

"If you were unsatisfied with my delay, why didn't you ask your father to break the engagement? I would have been amenable to that, I assure you."

"My father thought about that. In truth, I have been content to live at home with Papa since he has been unwell for some time now. I read books, write poetry, and do my needlework. I call on friends and have tea."

"And kiss strangers on the streets?"

Seemingly unmoved by his accusation, except for the creeping blush that rose up her neck and flooded her cheeks, she said, "I have no excuse. You were so engaging I couldn't resist. You are the only stranger I have ever kissed."

Her poise hadn't faltered. Camden took a step back and shook his head. This wasn't going the way he had planned. What he was saying to her was not going to win her over to his way of thinking.

He looked back at her and said, "I believe you about that."

She nodded once. "I have a full life, and I'm not opposed to spending the rest of it without a husband."

That explained why she took the chance of ruining her reputation. She wanted to be kissed before she settled into spinsterhood. He felt a certain admiration for her. If she were going to be doomed to the life of an old maid, she obviously wanted to live a little first.

"You are a woman of rare courage, Miss Whittingham. Bold and daring to a fault."

"I'll consider that a compliment, sir."

"Indeed it was. I daresay most young ladies in your position would be looking forward to a home of their own and children to take care of rather than remaining under their father's guardianship."

"Once I was resigned to the fact that I would never be a bride, I refused to look back on what might have been."

Her wistful voice took Camden by surprise. His gaze swept down her face. He saw that even though her words were gallant she was vulnerable. A catch in his breath fastened inside his chest and wouldn't move. For all her brave talk, he knew she hadn't completely given up on the hope of a family.

Camden cleared his throat. "Your honesty forces me to admit that it would be better for me, Miss Whittingham, if we presented ourselves to be the happily betrothed couple a few more months. Therefore, I ask you to reconsider the answer you gave me and act as my fiancée through the end of the year and possibly into next spring."

"Are you speaking about what happened to you in the past, Lord Stonehurst?"

He wasn't about to let her get into that. "Obviously that is part of it," he said tightly. "There are other things I'd rather not go into at the moment. Suffice it to say that I need to be engaged to you. I need you to be my fiancée."

It seemed so callous when he said it like that, when he looked into her beautiful green eyes. He would have liked to tell her that she would be his bride before the year was out and would have, if she hadn't already proven herself to be a woman with a blemished reputation.

There was no doubt he was as drawn to her now as he had been the moment he first saw her. She was beautiful, intelligent, and courageous. But he couldn't consider marriage to a woman who had given her affections so freely to another gentleman. His ego wouldn't allow it years ago and not now.

"I understand that you are unhappy by this unfortunate turn of events, sir. I'm afraid I didn't consider you when I took the actions I did, and I am truly sorry for any embarrassment my behavior has caused. I would have never behaved as I did had I any hope you would come home."

"It's not so much me I'm concerned about, Miss Whittingham, as personal problems concerning my family."

She took a step closer to him and looked up into his eyes. "Then I shall be blunt. I want to be done with it, Lord Stonehurst. I've found no pleasure in being betrothed to you these past years. I see no reason to continue this charade, which will cause only more pain months from now for your family and mine. Let us end it here."

"You do not mince words, do you, Miss Whittingham?"

"There is no reason to. Because of recent circumstances, you know me far better than most."

"I'm beginning to."

"I suspect you had no intentions of marrying me when your father made the arrangement with my father. Isn't this true?"

"No, it's not," he said. "I assumed I would marry you one day."

"When you were old and gray?"

No words had haunted him more. "Yes, I did say that, but I've always looked at our marriage as in the future after I sought my fortune abroad. I admit that I never considered what your feelings might be while waiting here in England for me to return."

"That's perfectly clear, and I've already accepted your apology for that."

"Then let us continue the engagement for the time being."

"No."

Camden blew out his breath. She was a stubborn one. She was going to force him to tell her the truth. "Miss Whittingham, my father is not able to repay the dowry money your father advanced him at this time. I'd rather not go into all the financial details, for they are lengthy and private, but I ask for your consideration in this matter."

Her eyes searched his face for a moment. He didn't like feeling anger at his father for putting him in this position. Miss Whittingham and his father were the ones who had done wrong, and he was the one at the point of supplication.

"I see this is a delicate subject for you," she said.

"Aptly put."

"The only reason you want to continue this charade is because your family is financially embarrassed."

Mirabella could never be considered coy. Damn if she wasn't the most challenging person he had ever met. A shiver of awareness shook him as he looked at her. Long, dark brown lashes framed her lustrous green eyes. Her brows arched and fanned upward into a lovely shape.

"At the moment that is true. But there is more." He spoke from the heart, but had no way of knowing if she knew. "I've already mentioned the advantage to you. Beyond which, I find you extremely attractive, Miss Whittingham. I find you stimulating. You have managed to surprise me at every turn. Admirably so. I wouldn't consider our engagement a burden. I would be a dutiful lover. It would be a great benefit to both of us, Miss Whittingham."

"Your compliments are welcomed, Lord Stonehurst, but once again, I've made my choice. I'm afraid I can't turn back."

Camden could see she wasn't going to budge this time. But he wasn't ready to give up. Not just yet. He would come back tomorrow and try to get her to change her mind. She intrigued him. She challenged him. For reasons he couldn't understand, he wasn't so bothered by the fact that she wasn't willing to go through life never having been kissed. How many women in her position were brave enough to do that?

"Then there's nothing more to be said."

"I'll tell my father on my evening visit that our engagement is off. I'm sure he'll be most circumspect and compassionate about your family's financial position after I tell him what I must."

"Here are the tea and scones, Miss Bella. I'm sorry it took so long, but the cook was just about to take fresh biscuits from the oven." Lily looked over at Camden then back to her employer. "I knew you'd want to wait for the warm ones."

"Thank you, Lily. Put them on the table." The maid did as she was told, then turned and walked out, but not before looking Camden over from head to toe.

"Would you care for refreshment before you go?"

There was a soft feminine strength about Mirabella that drew him to her even when he knew there could never be anything between them. "No, thank you. I know where my hat and coat are. No need to see me out. Good-bye, Miss Whittingham."

❧

Mirabella took a deep breath before knocking on the door of her father's room. She was not looking forward to this meeting. She had been in her room rehearsing what to say to him since Lord Stonehurst left, trying in vain to come up with a way to make this turn of events more palatable to her father.

At best, she would only have to tell him that she didn't want to marry the viscount. At worst, she would have to tell her father the entire dreadful story of how Lord Stonehurst caught her in the arms of another man. She couldn't tell her father about Sarah. She had to keep that from him so she could continue her search.

Lord Stonehurst's surprising offer to remain engaged had been so very tempting. But he wasn't offering a solution to her predicament, only a postponement.

A pang of guilt struck her every time she thought about Lord Stonehurst. How she had ever found the courage to deny herself his company for a few months she didn't know. He was the most interesting gentleman she had ever met, and she would have loved the opportunity to get to know him better. After all the years she waited for him to come home, she would have enjoyed having him by her side—if only for a short time.

But she was committed to finding the rake who seduced Sarah and caused her death. She had gone too far to turn back now, and a fiancé would be a hindrance. Refusing the viscount was the only sensible thing she could do.

Mirabella strode into her father's room with all the courage she could muster. "Papa, how are you this evening?"

Her father closed the book he was reading and laid it on the covers in front of him. "I've had a good day, Daughter. How about you?"

She brushed aside his heavy blanket and a copy of *The History of England* and took a seat on the bed beside him. "I've had a most unusual day."

"Something out of the ordinary?" He placed a finger on his chin. "Sounds like a wonderful change to a sick old man who spends too much time in bed reading. Tell me how so?"

It was best for her to just be done with it and not play around with the news. "The Earl of Lockshaven's son has returned to London."

Bertram's expression questioned briefly, then brightened. "What's this? The viscount? Your fiancé has returned?"

"Yes."

His eyes widened and he leaned forward. "How do you know this? The earl has sent word? Are you certain?"

"Quite certain."

Bertram clasped his hands together and whispered, "Thank God. What took him so long?" Relief washed down his face, and his eyes pooled with moisture. "This is wonderful news." He quickly brushed his eyes before the glistening could become tears. "I'm overjoyed. Mirabella, I don't mind telling you that I had all but given up hope of him ever returning. I planned to speak to Archer about other eligible men who would be suitable to you and now I don't have to. This is the news we've been waiting for."

She hadn't expected her father to show so much enthusiasm over Lord Stonehurst's return.

"Where's Newton? I must send a note to the earl at once."

"Papa, wait."

"What for? Your fiancé has come to claim you for his bride. It's past time he decided to uphold his duty."

"I'd like to discuss this with you."

"Of course we will. Tell me, how did you find out he had returned? I haven't received a visit from the earl. Unless Newton failed to deliver his message to me." Bertram started searching the covers. "Where's my bell?"

"Papa, please wait before you summon Newton." She took hold of his hand and kept him from ringing the bell as his fingers closed over it.

"All right, let's start at the beginning. Tell me how you know that he is in Town."

"Lord Stonehurst was really quite shrewd." *Too designing.* "I met him at the first party I attended last night. Uncle Archer introduced us."

Bertram rose from his pillows. "Archer knew he was in Town and didn't take the time to tell me? I'll have a word with him about that."

"No. Apparently, Lord Stonehurst wanted to surprise all of us." *Indeed he had.* "He just showed up at the Worsters' party last night unannounced and demanded he be introduced to me with no forewarning."

All of a sudden Bertram laughed out loud, a rich healthy laugh. She was pleased to see her father display energy. Her spirits lifted just listening to him. She hadn't seen him so alive in months.

She didn't want to sound like a grumbling child but she hadn't expected her father to be so amused. "I didn't find his behavior humorous, Papa."

"Of course you didn't, but I do. What a clever man your fiancé is. That is exactly something I would have done in my younger years. I approve of his tactics. Maybe he will be a good match for you after all, dear girl. I like his style."

Her father seldom made her bristle, but his attitude about Lord Stonehurst's antics was not what she expected. "Only a man would appreciate that kind of behavior. I thought it not only inappropriate but inconsiderate as well."

Bertram chuckled again. "I'm sure you did. No doubt he watched you from afar before he approached.

I can understand him wanting to get a good look at you before he met you."

"That's exactly what he did." *Though Mirabella was sure he hadn't liked what he saw.*

She hated to tell her father what she must when he was feeling better than she had seen him in a long time. But it had to be said before he went any further. "Papa, I don't want to marry the viscount."

"Nonsense, girl. This has been set for years. You know how important it was to me that you have a titled husband worthy of you and your inheritance. From what you've just told me, this man is up to the task."

"I know it is what you have wanted all these years, Papa, but I find that it's not what I want."

"You are merely getting jittery now that he is here. Perfectly understandable." He patted her cheek with a warm hand and smiled gently at her. "Not to worry, they'll go away in time."

No, she just needed to be free of him so that she could continue her search for the man who seduced Sarah, and so she could stop thinking about how much she would have liked to get to know him.

"It's more than that." She paused and went over her speech in her mind, the same story she told Camden which was as close to the truth as she could get without mentioning Sarah.

I can't marry him, Papa, because I have disgraced you, myself, and my fiancé by allowing certain young gentlemen to walk with me in the gardens and kiss me. I assumed he would never return and claim me for his bride, and I didn't want to go through life without being kissed.

That made her sound and feel absolutely wretched. No wonder Society dictated young ladies shouldn't be left alone with a gentleman.

Her father took hold of her hand and held it in his. "Mirabella, I see this has upset you. Everything is going to be all right now. I was so afraid the viscount wouldn't return, and I knew I must see you wed before I die."

"Papa. Don't say things like that."

"It's true."

An ache started in her chest. How could she tell her father how unresponsive she'd been when Lord Stonehurst was giving her a way to spare her father the pain of her indiscretion? What if her admission of what she'd been doing made her father worse and shortened his life? That was a horrible thought.

"You have a long life ahead of you. You admitted that even today you are feeling better."

"Better, yes. But there is no cure for what ails me, Mirabella. My heart is weak." He took a deep breath. "I haven't been fooling myself for some time now, and I am not going to allow you to delude yourself any longer. I'm not going to die tonight, but I won't live to be a very old man. I won't have to worry about you now. Lord Stonehurst will see that you are well cared for."

Mirabella saw her plans for avenging Sarah's death slipping away. "Papa. I don't want to marry. I want to stay here with you."

"Poppycock. Women are made for marriage. I've allowed you certain freedoms—to read the *Times* and other papers and to write your poetry and to be clever with sums—because your mother wasn't here. It pleased me to teach you. But I never meant for you to be so strong and independent as to not want to marry one day. Now, be a dutiful daughter and make me happy. I don't want to hear any more about not marrying. We'll send word to your aunt Helen. I know she will want to come and help you make all the arrangements."

She had always been a dutiful daughter, until recently. It had always been her desire to make her father happy.

"And if you marry soon enough, I just might get to see my first grandchild. That would be such a blessing for me, dear girl. I can just see it now. A wee one for me to hold, then I could tell your mother all about him when I see her in Heaven."

This was harder than she thought it would be. Her father had laughed, really laughed, not just the light chuckle he'd given her the past few months. What was she to do? She'd told Lord Stonehurst no when he offered to extend the engagement. What was worse, making her father's last days happy or rejecting Lord Stonehurst?

A kiss crossed her mind. Lord Stonehurst's kiss. A masterful meeting of lips directed to show her what she had missed. Mirabella rose from the bed and walked over to her father's window and looked out to the quiet street below.

What should she do? Give her father the prepared speech and take the smile off his face forever or go to Lord Stonehurst and tell him she had changed her mind, and ask him to reconsider his proposal to her?

If they came to an agreement, she would have to find a way to be Lord Stonehurst's fiancée and also continue her search for Sarah's Prince Charming, too. The viscount's return had effectively ended her efforts of slipping her fingers down the neckcloths of the young men, but she couldn't give up the search. She'd been through too many on her list already. Besides, there was an unscrupulous scoundrel in the *ton*, and right now he could be seducing another young woman and leaving her to ruination.

Mirabella turned to her father. "All right. The engagement will stand, but I need time to get to know him, Papa. We've only just met. I can't marry him right away."

"Don't wait too long, Daughter. You might have plenty of time, but I don't. Now, you run along and send up Newton. I want to send a note to the earl and find out why he hasn't notified me of his son's return."

"Wait on that, Papa. I'm sure it's because Lord Stonehurst took some perverse pleasure in astounding me last evening. Give the earl a day or two to notify you. I'm sure he will be in touch."

She had to give herself time to speak to the viscount again. To tell him she would accept his proposal, assuming it was still offered. She wasn't fond of the idea of now going to him with the same request he presented her. She had turned him down and now he could very well turn her down.

"What time is Archer coming to escort you tonight?"

"The usual time of half past eight, but I think I'll skip the parties tonight. I've been out every night for more than a week. I'm very tired."

"That's a good idea. I was going to suggest it. I think the next time you go out it should be on the arm of your fiancé. The *ton* needs to know that the viscount has returned for you."

"Yes," she whispered, hurting because she was deceiving the man she most loved. "Would you like me to ask Uncle Archer to come up and see you when he arrives?"

"Yes, do tell him. This is a great day, Mirabella. Splendid."

"Very well. I'll see you after dinner."

Mirabella walked directly into her room and sat down at her writing desk. She had to immediately send a note to Lord Stonehurst and ask to see him right away. Her breath quickened. Merciful heavens, now that she'd made her decision to accept Lord Stonehurst's offer, she found she was looking forward to seeing the handsome viscount again.

She would talk to Uncle Archer tonight before he went to see her father. No doubt he'd be pleased to hear her news.

❦

Camden wasn't in the mood to face his family with Miss Whittingham's rejection so fresh on his mind. He decided to stop in at his club for a stout drink and time to brood. Damnation! Miss Whittingham was the one who had behaved improperly, and she was refusing to help him. Now that he had time to think on it, that young lady had some nerve.

It served her right to have her name bandied about in the gaming halls of London. Gone were his thoughts of trying to get her to change her mind. He was through with her. How could he have had such dastardly luck with women twice? He was also through trying to find a respectable woman to marry. He'd do far better looking into getting an agreeable mistress.

He shifted in his chair and felt the weight of the jewelry box in his coat pocket. He had selected the emeralds because they had reminded him of Mirabella's sparking eyes. Why did he find her so elusive?

"Camden, I thought I saw you walk in. Here, I took the liberty of having you a drink poured," Albert Farebrother, the new Earl of Glenbrighton said as he walked over to where Camden had sat in a far corner of the darkened room.

So much for being alone. Camden looked up at his old friend and knew immediately he hadn't come just to talk over old times. The hand that held the drink out to him shook.

Camden took the glass as sounds of laughter, loud talking and billiard balls smacking into one another drifted in from the room behind him.

"That was intuitive of you, Albert. I take it you want to join me."

"Do you mind?"

"Not at all," Camden said and took the drink his friend offered him. Something told Camden it didn't matter if he did mind. Albert was already taking the chair beside him. If Camden was going to brood over Mirabella's answer it wouldn't be at the club.

Albert clinked his glass against Camden's and said, "Welcome home, old chap."

"Thank you."

Albert settled into the carved mahogany, tapestry covered armchair beside Camden. "So tell me, how was America?"

"Big. Lots of land in that country. Pleasant weather, good people and growing rapidly from all I could tell."

"You stayed away a long time. You must have enjoyed it."

"Yes. You need to make the journey yourself one day."

"I plan to," Albert said with no enthusiasm for the subject. "When my son is old enough to travel."

Albert held his drink in one hand and played with his fancily tied cravat with the other. Camden noticed the gold signet ring he wore claiming to all the world that he was Earl of Glenbrighton. The man was damned nervous for some reason.

"You know, it might be a good thing you decided to come back when you did," Albert said. "There has been talk that you had given up claim to your title and your bride. The rumor was that you planned to stay in America with your jealous mistress."

Camden chuckled. "There never was a mistress in America. Beautiful women, to be sure. Plenty to keep me satisfied. A mistress? No. Pure gossip from tongues of people who have nothing better to do."

"Ah—speaking of gossip." Albert downed the rest of his drink and motioned for the server to bring him another glass. "I don't know quite how to mention this, but I think it needs to be said."

Camden didn't hesitate. "Out with it."

He cleared his throat and nervously fingered his cravat again. "There have been some unpleasant remarks going around the club. Perhaps your brother had wind of the rumor and told you about it."

"Hudson doesn't engage in gossip."

"Then perhaps I shouldn't, either."

Camden smiled indulgently at Albert. "No, please, now that you've started please continue. I rather enjoy hearing about these things that have never happened." Deciding to be deliberately dull-witted and further disconcert Albert, Camden said, "As you just said there have been numerous rumors about me. To which one specifically are you referring?"

Albert looked into his empty glass before meeting Camden's stare. "I'm afraid this one is not about you. It's about your fiancée. I thought you should know that there has been talk about Miss Whittingham."

Before Albert had said her complete name, Camden knew he didn't want Albert or anyone else saying anything about Mirabella. He had thought the young bachelors he'd overheard a couple of nights ago were talking about Mirabella. Now he was sure of it.

He didn't understand his need to stand up for her. Maybe it was because he sensed there was more going on than what she admitted. Maybe it was because he had stayed away so long. If she had allowed a kiss or two, maybe it was his fault for not returning in a timely fashion. Certainly it was none of the *ton's* concern.

Camden wasn't going to make it easy for his friend. He'd make Albert spell it out for him. Then he'd know exactly what kind of rumors and gossip he was dealing with.

"Talk about her? I should think so. She's an extraordinarily beautiful woman. As you and I know, most men like to talk about lovely ladies who are not within their reach. Makes the gossip all the more exciting, doesn't it?"

"Well—ah—this was not about her beauty, which, of course, she is lovely. I should like nothing more than to spare you the details, but if what I've heard is true, recently she has been less than circumspect in your absence. I'm afraid it has just begun to make the rounds."

Camden sipped his drink and willed his brows not to knit in anger. He let the burning liquor slowly slide down his throat and settle in his stomach.

"Unflattering gossip about Miss Whittingham?" he asked. "Are you sure?"

"Quite sure. I wouldn't mention it otherwise. Not pleasant news to come home to, I know. But the rumor is that she has allowed certain gentlemen to walk with her in the garden."

"I assume this hasn't hit the Society papers."

"No, I don't think so. But you know it's only a matter of time before someone speaks to the right, or should I say the wrong, person."

"I know Miss Whittingham would be crushed to hear of any gossip about her. I'll try to see that doesn't happen. Just because I delay a few years returning home, the gossipmongers think they can ruin her reputation. I won't let it happen. The devil be damned. Is there no one else to talk about this Season, or is it because I've been gone so long the *ton* considered her fair game?"

Albert stirred in his chair uncomfortably. Camden enjoyed making Albert squirm. Knowing Miss Whittingham and her independent nature, she probably wouldn't even appreciate that he was trying to help her. In fact, he was sure of it. She would tell him in no uncertain terms that she knew what she was doing, and that she didn't need him to speak up for her.

"I'm not sure. Plenty of gossip to go around the *ton* from what I've heard. And I'm certainly not assuming any of the things I've heard about Miss Whittingham are true."

"I should think not," Camden said in disgust. "What rubbish the young bachelors spread about innocents these days. By the sound of things, I came home just in time to put a stop to this vilification. Please tell any and all who may approach you that Miss Whittingham is a lady with spotless character and above reproach."

Albert took the glass from the server, nervous as a cat in a room full of dogs. "You're certain of this?"

"Most certainly. I trust her implicitly," he said, knowing that couldn't be further from the truth. Mirabella had given him ample reason to not trust her, but there was no way he was going to let Albert know that.

"I think you might be a bit too accepting, Stonehurst, considering you've been gone for six years and considering your past with your first fiancée."

Past indeed. Maybe that was the reason he was defending Miss Whittingham so staunchly. He'd had one woman make a fool out of him in front of all Society.

He'd be damned if he'd let another. If there was any way he could quell the rumors, he was going to do it.

Camden remained calm. "Talk was bound to happen. I stayed away too long. I can see that now. Miss Whittingham has told me she has flirted and danced with many gentlemen of the *ton* while I've been away. I'm perfectly fine with this, I assure you."

"I trust your judgment, Stonehurst. I'll say nothing more on the subject."

"Thank you. If you hear any more such gossip smearing her good name, I know I can trust you to set the gossipmongers right immediately."

Albert was obviously stunned by Camden's reaction and didn't speak right away.

"Can't I?" Camden demanded, more forcibly than he should.

"Yes, by all means you can count on me, Camden. Oh, look. There's Sir Billingsly. I'm to have a round of billiards with him. Would you excuse me?"

"Of course."

"I must run now, Camden. I'll see you by the by." He rose and gave Camden a good-natured pat on his upper arm. "And welcome back."

As soon as Albert had his back turned Camden downed his drink, emptying the glass. He must be the biggest of fools. The devil take him. What was he doing defending a woman who so obviously didn't want it? She didn't want any part of him, and didn't deserve his protection. Mirabella had made it quite clear her reputation didn't matter.

Damnation. It wasn't so much that he didn't want anyone knowing he'd been fooled by yet another young lady. He didn't want anyone speaking ill of Mirabella. And he believed her when she said she had had no hope of his return. But how many young gentlemen had she kissed?

And what about her father? Did it matter to her if he knew she was being talked about in a way that would keep her from making a suitable match?

Blast it! Was he smitten by her?

Maybe he should try one more time to reason with her before he told his parents he had failed to win Miss Whittingham over. At this point he had nothing to lose. He was defending her anyway.

He remembered her words when he'd foolishly kissed her. *I feel as if I haven't ever been kissed before you.*

Those words had washed over him like warm water on a cold day. He remembered how easily her lips melted against his and how soft she felt pressed against his chest. He liked looking at the sparkle in her green eyes. He even liked the way she stood up to him and forced him to shoulder some of the blame for the situation she found herself in.

No, God help him, he wasn't ready to give up on Miss Mirabella Whittingham.

Seven

"Lord Stonehurst, thank you for coming so quickly," Mirabella said as the viscount handed his hat, gloves and overcoat to a servant.

Concern showed in his eyes. "How could I not? I had just arrived home when I received your message saying that it was urgent you speak to me before I talked to my father about our discussion."

"Yes." Mirabella paused and waited until the servant left the foyer before she continued. "It wasn't my intention to worry you."

"More intrigued, I would say."

"No doubt."

"You were adamant at the end of our last conversation."

She caught her bottom lip for a moment. "Let's go into the drawing room where we'll have more privacy. It's late for tea. Would you care for something stronger?"

"Do I need it to fortify me for what you are about to say?"

An amused smile played on his lips and in his eyes. It took her aback for a moment. Did he think this a game? "I believe you are flirting with me, sir."

"Perhaps I am."

So he wasn't too angry with her for rejecting his proposal. "That's very kind of you after the way I've treated you."

"I've been dealt worse and lived through it."

"I'm sure that's true."

"So, do I need that drink?"

Her tense mood lightened. How could she stay serious when he had such a delightful twinkle in his eyes? It certainly wasn't there when he'd left her earlier that day.

She responded to his question by saying, "I believe you might want a shot of something, Lord Stonehurst. I'm thinking of asking you to remain engaged to me for a time."

"Then by all means let me have a drink."

Mirabella should have been nervous, but she wasn't as she led him into the drawing room. She had hoped to be done with him but her father's reaction to the viscount's return had left her no choice but to ask him to do what he had suggested and renew their engagement.

"Shall I pour?" he asked.

"Please do."

"How about you? Care for a sherry?"

"No, thank you. I'm fortified enough."

Camden picked up the crystal decanter and poured, barely covering the bottom of the glass with the dark liquor. Obviously he didn't need liquor to give him courage. That pleased her.

"If you will sit down, I'll get right to the point. I don't want to take up any more of your time than necessary."

He remained standing by the sideboard and let his dark brown gaze sweep down her face. A tingle of awareness pricked her skin. His hat or the wind had blown a lock of his hair out of place, and she ached to walk over and comb it with her fingers for him.

"No hurry, Miss Whittingham. My social calendar isn't yet full." He touched the rim of the glass to his lips and sipped the drink without taking his gaze off her. "You look lovely tonight. What is that color of your dress? Yellow or beige?"

Mirabella looked down at her flounced skirt and saw that it shimmered elegantly in the candlelight. "I believe the dressmakers are calling it buttercream this year."

"Yes, that's the perfect name for it. Very becoming." He took a seat on the floral-printed settee.

"Thank you." She cleared her throat and said, "I now believe I might have been too hasty in making my decision not to continue with our engagement for a few months longer."

"Really?" The corners of his lips twitched with humor.

He was teasing her, but she didn't mind. "As surprising as it must be, considering how unbending I was earlier in the day, I find that your proposal now suits my needs. I would like to take you up on your offer."

He didn't say a word, only continued to search her face with a thoughtful expression, giving her reason to doubt her wisdom in approaching him.

Unable to wait him out, Mirabella hurried to say, "That is if the offer you made is still on the table, sir."

"Just so we are clear on this, specifically, how did you remember the offer as being made?"

She thought back. "You suggested that we continue with the pretense of an engaged couple. We would attend parties and balls, stroll in the park, and take rides down Rotten Row. We would also make a few wedding plans to make it all seem very legitimate."

"I remember it that way as well. Is this what you are proposing," he paused, "or is it something more?"

An unexpected rush of anticipation filled Mirabella's chest. She wondered if he were aware of how he affected her. "No, no more. Just as you had stated it."

"Since you have come to me this time, I feel free to inquire what happened that you have so sudden a change of heart."

"I agree. That's a reasonable question, and it has a very simple answer. My father is the reason. I'm afraid I don't have that rare courage you suspected me of having."

His eyes narrowed. "How so?"

She took a seat in the oval-back, tapestry covered armchair facing him. "My father has not been well recently. His physician has him on strong medication, and we hope that he will be well again, but as time progresses and there is little improvement, his future health is doubtful."

"What is his problem?"

"The doctor says his heart is weak. He has very little energy to do the smallest tasks. Even though he has been ill, he has looked forward to your return with great anticipation."

"Something you failed to do."

She stiffened a little, but tried not to show it. "I didn't give up on you, my lord, until after years of futile hope had passed."

"Perhaps now you know that one must never give up hope."

"If ever again I think I might, rest assured I will remember your unexpected return and renew my expectation with vigor."

He lifted his drink in a toast to her and took a sip as their eyes met again and held. Lord Stonehurst was such a powerful looking man dressed in fawn-colored riding breeches, casually-styled cravat and black coat. Even though his words were a bit harsh, the sparkle never left his dark brown eyes. Mirabella felt an unexpected sense of loss, knowing she would never really be able to have a relationship of any significance with this gentleman.

He would surely be an easy man to get to know and banter with if fate hadn't stepped in their way. She put aside thoughts of what might have been. The die had been cast, and she couldn't go back and change her damaged reputation. Her only course was to go forward with her plans.

Mirabella cleared her throat. He kept leading her off the subject at hand. She had to focus. "This afternoon when I went up to visit with my father, I told him you had returned, but that I didn't want to marry you. He refused to listen to any of my arguments about why we shouldn't marry."

"I assume not a one of your arguments was the truth."

"All were truthful, sir, but none of them hinted at what you witnessed last night."

"I'm sure."

"My father was absolutely exuberant about the news of your arrival. I have not seen him this happy in years. He laughed out loud for the first time in many months."

"I can see how much that pleased you by the glow that has lighted in your eyes."

"Oh, yes." She smiled at Camden. "It's as if your returning has given my father a new lease on life. He now has reason to fight this weakness that grips him. I'm sure my father will live many more happy years, but he had convinced himself that his days were short. If you are still willing, I would like to continue the engagement until my father is well and better able to handle the truth of why we can't possibly marry."

"I see."

"I hoped you would understand."

He placed his glass on the table in front of him and asked, "What would you say if I told you that my offer was no longer available?"

Her smile slowly faded, her shoulders slumped ever so slightly. "I would be gravely disappointed."

"And?"

"I would be forced to tell my father the truth of my recent actions and admit that you don't want to marry me because of them." A new urgency bolted inside her. Mirabella rose from her chair and seated herself on the settee beside him. "I would rather not put either of us through this unnecessary ruse, my lord. I have no great desire to falsely portray ourselves as something we're not, an engaged couple. That is the main reason I declined your offer in the first place, but as you said, this would be good for both of us."

"I did say that."

"I believe that to be true. I really see no other way to make my father happy and give your father the time he needs to get his financial affairs in proper order."

Camden listened intently, and then asked, "So now, if I don't agree, you will be forced to tell your father the truth?"

"Yes."

"And what exactly is the truth, Miss Whittingham?"

Was he trying to corner her for more details? "That I allowed certain liberties, a kiss or two." *Or three.*

"Is that the whole truth?"

"What do you mean?"

He leaned in close to her, lowered his voice and asked, "Just how many men have kissed you, Miss Whittingham?"

Mirabella didn't shrink from his question or his imposing nearness which had her pulse racing. She didn't know the answer to that question without looking at her list of suspects. Possibly eight or ten, but she couldn't be sure because she hadn't counted them.

They were only brief little kisses and embraces, lasting only long enough for her to slip her little finger down the gentleman's neckcloth to search for a scar. Would he think any worse of her if he knew she was the one who had initiated the kisses from the young gentlemen?

"Obviously one was enough to ruin my reputation in your eyes and deem me unfit to be your bride,

Lord Stonehurst. What would be the point in admitting to more?"

"So there were more than the one young man I saw with you last night?"

"Yes." She lifted her shoulder to a more rigid pose. "Either your offer is still open, or it isn't. Although I would be disappointed to do so, I'm quite prepared for us to go our separate ways."

"I believe you are."

He had keen, observant eyes, and he studied her thoroughly.

"You're not going to let me forget that I rejected your earlier offer, are you?"

"No one likes rejection."

"And no one knows that better than I. Believe me, I am now wishing I had been more generous with my sympathy when you were here this afternoon."

"So do I, Miss Whittingham. My offer is good. Our engagement will not be broken right away."

Mirabella let out a shaky breath. "Thank you," she whispered softly.

"You are welcome."

She moistened her lips and said, "I would like to make a stipulation."

"You have some nerve, Miss Whittingham, wanting to add a stipulation after I've agreed to your counteroffer."

"It's one I think you will be pleased with."

"I'm listening."

"I would like for us to be completely honest with each other. There's no reason for us to be coy or elusive since we both know this will be a ruse."

"I like the sound of it."

"I would like to ask that if at any time you feel you can't go on with this subterfuge, you will give me time to speak to my father."

"I concur." He rubbed his chin absently. "Completely honest, you say?"

"Yes."

"How many gentlemen have you kissed, Miss Whittingham?"

"Does the answer to that have a bearing on our agreement, or are you merely curious?"

"Given our promise to total honesty I have to admit to curiosity."

"So our agreement stands no matter my answer."

He pursed his lips attractively, causing Mirabella to capture her bottom lip with her teeth and hold it a moment before letting go. She remembered those beautiful lips of his massaging hers with demanding pressure. She remembered feeling things deep inside herself that she'd never felt before even though the kiss was very brief.

"I might end up regretting this, but yes, our agreement stands no matter your answer."

"In that case, my complete honest answer is that I've said all I intend to say on the subject."

Camden grinned. "You tricked me. I thought you were going to confess."

"I didn't trick you," Mirabella said, feeling a good measure of satisfaction, and a breathless excitement that she was going to spend time with this man. "I answered you honestly."

"I have a stipulation of my own."

"What is that?" she asked, her voice a little huskier than she would have liked.

"I don't want anyone to know that this is not a real engagement. This includes your uncle, your maid, your friends, or anyone else you might be tempted to confide in."

"I think that is a very good idea."

"Good. Since you are my fiancée, I think you should call me Camden, and I will refer to you as Mirabella."

She liked the way he said her name with an American flavor to the roll of it. "Very well."

"I also think we both should skip the parties for the next few nights and attend the Chesterfields' soiree on Saturday night. Everyone we know should be at that one. I'll see to it that my parents and my brother attend, and I'll make a point of introducing you to them."

"That sounds the sensible thing to do."

"I think Mr. Hornbeck should continue to escort you to the events and chaperone you."

"I think he will agree to that."

"I want you to arrive exactly at half past ten. Wait in the foyer until I come for you. The more people who know you have arrived, the better. Your entrance will be when I go and claim your hand."

"I understand."

"This will be a signal to the *ton* that my entire family is in agreement and happy about this engagement. That should help stanch the flow of gossip about you that's making the rounds."

"It's most kind of you to do this, Lord Stonehurst. After seeing how happy my father was, I dreaded telling him about the incident you witnessed last evening."

"It's Camden, remember? And I don't expect there will be a repeat of anything that happened while I was away."

"You have my word on that." Her kissing days were over. Now that Camden had shown her what kissing was really like, she couldn't bear the thought of any other man pressing his lips to hers.

The next step in finding Sarah's seducer would be finding a way to get into a gentlemen's club so that she could get a look at the necks of the men. She couldn't trust Lily to look the gentlemen over thoroughly. Mirabella would wear a disguise so no one recognized her.

Camden reached into his coat pocket and pulled from it a small black box. "This is a gift for you."

"For me?" She took the case and stared into his eyes. "I don't understand."

"I had it with me when I came earlier today."

"But... I thought your finances were low, sir."

"That is true, but it doesn't mean that certain proprieties shouldn't be observed. I've not been here to court you properly. You are my fiancée, and I intend to act the part. That includes giving you flowers and gifts, as well as being seen with you all over Town."

"Oh, but our engagement's not real."

He gently laid his forefinger upon her lips. The pressure was slight but heady. Pleasure filled her. At that moment, Mirabella knew she desired Camden the way a woman should want the man she was to marry. He stirred her like no other man ever had. She hardly dared breathe. She didn't move or twitch, not wanting to break this seductive contact with him.

"Not even to ourselves will we entertain the thought that this is not a proper engagement," he whispered. "In all ways, everyone, including you and I, will be thinking this engagement will end in marriage. From this day forward we will act and plan as if we'll be married next spring. Understand?"

She nodded.

"You have beautiful lips," Camden said and ran his finger across them, down her chin and neck to the hollow of her throat and let it rest there.

Mirabella wasn't sure she was breathing. His caress stirred wonderful sensations deep in her abdomen. "You have a gentle touch, sir."

She heard his shaky intake of breath.

"You are a mystery, Mirabella, with your beautiful green eyes and tempting lips. It's no wonder every worthy gentleman in London was gaming for your attention when the years passed and I failed to show up and claim you for my bride."

A mystery. If only she could tell him about Sarah, she wouldn't be a puzzle to him any longer. But she couldn't. He would demand that she stop and make her promise not to continue her search. She couldn't give up until she had found the vile man and made him pay.

Remaining very close to her he said, "Open your gift."

She peeled back the top of the box and exposed a delicately fashioned necklace of emerald and diamonds with matching earrings lying on a bed of black velvet. She looked up at him with wonder in her eyes.

"They are lovely, my lord. This is so unexpected. I don't know what to say."

"'Thank you' is usually appropriate."

"Indeed it is, and I am most grateful, but I'm afraid I also feel undeserving."

"My fiancée deserves the best and more. Everyone has made me feel like a schoolboy whose knuckles have been rapped. I have a lot of catching up to do. I should like for you to wear them on Saturday evening."

She gave him an appreciative smile. "You have excellent taste, sir. I shall be happy to."

"All I needed was to look at you. Your eyes are much lighter in color than the emeralds, but the beauty of the stones perfectly matches your lovely face."

She blushed at his comment and looked down at the precious stones again. She felt totally undeserving of his generosity. She would give the jewelry back to him once the engagement was broken.

"So, what do you think, Mirabella? Should we seal our new engagement with a kiss?"

Her heart fluttered. "You mean you want to kiss me again?"

"Oh, yes," he whispered. "You are my fiancée, and a beautiful lady. Why wouldn't I want to kiss you?"

"You know I have allowed other gentlemen to kiss me."

"That doesn't lessen a man's desire to capture the lips of a ravishing lady."

"I find that strange, my lord. You don't want to marry me because I've kissed another gentleman, but you don't mind kissing me."

He seemed to study the point for a moment. "That is because you are taught such things in polite society.

That is not the case in real life. One man's lips do not poison a lady's lips for all other men."

She took a deep breath and lifted her face toward his. "Then by all means, I believe that one kiss is usually appropriate after a renewed engagement."

"Then let it be a long one," he whispered.

Eight

CAMDEN PLACED HIS HANDS ON HER SHOULDERS AND bent his head low, gently pulling her to him. His lips grazed lightly but constantly over hers. She leaned toward him accepting and accelerating the power of the kiss, not wanting it to end too soon. She felt strength from his hands, which gripped her tightly.

Mirabella was filled with a longing and a hunger she didn't understand, but knew she didn't want these feelings to go away, and she hadn't felt such wonderful sensations with any other man's kiss. A thrilling warmth spread throughout her as all her senses burst to life. She loved the touch of his hands on her arms and the taste of his lips on hers. She caught the fresh scent of shaving soap and heard the soft sound of his breathing. Her lashes fluttered upward, and she saw his handsome face so very close to her own.

She lifted her arms and let them circle his neck. His hands slid down her back to cup her waist and bring her up tighter against him. The kiss deepened. Mirabella didn't know why, but she parted her lips. Camden slipped his tongue into her mouth. She gasped as something wonderful happened to her insides.

He must have assumed her intake of breath was a sign he'd gone too far because he slowly let go of her and backed away.

Mirabella's cheeks heated. Did he know how tantalizing the kiss had been for her? She felt as if pleasure radiated from her and she didn't want the feelings to end.

She didn't know why she'd encouraged his kiss. Oh heavens, what a wanton he must think her to be. She wished she could tell him that he was the only man she had ever kissed because she wanted to.

"You have sweet lips, Mirabella," he said.

"You are a most delightful kisser, sir. For a moment I thought my heart might stop beating."

Camden cleared his throat and glanced away from her as he said, "Yes, well."

"Did you not like what I said?"

"No, of course I did. I'm flattered."

"And embarrassed I was so truthful?"

He smiled sweetly at her. "I assure you, Mirabella, it is every man's desire to give heart-stopping kisses."

"Yes, I suppose it would be."

Camden rose from the settee. "I must go tell my family the good news of our renewed engagement."

"So, you are sure they will be pleased?"

"Definitely."

"And we know where we stand. You are doing this for your father, and I'm doing this for mine."

His eyes suddenly had a faraway look to them. "I believe that's where we were six years ago, isn't it? Becoming engaged to please our parents."

"Yes, I guess it's comforting to know that some things don't change."

"Some things don't need to. Good night, Mirabella."

"Good night, Camden."

She walked with him to the door. She took his hat and gloves off the entrance table and his fine wool coat off the hall stand and handed them to him.

"I feel quite indebted to you, sir."

"Likewise. I'll see you at half past ten Saturday evening."

"I'll be there."

Camden opened the door, and Mirabella saw Archer walking up the front steps dressed in evening attire. Merciful heavens. She had failed to send word to her uncle that she wouldn't be going out this evening.

"Good evening, Mr. Hornbeck."

"Lord Stonehurst," Archer acknowledged the viscount by taking off his hat as they passed each other on the landing. He stopped and watched Camden climb into a carriage.

"Do come in, Uncle."

Archer stepped into the entrance way and hung his own hat and coat while Mirabella closed the door. He turned to her with his pale blue eyes wide with surprise.

"Bless the saints," Archer said, "he looked chipper enough for a man who's been made the fool by a woman for the second time."

Mirabella bristled at her uncle's choice of words. "Please, Uncle. Those words were most uncalled for. Lord Stonehurst is more courageous and generous than you might imagine."

"Do tell."

"He does not deserve callous remarks from you or anyone."

"As you say, but never mind the viscount. How did it go with your father? I tried to warn you not to be so free with your kisses, Mirabella, more than once. I simply don't recognize you anymore."

"I hardly recognize myself. It's most unfortunate that Camden chose a most inopportune time to return."

"I'll say. I've been in a dither about this all day. Couldn't eat a bite, knowing I failed you and your father."

"Actually, Uncle, you have failed no one. You can relax and not worry. Everything has been worked out satisfactorily."

"Does that mean your father is sending you to the country to be with your aunt Helen?"

"Dear me, no. Lord Stonehurst and I have worked everything out. He and I have decided not to break our engagement, and my father doesn't know anything about what happened last evening. I intend to keep it that way."

"What a turn of events." Archer shook his head absently. "Last night, when I left, I would have sworn on the Holy Book that your life would be a shambles and you would be in tears today. What's this all about?"

She promised Camden she would tell no one, but would have loved to confide everything to Archer. But she would keep her vow of silence. "We talked and made some decisions. Lord Stonehurst and I understand each other, and we are in full agreement that we will be married next spring as planned."

Archer's face flamed red and his eyes bulged. "I don't believe it. It can't be true. I saw—he saw you in the arms of another man. The last time that happened to him he sailed for America within a month."

"Shh, Uncle, please." She put a finger to her lips. "Lower your voice. I've kept my behavior from Papa this long and now that things are worked out, I don't intend for him to overhear your outbursts."

"I'm sorry," he said, pulling his handkerchief from his pocket and dabbing his forehead. "Tell me how. Why? I don't understand. I came here fully prepared to tell your father that I would marry you to save your reputation from complete ruination."

Shock caught in her throat. Her uncle was far too old for her to even consider such an arrangement. She gave him a grateful smile. "What a dear you are, but as you can see, your chivalry is not needed. Lord Stonehurst is a very astute and understanding man. Quite modern, too, I might add. I simply told him the truth." *Part of it.* "I had given up all hope of being a bride, but I didn't want to go through life never being kissed."

"And he accepted that?"

"With what I've just told you, do you doubt it's true?"

"No, no. Not at all," he said, mopping his face, though there was no sign of perspiration. "I—just—I'm surprised that he accepted your explanation so quickly. But, as you said, he is a man of modern times. No doubt the Americans with their loose ways got to him."

Mirabella laughed. "You are so flustered, Uncle, you aren't making sense."

"Well, dear girl, I have reason to be perplexed. I thought I would come here tonight and have to explain to your father why your reputation was in shambles and beg him to forgive me for not taking better care of you. Yes, I believe this has quite undone me."

She smiled. "Not to worry now," she said with complete confidence.

"And I am happy about that, but you're not dressed. Why aren't you ready to go out to the parties tonight?"

"Lord Stonehurst thought it best if he and I stay away from the parties until the Chesterfields have their grand soiree on Saturday evening. You and I will go to the ballroom as planned. We will wait in the entrance until Lord Stonehurst comes for me. We shall attend that ball together and others. We want to show Society that all is well with us."

"A very good idea. But I will continue to be your chaperone and not let you out of my sight for a moment. No more trips to the garden for you."

"Absolutely, Uncle."

"Good."

"Now, Papa wants to see you. I must have your word that you will not say anything to him about what happened last night with Mr. Farthingdale or anything else you may have heard."

"I assure you, I don't want him knowing about that any more than you do, but what's to keep Mr. Farthingdale from spilling all?"

"Nothing, of course, and I do realize this whole affair could end up in the Society columns tomorrow morning. But Mr. Farthingdale did seem quite upset that Camden came upon us in the garden. I would like to think he will be a gentleman about this and remain quiet."

"I fear that is too much to ask, but we can hope." Archer turned to go up the stairs when he stopped and asked, "What is it that you hold in your hand?"

Mirabella carefully took off the lid and revealed the emerald and diamond necklace and earrings.

"An engagement gift from Lord Stonehurst?"

She nodded, knowing that appreciation sparkled in her eyes. His family's income wasn't what it once was, yet he bought her the most beautiful jewelry she had ever seen.

"About time," Archer mumbled and looked down at the jewelry. "Dear girl, I do hope you know what you almost lost and that you will be the epitome of propriety from now until you are safely married."

A sudden feeling of guilt robbed her of any feeling of victory over keeping the engagement sound.

Mirabella watched her uncle walk up the stairs and whispered to his back, "No, not yet, Uncle. I cannot give up my quest to find Sarah's seducer and have him banished from Society."

❧

Camden took off his coat and hat and placed them on the hall stand in the corner of the small foyer of his parents' town home. He noticed that the flocked wallpaper was peeling away from the corners of the walls. A fine layer of dust covered the marble-topped pedestal in the center of the room.

As soon as he had his father's pressing financial matters under control, he would concentrate on getting the maid some help with the cleaning, cooking and clothing. He also wanted to do things like refurbish the town house for his parents. It had been neglected for too long.

He stood in the foyer for a moment longer and looked at a vase of flowers sitting on the table, no doubt cut by his mother that morning. He couldn't help but notice their color was the same shade of pink as Mirabella's lips. He relaxed and let his mind drift back over his conversation with her, and their kiss. She was a fascinating woman.

If for no other reason than he was going to enjoy getting to know her, he was glad they were to continue their engagement. He had a feeling there wouldn't be a dull moment with her. She wouldn't tell him how many men she had kissed. Why? Was it two? Three? A dozen? And why did he need to know? He certainly didn't want to have to divulge to her how many women he'd kissed since their engagement.

There was Albert, too, and his malicious ramblings about Mirabella's impropriety. How many other gentlemen were talking about Mirabella? No matter. He had to stop it immediately, and he needed his family's help to do that.

He didn't know why he felt so satisfied about having Mirabella as his fiancée. In truth, he should be smarting about the whole affair. Maybe his stint in America had changed him. Mirabella was lovely, desirable, and captivating. Damnation, the list could go on forever. He couldn't blame the men for wanting to kiss her. He couldn't blame her for not wanting to go through life never having been kissed.

It puzzled him that he had not been repulsed by her as he had been by Hortense six years ago. He had had no desire to kiss *her* after she was caught in another man's arms, but Mirabella still fascinated him, still tempted him. Maybe it wasn't as important the second time around, or maybe it was that this time Mr. Hornbeck had been the only other witness and not half the *ton*. He didn't know the answer yet and maybe that was what made her so intriguing.

He strode into the parlor and found his father reading and his mother doing needlework. "Good evening," he greeted them.

His mother looked grave and laid her sewing aside. "Hello, Camden."

"Evening, Son. I trust you had a good day."

His father had the look of a man beaten down. Perhaps this time he was truly sorry for having squandered his inheritance and putting his family in dire jeopardy from gambling and fools' games. Camden could only hope it wasn't too late to save them from the creditors.

"We've been waiting for your return," his mother said. "Betty told us you had come in for a little while, but that you left suddenly without a word after reading a note that had been delivered. She has held dinner for you."

"Perhaps you'd like a drink first?" his father asked, rising from his chair and heading for the satinwood sideboard.

Mirabella had fortified him with all he needed. "No, thank you. I'm fine. I have just come from a long discussion with Miss Whittingham." His mother straightened. His father returned to his chair. "As you can imagine, we had many things to discuss."

"We know, dear. Your father and I had a long talk, too. We want you to know we understand why you can't go through with the wedding, all things considered. Your father and I will manage somehow."

"No, Mama. Miss Whittingham and I decided to continue our engagement. Although she and I will not marry in the near future."

Norine's eyes brightened. "Oh, Camden. Are you sure about this?" She put her face into her handkerchief.

He walked over and took her hand from her face. "Don't cry, Mama. Of course, I'm sure. This is not a time for tears."

"Thank you, Son," his father said. "I'm sure the gossip about her will die down now."

"What gossip?" his mother asked, lifting her head.

"Well—er—I only meant that if Camden caught her in the arms of another man, surely someone else saw them. You know how things like that get around the *ton*. There's bound to be talk."

So his father had heard about Mirabella's indiscretions. No doubt several people had, which was why Albert felt comfortable in bringing it up to Camden. Why it hadn't hit the Society columns, he didn't know.

"There are some conditions to my agreeing to this, Father."

"What does the chit want in return?"

"Mirabella?" Camden frowned. He didn't like the tone of voice his father used when he referred to her. "The conditions are from me, not her."

"Oh, of course, I see."

"Starting tomorrow morning, I will be in complete charge of the finances in this family. You are to have papers drawn up and signed tomorrow morning giving me control over your accounts, your debts, your holdings."

His father rose from his chair. "See here, Camden. That's going too far."

Camden kept his gaze steady on his father's. "Maybe, but that's the way it has to be. I want to meet with all your creditors. First on the list will be the man who holds the mortgage on your lands. I only hope I have enough funds to take care of immediate needs, buy back the mortgages and keep the town house, too."

"Listen to him, Wilson," his mother said. "I think it's time you do this. You have never had control when it comes to money."

The earl nodded.

"Mama, on the way home I stopped by a dress-maker and made arrangements for a seamstress to be here at eleven o'clock tomorrow morning. She will fit you for new gowns and dresses." He looked at his father. "And you, sir, need a new suit of clothes, too."

"Oh, Camden, you know we don't have the money."

"Any money you were to spend on us, put it to Hudson. He needs it. We don't go out anymore."

"That is about to change. We will all attend the party at the Chesterfields' Saturday night, and my fiancée will be on my arm. It's time the two of you came out of hiding. We have to show a united front to the *ton* that we are delighted to welcome Miss Whittingham into our hearts and our family. She is my fiancée, and I don't want any more gossip about her. I need you to help me stop that. Is that understood? If anyone should hint at any indiscretion by her, you are to shame them and tell them they are out of line."

"But of course. We understand, and we'll do whatever you want us to."

"Now, if Hudson needs a new suit of clothes, I'll see he gets them after you two are taken care of."

"Oh, Camden, I knew things would be better when you came home. I knew you would take care of everything. Thank you for coming home to save us."

"Wait, Mama. Father hasn't agreed to my conditions."

Camden and his mother turned to the earl, but he remained quiet.

"Wilson?" his wife said.

"I don't think our son's conditions are necessary, but all right. I'll sign everything over to you as soon as the papers are ready. I've made such a mess of everything that, without your help, I don't have anything anyway. I just want your mother to be properly cared for."

"Father, we need to pay the most pressing debts. We'll work on that tomorrow. Now, there's one other thing."

"What's that?"

"I want to know if you have been putting pressure on Hudson to offer for Miss Pemberton?"

"What? No pressure was needed. He loves that young lady, and she is a perfect match."

Camden saw guilt in his father's eyes. He knew what he was about to do was best. "He may. But I won't allow you to let him offer for her until the family finances are out of trouble."

"That's madness. What if someone else offers for her in the duration? He'll never forgive us. It could very well happen. She's a catch."

Camden remembered the way they looked at each other and felt a moment of guilt himself. He wasn't thrilled to be doing this to Hudson.

"If she loves only him, she'll ask her father to wait. In the meantime, if that does happen, we will surely get wind of it and can proceed as necessary. I'm sure Miss Pemberton has already made it clear to her father that she wants to hear from no one but Hudson."

"We could use the money we'd get from her dowry to help pay our creditors, Camden. This is insane."

"No, Father. Getting money by dowry to pay your gaming debts is what's insane. And we won't do it again. Once was enough. Now, are we in complete agreement?"

His father stood his ground for a moment. Norine eased to the edge of her chair.

"Yes," the earl finally answered.

Camden breathed a sigh of relief. "I'm going up to my room. Have dinner sent up to me."

Turning from his parents, Camden headed up the short flight of stairs. There was no turning back for him. He would have to send word to his lawyer in America tomorrow to start liquidating his holdings over there.

He had enough cash in London to take care of the most immediate needs of his family, but to completely clear his family of all the debt his father had incurred through the years, he needed the assets he had built up in America—and he needed them fast.

It was a bitter pill to swallow. He had hoped to have the money to be his own man and not depend on his father's title or lands. Instead, he found himself making his family whole again. But now he would manage the lands and not let his father have enough money to gamble away.

He had also done something else he never expected to do. He had put himself at the mercy of a woman.

His stomach tightened. A very desirable woman.

Nine

MIRABELLA WAS SELDOM NERVOUS. SHE DIDN'T MAKE decisions lightly. She always thought them over carefully, in detail, which gave her ample reason to believe she would always make the right choice, thereby giving her confidence in whatever was at hand. But standing in the foyer of the Chesterfields' home in her sage-colored evening gown, with diamonds and emeralds sparkling from her ears and around her neck, her insides were trembling.

It was later than half past ten and there was no sign of Camden. A crowd of curious onlookers gathered round, desperately trying not to look like they were watching her, but she knew they were. Some threw curious glimpses her way and others issued chilly stares. She had noticed older ladies talking behind their wide-spreading fans and debutantes whispering behind gloved hands.

And why not? She and Archer had remained just inside the doorway since their entrance fifteen minutes ago.

Yellow light from the candles lit the gilt and marble room with a soft, romantic glow. Music from softly played violins could barely be heard above the constant roar of talking, laughing and moving about of the more than two hundred people who filled the grand house.

Archer coughed into his handkerchief, and then said to Mirabella, "Maybe we should go inside and find Lord Stonehurst. I don't like the draft here at the door, and I'm beginning to feel like a small fish in a rather large bowl."

Mirabella smiled at him. He was such a dear, patient gentleman to put up with all that she had put him through these last few days. He was a true friend to her and her father.

"No, Uncle. The plan is for us to wait for him here. I think it was his desire that we be the center of attention before he shows."

"If that's the case, we're a huge success." In a lower voice he grumbled, "However, it's easy for him to tell us what we must do when he's not the one standing here just inside the doorway looking like a piece of the statuary."

Mirabella laughed as she imagined a statue of Archer. He was short for a man and more than a bit paunchy around his middle. Most of the statuary Mirabella had seen showed the male form looking like Adonis or Michelangelo's great statue of David. Archer didn't have the physique to compete.

"I have total trust that Camden knows what he is doing."

"Hmm. No doubt whatever it is, it's something he picked up when he was across the sea with the unmannerly Americans."

"My faith in him is not diminished because he is late or because of what he may have learned while he was away."

Archer sniffed. "Your confidence is admirable. Yes, well, since he is the one doing us the favor in rescuing your reputation from certain ruin, we do need to allow him to do it his way."

"Exactly."

"I do wish he'd get on with it."

"Oh, Uncle, you have no patience. I've seen at least two young ladies walking by and giving me unpleasant expressions. I think it must be that they are not happy I'm keeping you so long from the party."

He quirked a bushy eyebrow at her and glowed with pleasure. "Truly? I hadn't noticed."

Mirabella smiled, then softly laughed out loud. Archer couldn't fib any better than she could.

A few minutes later, she watched as a young gentleman named Sir Thomas Rollinson approached her. He had dashing good looks with sky blue eyes, soft brown hair and was well below the average height of most young men. Her senses heightened. He was on her list of possible suspects.

Good heavens, what was she thinking? There would be no trips into the garden with him tonight or ever, thanks to Camden's return. She had to find some other way to see the crook of his neck and the only idea she had at present was to sneak her way into the gentlemen's clubs.

"Good evening, Miss Whittingham. Mr. Hornbeck."

Archer barely nodded to the young man. Mirabella said, "How do you do, Mr. Rollinson?"

"Very well, thank you. Lovely weather we're having tonight."

"Indeed," Archer said in a bored-to-tears tone.

Mr. Rollinson cleared his throat uncomfortably. "Might I say you look simply ravishing this evening, Miss Whittingham."

Mirabella smiled at him. "Thank you, sir. That is most kind of you."

"I couldn't help but notice you've been standing here for a few minutes. The buffet is being served. Mr. Hornbeck, I was wondering if you would allow me to escort Miss Whittingham inside for you?"

Archer patted his forehead with his handkerchief, before giving the young man a look of dismissal. "No, I'm afraid I can't do that, Mr. Rollinson. We're waiting for someone."

Undaunted, Mr. Rollinson said, "And may I ask who that might be?"

"That would be Viscount Stonehurst, sir," Camden said walking up behind Mr. Rollinson. "And I am present. You will excuse us, won't you, while I escort Miss Whittingham inside?"

"By all means, my lord. I didn't realize you were here. Pardon me for intruding." He smiled at Mirabella, bowed and walked away.

"You are late, sir," Archer grumbled.

"I'm afraid that is the story of my life, Mr. Hornbeck. I offer apologies to you and Miss Whittingham."

Archer lifted Mirabella's hand and delivered her over to Camden who wrapped her fingers in the palm of his hand and gave her fingers a slight squeeze. Mirabella felt a delicious skittering of desire tighten her insides at his touch. Pleasing warmth spread through her.

She curtsied before him and whispered, "My lord."

He kissed the back of first one hand and then the other while keeping his gaze only on her face. "You are very lovely tonight, Mirabella. I don't know which is sparkling more, your eyes or the emeralds and diamonds you wear."

"Nothing could outshine your gift. Thank you again. They are beautiful. My father was most impressed."

"It's about time I did something to impress him." Camden turned to the older, impeccably dressed man standing beside him. Without introduction, Mirabella knew him to be Camden's father, and the quite pale and frail looking woman standing beside the earl had to be Camden's mother. If not for the grape-colored gown she wore and the colorful flowers in her headpiece, Mirabella was sure the countess would not have a hint of pink in her cheeks. "May I present my father, Earl Lockshaven. Father, this is Miss Mirabella Whittingham, and her chaperone, Mr. Archer Hornbeck."

The earl took her hand and kissed it. They exchanged polite greetings and smiles.

"May I present Countess Lockshaven."

"How do you do, Countess?" Mirabella greeted her with a curtsy.

"You are as lovely as I've heard," the countess said with a beaming smile. "We welcome you to our family."

"Thank you, my lady. It is my pleasure to meet you at last. My father has spoken well of your family for years."

"And I believe you've met my brother, Hudson," Camden said.

"Yes, we were introduced last Season."

"Indeed, we were introduced. I believe I met your cousin as well. My condolences. I heard of her untimely death."

Shock thundered through Mirabella. He had mentioned Sarah. She couldn't believe it. "Thank you," she mumbled. "It's very kind of you to remember her."

Over the years, she'd found that most people chose to pretend that Sarah wasn't around. At their parents' urgings, young bachelors would dance with Sarah, but not a one had ever called on her. No one except Prince Charming, and he had come to their house in the dark of night entirely in secret. Only a few of the older ladies of the *ton,* with unmarried daughters of their own, had even mentioned Sarah since the current Season started.

"How are you, Miss Whittingham?" Hudson bowed and kissed her hand.

"Very well, thank you." As the words faded from her lips, she saw a red patch of skin just above his neckcloth on the left side of his neck.

Mirabella's breath quickened. Could that be the beginning of a raised thick scar? Her mind swirled with possibilities. She thought back. Lord Hudson wasn't on her list of suspects, but that was only because Mirabella hadn't found his name on any of Sarah's dance cards, and he was quite tall.

Sarah had mentioned that her Prince Charming was shorter than most men. Mirabella wouldn't have considered Hudson short, but he had been one of the few members of the *ton* to even mention Sarah. Was it possible that Sarah's seducer was the brother of her betrothed? Merciful heavens! She had to know. But how?

The conversation continued around her, and Mirabella didn't know how but was sure she answered each question appropriately. She couldn't avert her attention from Hudson's neck. What she wouldn't do to reach over and slip her little finger down his neckcloth and search down to his collarbone as she had with the others. She couldn't very well do that for a number of reasons, not the least of which was that his entire family had her surrounded.

"Mirabella?"

Her gaze snapped to Camden. "Oh, I'm sorry, what did you say?"

"Are you ready to go in and dance before we dine?"

"Yes, I'd like that."

"Why don't you let me escort her in, Camden?" his father said. "And I would like a dance with her, too, if you don't mind."

Camden looked at his father and nodded. "I think that both would be good and appropriate."

The earl offered his arm to Mirabella and Camden offered his to Countess Lockshaven. The people who had gathered around the entrance to watch them parted and backed away. Mirabella and the earl walked through the opening in the crowd and made their way to the dance floor.

Mirabella heard her name whispered and gasps of surprise as she passed the curious partygoers, but the only thing on her mind was how in the world was she going to find out if Camden's younger brother had a scar on his neck?

The evening progressed much as they all had since Mirabella debuted four years ago. She twirled, swayed, skipped and glided as Camden and other young gentlemen led her across the dance floor into every appropriate turn, dance after dance. Camden was charming and attentive but not overly so.

Some of the guests must have heard that she had allowed certain liberties, but it was clear not everyone had. She was too well received for that to have happened. For the first time since her father had made the match, she felt as if she truly was engaged. It was a bittersweet feeling because she knew it wouldn't last.

Camden was an excellent dancer, not missing a step when she danced with him. Even though their engagement was a stratagem, Mirabella felt secure with him. She liked the strength she felt in him when he took hold of her gloved hands or when his hand lightly touched the small of her back or skimmed the top of her shoulder. She loved it when he smiled at her and, when he was talking with someone else, how his eyes searched for her among the crowd.

Shortly after midnight, they joined his parents again and dined from a buffet table laden with fish that had simmered in a wine sauce, pheasant covered in sherry-raisin gravy and a platter of braised beef surrounded by tenderly cooked vegetables.

After the meal they said good-bye to his family, but she and Camden stayed at the ball and danced again with each other and with other partners. They walked the ballroom and chatted with dukes, earls and a host of untitled attendees. Most of the ladies greeted her with friendly smiles and pleasant words. Only one countess had been cold as a cod and seemed to want to be anywhere but in Mirabella's presence.

Finally Mirabella pleaded that she needed to go to the ladies' retiring room. Once there, she sat down on one of the moiré-covered benches and closed her eyes for a moment to collect herself. Maybe, with Camden's help, she could salvage her reputation after all. Maybe the gossip about her escapades hadn't started and wouldn't.

"Miss Whittingham?"

Mirabella's eyes fluttered open. A short, slightly rounded young lady with beautiful red hair and light brown eyes stood before her. Mirabella didn't recognize her, but she wore a friendly expression.

Mirabella smiled and said, "Yes?"

"I'm Countess Glenbrighton. You might not remember me, but we were introduced two years ago. My husband, Albert Farebrother, Earl of Glenbrighton, and your fiancé have been friends since boyhood. And, I believe, their fathers were friends since childhood."

"Yes, I remember we met some time ago," Mirabella said, but truly could not place ever having met the countess. She rose to stand with the young lady. "How have you been?"

"Oh, perfect. I delivered my first child, a boy, ten months ago."

It was clear from the glow on Countess Glenbrighton's face that this baby was the joy of her life. "Wonderful for you and the earl," Mirabella said. "I'm sure your babe is strong and healthy and a constant pleasure."

"He is, thank you. I've just discovered I'm expecting again."

"You have reason to celebrate. That is happy news for you and your husband."

"Yes. He's thrilled. I wanted to renew our acquaintance in hopes the earl and I could have a small dinner party for you and Lord Stonehurst in honor of his return and your engagement."

"What a lovely thing to want to do, Countess." Mirabella was touched by the woman's generous offer. Because Mirabella had always had Sarah in whom to confide, she hadn't made a lot of friends since her debut.

Countess Glenbrighton laid a gloved hand on Mirabella's forearm. "Please call me Irene. I know we will be good friends because our husbands are so close."

"All right, Irene. I have to admit that I'm still getting used to the idea of Lord Stonehurst being home."

"And no wonder. His absence must have been troublesome for you. As soon as Albert and I made the match, we were able to begin our wedding plans, and now we have a handsome son."

"There are truly advantages to a fiancé being available."

"I know you must be eager to get started on your arrangements."

Mirabella smiled. She might as well get used to these kinds of comments. She had to pretend her wedding would occur. "Yes, though we haven't begun yet. He's so recently returned. Perhaps I could call on you one afternoon."

"Countess Glenbrighton!" a woman's shrill voice rang sharply throughout the small room.

Startled, they both turned to see a stern-looking, heavy-set older woman with a lace scarf covering most of her graying hair. Heavy red jewels circled her neck and dangled from her ears. Mirabella recognized her as the wife of the Duke of Highbury.

"Oh, Duchess, come let me present you to Miss Mirabella Whittingham."

The woman sniffed so hard her nose pinched unattractively. "No, thank you. I hear your husband is looking for you, Countess Glenbrighton. You are to go to him at once."

Irene looked at Mirabella with stunned embarrassment. The duchess had made her disapproval of the countess talking to Mirabella painfully clear.

"I'm sorry, I have to go. Perhaps the earl is ready to go on to another party."

Mirabella smiled sweetly at the kindly countess who had offered her friendship. It had felt wonderful. But she had a feeling this was as far as a relationship with Irene would go.

"I understand. Please go to your husband."

Irene glanced at the duchess then quickly back to Mirabella. "Do watch out for Lady Gwyneth Sackville. She's the belle of the Season this year and can have her pick of the beaux. Word is that she took one look at Lord Stonehurst when he was at the Worsters' the other night and set her cap for him. Do not be fooled by her charming smile."

A stab of jealousy tore through Mirabella at the thought that another young lady had designs on Camden.

She tried to blunt the pain by taking a deep breath and saying, "Thank you. I'll consider myself warned. You can be certain I will watch her with all diligence."

"I'll pay you a call one day soon," Irene said with a smile and turned away.

The duchess lifted her chin and jerked her head around stiffly and marched out of the retiring room behind Irene. Mirabella had never been so royally snubbed in her life.

A chill pricked her skin and the warm smile she had given her new friend faded from her lips. Clearly word of her indiscretions with the young gentlemen in the gardens had made its way to Duchess Highbury, and Mirabella couldn't help but wonder how many other ladies of the *ton*.

Mirabella plopped down on the bench and took another deep breath. She had given up all hope of a life with Camden weeks ago when she began her search for Sarah's seducer. She couldn't start thinking she had any claim on him now that he had returned.

What did it matter what the old *ton* thought about her? It didn't. Camden already knew about her indiscretions and was willing to continue acting as her betrothed. His and her father's opinions of her were the only two she worried about. They were the only two important people in her life.

The sting of the duchess's affront jabbed Mirabella anew. It was difficult to hold the doubts at bay. Were she and Camden only fooling themselves in thinking her reputation could be salvaged so she could finish this Season unblemished?

Mirabella feared this slight was only the beginning.

❧

Candles had burned low and early morning was on the rise when Camden shrugged off the group of gentlemen he was with and walked outside for fresh air. As soon as Mirabella returned he would suggest they leave. By all accounts, it appeared from the way she had been received by everyone they talked to that the evening had been a complete success. Mirabella had been delightful all night, a fiancée any man would want to have by his side.

Camden looked up at the early morning sky. He welcomed the chill in the air and let out a long deep sigh of discontent. How long had it been since he found delight in a woman? Correction. In a lady. Many women of the evening and a few wealthy widows had pleased him in America over the years he was there.

Tonight, Mirabella had pleased him more than he had expected. He hadn't planned on being smitten by her, but after dancing with her, holding her, touching her, he found he didn't want the evening to end— even though it was past four in the morning.

Still, there were lingering doubts about her that he couldn't shake. What had made her allow gentlemen to take her into the gardens and kiss her? Was it only that she wanted to be kissed or was there more as he suspected? Had she only kissed one or two, or had there been more gentlemen? Would he ever know?

Blast her, she was right when she said one was enough to ruin her name. The number didn't matter. That she kissed one man was unbelievable, inexcusable and unforgivable, but the problem was that she was

unforgettable. Mirabella had intrigued him the first night
they had met and that hadn't changed. In fact, he feared
he was even more intrigued by her. And, like it or not,
she had become a part of his life and would be for the
next several months. And that pleased him greatly.

"Stonehurst, over here."

Damnation. It was Albert, whom Camden had
successfully avoided all evening, calling and motioning
to Camden to join him and none other than Mr.
Farthingdale, the young man who was with Mirabella
in the garden a few nights ago.

Obviously Albert had been avoiding Camden, too.
It was no wonder considering all the things he'd said
about Mirabella that day at the club. Camden had felt
that he had left Albert feeling thoroughly shamed. No
doubt Albert had heard that he and Mirabella were a
smashing success tonight, and this was Albert's way of
getting back at him.

Camden suddenly had the feeling there was going
to be a bad ending to an otherwise pleasant party.

There was nothing to do but walk over and act as if
nothing out of the ordinary had happened with either
of the two men. It was clear to them that Camden had
seen them so there was no getting out of this meeting.

"Stonehurst, you're still here. Good. Somehow,
I've been missing you all evening."

Camden and Farthingdale barely nodded a greeting
to each other.

"I assume you two know each other," Albert said.

"Yes, we met briefly," Farthingdale said, a nervous
edge to his voice.

"Very briefly," Camden answered tightly.

"Seems you two have a lot in common."

"Is that right?" Camden's words got tighter.

"Both of you full of lust, don't you know."

Farthingdale's mouth gaped. His face paled at Albert's choice of words. "What do you mean?"

Camden glared at his friend, hoping Albert would stop this foolishness before Camden had to put a stop to it. Obviously Albert knew of Mirabella's liaison with Farthingdale in the Worsters' garden, and he wanted to have a little fun. Camden was in no mood to be the brunt of Albert's game.

"Wanderlust, that is." Albert laughed but didn't seem to notice that neither Farthingdale nor Camden cracked so much as a smile.

"Farthingdale was just telling me how he hopes to visit America one day," Albert continued, seeming oblivious to the strained atmosphere surrounding the two men standing with him. "Tell him, Farthingdale."

"Yes, it is true that I would like to travel there one day," the man said with an uncomfortable edge still in his voice.

Camden's gaze bored into Farthingdale's, hoping the man could see how much strength it was taking for Camden to keep his anger under control and make a hasty retreat. "Let me suggest that this is an excellent time of year to travel the seas and the land. Do plan to stay for a long time. There's so much to see."

"Oh, excuse me," Albert said. "There goes the Duke of Highbury. I need to speak to him. I must hurry."

Albert rushed away, leaving Camden feeling as if his friend had staged this undesirable meeting with the man who had so recently kissed Mirabella's lips. Suddenly Camden didn't know who he wanted to strangle more—Albert or Farthingdale.

"Farthingdale, I'm glad I caught up with you." A handsome young gentleman with a fair complexion came running up to them before either had the opportunity to take their leave. "I must ask if you were able to steal a kiss from Miss Whittingham the other night."

"Ah—no. No," he choked out. "She was a perfect lady. Perfect. I must introduce—"

"Do say?" the man interrupted, clearly not interested in who Camden was at the moment. "When I was in the garden with her she purred like a kitten in my arms."

Camden saw red.

Hell and damnation! How many men had Mirabella been with?

"Stephenson, stop. Please," Farthingdale said in a squeaky voice, his gaze jumping wildly from his friend to Camden. "I don't believe you've heard Miss Whittingham's fiancé is back in Town."

"And standing right beside you," Camden ground out, unable to hold on to his anger any longer.

In one fluid motion Camden grabbed Stephenson by the shoulders, pushed him backward, and then shoved him up against the side of the stone house. Without conscious thought, he rammed his forearm against the man's throat.

Stephenson's eyes bulged as his head smacked against the wall. With trembling hands and grasping fingers, he tried to rip Camden's arm away from his neck. Camden pressed harder with his arm.

"I don't believe anyone wants to hear anything you have to say about Miss Whittingham. Not now. Not ever," Camden said in a growling voice. "Do I make myself clear?"

Farthingdale drew in close to the two but didn't attempt to stop Camden. "I tried to warn you, you ninny. May I present Viscount Stonehurst, Miss Whittingham's fiancé, just back from the wild new land across the sea."

"This is—not the time for proper—introductions, Farthing—dale," Stephenson managed to say between gasps of much-needed air. "Help me, you jackass."

"Damnation, Lord Stonehurst," Farthingdale said. "This has gone far enough. Be done with it and let him go. You are choking him."

"That is my intention," Camden answered Farthingdale but kept his gaze on Stephenson. "Maybe he'd rather I call him out?"

"No, no." Stephenson shook his head, strangling with fear and pain and unable to speak more than a mumble.

"Dueling is against the law, and you know it," Farthingdale said.

"That doesn't keep it from happening to ill-mannered oafs who try to sabotage the reputations of properly brought up young ladies."

Camden moved his face closer to Stephenson's. "If you have anything to say about Miss Whittingham, say it now. I am the only one who wants to hear it."

"He will not say anything else," Farthingdale offered. "He doesn't have a death wish. Neither of us do."

"Good. So I can assume you will not mention her name again to anyone in public or private?"

Stephenson nodded, clearly in pain.

"And should anyone mention her name to you, you will only have very nice, very *appropriate* things to say, is that not right?"

Stephenson nodded again.

"Good. I'm glad we understand each other."

Camden turned to Farthingdale. "Do you and I understand each other?"

Farthingdale swallowed hard. "Yes, my lord."

Camden let go of Stephenson and backed away.

The man grabbed his throat and coughed as he moved away from Camden. Between broken gasps he said, "You... sir, are no gentle... man."

"Remember that."

"I couldn't breathe, you bastard. You almost killed me."

"I still might. You would do good to remember that as well."

"You wouldn't dare harm me."

The man obviously didn't know when he had gotten off easy. Camden took a step toward him and Stephenson backed up like the scared rabbit he was.

"Would you like to make a bet on that?" Camden said as coldly as he felt. "Make no mistake, Stephenson, I don't want to hear another unkind word about Miss Whittingham's reputation. If this talk about her doesn't stop immediately, I'll find you the next time you're walking past a narrow alley, riding alone in the dark, or so deep in your ale that you can't see straight. I will come for you and I will get you."

"You're a madman," he hissed.

"Then you are a brave man to test me."

"You are completely uncivilized."

"Some might say that. But make no mistake about this. I will not have you breathing an unkind word about Miss Whittingham again. I will do whatever I must for her. Are we clear on this?"

"Perfectly," Farthingdale said. "We're perfectly clear, aren't we, Stephenson?"

Stephenson wiped the corner of his mouth with the back of his hand and waited. He looked at Farthingdale, then back to Camden as if trying to decide what he wanted to say, how he wanted to react, and whether he had the courage to take Camden on again.

At last he said, "Miss Whittingham was a perfect lady when we met, Lord Stonehurst. I shall be happy to tell anyone who asks about her."

"Remember that when the poison-pen Society writers speak to you about Miss Whittingham. She is mine, and I will not have her reputation in tatters because of a couple of loose-tongued gabble-grinders."

Farthingdale and Stephenson backed away from him a few steps before turning and hurrying away. Camden took a deep breath. What the hell had gotten into him? He hadn't been this out of control when Hortense had been caught kissing that chap in front of half the *ton*.

Camden raked both hands through his hair. He knew the answer. Mirabella was different.

He felt differently about her. He sensed something was going on with her that she didn't want him to know about. He now knew she had kissed at least two men, yet she seemed so innocent.

He simply should be trying to save her reputation and buy himself time to get his money from America. Instead, he was drawn to her, and he didn't know what he was going to do about it.

Ten

CAMDEN FELT STIFF AS HE WALKED WITH MIRABELLA and her uncle out the front door of the grand ball-room and down the stone steps to where the drivers waited for their employers' evening to end. He saw his driver and Mr. Hornbeck's take off running to fetch their carriages.

While Camden helped Mirabella put on her satin-lined pelisse, he said to Mr. Hornbeck, "I would like for Mirabella to ride with me. Do you mind following in your carriage?"

"Yes, I do, my lord. It's not appropriate. If you want her to ride with you, I shall also so she can be properly chaperoned. My driver can follow us."

Camden was not going to let this short, untitled man set the rules tonight. "Nonsense, we are engaged, soon to be married. She should be allowed more freedoms. I believe it's perfectly acceptable."

"No, no. We are not having any of that. Too risky under the circumstances."

How much worse did he think her reputation could get!

"I give my word as a gentleman that Miss

Whittingham will not be harmed or compromised by riding in a closed carriage with me tonight."

Mr. Hornbeck snorted. "Mirabella has trod the fringes of respectability more than once. Every day I expect her father to call me in and give me a dressing down for not properly watching over her."

"I take full responsibility for her, Mr. Hornbeck," Camden said in a tone that really left no room for argument. "And should her father insist I would marry her within the week."

Mr. Hornbeck looked at Mirabella and blew out his breath loudly. "Very well," he said. "I've done all I can do to protect her. I can't do more. I'm most happy to give her over to your care, Lord Stonehurst. But remember, I'll be right behind you in my hack."

"I expect it."

Camden's hired carriage pulled up. The driver jumped down and opened the door for them. Camden helped Mirabella inside, then turned back to his driver and spoke softly so Mr. Hornbeck wouldn't overhear, "Take the long way to Miss Whittingham's home, and take it slowly."

Mirabella's uncle was going to be upset about that, but it would be too late to change course by the time he realized it. Blast it, Camden didn't really care what the old chap thought. After the disastrous debacle with Stephenson and Farthingdale, he needed to spend some time alone with Mirabella. He needed to know that he wasn't losing his mind in defending her. Maybe he should have just called Mr. Farthingdale out that night in the garden and been done with it quickly.

But no, he'd done that last time and had ended up sour with himself over what he'd done. And, afterward, he had realized Hortense hadn't been worth his honor. The poor man he challenged had been a mere eighteen and scared out of his trousers. He made it to the dueling site, but before it began, he threw down his weapon and ran. Camden was told he left for France that day and, as far as Camden knew, he'd never returned.

While he'd been abroad, his mother wrote and told him that Hortense had married a knight whose wife had died. He had been left with three small children. Shortly after the ceremony, they moved up to the North Country.

Camden shook off remnants of the past and climbed in after Mirabella, taking the seat opposite her. The driver shut the door soundly behind them. Seconds later, they started the jostling ride to her house. Faded yellow light from the outside lanterns streamed in through the cloudy windows on each door. The closed coach smelled of worn leather and clippings of evergreen twigs the driver must have thrown inside to freshen the small compartment.

Mirabella looked flushed. From dancing or something else? Damnation, would he always wonder with her? The gentle rocking of the carriage soothed him. In the dim light, he studied Mirabella as she settled her skirts and wrap about her legs. There was something intimately charging about being alone with her.

Her lips were full and a delicate shade of pink he found very tempting. Her eyes were wide and luminous, sparkling more than the jewels around her porcelain-looking neck. He liked the way her soft auburn curls fell out from under her ribbon hairpiece and framed her heart-shaped face.

It was a damnable thing, but he wanted to pull her into his arms and kiss her. Maybe he was a madman as Stephenson had suggested. He thought back to his altercation with the bachelors. Why had he bothered terrorizing the hell out of those worked up dandies? Was it simply a jealous binge because Mirabella was his fiancée, or was it more? Was it because he desired her?

That was why he'd wanted her to ride with him. He wanted to kiss her, make love to her, and make her forget any other man whose lips might have touched hers.

She is a temptress. A very desirable temptress.

"I think our first evening together as an engaged couple went very well," he finally said when he realized he couldn't continue to watch her and brood without saying anything to her.

"So do I, my lord. The party was a smashing hit."

She smiled at him and Camden felt his chest and his lower body tighten. "Do you really think so?"

Her gaze swept up and down his face before holding steady on his eyes. "Yes."

He chose his words carefully when he asked, "So no one said anything out of the ordinary to you?"

Her eyebrows rose a little. "Why do you ask? Did someone say something out of line to you?"

"To me? I was concerned about you."

"You needn't have been," she answered, keeping her gaze locked on his. "Nothing was said tonight that I couldn't handle."

Camden tensed. "So someone did say something beyond the line. Something happened. What?"

"Many things happened, sir. I danced until my feet hurt. I ate until there was no room left to breathe. I drank two glasses of champagne and felt dizzy. I met and talked with many nice people."

He sighed. "And some not so nice?"

"I didn't say that."

"You don't have to. You have cleverly avoided answering my question, Mirabella."

"So have you avoided mine."

Fighting twinges of guilt, he hesitated, but finally said, "Then I suppose that is the way we want it."

"Yes. I believe it is."

"So much for the complete honesty we vowed would be between us just a few days ago."

"I beg your pardon, sir. I am not being dishonest in what I say. Are you?"

"Certainly not. But I take it you are not telling me everything that you could tell me about the subject."

"I get that same feeling from you."

Camden nodded. He certainly didn't want her knowing how he'd roughed up Stephenson like he was a cheating drunkard in a gentlemen's card game. But he did want to know who had the gall to corner Mirabella, and he wanted to know what had been said to her. This protectiveness he had for her astonished him, and it confused him. But the fact that he felt it was indisputable.

Without reason, she reached over and laid her gloved hand upon his. "You look strained, Camden."

He was.

Camden wanted to grasp her hand and close it in his but resisted for fear that if he held her hand, he wouldn't turn her loose until he had kissed her, too. His breathing came faster. Suddenly it grew warm inside the carriage. His hand tingled where she touched him. Her nearness overwhelmed him and threatened his control over his natural urgings.

Her eyes never left his. She held him captive with her feminine concern.

The moment passed and Mirabella slowly removed her hand and leaned back in her seat. "All in all, it was a wonderful evening, my lord," she said when he continued to watch her again without speaking. "You dance very well."

Her voice was soft and alluring. The compliment surprised him. He had no idea why such a little thing made him feel good, warm inside. And, like her, he was happy to change the subject. It was getting too damn hot in the carriage.

"So do you, Mirabella. I'm happy to know I didn't forget everything I was taught during the years I spent in America. I did very little dancing while I was there."

"It doesn't show. From all I saw and heard tonight, the *ton* is happy to have you home." She looked right into his eyes and said, "I noticed that Miss Milhouse, Miss Clayton and Lady Gwyneth watched every move you made, and the Duchess of Westmorely was standing close to you whispering in your ear on more than one occasion."

"She's a charming lady, difficult to get away from."

"No doubt she was extolling the virtues of some new debutante she's supporting. Perhaps one of the young ladies I mentioned?"

Camden took note and gave Mirabella a slight grin. "Perhaps."

Had Mirabella really noticed all that? He had been bored with all the attention he'd been given by the eligible ladies, and their mamas nudging him at the end of every dance. He had no idea that Mirabella had been so aware of what was happening. He had thought her too busy with all the young beaux after her for a dance.

"No doubt you were delighted with all the attention you were receiving from so many beautiful ladies tonight."

What happened with Farthingdale and Stephenson faded from his mind as calmly as clouds passed over the moon. He was only aware of Mirabella.

"Careful, Miss Whittingham. I do believe those could be considered jealous remarks."

A slow smile lifted the corners of her mouth. "Oh, I think you should take them that way."

He returned her smile. "Then I will."

"I'm certain you were flirting with Lady Gwyneth at one point this evening."

"Certain, are you?"

Mirabella folded her gloved hands demurely in her silk lap and said, "Very much so. Were you not flirting?"

"Friends of the family catching up. That's all."

"And what about Miss Milhouse?"

"What about her?"

"Really, Camden. She is lovely, but I would think you are too old and too wise to succumb to machinations as simple as a young lady dropping her handkerchief to gain your attention."

His brow furrowed into an elaborate, fake frown. "Too wise, yes, but old? You wound me, Mirabella."

"Yes, well, only you know whether or not that is true, my lord."

She smiled again, and Camden knew why he was captivated by her. She was not only beautiful, she was downright charming. He was beginning to believe that the reason he wanted to continue with this pretend engagement had very little to do with the fact that his money wasn't yet available to repay her father the dowry and help his family.

Mirabella enchanted him.

Camden settled more comfortably on the too small seat and laughed, enjoying their tête-à-tête. "I wouldn't have been a gentleman had I not stopped and picked up the handkerchief for the clumsy Miss Milhouse."

"Clumsy, is she? I'd call her clever. Her tactics worked. You must have talked to her for five minutes before handing back her lace handkerchief."

He laughed softly. "Counting the minutes, were you?"

"Every one. But only because she was so obviously trying to steal you away from me."

"You can be assured that I made everyone I met aware my affections for you are true and without reservation. I have no desire to desert you and elope with a young lady making her debut."

"And the doubting Duchess of Westmorely?"

"She's quite a pusher once her mind is made up. I had to be firm on the matter."

Mirabella lay her head back against the seat and laughed gently, though she didn't take her eyes off him. And Camden couldn't stop watching her. He liked the way her lips parted slightly when she smiled. He especially liked the way he felt contented with her.

"That was delightful, my lord. Did I play the part of the jealous fiancée convincingly?"

Camden's breath halted in his throat. "Very well." *Too well.* He was eating up her comments like a street urchin with a handful of sweet bread.

What was he thinking, falling victim to her charms? Of course she was teasing him, flirting about her possessiveness. How could he have forgotten they were only acting a part?

"Your popularity this evening made it easy. Surely, Lord Stonehurst, you will not want for a proper match when our liaison is finished."

She spoke softly, seductively and truthfully, he realized. Was she as strong and capable as she always appeared, or was there a vulnerable spot inside her that he had seen hints of but hadn't yet discovered?

"Nor will you. Which I believe is part of our plan."

"Yes, our plan."

Mirabella didn't want their repartee to end but knew it must. She had been captivated by Camden all evening. This teasing and flirting side of him was very attractive.

At the back of her mind, she had been waiting all night for the right time to question Camden about his brother. She would rather continue with their playful witticisms, but knew they would be arriving at her door soon. Duty called her to change the course of the conversation.

"Tell me, Camden, your brother, Lord Hudson, is he about six or eight years younger than you?"

"Eight."

"That's quite an age difference."

He shrugged. "There were other babies between the two of us, but none that lived. Why do you ask?"

For the first time since they climbed into the carriage, she didn't look him in the eye. She didn't want him to see the importance of his answers to these questions. "I want to know more about your family. Was he a hellion in his early years, getting in fights or trouble at school?"

"My brother? Certainly not, just the opposite."

She appreciated the fervor with which he defended Hudson. "A lover, then?"

"A lover?" Camden leaned forward. The frown returned to his brow, but this time it wasn't in jest. "What kind of question is that for you to ask? Does my brother interest you so?"

"Not overly much," she hedged. "He's quite handsome, as you are. I wondered if he was considered a man of pleasure like poets enjoy writing about."

"Poets? Your imagination works overtime, Mirabella. Hudson is handsome. I'm sure he has attracted a few ladies in his time. Though this isn't a subject I intend to discuss with you."

"How about accidents? Was he ever burned or cut badly when he was younger? Does he have any scars on his body?"

"What the devil? Blast it, Mirabella. What kind of questions are these to be asking about my brother? Just how are these kinds of questions going to help you know me or him any better?"

"It seems perfectly logical to me. Considering if he was a bully or accident prone would help me to know about his character."

"He wasn't either of those. And his character is in fine order, thank you very much. He's a personable chap who at this very moment insists he is in love with Miss Paulette Pemberton."

"I know of her. She's very beautiful. Does he plan to offer for her hand?"

"Yes, I'm afraid he does. But not until the time is right."

"So he has no unusual scars or birthmarks or scarring on his neck?"

"How the devil should I know? And don't ask me any more personal questions about him, Mirabella, this is farther beyond the pale than I want to go. What Hudson has or has not on his body is no concern of yours."

She knew she had said enough and had found out nothing from Camden. Surely if Sarah had danced with Hudson, Mirabella's fiancé's brother, she would have mentioned it. Perhaps she was taking her suspect list too far.

"You are right, of course."

"I suggest you don't turn your designs toward him."

Mirabella stiffened. "As if I would. I have no such intentions."

Camden quickly reached over and brushed her skirts aside and moved onto the seat beside her. He took hold of her upper arms and turned her to face him. He forced her to look into his eyes and said, "You provoke me, Mirabella."

She was intensely aware of how close his face was to hers. She moistened her lips and said, "No."

"Yes. You have gone from a tempting seductress who had me eating out of her hand to a maid asking indecorous questions about Hudson. Do not attempt to make me jealous using my own brother."

She gasped. "You misunderstand me again. It wasn't my intention to make you jealous."

"How can you say that when you must have known that this entire evening I've wanted to do this?"

His arms snaked around to her back, cupping her, pulling her up to his chest. His hand held the back of her head as his lips captured hers. Teasing warmth tingled across her breasts and settled low in her abdomen. She yielded to his kiss. She leaned into his embrace and savored every taste, every breath.

The kiss was hungry and powerful. His lips moved back and forth over hers with such intensity it took her breath away. Instead of pushing him away, her hands slipped around his neck. One hand played in the back of his hair while the other ran up and down his strong back, discovering the width of his shoulders, the firmness of his muscles beneath the expensive feel of his evening coat.

Mirabella melted against him. She wanted the exquisite kiss to go slowly. She loved the feel of his lips melting against his. She had never before felt this burning intensity inside her body. It was as if she wanted Camden to consume her.

With the tip of his tongue, he urged her lips apart, and she willingly opened her mouth to him. He sank his tongue deep inside. Mirabella moaned from pleasure that erupted from her breasts to the womanly spot between her legs. She arched her back to get closer to him. Sensations she welcomed surrounded her and speared her with unbelievable craving to allow this man all the freedoms he wanted.

She tried to call his name, but her words were caught by his breath. His hand slid around her rib cage and covered her breast. With firm pressure, he caressed her and the delectation was so sweet Mirabella felt she was going to faint. She was limp with craving—for what she didn't know. She only knew she didn't want him to stop kissing or touching her.

Their kiss deepened, hardened for a moment longer before he placed his hands on either side of her face and dragged his lips from hers. He dropped his forehead against hers. Mirabella felt him tremble. She heard his short, shallow breaths even as she tried to calm her own breathing.

"Oh, God, Mirabella," he whispered as his thumbs drew lazy circles on her cheeks. His fingers caressed that soft skin behind her ears, sending chills of desire coursing through her, tempting her to lift her lips once again to his and beg him to kiss her over and over again.

With his head resting against hers, he said, "Tell me you didn't respond to those other men this way. Tell me you did not drive them crazy with need."

Her heart stalled in her chest at the pain she heard in his voice. "I swear, Camden." She moved her head so that she could look into his eyes as she said, "I swear they were only chaste kisses. I felt none of the overpowering sensations I have enjoyed in your arms with your touch and your kisses. You leave me wanting more. No one else has ever left me with that feeling before."

He matched the depth with which she looked into his eyes. "Then why?"

She opened her mouth, thinking to tell him about Sarah. "I have been in search——" She stopped. If he knew what she was doing, he would surely forbid her to continue her search. She had only a few more men on her list, and she had to continue. She couldn't tell him what she was doing.

"I can't take back what I have done," she said.

"I know."

The carriage jerked to a stop. Camden moved to the other seat and pulled on his overcoat.

Mirabella felt bereft. "It's too late for the reason to change the outcome, isn't it, Lord Stonehurst?"

He slowly nodded.

He stared out the window. He looked so forlorn that it hurt down to her soul. "You must believe me when I say that I truly believed you would never be hurt by my actions."

Camden glanced at her as the driver opened the door to the carriage. "I do believe that, Mirabella. I'll stop by for you at half past three this afternoon. We'll take a ride to Hyde Park and maybe have a stroll if anyone is about."

Mirabella put on her brave face to cover the pain in her heart. "I'll be ready."

❧

The edge of dawn lay on the sky and streamed through the bedroom window mixing with the light from a single candle that burned on the bedside table. Lily hummed, soft and melodious, as she unfastened the hooks that held Mirabella's dress together.

Mirabella fingered the emerald and diamond necklace she had just removed from her neck. She would never forget the wondrous sensations that spiraled through her when Camden kissed her. She would never forget how his body trembled for her and how she went limp with longing for him at his touch.

She dropped the necklace into the satin-lined box with the earrings. She would have to force herself not to dwell on Camden's parting words. They wounded her deeply, but it was best for her to forget about Camden and concentrate on what she had to do for Sarah.

Mirabella knew there wasn't going to be a better time to approach her maid so she said, "Lily, I want you to help me with something."

"What can I do for you, Miss Bella?"

She took a deep breath as she slipped the bodice off her shoulders. "I want you to bring me some of your clothes."

Lily's hands went still. She walked around to face Mirabella and pursed her twisted lips into the shape of a tight bud. "With all these beautiful clothes you have, you want some of mine? Are you going daft?"

"No, of course not." Mirabella stepped out of her skirt and turned for Lily to unlace her corset. "I plan to go with you to the tavern where you work and help you."

Lily walked around Mirabella and faced her again. "No, no. Not with me you won't, Miss Bella." She shook her head. "I'm not going to bring you any of my clothes, and you are not going to work with me in that place."

"Now, Lily. Don't question me on this."

"I have to, Miss Bella. I don't know what you're planning, but I'm not helping you do it."

"You must. If you don't, I'll simply find someone who will do this for me—even if it is someone I don't know."

"You wouldn't do that."

"If I have to, yes, I will. What I must do is that important to me. I can't leave this undone."

"A proper lady like you, betrothed to a fine-looking man like Lord Stonehurst, going to work as a servant in a tavern. I'd be fired for sure if your father found out."

"He won't." Mirabella turned her back to Lily again. This time Lily began unlacing her. "You know you can trust me to take care of you, Lily. If I'm caught, I will make sure Papa knows that you helped me only on fear that I would dismiss you if you didn't."

Lily's hand stopped again. "You wouldn't dismiss me, would you, Miss Bella?"

"I need help." Feeling as she did right now, Mirabella knew her voice had the right amount of certainty to it that Lily was bound to hear.

"You know my mama needs the money I make."

Mirabella felt dreadful treating Lily this way, and she was glad her back was to her maid. Even though her voice held conviction, she wasn't sure her eyes did. "I do, Lily. Now, can I count on you, or do I have to solicit someone else's help?"

"I'm thinking about it."

Relief melted through her. That meant she had won over her maid. "Good. You think about it." Feeling sorry for how she had treated Lily, Mirabella added, "You act like you think I'll be alone. I won't. I'll have you with me. And I have no doubt that you can take care of me. I trust you."

Lily continued to pull on the strings. "What if someone you know recognizes you?"

"With your clothes and my hair covered, I don't believe anyone will. If you think it's necessary, I'll put a little dirt on my face. Besides, all I want to do is take a peek at the gentlemen inside the gaming rooms."

"You can look at the gentlemen at parties."

"Not without their collars and neckcloths on."

"Their collars? Why are you so interested in men's necks?"

Mirabella sighed. "You don't need to know that."

"It just doesn't sound natural to me, Miss Bella."

She slipped out of her corset and lifted her chemise over her head, tossing it on the daybed with the rest of her clothing. Lily handed her a freshly laundered night rail. She pulled it on over her head and let the fine muslin fall to the floor.

"It doesn't have to. Now, are you going to help me?"

"I don't like this, but I don't have a choice. The Deity only knows who you will get to help you if I don't. I guess your papa would be angrier with me if I let you do something like this on your own than if I didn't help you."

"Don't fret, Lily. I know what I'm doing." *And why.* "Now you go back to bed. I can finish from here by myself."

Mirabella blew out the candle Lily had lit, and shadowed moonlight filtered into the room. She crawled into her bed and lay on her back, staring at the ceiling. She lifted her fingers to her lips and kissed them, but there was no way she could make the pads of her fingers feel like Camden's urgent kisses. She would have to close her eyes and remember each touch.

She had ached inside for him to forgive her and to say the past didn't matter, that they would only look to the future—but that wasn't going to happen. So she had to go on only playing a part.

She thought back to what she had heard about his first engagement. Rumor had it that Camden had called out the young gentleman who had been caught kissing his fiancée, but that the man proved himself a coward. He fled to France and his parents never mentioned his name in public again. Only a few days later, Camden's father had made the arrangement with her father, and Camden had left for America. His fiancée had married an older gentleman who already had several children, and they moved up north.

Knowing his past, it was no wonder Camden couldn't find it in his heart to forgive her.

Eleven

WILL MISS WHITTINGHAM EVER BE A BRIDE?

Reports are in from Lord Stonehurst and Miss Whittingham's first ball together since his return. It appears all is not well with the engaged couple. It was reported that the viscount spent much of the evening in the company of three beautiful debutantes. Hmm. Could it be because there have been hints that Miss Whittingham wasn't as patient as we thought? We are looking for answers as I write this. Do tell if you have any information on the viscount and the Miss.

—Lord Truefitt, *Society's Daily Column*

"PAPA!" MIRABELLA EXCLAIMED. SHE PICKED UP THE hem of her carriage dress and rushed over to the chair in the drawing room where her father was seated. She threw her arms around him and hugged him, kissed his cheek, then hugged him again for good measure.

"Heavens to madness, girl, you're going to suffocate me with all this blustering. Be done with it."

"But, Papa, I haven't seen you downstairs in weeks. Months. This is so very wonderful!"

"Well, there's no cause to be frolicsome, young lady. You're acting like I've been on my deathbed, not just ailing."

"I've been praying for the day I would come downstairs and see you in your favorite chair again."

"Be sensible. I didn't want to meet the viscount for the first time in years up in my bedroom. That would have been dreadful, don't you know. I wanted him to see me dressed and looking as fit as possible."

She smiled at him with all the love she felt. Her father must truly be getting better after almost two years of pain and debilitating weakness. She was so grateful, and she believed she owed her father's remarkable recovery to Lord Stonehurst. Camden's return might have caused her much distress, but his sudden appearance had rejuvenated her father and given him a new life. She didn't know how she could repay Camden.

"You look much more than fit this afternoon. You are perfectly handsome in your new brocade waistcoat and silk neckcloth. And you look simply dashing in that cutaway jacket with double buttons."

"Stop that poppycock talk. I haven't been handsome, dashing, or splendid for the past two years."

"Nonsense. You would have all the lovely widows chasing after you again if you were only able to attend the parties in the evenings." Mirabella fluffed his cravat.

"Don't fuss." He brushed her hand away.

She knelt at his feet and clasped one of his hands in

hers. She looked up at him. Not a gray hair was out of place, and his beard had just the right amount of grooming wax.

"Why not? It's what daughters do," she said, feeling quite pleased with herself for reminding him of one of his favorite phrases.

"Because I don't want it. That's why. And until you marry, you have to do as I say," he grumbled, though fondness shone in his eyes.

"You cannot burst my bubble of happiness. You know how delighted it makes me to see you down here, Papa. For the first time in so long, I'm really beginning to feel that you are getting better."

He pointed a straight, but trembling, finger at her. "Do not pin your hopes on that, Daughter."

"I have to, Papa. I want it to be so."

He looked down at her and caressed her cheek with the back of his hand, then cupped her chin, tilting her head back a little farther. "I know that Lord Stonehurst will have heard that I've not been well. But I don't want him to know exactly how ill I've been. Let's keep that between us, shall we."

She nodded, knowing that no man liked for his weaknesses to show.

"So tell me, what do you think about Viscount Stonehurst?"

Oh, Papa, he is remarkable, dreamy and desirable.

"He is a nice gentleman," she offered instead of what was on her mind.

"That I assumed, given he's titled and that he's well educated. Tell me something I don't know."

He's divinely handsome, enchanting, and seductive.

"Let me think."

"You have to think about his attributes? Surely you must have noticed something right away."

"Well, we've spent so little time together." She sank her teeth into her bottom lip for a moment and drew her eyebrows together as if studying hard over the question. "He is also charming."

"Botheration, you do try my patience, girl. I expected that, too. What else do you have to say about him?"

He's the best kisser in all of London, and that I'm certain of, having kissed several other gentlemen in Town.

"Oh, Papa, I don't know what you want me to say." She patted his knee and rose. "He's a man. Isn't that enough?"

"Good heavens, no."

Mirabella couldn't tell her father what she really felt about Camden. That would be scandalous. She looked down at him and said, "I guess the best way to say it is that he is acceptable. No, more than acceptable. He's a gentleman I think I could be contented to spend the rest of my life with."

If only there was a chance for us. I believe I could make him happy.

"Now, that is what I was waiting to hear. I expect a gentleman of his breeding to be honorable, charming, and nice. I'm glad to hear you think you can be content with him. Believe it or not, Mirabella, your satisfaction is important to me. That's one of the reasons I wanted you to have a husband who wasn't twenty years older than you."

For her father's sake, she wanted this liaison she had concocted with Camden to succeed so that her father would never have to know what she had done to avenge Sarah's death. "You did well, Papa."

"Be that as it may. I do want to see the viscount and make my own judgment of him since so much time has passed." Her father chuckled and shook his head once. "I approve of his method of meeting you."

"Yes, I remember. I thought it something only an unmannerly scoundrel would do."

"It was devilishly clever."

"It was perverse," she insisted, remembering how mortified she'd been in the garden that night with Mr. Farthingdale while Camden and her uncle both stared at her as if she were a soiled lady of the evening. She considered herself lucky that Camden ever spoke to her again.

"It was sagacious."

"Yes, if he hadn't approved of me, he would have gone back to America and we would have never been the wiser about his return."

"How could any man not approve of you, dear child? Besides, you would have delighted in doing the same thing to him I'm sure, had it been possible. Now stand over there and turn around. I want to have a look at you."

Mirabella twirled for her father in her light pink gown. Each flounce on her skirt was edged with a delicate white lace. A wide, white satin ribbon banded the high waist and cuffs on the sleeves of her pelisse. Her parasol and matching broad brimmed, feather-and-ribbon bonnet lay on the sofa ready to be put on.

"I plan to send a letter to your aunt Helen tomorrow asking that she return immediately to help you prepare for your wedding."

"She is still in mourning. I don't think we should disturb her right now. There isn't any reason to hurry her."

"I couldn't hurry Helen if I put a pair of prize-winning Thoroughbreds underneath her. No doubt it will take her weeks just to get her trunks packed and on the coach."

"But really, Papa, Lord Stonehurst and I don't plan to marry before next spring."

"Spring? Good heavens! That's a year away. I could be dead by then. I won't hear of it taking that long, Mirabella. You should have been wed three years ago. If you insist on a big wedding with all the pomp and fluff, I'm willing, but I must insist that it be before next spring."

"Papa, I need time to get to know him."

"Nonsense. You've already said he was accept-able. That's all I needed to hear. Don't put a line of worry in your face about this. I'll handle it with Lord Stonehurst."

Mirabella had no idea that her father would use her words against her. She picked up her bonnet and dusted a piece of lint off the ribbon. There was no way Camden would agree to hurrying up plans for a wedding they didn't plan to hold. And already her father was showing signs of recovery. She would talk to Camden and they would have to come up with a reason they couldn't marry before next year.

"I think I heard a knock at the door." Bertram looked at the brass clock on the mantel. "That must be him, and he's right on time. Another fine attribute to add to charming, nice and acceptable."

Mirabella walked over to stand beside her father's chair. Excitement welled within her at the prospect of spending the afternoon in an open rig with Camden, riding in Hyde Park. She had seen lovers make their trace around the park through the years but, of course, had never experienced the pleasure firsthand.

She knew all the reasons she shouldn't allow herself to indulge in the sweet sensations being escorted by him would bring, but if the faster beat of her pulse was any indication, she was looking forward to being Camden's fiancée for however much time they had.

"Mr. Whittingham," Newton said from the doorway. "Viscount Stonehurst here to see you and Miss Whittingham."

Newton couldn't have been any stiffer if he tried. He was tall and thin with closely trimmed mustache and beard. He had been with her father as long as Mirabella could remember. She seldom saw him smile and often wondered how a man with such a dour disposition could be happy. He was the complete opposite of her maid, Lily, who constantly hummed gaily. Even when Lily was awakened in the predawn hours to help Mirabella undress after a night of parties, Lily was always cheerful and pleasant.

Her father rose. "Show him in."

Camden came through the doorway into the parlor. The masculine boldness with which he took every step was hard to miss. Mirabella's breath caught in her throat. Her pulse thudded crazily. He was masterfully dressed in a fashionably dark gray suit with a white shirt and a blue silk waistcoat that was fastened with monogrammed buttons. His neckcloth was wrapped high on his neck, and the sash of the bow lay perfectly on each side of the center.

He stopped just inside the room. His gaze skimmed over her father and immediately found Mirabella. He walked straight to her and held out a bouquet of tulips almost the same pink color as her dress.

"Good afternoon, Mirabella. These are for you."

She curtsied. "Good afternoon, my lord." She smiled up at him, and he returned the smile. "They are lovely and fragrant. Thank you." She plucked one of the blooms from the bouquet and handed the rest of them to Newton. "Would you please put these in water for me and have Lily take them up to my room?"

"Yes, Miss Bella," Newton said and turned away.

Mirabella listened while her father and Camden exchanged greetings and pleasantries.

A smile came to her father's face when Camden presented him with a bottle of fine brandy and said, "My apologies, sir, for being late to claim my bride."

"I'm glad you finally saw fit to return to London, Lord Stonehurst. We'll let the past stay buried where it is and consider only the future. I assume, Lord Stonehurst, that whatever took you to America has been settled, and you are now ready to forsake those things and take your responsibilities to my daughter seriously."

"That is correct, sir." Camden glanced at Mirabella before adding, "I'm happy to present her to my family, my friends and the *ton* as my bride-to-be."

"Glad to hear it."

Suddenly it was difficult for Mirabella to keep the smile on her face. A wistful feeling settled over her as she looked at Camden and her father standing together. She supposed, at times like these, it was natural for her to wish things were different.

For Sarah there had been no hope of setting things right. Drinking a bottle of laudanum and going to sleep was the only way out Sarah could see. Now there was a dandy strolling the balls and parties who had seduced her and then left her on her own. He needed to be punished and Mirabella was the only one who could do it.

"Isn't that right, Mirabella?"

"I'm sorry, Papa. What did you say?"

"I was telling Lord Stonehurst that you write beautiful poetry."

Mirabella felt the color rise to her cheeks and neck. "Oh, well, I only dabble in it from time to time. I'm not devoted to it as some people are. You know that, Papa."

"Yes, but you would be excellent at it if you gave it more of your time."

"It takes *courage,* which I'm certain you have, to even attempt to create beauty with words. I'd enjoy reading some of your verses," Camden said.

His comment and the way he looked at her with his dark eyes sent her pulse dancing with excitement, but she said, "I fear I'm not as courageous as you think, my lord."

"I don't believe that for a moment. I think you are also resourceful and intelligent."

"I've tried to talk her into having some of the poems published, but she won't hear of it."

Mirabella smiled at her father, thankful he chose that moment to join the conversation. Another word of praise from Camden, and Mirabella would be ready to rush into his arms right there in front of her father.

She turned back to Camden and said, "I'm afraid it's the kind of poetry that only a father could love." She picked up her bonnet and stuck the stem of the tulip beneath the hatband and pulled it through until only the bloom of the flower showed on the band. "Now, if you two will excuse me, I'll go put on my bonnet, and then I'll be ready to go."

❧

The sky was an unusually light shade of blue. Streaks of cloud-filtered sunlight glinted off Mirabella's face even though she had her parasol open. It was a warm, lovely day. The smell of horse mingled with the scent of blooming primrose and flowering shrubs. The sounds of conversations and laughter mingled with the creaks of carriage wheels and horses' hooves clopping along the soft ground.

"It's a perfect, perfect afternoon for an open carriage ride in the park," Mirabella said as the two bays plodded along in the tight line of fancy carriages making the rounds.

Camden suddenly pulled the ribbons tight when the red-painted gig in front of them stopped without warning. Mirabella braced herself with her feet to keep from being thrown forward. The horses protested with snorts and jerking, but Camden held them in check.

"It would be if not for the traffic. Half the population of London must be in the park today and most of them in rigs. I don't remember it being this crowded years ago."

The throngs of people, carriages and horses didn't bother Mirabella. She loved the hustle and bustle of all the people milling around the park dressed in their fashionable, late-spring clothing. Walking the streets of London and looking in all the shops, listening to all the sounds was one of her favorite things to do.

Mirabella and Camden waved and smiled at acquaintances as he drove the two-wheeled curricle around the park, but she could tell that Camden didn't have his heart in what they were doing. She had seen his mood shift when the Earl of Glenbrighton and Countess Irene had passed them and waved without any true friendliness in their manner. Mirabella feared news of her indiscretions were becoming widely known. She could only hope Camden's close friends would forgive him and welcome him back into their circle once he had broken his engagement to her.

"If the heavy traffic is disturbing you, perhaps we should park and walk for a little while," Mirabella said.

"No. If we take a stroll, we will be obliged to stop and talk to those we know."

"And you don't want to do that?"

"I was more concerned about you not wanting to talk to those we might meet. I know something happened last night, even though you wouldn't tell me what was said. But we can stop, if you prefer."

How could she tell him that the wife of one of his childhood chums was prevented from talking to her? "No, no. You are quite right, and this is fine with me. This is actually better. We have to handle enough conversation at the parties and balls. No need to add to it here on such a lovely afternoon."

And too, she had him all to herself and didn't have to share his attention with anyone but the excitable horses.

They were both quiet for a few moments before she asked, "Do you really think attending the parties and riding in the park is going to help silence the talk that has started about me?"

He glanced over at her, but only for a second. The carriages were so close together he had to struggle to keep the horses from getting skittish. "Let us hope it works. That's one of the reasons we are doing this."

"How could I forget?"

"What we are doing benefits my family as well," he added. "I felt it was a good sign when there wasn't very much written about us in the Society columns this morning other than we attended our first ball together."

"And, obviously, I'm not the only one who noticed the time you spent with Lady Gwyneth."

"Not of my own choosing, I assure you. She was at my elbow every time I turned around."

"You were worried there might have been something about you?"

"Could have been."

"Other than mention of our attendance last evening and your return to London last week, there's not been a hint of real scandal. Sometimes it takes a few days for the gossip to make it to the columns. What happened last night that you didn't tell me?"

"Nothing that I intend to tell you. Was there anything you wanted to tell me?"

"Not a thing."

"I suspected as much, but something tells me we will both be watching the papers."

He was as closemouthed as she. Mirabella wondered what could have happened. Mr. Farthingdale was present last night, but so were at least three other gentlemen she had kissed. Merciful heavens. What if they had all told Camden they had kissed her? The number of gentlemen she had kissed was important to him. Almost anything could have happened.

"I suppose I should tell you that my father plans to put pressure on you to make it a fall wedding," she said, changing the subject. "We'll have to come up with something to change his mind about that."

"He said as much to me when you were putting on your bonnet. We've plenty of—Damnation!"

The carriage jolted. He jerked the ribbons hard and barely stopped the horses in time to keep them from plowing into the gig ahead of them. One bay reared and tried to bolt, but Camden held tight and kept the animal in line.

"Sorry about my language, Mirabella, but this wretched traffic is unbelievable. Hold on, we're getting out of here."

He turned the horses off of the regular path and started across the grassy lawn at a fast clip. She held on to her bonnet with one hand and the seat arm with the other.

"Your language is understandable, but what are you doing? You're not supposed to drive on that part of the— look out!" Mirabella gasped loudly as Camden narrowly missed two strolling couples. One lady lost her parasol and the other swerved into her escort's shoulder and knocked him to the ground.

Camden drove the curricle over bumps, around

benches and onto the walking path. Several more people had to hurry to get out of his way.

"Careful. You're going to run someone down before you get out of the park."

"I've had enough of this parade," he said and guided the horses off the footpath and back on to the road leading out of the park. "I'm going to head to the outskirts of town and get away from these bucks who haven't been taught how to properly drive a carriage or handle a pair of horses."

Mirabella looked back at the people staring after them. "That should make us hit the Society papers."

He looked at her and smiled. "You really think so?"

She nodded.

"I can see it now. Lord Stonehurst's fiancée must have had a bee in her bonnet. The viscount fled the park, nearly trampling more than half a dozen people."

Mirabella laughed.

Camden returned to his driving. She remained quiet and thoughtful. She left Camden free to work their way out of the park and toward the end of Town turning left, then right and left again. She was enjoying watching the people and the carriages decked out in their finest. She didn't mind the ride through the crowded streets of London. The farther out they went the less traffic they encountered, and soon the busy streets with their noise and smells were left behind for a quieter, peaceful ride.

Camden slowed the bays and turned to Mirabella and said, "Why don't you tell me about the young lady named Sarah."

"My aunt's ward, Sarah?" Mirabella hadn't expected the question. It took her by surprise.

"If there are no others." He glanced over at her again, the horses now easier to manage. "I heard Hudson give you condolences last evening when he met you."

Mirabella's throat was suddenly dry. "She was a part of our household for thirteen years. Only two years older than me. We developed a close friendship. We were like sisters in a lot of ways." Mirabella hesitated. "There's really not much to tell. She died in her sleep."

"I saw in your face last night that you were stunned when Hudson mentioned her. I could tell that her death still saddens you."

"Very much so. It was extremely sad and difficult to see someone so young pass on." How could she tell Camden that Sarah was such a sweet and thoughtful young lady that she would rather take her own life than bring shame to the Whittingham house?

"I take it she hadn't been ill a long time."

Sarah guessed she was three months pregnant.

"No. Not long at all."

"Was she betrothed?"

Mirabella's chest felt heavy. "No. You see Sarah wasn't beautiful, wealthy or from a titled family. One of her eyes was defective and no one wanted to—" Mirabella stopped.

"To marry her."

"Yes. Her dowry wasn't very large. My aunt had been able to save a little for her from what Sarah's father had left and my father had always said he would contribute, but there wasn't enough for any young man of means to seriously consider her a match. I find it dreadful that the eligible men couldn't get past her plainness to see the beautiful person she was inside."

"I agree and it's a shame she died so young. From what you say, she made a wonderful companion for you."

"Oh, she did. During the Season, we would talk about the latest young ladies making their debuts, their dresses and hairstyles. We discussed the bachelors. In the winter, we would take long walks and read to each other and—" Mirabella stopped. "I still miss her and will for a long time."

He glanced at her and gave her a comforting smile. "Tell me what kinds of things would you discuss about the young blades?"

Mirabella was relieved to redirect the conversation. "Let me see. We talked the usual things ladies discuss. Sometimes we'd try to guess if the gentleman was dashing and dapper, or solemn and ill-mannered. But I'm sure you don't want to hear all that. We both know what London is about. Why don't you tell me about America, a place I've never been. Are their parties as grand as ours? How do they get along without the peerage?"

Camden drove the horses and talked about the new land across the sea. Mirabella clung to every word. She didn't know how long they had been at their leisurely ride when Camden stopped the horses. He looked around them and so did Mirabella. The sky had turned a dark shade of gray. There were no houses or buildings anywhere in sight. It appeared as if they'd ended up on some desolate country road.

She hadn't noticed until they stopped, but the wind had picked up and the temperature had cooled since they left the city. She was hugging her arms to herself. Her pelisse was almost as thin as the material of her dress.

"You're cold. Here, take this." He took off his coat and put it around her shoulders. She immediately felt his warmth.

"Thank you, Camden, but you will be cold."

"No, I'm fine."

"Do you know where we are?" she asked.

"Afraid not. I was too busy talking and not noticing which roads we took."

"Are we lost?" she asked.

"Certainly not. I know we are on the outskirts of Town."

She searched his face. He didn't look worried, which gave her some comfort. "I hear a but at the end of that sentence."

"It's just that the landscape has changed in the six years I've been away from London, and I'm not sure exactly what road we are on."

"Do you know how to get us back to the city?"

"No, but I'm sure there will be signs enough pointing us in the right direction. Don't worry. I'll have you home before dark." He looked over and grinned at her. "I wouldn't want to ruin your reputation."

She couldn't take this as lightly as Camden seemed to. This could be another serious infraction. "This is not something to poke fun at, Camden. If I'm not home by dark, my father could very well insist you marry me immediately and neither of us wants that."

"Don't fret, Mirabella. All is well. I do believe we've traveled quite a distance from the city, but the horses are in good shape so I'm going to let them run," he said, starting to turn the horses around.

"Do you think we can make it back to London before the rain starts?"

"I have great doubts about that, but I do believe I will have you home before dark. Hold on to your hat. It's going to be a wild ride." He snapped the ribbons against the bays' rumps, and they took off at a fast trot.

Mirabella slipped her arms into the sleeves of his coat and opened her parasol as the first drops of rain landed on their heads.

Twelve

THEY DROVE RIGHT THROUGH THE RAIN. IN NO TIME AT all, Mirabella's skirt was soaked to the skin.

The wide brim of her bonnet helped shield her eyes from the stinging drops as long as she kept her chin pointed toward her chest. Her silk and fringe parasol quickly became a soggy mess and was difficult to hold on to because of the wind.

Camden drove the horses at a fast clip but not dangerously so. The bays stayed in the ruts and trotted along at his direction, as if they were enjoying the late afternoon jaunt in the spring shower.

The cushioned seat on the curricle did little to keep her posterior from bouncing up and down as they covered the rough and uneven road. With each jar, Mirabella felt as if the whole of her bone structure would collapse at any moment and crumple in a heap.

The rain slashed down on them. Even with Camden's coat to protect her, in a matter of moments she was chilled. A gust of wind caught under her bonnet and lifted and dropped it behind her shoulders. While she was trying to put it on her head, she lost her grip on the cane handle of her parasol and it went flying over the side of the carriage. She watched the beautiful pink fluff land with a splat in the mud.

Camden made a move to stop the horses.

"No, don't," she said, turning quickly to him. "Keep going. It's not worth going back for."

Taking his gaze off the road only for a quick glimpse in her direction, he said, "I'm going to try to find shelter for us."

Mirabella didn't know how Camden was keeping his eyes open against the hard rain, but he easily handled the ribbons and kept the bays in line.

She pulled her bonnet back on top of her wet hair. Her cold fingers fumbled with the bow under her chin. She wanted to untie it so she could tighten the sash. Just as she managed to unfasten it one of the wheels hit a large hole.

The jolt threw her forward. She grabbed the arm of the carriage seat with one hand and Camden's arm with the other and lost her grip on her bonnet. She gasped in frustration as it went the way of the parasol and left her with nothing to protect her from the sky emptying itself on top of her head.

"Over there," Camden said. "I think the branches of that tree are high enough we can park under it and have a little protection until the rain eases."

Camden slowed the horses and carefully guided them off the road toward their shelter. Mirabella didn't know how Camden had seen the tree with the rain so thick and the air already getting foggy.

He pulled the horses to a stop as close to the trunk of the tree as he could get and set the brake.

The horses shuddered and nickered, obviously as delighted as she was to have a little shelter from the constant onslaught. The branches were quite low and Mirabella realized there was less rain hitting her, but the drops were bigger when one plopped in the middle of her forehead.

"Take my coat off and I'll hold it up like an umbrella," Camden said.

Mirabella allowed him to help her peel the soggy coat off her arms. He moved very close to her, lining his thigh tightly against the length of hers. He held the coat up like a roof over her head. She was immediately thankful that the rain was no longer drenching her.

"I'm supposed to know better than to let a young lady get caught out in the rain," he complained in a low voice, mostly to himself.

"My father likes to say a little rain never hurt anyone. Let us hope he is right."

"Let's do, because it's my ego that feels bruised at the moment."

She saw Camden's head was still exposed to the heavy sprinkling so she reached up and moved his arms higher so the makeshift roof shielded him, too. It brought him extremely close to her.

As she brought her arms down, Mirabella looked at Camden. Like her clothes, his were saturated. His white shirt was plastered to him, appearing like a second skin for his arms and shoulders. She could make out the outline of firm, slightly bulging muscles across his chest.

Camden's hair lay flat, dark and wet against his head. Water dripped from his nose and chin and ran down his forehead and cheeks. She noticed he stared at her and knew she must look as soaked and rumpled as he.

Mirabella smiled and bit down on her bottom lip to keep from laughing at the predicament in which they found themselves.

Camden quickly scanned her from head to toe. He smiled, and then chuckled, too.

"You look a bit mussed, Lord Stonehurst," she teased.

"As bad luck would have it, Miss Whittingham, I believe I am."

"I don't believe I've ever seen a gentleman so wet."

He looked the length of her again, but this time it wasn't a quick glance. He took his time, letting his gaze linger on her face, her breasts, and her hands, which lay cupped together in the center of her lap. It was the expression of desire in his eyes that made her shiver, not the wet clothes or the chill in the late afternoon air.

"I don't believe I've ever seen a lady look so lovely in a wet dress." His voice softened and his gaze caressed her face as he said, "Wet or dry, Mirabella, you're beautiful."

"You lie, sir," she said, feeling the telltale rise of a blush in her cheeks at his thorough inspection.

"No."

She heard the soft patter of rain falling on foliage and smelled the damp scent of wet horse and drenched clothing, but the only thing she could do was concentrate on Camden's moist lips. They seemed to be inviting her to kiss him.

"I must look like a bedraggled cat who's been thrown in the Thames and left there for several days before being fished out," she said.

"To me, you look like you need to be kissed."

Her heart rate increased and her stomach fluttered crazily. "I do?"

"Oh, yes. You do."

Mirabella felt as if she were on the edge of a cliff and at any moment she was going to fall. "Is there anyone in this carriage who would want to kiss me?"

"I believe you are looking at him, Miss Whittingham."

The tone of his voice warmed her like flames from an open fire. Heat rose from deep within her, and she no longer felt the breezy wind or the cold drops of rain. Did he know she had thought about a kiss from him only moments before?

He lowered his arms and let the coat drop back around her shoulders. He took a deep breath and pushed his dripping hair away from his face with both his hands, showing a wide forehead, and making him look younger, even more handsome. Suddenly Mirabella was filled with an intense craving to feel his lips on hers.

Camden must have felt the same because his eyes darkened and his lips parted slightly. He bent his head and lowered his lips toward hers. Mirabella's breaths became short and rapid in anticipation.

But instead of kissing her, he gently placed the tips of his fingers on her cheek and wiped them down her face. He watched the trail of his light touch. His palm was warm and smelled of the leather he'd worked in his hands. He let his fingers slip lightly over her chin, down her neck to the wet skin of her chest exposed by the square-cut neckline of her dress.

When he reached the swell of her breast he paused and opened his palm, flattening his hand against her breast. The weight of his hand on her skin made her heartbeat race even faster.

She knew she should slap his hand, move as far away from him as she possibly could, and admonish him with strong words for his forward behavior. She could do none of those things because she wasn't offended by the way he touched her. Mirabella felt only desire.

She looked down and saw that her pelisse was open. The thin material of her carriage dress was saturated, perfectly outlining her lace-trimmed undergarments. Camden's hand lay resting on her breast, over her heart, moving only with the heavy, erratic rise and fall of her chest.

Oh, yes, her pulse was beating fast. Fast from the dash to get out of the rain, faster from the heat of his touch. Her gaze met his and held.

She should have felt soggy and frumpy but she felt beautiful.

"I'm going to kiss you," he whispered.

"Please do."

He moved his face closer to hers. Their breaths mingled. Their eyes searched. Suddenly their lips were together, fusing tightly.

It was an immediate, urgent kiss that made her body temperature soar. More demanding, more fascinating, more desperate than the other kisses they had shared. She welcomed his aggressiveness. Her mouth opened, and his tongue drove inside, filling her, teasing her with the taste of him.

With one hand, he held her to his chest, while with the other, he caressed her breast with such skill that she wanted to cry out from the pleasure, the excitement, the urgency he was creating inside her.

Mirabella needed to touch him as he was touching her. She tugged his shirt from the waistband of his trousers and yanked it free. With driving anticipation, she shoved her hands beneath his shirt and gasped from the ardor that rippled through her as she splayed her hands on his bare chest.

His skin was damp, cool, exhilarating. The muscles beneath his taut skin were full and firm. She ran her palms up and down, over and around his rib cage and slid her hands up until her fingertips found the swell of his upper chest.

Camden moaned his approval and whispered against her lips. "Yes, Mirabella. Feel my heart. Oh, my lady, feel what you do to me."

"My heart races, too, my lord."

"Touch me wherever you want."

His husky voice was all the encouragement Mirabella needed to continue her thorough examination of his upper body.

His lips left hers, and he kissed her eyes. His tongue raked across her cheeks, her neck and her chest, drinking the rain from her skin. With his mouth, he lightly pulled on first her upper lip, then her bottom lip and gently sucked before releasing them.

Mirabella shuddered with pleasure.

"I love the taste of you," he murmured.

"You taste of cool rainwater," she answered in a breathless whisper.

Mirabella ached to touch all of Camden's body but was fearful to let her hand slip below his waist. She couldn't have dreamed that stroking a man so intimately could push all rational thought out of propriety from her mind and make her happy and excited to feel so wanton.

She knew she didn't want to think. She only wanted to touch, experience and enjoy what this man was doing to her and how touching and exploring him made her feel. She wanted the sensations he created in her to go on forever.

"I know we shouldn't be doing this," she managed to say between fervent kisses. "But I have no will to decline my fancy."

"Thank God," he mumbled against her lips. "I have no will to stop either."

Camden was hungry, desperate to feel the length of Mirabella's softness beneath him, pressing against him with uncontrolled desire, but the seat was simply too small to lay her down. His lower body was hard and huge, straining against the wet material of his trousers. Not even in his youth had he wanted a woman as desperately as he wanted Mirabella right now.

He pushed the sleeve of her dress and pelisse off one shoulder and pulled on the front of her dress and undergarments exposing a soft, full beautiful breast that seemed to be yearning for his possession. Her beautiful breast lay before him expecting his touch, willing his possession. He was torn between cupping her breast and feeling its weight in his hand and taking it into his mouth for a taste of her.

Camden desired both.

"Are you cold?" he whispered huskily.

"No. Hotter than I've ever been, sir."

"Me, too."

He bent his head and took the erect nipple into his mouth. Mirabella gasped with pleasure and arched toward him. Her whole body trembled with delight. He tore the other side of her clothing away from the yielding breast and covered it hard and fully with his palm.

Instinctively Mirabella pressed closer to him.

Pleasure mixed with confidence and satisfaction welled up inside Camden. Mirabella had no aversion to lovemaking. With her movements, her sounds and her intimate responses, she let him know that he had the power to thrill her. That excited him all the more.

Unlike some men, he was not afraid to admit that a woman, be she wife, mistress, or lady of the evening, should enjoy sexual bliss as much as a man. He found no joy and little gratification in a woman who failed to luxuriate in his ability to give her pleasure.

The feel of the tight, damp nipple in the warmth of his mouth almost sent him over the edge. He gently pulled and sucked on it, drawing out her enjoyment and his. He wanted her so desperately. Right here. Right now. He wanted to drive deep inside her and watch the delight play out on her lovely face.

Water dripped from his hair onto her breast, and Camden lapped it, needing the moisture to quench the fire burning inside him. He felt as if he was going to burst out of his breeches.

"Mirabella, you know what I want to do to you, don't you?"

"I believe so."

"I want to take you the way a man takes a woman." His breath was shaky and mere gasps, he needed her so badly. "Tell me that you have been this far with a man before so that I can satisfy us both with no retribution."

Desire swept out of her eyes like a piece of flaming paper turning to ash. "I can't tell you that, for I haven't."

He squeezed his eyes shut only for a moment then opened them against the throb of his craving.

"I didn't think so."

Niggling doubts of his admirable gesture crept into his mind and threatened to snare his appetite to continue. Was she being truthful? He had proof she'd kissed more than one other man.

Her reputation was already on the brink of unrecoverable injury. It was just that so far they'd kept what she had done from the *ton*. If anyone knew what they were doing right now, her reputation would be beyond repair.

Camden's desire to possess her was strong. Surely no one would know if he took her virginity. He wanted her. He was frantic for release, desperate for her total surrender to him. He was hard for her—not just for any woman. This one. Mirabella.

Her eyes were bright with wonder, acceptance. She was willing. He had no doubt of that. Her lips were red and full, her hair an attractively wet, tangled mass. The pale skin of her neck and chest were flushed from the rub of his faint beard. If anyone saw her right now, they would not doubt that she had just been thoroughly kissed and plundered.

He swallowed a cold lump of desire that had frozen in his throat. He was a gentleman, not a ravager of innocents.

He lifted his head. "Much as I want to continue, we cannot go any further. We're trying to salvage your reputation, not vandalize it."

Mirabella pushed away from him and pulled her clothing back over her shoulder. The rain had slowed to a heavy mist, but the chill of the dampness lingered in the air.

Almost gasping for breath she managed to say, "You are right, Camden." Her gaze dropped to the bulge in his lap.

The heat of her gaze on his arousal only served to make him harder. He moved his hand to cover himself.

"I don't know what came over us," she continued. "We were about to sabotage ourselves."

Most young ladies would have been furious that he'd almost ravished them. "I know, but you test my willpower, Mirabella, and I'm afraid it comes up lacking. I still want you."

She stopped adjusting her dress. "But you don't want to marry me."

How could he tell her that after what his first fiancée had done to him, he wanted a wife he could trust to be faithful. It sounded so pompous, even to himself, that he only said, "You know that I can't."

She stared up at him and said, "Is this the reason women become mistresses?"

"What?"

"Maybe I am supposed to be a mistress."

"What the devil did you say?"

"Maybe I'm supposed to b—"

"Damnation, Mirabella, you don't have to say it again. I heard you. I just can't believe you said it." He reached over and pulled up the neckline of her bodice, in an attempt to cover more of her breasts than she had when repairing her clothing.

"I am sorry, my lord."

"I should think so."

"Did I make you angry?"

"No. Yes. What would make you think about being a mistress? You are a lady of quality and breeding."

"You are a true gentleman to say that when you know I have been less than circumspect in my behavior with certain gentlemen—and with you, my lord."

"What you do with me is different. We are engaged." He straightened. "And a few stolen kisses in a quiet garden don't qualify you to be a mistress."

"But they do keep me from being a bride."

"Not a bride, Mirabella. They keep you from being *my* bride."

He realized how harsh his words had sounded when the sparkle went out of her eyes and a heart-wrenched gasp escaped her lips. She looked out into the gray mist. This was not the kind of conversation he wanted to have with her. Especially after the passion they had shared.

"Is it wrong for a man to want a wife he can trust? A lady who has been true to him?"

"Not at all. I understand perfectly."

He knew she wasn't telling the truth. His voice softened, though he knew he could not take the sting out of the words he'd just said to her. "Such thoughts of being a mistress should never enter your mind. And if they do, you shouldn't ever say them out loud to anyone."

She turned to stare into his eyes. "It's just that after the pleasures you have shown me today, I know that I would not want to live the rest of my life and never experience again the way you made me feel just now."

Her words sucked the breath out of him. Heat fused him, and his wet clothes suddenly felt damned uncomfortable.

He reached down for the ribbons and released the brake handle. "You honor me by complimenting my—skills, Mirabella. However, you deserve to be a wife who is loved and cared for by a husband who will give you children. You should not simply be a man's indulgence."

"Camden, would you want me for a mistress?"

He jerked back toward her. She was driving him crazy with her innocent remarks. "Mirabella, I'm not going to answer that question and there will be no more talk of mistresses."

He laid down the leather on the horses' rumps and headed back toward the road at a jaunty clip. Mirabella had his mind whirling in so many directions he couldn't talk straight. He couldn't even think straight. Mistress indeed! As if he or her father would allow such a thing!

Camden maneuvered the bays back onto the road and started the journey back into Town. The graying mist spread over the land before them like a wet blanket. He was afraid to even steal a glimpse of Mirabella. But he had to admit to himself that he couldn't stop thinking about the possibility of her outrageous question.

Suddenly there was a large jolt and crack, then the carriage rumbled to a halt.

"Oh, hell!"

"What happened?"

Camden pushed his wet hair away from his face. He felt like swearing long and loud but calmly said, "I don't know. I think we hit a hole. We might have damaged a wheel. Sit here while I have a look."

He set the brake again and jumped down. The left wheel was in a deep hole and hopelessly broken. He looked all around him but saw only gray mist. Night was falling fast. He had to get Mirabella home.

"I can help you push the carriage out of the mud," Mirabella said from her perch on the seat.

Through clinched teeth he said, "We're not stuck in the mud. This wheel is broken, and we are not going anywhere in this carriage."

"What are we going to do? How far are we from Town?"

"Too far to walk."

"Camden, we can't be out after dark. It will give my father cause to apply for a special license and force us to marry. You must do something immediately."

He didn't know if he was relieved or upset that she was as eager not to marry him as he was not to marry her. No way in hell did he want to be forced into marrying Mirabella, no matter how much he desired her.

She had already told him that her father wanted them to marry sooner than next spring. No doubt the old man was looking for a reason just like this to press his advantage.

Camden looked around to see if he could spot a light in the distance. There was nothing to show signs of a house where he might leave one of the bays and borrow a rig.

He looked at the two horses, then up to Mirabella. "Can you ride?" he asked.

"A horse?" she asked.

He nodded.

"I haven't ridden often and certainly not without benefit of proper clothing, a saddle and a gentle, well-schooled mare."

Camden strode over to the harness and started unfastening it. "Something tells me you learn quickly. We could make better time if we rode together, but I really can't leave one of the bays here. You'll have to ride one of the horses."

Mirabella stood up in the carriage. "You plan for us to ride through the streets of London and up to my father's house astride a horse? That will not make my father happy, my lord."

"Of course not. We'll stop at the first livery we come to, and I'll hire a carriage and take you home properly. We must hurry. After all I've been through with Stephenson and Farthingdale, I'm determined this outing will not end in marriage or be the death of your reputation."

She gasped. "What do you know about Sir Patrick Stephenson?"

"Nothing," he mumbled, realizing his error.

"That you mention his name indicates you know something."

"Forget I said it. I haven't time for long explanations, Mirabella. With the mist, darkness will fall fast."

As it was, he feared there was no way they would make it back before dark. How had he become so caught up with Mirabella that he forgot about time? But he knew. Mirabella made him forget everything but her. But now wasn't the time to worry about that. He *must* get her home on time.

He was aware of everywhere he touched Mirabella. Her waist when he helped her down from the carriage. Her buttocks as he shoved her up and onto the back of the horse. Her thigh as he helped pull her undergarments, dress and pelisse down her legs as far as they would go. But he had no time to linger over any of the feelings she stirred inside him.

Within a couple of minutes he mounted the other horse and they took off down the road. There was a rush of excitement in the way they raced side by side. It pleased him that Mirabella had no trouble keeping pace with him.

On the edge of Town they came to a livery where Camden quickly made arrangements with the tradesman to hire a carriage. The stable owner was happy to receive an extra shilling to forget he ever saw the young lady riding with Camden.

Camden kept the horses at a mad dash through the streets while Mirabella tried to hold on and re-pin her hair up on top of her head with the one comb that hadn't been lost during the strong winds and their passionate lovemaking. In his haste, Camden overtook and passed several carriages along the way, but never slowed his pace. He was racing the darkness, and for a time, it looked like his opponent was going to win.

There were no seconds to spare when he pulled the hired rig to a jerky halt outside her town house. It was such a black shade of gray anyone could have said it was night and no one would have argued—except Camden. He would swear on the Holy Book it was merely dusk.

Camden jumped down and ran around to Mirabella. She flew into his arms. He set her on her feet, grabbed her hand and they raced up the steps together. Camden's heart beat frantically in his chest as he opened the door. They stepped inside the small foyer where a lamp had been lit.

He took a deep, drawing breath and combed through his damp hair with his fingers. The house was too quiet.

"I half expected my father to be standing here waiting for a chance to demand we marry."

"We're not out of the woods on that yet, Mirabella," Camden cautioned.

There was the sound of voices and Newton and Lily came walking down the hallway from the back of the house.

"There you are, Miss Bella," the maid said. "We've been worried about you."

"Yes, Lily, I'm sure you were. As you can see, I'm fine."

Mirabella's maid was clearly shocked at her employer's appearance, and the butler was giving Camden the evil eye. And no wonder, Mirabella looked like she had been dragged through a horrific storm.

"You don't look fine. What happened to you?"

"We were caught in the rain is all. The wind was so fierce I lost my parasol and my bonnet."

Lily looked from Mirabella to Camden. "We were just talking about you and wondering why you didn't come home the minute the rain started. We were on our way up to tell your papa you hadn't returned from your afternoon ride."

"I'm glad you didn't. We tried to wait out the worst of the rain under a tree. Then we had a little carriage trouble—"

"That turned into big trouble," Camden said, interrupting Mirabella. The least said the better. "A broken wheel delayed us, but thank God, I found a livery and was able to deliver Miss Whittingham back safe, sound and on time."

"That's right," Mirabella added. "Thank goodness we returned before you disturbed my father. Newton, we're chilled, please have Cook make us some hot tea, and Lily, please get a towel for Lord Stonehurst."

"I was sure you would be damp when you came in, Miss Bella. I had a fire lit in the drawing room for you a little bit ago."

"Bless you, Newton. We'll go there now."

The butler and maid hurried away, and Camden followed Mirabella into the drawing room. Camden took a deep breath and relaxed. It looked as if no one was going to challenge their lateness. They walked over to the fireplace and stood before it. The warmth was inviting. The lamps had been lit and the glow from the fire made the room seem cozy, but Camden knew he could not get comfortable.

Mirabella looked up at him and smiled.

"Don't start that again, dear Mirabella. This is not the place, and we are not alone."

"Whatever do you mean?"

"The last time you smiled at me like that you ended up in an alarming state of dishabille."

She deliberately furrowed her brow into a mock frown. "You are quite right, my lord."

"No doubt we both look exceptionally haggard."

"No doubt."

"You are the most desirable woman I have ever had the misfortune to meet."

"Is that a compliment?"

"It is simply the truth."

Her expression turned serious. "Camden. Why was our kiss so intense?"

He raised an eyebrow and gave her a curious look. "You are such an innocent to have been kissed so many times."

"The number of times has nothing to do with it. I felt like I wanted to devour you, to bring you into my body, I couldn't get enough of—"

He placed his fingertips on her lips and silenced her. "You don't know what you are saying." *And I pray you don't know what your words are doing to me.*

"It's how I felt. I don't understand it. I have never felt that way before."

"That, I'm glad to hear." He looked back at the doorway. If she kept up this kind of talk, he would be embarrassing himself in front of the maid and the butler. "We shouldn't be discussing this. Especially not here in your home where someone can overhear us."

She stepped away from him. "I just wanted you to know how I felt."

He needed to get away from her and cool off. "I'm not going to wait for the towels or the tea."

"Why?"

"If I stay any longer and listen to your words, I'll need another wild ride in the cold rain."

"You are quite wet enough, Lord Stonehurst."

"Quite. I have important business to conduct with my father tomorrow, so I won't be free until evening. Shall we meet at the Prestwicks' at half past ten?"

She slowly nodded. "I'll be there. But be sure you save a dance for me."

"As if I wouldn't."

"I'm certain Lady Gwyneth will have the Duchess at your ear, and Miss Milhouse will have her handkerchief ready. They both have their caps set to see if they can take you away from me."

"You jest, Mirabella."

"You turn a blind eye, Camden. Mark my word. Lady Gwyneth is desperate to get your attention."

"I've no time for her silly games. I've told everyone I'm devoted to you."

"I want you to know I think she is beautiful and proper to a fault."

"I'm sure she would love to hear you think so, but I won't be telling her."

She took in a deep breath and cupped her hands together in front of her. "I think she will be an excellent bride for you."

Mirabella was full of surprises. "Do you now?"

"Indeed."

"Let's see." He pushed his damp hair away from his face and pretended to ponder her words. "I picked my first fiancée. My father picked my second. And now you feel qualified to pick my third chance at a bride?"

"Oh, yes. I, above all, know what you are looking for in a bride."

He chuckled. "Thank you, Mirabella, but I think I'll wait a few years before considering a bride again."

"Perhaps when you are old and gray, my lord, would be a good time."

"No truer words have been said this day. I think that is exactly what I'll do. Good evening, Mirabella."

Thirteen

VISCOUNT'S MAD DASH THROUGH HYDE PARK

Was this writer the only one who heard about Lord Stonehurst's wild spurt across Hyde Park yesterday afternoon? The newly returned-to-Town viscount nearly ran down three strolling couples, two earls, a countess, and a duchess before he dashed out of sight. Hmm. One wonders if he had just heard the same bit of news this writer was made privy to late yesterday. It seems the reports are that the viscount was all but brought to dueling (for the second time!) with two of the Season's most eligible gentlemen over reports that his fiancée had been seen walking with them in the garden. But, of course, both gentlemen who were said to be in attendance swore the scuffle never happened, and that as far as they knew, Miss Whittingham was a perfect lady. Makes one wonder how gossip gets started if there is no basis in the foundation. Hmm. Or does it?

—Lord Truefitt, *Society's Daily Column*

Camden slammed the paper down on his father's desk in the small office of their town house. He took a deep breath and muttered a few choice words under his breath. Why did he even read the rags? They were nothing but scandal sheets, and he had better use of his time than to read such drivel.

He didn't come close to running anyone down when he left the park. Well, maybe one or two. And he'd like to know who the talebearer was that had witnessed his scuffle with Stephenson and told about it. Camden would have a private talk with him if he ever found out.

It was no wonder most of the people who wrote the gossip columns kept their true names private. They didn't want anyone asking them how much money they paid out each year for the unsubstantiated balderdash they printed. Someone had to know who the evildoers were.

There was one good thing about all of this. Apparently his talk with Farthingdale and Stephenson had paid off. According to the gossip pages, the young men were mum about their intimacy with Mirabella. But were there other men he didn't know about?

Mirabella wouldn't tell him. By her silence he could only assume there were others. Why wouldn't she tell him? Were there too many to count? He couldn't even think about that possibility.

He could understand her not wanting to go through life without a kiss, but did she have to kiss more than one man? More than two? Just how damn many men had she kissed? Camden had to stop thinking about it. It was driving him to distraction.

He laid his head against the tuft of the chair and thought back to yesterday afternoon. She had demonstrated that she was a woman of rare passion, eager to participate in lovemaking. No doubt, any man would have his hands full with a woman such as she.

A *mistress?* Mirabella?

He supposed it was logical that she might think she was born to be a mistress because she enjoyed a man's touch. From what Camden understood most wives were passive, not active in the marriage bed. It was a longstanding rule among some men that the finer pleasures of lovemaking were for their mistresses' beds, not their wives' bedrooms.

Perhaps it was a reasonable deduction for Mirabella to think that, because he didn't want to marry her, the life of a mistress would be an acceptable alternative considering her erotically appealing side. But why did the idea of Mirabella as a wealthy man's mistress distress him almost to the point of madness? The very thought of it wrenched his gut into hard knots.

He'd be a fool not to think about the possibility of Mirabella becoming his mistress as she had all but suggested. Camden felt stirrings in his lower body.

No, he didn't want to consider Mirabella as a mistress for himself or any other man. He wanted her because she was a beautiful, utterly engaging young lady. She matched his intellect and his desires. However, her inappropriate behavior with the other men made her unacceptable as his wife. So why didn't he like the thought of her being his mistress any better than the thought of her being someone else's courtesan?

Camden closed his eyes and remembered snippets

from yesterday afternoon. He savored each image that came to mind: the chilling rain and the hot kisses. He'd never forget the smell of damp foliage, the taste of her wet skin, or the vigorous wanting and the denied ecstasy.

One minute she was teasing him with her banter; the next she was an impassioned woman, malleable to his manly needs and her own womanly pleasures; and in the next minute she was reminding him why she would never be his. By the end of the day, she was talking of mistresses and suggesting the name of a proper young lady who would make him a good wife. She was almost too much for him.

Almost.

Camden chuckled.

There was a knock on the door of his father's small office. Camden opened his eyes and leaned forward.

"Having a good laugh all by yourself, are you?" Hudson asked as he walked into the room.

Camden cleared his throat and straightened in his chair. "Yes, I was."

"Care to share?"

"I don't think so."

Hudson reached over and picked up the scandal sheet from the desk. "I saw this earlier. Good you can get such enjoyment out of being dragged through the muck."

"No doubt the wretched souls have nothing else to occupy their time."

"May I sit down?"

"Certainly. How was your afternoon?"

Camden gave his attention to his brother and brushed aside the papers he had been going through before his mind had wandered. Hudson made himself comfortable in the armchair on the other side of their father's desk.

"Splendid when I called on Miss Pemberton and a holy debacle when I called on Lady Gwyneth."

"Miss Pemberton, I understand, but what's this about Lady Gwyneth?"

"I was hoping you would ask."

"How could I not? It surprises me that things aren't as serious with you and Miss Pemberton as I thought." Camden breathed a silent sigh of relief, thinking it was good that Hudson wasn't ready to offer for the young lady's hand.

"Oh, I was astonished anyone would think that, too," Hudson said. "It was made known to me last night, by an acquaintance, that Lady Gwyneth would welcome a call from me. So, even though I'm quite devoted to Miss Pemberton, naturally, I didn't want to disappoint Lady Gwyneth, since she had gone to such lengths to gain my attention."

"I should think not. No reason not to keep your options open until a match has been made. She is a beautiful young lady."

"You think so?"

"Yes. If she asked someone to speak to you, she was most definitely interested in you. I'm glad you went, Hudson."

Hudson expelled a heavy breath. "You may not think that when you hear what I have to say."

Camden tensed and braced himself. He wondered if she'd heard something about Mirabella's indiscretions or his fight with Sir Patrick Stephenson and decided to tattle to his brother.

Camden managed to keep his expression blank and asked, "What is that?"

"What, indeed. It was pure insanity. The wretched fellow who gave me the tip got me confused with you. She welcomed a call from Lord Stonehurst. Not his brother, Hudson."

"The devil, you say?"

"It's true. She was most outraged about the whole misunderstanding."

"But she knows I'm betrothed."

"But not married. People change their minds and lovers elope to Gretna Green. It is still as popular as ever for those who wish to marry without their fathers' blessings."

Camden laughed. "Well, I hope you set her straight. I don't intend to leave Mirabella and run away with Lady Gwyneth Sackville."

"She did most of the talking, I'm afraid. She's quite adept at getting her point across."

"Yes, she is a determined young lady."

"At first she thought you had sent me in your place and, I swear, she was on the verge of throwing back the flowers I gave her."

Camden thought about chuckling again but thought better of it. Hudson was truly in a dither over the matter. "What a scene that must have been."

"Not one I want to repeat. When she walked into the parlor, and I was standing there, her face turned as pink as the gown she was wearing. She was quite annoyed that she'd spent so much time getting ready for the wrong person. I made my leave as soon as I could once I was aware a mistake had been made."

Camden deliberately focused on shuffling through some papers on the desk to keep from smiling again. Beautiful and wealthy young ladies could be spoiled chits when they wanted to be.

"No worry now. It looks to me as if you made it out of the situation with your neckcloth in place. So all is well."

"That remains to be seen. I think she's set her cap for you, Camden."

"That's ridiculous. I have no interest in her and have shown no interest in her."

"Be that as it may, consider yourself warned. Don't be caught alone with her, or you'll find yourself in a compromising position and end up having to marry the wrong girl."

God forbid.

"Wise words I'll keep in mind, Hudson."

Camden wanted to marry someday and have an heir, but, blast it, he had no desire for a pouty eighteen-year-old who couldn't bow out of a misunderstanding graciously. No doubt Mirabella had already heard about Lady Gwyneth's intentions about him, and that was why she suggested the girl might be a good wife for him.

He had no doubts Lady Gwyneth would be a dreadful choice.

He could only hope that she didn't get wind of any specific details of Mirabella's rendezvous with the gentlemen in the gardens. She wouldn't stop until Mirabella couldn't show her face in Town.

Hudson rose. "Well, I'm going up to get ready for tonight's parties." He started untying his neckcloth.

"While you're here, Hudson, I'd like a word more with you."

"You sound serious."

"No, not really. I need to tell you that first thing tomorrow morning our parents will be traveling to our estate in Lockshaven."

"They are? Before the Season is out? Why? They never leave Town before the end of the Season." Hudson leaned a slim hip against the desk.

"There are pressing business matters that need the earl's immediate attention." Camden didn't want to tell Hudson that he was sending his father with the money to buy back the land he'd lost. Camden could only hope it would be enough. If not, he gave his father leave to ensure there would be more in the coming months.

"But I thought that land was mortgaged and lost—" He let the last word trail off, his hands stilled on his neckcloth.

"Yes. It was. Perhaps you know more about the family finances than I realized."

"I know our funds are limited but not all the reasons why. Father assured me all would be well in due time. And that it would not keep us from living the lives a titled gentleman's sons should live."

That was only mere days from being not true. Camden saw no reason to tell Hudson what he didn't already know. With the money Camden had brought with him from America, he had stopped the foreclosure on the town house. There were still many other smaller debts to be paid. His main objective was to regain all the estates and lands that his father had lost over the years.

Only a day after his return, he had sent a letter to his solicitor in America asking him to sell his stake in the Maryland Ship Building Company. Camden knew selling meant he would take a huge financial loss. With the new steam engines that were being built, hauling cargo would be more profitable than ever, but he couldn't keep his holdings there and let his family lose their ancestral home. And, of course, the dowry had to be repaid to Mirabella's father.

"I had hoped that I would be able to talk to him about asking for Miss Pemberton's hand before the Season was over. You know the truly exceptional girls are all matched their first Season. I'd hate for her to think that she's not among the best."

Camden felt a twinge of guilt. It wasn't Hudson's fault that their father had been so derelict in his financial duty to the family.

"Well, we don't have to make a decision about that right now. There's time left in the Season. Let's wait and see how well things come along. I know you would want to wait until you could properly take care of a wife, and we are not in that position yet."

"I see."

"Don't look so downhearted. We're going to be all right, but it will take a few months."

"Months?"

"Yes, it could take that long. We've enough to manage until the end of the Season. Don't worry."

Hudson seemed to consider Camden's words. "I suppose I'll just have to persuade Miss Pemberton to wait for me."

"I'm sure she'll understand, and that she will be

happy to. She seemed utterly devoted to you when I met her the other evening."

Hudson smiled at Camden's words and slid his neckcloth from around his neck. Camden's eyes zeroed in on a long, thin scratch on the side of his brother's neck just above his collarbone. It was red and angry looking.

He immediately thought of Mirabella's strange questioning about scars and birthmarks on Hudson's body. There had to be a reason she asked about that. But what?

"You're looking at me as if you've seen Lord Pinkwater's ghost, Camden. Did I suddenly grow a horn?"

"No. A bad scratch. What happened to your neck?"

He put his hand up to the wound and winced. "Ah— at last, I think it's healing. Wretched thing. I might have a scar. Two weeks ago I was riding like the wind, racing Lord Standbringer, when a low branch from a tree caught me. I didn't see it because there were no leaves on the limb. It was really quite alarming. I was jerked off the horse and wrenched my knee, causing me to limp for a day or two. I was damned lucky my cravat didn't tangle in the branches and hang me."

"Damned lucky indeed."

How could Mirabella have known about Hudson's wound?

"Is Standbringer married?"

"The devil no. Swears he loves too many women to settle for just one."

Camden wondered if perhaps Mirabella walked in

the garden with Standbringer, and she had learned about Hudson's wound from him. Camden shook his head in anger.

Damnation! Would he now suspect every man of having kissed Mirabella?

Why did it eat at him so that he didn't know all the men who had kissed her? It was giving him a devil of a fit.

∝∽

Mirabella sat at her dressing table, her eyelids drooping while Lily took care with pinning Mirabella's hair on top of her head in a mound of curls. She was so tired she could hardly keep her eyes open. She didn't know how Lily managed to hum after such a day. She must be dead on her feet, yet no one would know it from the way she went cheerfully about her duties.

Mirabella didn't know how she was going to make it through the long evening of parties that lay ahead of her. If not for the longing to see Camden and spend time with him, she would have sent a note to him and Uncle Archer that she had a headache.

She thought back over her laborious day. She'd spent the entirety of it at the tavern with Lily. Her hands were red and sore from washing glasses, dinnerware, large pots and floors. She was yelled at, cursed and pinched on her bottom more than once by the foul-smelling curmudgeon who had no smiles or kind words for any of the workers in his charge.

It had been gravely disappointing to discover that she would not be allowed to step one foot inside the gaming, reading, or smoking rooms as she had hoped.

Only the male servers who were fashionably dressed were allowed in there. A fact that Lily knew but failed to make clear to Mirabella. She had managed to look through the doors several times, but couldn't get close enough to see the necks of any of the men.

She certainly couldn't consider the day a total waste of her time. She was able to mark Sir William Jackson off her list. Fate had smiled upon her when at the end of the day, as she was getting ready to leave, he came to the doorway of the kitchen and called for one of the servers. His collar and cravat were off, and his neck was clearly visible and clearly free of scars. She had only a handful of men left to inspect, and she was certain the man she sought had to be one of them.

Playing the part of the maid would not go as fast as the kissing and that had been painfully slow. What she discovered from one of the older maids who worked there was that most men seldom relaxed enough to take off their collars and neckcloths and if any of them did, it was usually late into the evenings, and never during the day.

At the rate she was going, the rest of the gentlemen on her list would be retiring to their summer homes before she found the one she sought.

Mirabella had to turn to her other idea. There was no choice really. She had to do it. She would gain entrance to the gentleman's club her father belonged to as one of his relatives. She would dress as a proper gentleman. As a male, she could walk around the gaming rooms and check every man in attendance. She'd watch them and wait until she'd seen all who chose to bare their necks.

She didn't know why she hadn't thought about this idea before she spent all day at the men's club doing the work of the lowest paid servants. Now getting men's clothes was the key to her success. The only place she knew to go was her father's wardrobe. She would have Lily pilfer a suit of his clothing and cut it down to fit her.

She looked at her maid in the mirror. Lily hummed as she arranged small flowers in Mirabella's hair.

"Lily, I need you to do something for me tonight while I'm out."

"Yes, Miss Bella."

She took a deep breath. "I want you to obtain a pair of my father's trousers, a shirt, waistcoat, neckcloth and a well-cut jacket from his wardrobe."

Lily stared at Mirabella's reflection in the mirror for a moment. "You know I don't have anything to do with your papa's clothes. He's very particular about who takes care of his things."

"I know. That is why you will have to sneak into his room tonight after he has gone to sleep and get the clothing for me."

The maid's eyes widened in shock. "Sneak into your papa's room? Miss Bella, you know I can't do anything like that. You want to get me put off?"

"That is preposterous. Why would I want to get you fired? With you gone, I would have no one to be my partner in this scheme. I need you to help me accomplish this. Don't worry about yourself. I'll protect you."

"See, even you realize it is a misdeed for me to go into your papa's room and steal his clothes."

"Oh, it's not stealing, Lily. I'm not going to keep them."

"Then what do you call taking what doesn't belong to you without permission?"

"I'm merely borrowing them with no expectations of returning them anytime soon."

"I don't know why you keep having me do all these things that aren't right. You are up to something, Miss Bella, and I don't know what you are trying to do."

Mirabella rose from her stool and looked down at her maid. "Lily, I don't want you to question me on this. I know what I'm doing. You must trust me and do exactly as I say. Now, tonight, while I am out of the house, I want you hemming trousers and remaking one of Papa's shirts to fit me."

"If your papa wakes and finds me in his room, plundering through his private things, I'll be thrown out into the streets before you even get home."

Lily put the back of her hand to her forehead as if she was going to faint. Mirabella knew she was too stout a girl for a trick such as that, but she was trying to send Mirabella a message.

"Nonsense. Don't be a weak-kneed ninny, Lily. That's not going to happen."

"I know, because I can't do it."

"Of course you can. Just stay calm. You know my father's medication makes him sleep soundly and Newton seldom stirs in the night, either. No one will know you have been in Papa's room."

Lily picked up her apron and twisted the hem in her hands. "I have done a lot of things for you, but I don't know if I can steal your papa's clothing."

Poor Lily must think her insane, and maybe she was, but she wasn't about to stop now. "For the last time, it is not stealing. And you have to do this. I can't explain why I must do this, Lily. I'm asking you to trust that I know what I'm doing."

Lily huffed loudly and dropped her hands to her sides. "I'll try, but I'm not making any promises."

Mirabella inhaled an uneasy breath. It would be simple enough. Tomorrow evening, she would plead to Camden that she wasn't feeling well and needed to go home early. She would don her father's clothing and head for the club and return home in the wee hours of the morning before the household awakened. Yes, that should work.

"I know you won't let me down. Oh, and Lily, I'll need a nice gentleman's wig. Check the attic. One of Papa's old ones should be up there."

"Oh, my saints," Lily exclaimed. She cupped her hand over her now-gaping mouth. "You're going to dress up like a gentleman and go back to the tavern."

"Yes, Lily, I am going to dress as a gentleman but this time I'm going to Papa's club."

Fourteen

It was well past midnight as Mirabella stood in front of the mirror in her bedroom. She didn't recognize herself. Instead, in the looking glass before her, she saw a boy on the brink of manhood. The transformation was miraculous.

She ran her hand down the shiny brass buttons of the double-breasted waistcoat that hid her breasts. The metal was cold to her touch, but strangely made her think of Camden's cool, damp skin on Sunday afternoon. She was certain she would never feel that wonderful again. She closed her eyes for a moment and remembered the taste of him on her lips, the feel of his mouth on her skin.

A noise sounded behind her, and her eyes popped open. She realized it was Lily humming, again. Mirabella took a deep breath and put away her womanly notions of steamy passion. In the mirror, she noticed that her hands looked very feminine. She would remember to keep them by her sides at all times. They were a telling sign that she was a lady.

It had taken Lily more than an hour to make over

Mirabella. She had bound her breasts to her chest before she donned the shirt. Lily had wrapped her hair tightly so none of it would fall from under the powdered wig she'd fit snugly around her head. With care they had dusted her cheeks with cosmetic powder, trying to cover the natural pink tint of her skin. With a small paintbrush and smut from the fireplace, Lily had cautiously darkened Mirabella's eyebrows and made them look larger and thicker. Using the white powder, her full lips had disappeared into a thin line.

They had taken great pains to make sure the cravat was stylishly tied in a shape most dandies would envy. Lily had turned out to be an expert with a needle. She left the hips and thighs of the trousers wide so her legs would look more muscular. After she attached a wide brass buckle to plain black boots the metamorphosis was complete.

Mirabella had watched enough men at parties to know that most of them stood with one leg cocked to the side at a stance. She had made countless trips from one side of her bedroom to the other practicing walking with more of a stride than a glide. She had even shut herself in her wardrobe and rehearsed in a low raspy voice what she planned to say to the doorman to gain entrance to the club.

Apprehension ran rampant inside her, but she calmed her fears by thinking that if luck were with her, most of the gentlemen at the club would be too busy playing at the gaming tables, or talking with their friends, to notice her. Her worst fear was that she would see none of the men who were still on her list. London was home to many private gentlemen's clubs and she had to have faith that at least one on her list belonged to her father's club.

"I never would have believed we could make you look like a man," Lily said, walking up behind Mirabella. "You look just like a young Mr. Whittingham."

Feeling confident, Mirabella turned away from the mirror. "Well, now I know how I would have looked if my father had had a son. Thank you, Lily. I never could have done this without your help."

Lily's dark eyes narrowed and her lips pursed before she said, "Just don't get caught, Miss Bella. Mark my word, if you do, we're both going to be in more trouble than we can get out of."

"I won't. I know what I'm doing." *And why*. Mirabella picked up the great coat, felt top hat, and said, "Let's go."

Lily led the way down the back stairs to the kitchen without lighting a lamp. She motioned to Mirabella that the room was clear. Mirabella hurried across the floor to the door, opened it and quickly stepped outside. The sky was dark with only a small slice of moon and very few stars to light her way. A damp chill hung in the air, but with all the clothing she had on she didn't feel the cold.

Once Mirabella was free of the house, she didn't look back. With the long strides she had practiced in her room, she walked down the street toward the main thoroughfare, which led to the business district of Town. Within a couple of minutes, she had flagged a hired rig to drive her to the club.

A few minutes later, she arrived and paid the driver from the coins Lily had given her. Mirabella had promised to see that Lily was repaid every shilling.

She was pleased to hear the man say, "Thank you, sir," when she gave him the fare. She knew she looked like a man to herself and to Lily, but to fool another man meant she'd passed the first crucial test of the evening.

It seemed as if she stood in front of the men's club for hours, but it couldn't have been more than a minute or two. If things went well for her at this smaller, private club maybe she would get brave enough to go to White's. She had thought that a smaller one would be less intimidating, but now she wasn't so sure. This gentlemen's club might be more discriminating, too. Her father had been a member at this one for years, although it had been well over a year since he had ventured out to spend an evening at the gaming tables.

A carriage pulled up in front of the building and three men got out. Not a one of them gave her more than a cursory glance and slight nod. That should have bolstered her courage, and it did, but not enough to make her take the step that would put her inside the club. She ran her hands down the sides of her coat and took a deep breath.

She gave herself a mental shake. With what had come out in the scandal sheets yesterday morning, she had nothing to lose by going inside. There was already the breath of scandal about her among the *ton*. The only thing left to lose was her father's pride in her, so she had to make sure she didn't get caught.

Taking a deep steadying breath, she opened the door and stepped inside. A well-dressed older gentleman immediately walked up to her and asked, "May I 'elp ye, sir?"

Mirabella cleared her throat and lowered her voice just as she had rehearsed. "Yes. I'm Adam Moore from Kent, nephew to Bertram Whittingham, here as his guest for the evening."

Keeping her head bowed, Mirabella held out her hand palm up. The man knew exactly what to do and took the money she offered along with her hat and coat.

"Oh, cert'nly, I know 'im. 'Ow is yer uncle these days? I 'aven't seen the ol' chap in months."

She lifted her head slightly. The man never blinked. He took the coin and dropped it into the pocket of his coat. Mirabella took a much needed, relaxing breath. Listening to her father's conversations over the years had paid off. The money worked like a charm.

"Feeling better than he has in weeks," Mirabella said, hoping her happiness at her father's improved health didn't sound any alarms for this man.

"Splendid to 'ear. Tell 'im ol' Charles asked about 'im, will ye?"

"You can be sure I will."

The conversation with Charles went so well that Mirabella's courage soared. She had passed another big test and was inside the club.

The older gentleman ushered her inside a dimly lit room filled with muffled sounds and lingering smells of burned wood and ale.

"'Ave ye been with us before, sir?"

"No, first time."

"Well, this 'ere is probably the first room ye want to go. Get yer spirits over there." He pointed to a long oak bar, crowded with men. "Billiards will be through there, an' the card games that way. Ye'll find the rest of 'em as ye walk around. If ye 'ave any bit o' trouble, come find me."

"Thank you. I will."

Mirabella hadn't taken her eyes off the bar area since she'd walked inside the taproom. Hanging on the wall was a life-size portrait of a dark-haired lady lying nude on a red sofa. A black cloth draped across her body, but it was only covering her waist, not her private parts!

As soon as Charles walked off, Mirabella turned away. She feared she glowed crimson beneath the white powder she wore. *That* must be the reason ladies were not allowed in gentlemen's clubs.

Mirabella knew she couldn't continue to stand just inside the doorway and act like a ninny who had never been in a place like this before. She heard the sound of billiard balls smacking together. So she took a deep breath and headed in that direction with her newly learned, swinging stride. She hoped that would be a more respectable place for a young lady than hanging around a painting of a well-endowed nude.

She stepped into the room and lingered near the doorway at the back while her eyes adjusted to the dim lighting. The chamber was small, but elaborately decorated with a thick carpet, marble fireplace and costly upholstery on the comfortable-looking chairs. There were two tables with three and four men surrounding each table. Only two of them had taken off their collars and neckcloths.

All the gentlemen appeared casual with good-natured talking and genuine laughter mixing among them, filling the room. After a minute or two, she decided to walk closer and to pretend to be watching their game. It pleased her that no one seemed to pay her any attention. She was too cautious for any sign of a problem to listen to their conversations. She kept her eyes trained on the necks of those which were bare, even though none of the men she saw were on her list of possible suspects.

It was surprising how little attention they paid her, and she soon relaxed and became comfortable enough to move into the reading rooms to see if there were anyone she recognized in there. Those areas were occupied mostly by older gentlemen who were far less relaxed with all their necks wrapped with varying styles of cravats.

The younger men seemed to gather where the liquor was served and in the billiard and card rooms, so she took her time and slowly made her way from one room to the other, constantly watching for one of her suspects. Only one or two of the gentlemen at the gaming tables had removed their neckcloths.

After more than an hour, her heartbeat jumped rapidly in her chest when she spotted a young man on her list in one of the card rooms. She took her time and casually walked by the table where he sat and stopped to look him over carefully.

She saw no signs of a scar, but noticed one of the other men staring at her. She tensed. He moved his cards closer to his chest and Mirabella realized his problem. She didn't want to be accused of trying to read anyone's cards, so she made her way back to the billiard room.

As she slowly sauntered into another room, she was congratulating herself on how easy this was compared to the kissing and servant's work. Why hadn't she thought about this before?

The only problem with this plan was whether the right young men would come in and bare their necks. There were less than five gentlemen left on her list of suspects. Would it be her luck that the very last man she saw would be the man she sought?

The night wore on, and Mirabella became quite comfortable. Occasionally someone would speak to her, but for the most part, she was left alone. She often heard language that was seldom used in front of a woman, but other than that and the nude painting, she didn't understand why women were not allowed beyond the front doors.

There was a concern though. She couldn't very well plead a headache every night to get away from Camden early enough to visit the clubs. But she wouldn't worry about that right now. The evening was going so well she would figure out how to do that tomorrow.

જીજી

Camden left White's and had the driver take him to the smaller private club a few streets over. He was tired of the noisy club but wasn't yet ready to go home and sleep. He couldn't get Mirabella off his mind. She had pleaded a headache early in the evening and had left for home with her uncle.

Camden couldn't help but be worried about her. He was sure she wasn't the kind to use the headache or vapors as an excuse. She had seemed preoccupied when they were together during the evening. He wondered if she was upset about something.

She could have been upset about their passionate affair in the rain on Sunday afternoon. He'd never meant to get so carried away, and he certainly never dreamed she would be so warm, receptive and eager for his kisses—as he had been for hers. But their time alone together had been such sweet ravishment. She'd had time to think about the afternoon and it could be she regretted it.

Shaking off thoughts of the siren, Camden walked into the club and nodded to the doorman. The first member he saw was Albert Farebrother on his way out. What damnable luck. The man seemed to be everywhere.

Albert was the last person Camden wanted to see. No doubt he would gloat that what he had mentioned to Camden about Mirabella last week had finally hit the gossip columns. Camden had hoped to avoid the man, but there was no doing that now.

He walked right up to him and said, "Albert, so glad to run into you. Let me buy you a drink."

"Good heavens, no, my cup is full, but I should buy you a round after the day you must have had."

Camden pleaded innocent. "I had a pleasant enough day. What are you referring to?"

"Ah—well." Albert stumbled over his words and looked around the room as if someone would know he was in trouble and come to his rescue. "Surely you saw the papers, man?"

"I read the *Times*. The Lord Mayor's money troubles have nothing to do with me. Didn't give it a passing thought, why did you?"

"I—I was talking about the Society paper."

Camden wondered if Albert had always been so easy to read and so easy to dupe. "Oh, you mean the scandal sheets all the ladies of the *ton* live and die by? I had no idea you read them."

"Er... yes." Albert's cheeks flushed pink. "Surely you saw or, at least, heard about what was written. Simply dreadful what they had to say about you and Miss Whittingham."

"You know, Albert, I seldom read them, and you must know why," Camden said tightly, wondering if he had ever been as close to Albert as he remembered.

"I'm sure there wasn't a shred of truth in what was reported about a scuffle between you and some unnamed gentlemen," he added as more of an afterthought.

"Glad you realize that, Albert. I'm sure all my old friends will."

"Yes. It was nothing like what happened six years ago. Back then the gossips were appalling to you and the poor, wretched girl, Hortense. And, well, that young man she was caught with, who proved himself such a coward, could never show his face in England again. I hear he lives the life of a recluse in Paris. With all that was written about the three of you, it's no wonder you stayed in America so long."

"I see you haven't forgotten a morsel about that time, Albert."

"How could I? There hasn't been a bigger scandal in Town since."

"No doubt because good friends like you keep that one alive."

Albert's chin dropped. The pink in his cheeks flamed red.

"But don't give it another thought, Albert. That's all over now," Camden said when what he really wanted to do was ram his fist in Albert's face. "I have a perfect lady now who is simply the toast of the *ton,* and I refuse to let this breath of scandal sully her spotless character. What are you drinking these days, old chap? Port, ale or brandy? I'm buying."

"Port, but I can't stay. Truly. I was on my way out the door." He laughed. "The wife, you know, gets worried if I stay out too late. She swears she can't sleep until she hears me come into my rooms."

Albert clapped Camden on the shoulder and it took all his willpower not to throw off the offending hand.

"Yes, the wife. Something I have to look forward to, no doubt."

"To be sure. They do like for their husbands to keep certain hours. It's such a bore. I'm not sure you'll look forward to it, if you know what I mean." He winked at Camden. "Enjoy yourself while you can, old man."

"I shall."

"I find it's quite difficult to divide my time between a wife, a mistress, and the clubs. But I do try hard to be fair to all."

"I'm sure they appreciate your efforts."

Albert smiled broadly. "They seem to."

"My regards to the countess."

Camden watched his old friend walk away and wondered if he was the one who had changed or if the new earl had changed. What had happened? He and Albert used to stay out until sunup and share a pint of ale and a loaf of bread before going home. Camden heard a clock strike three. He supposed a man with a wife and family should be home by three in the morning.

Refusing to let Albert sour him completely, he picked up a glass of brandy at the bar and decided to watch a game of billiards. Surely there would be enough noise in there to drown out Albert's words from his mind. If he was lucky, no one would approach him, and he could sit and enjoy his drink before he went home.

He found a dark corner and sat down. Now he knew why Mirabella went home early. She probably did have a headache. No doubt she was harassed by someone the way Albert had just troubled him. Why was he so worried about her? She had brought all this on herself. She had to know that though everyone broke the rules, Society was only unforgiving when you were unfortunate enough to get caught and have your indiscretion talked about among the *ton* or in the scandal sheets.

Camden took a swallow of his drink. Over the rim of his glass, he saw a young man walk through the doorway and immediately thought he was too young to be in the club. He couldn't stop watching the youth. There was something vaguely familiar about him, but Camden couldn't bring a name to mind.

The lad made his way slowly around the first table, looking each man over carefully. That was odd. Most spectators looked at the table, not the players. The youth was so unobtrusively clever, not one of the gamesters noticed him. It was odd to say the least. Was he a young man whose tastes leaned toward older, wealthy men? The hair on the back of Camden's neck spiked. This club was no place for the likes of him and his feminine ways.

Camden started to tell Charles to question the lad, but decided to handle the interloper himself. He'd put a scare into the youth, and he wouldn't be back to prey on anyone in this club.

Camden followed him out the doorway and, at the dark, shadowy end of the hallway between the card and billiard rooms, he called to him.

"Hey there. You. Young man."

The stranger turned around. When he saw Camden, he could have sworn the lad swallowed his tongue. He turned and fled. Camden gave chase and reached out and caught him by the arm, yanking him around just before he made it inside the card room.

They stood in the dimly lit hallway. The young fellow kept his face down and didn't meet Camden's eyes. Camden was sure the lad was trembling. He hadn't meant to scare him so badly.

Feeling a bit of remorse Camden politely said, "Just a moment please. You look lost. May I help you?"

"No," came the raspy reply.

He must have been a surly, ill-bred youth. He didn't look up to speak. Camden didn't even know why he was bothering with the chap. Dealing with the likes of him was Charles's job.

"I've watched you walk around the tables. You seem to be looking for someone. Maybe I can help you."

"No. Thank you, sir. I need to go."

He turned quickly to walk away and, when he did, Camden's heart slammed against his chest. He clearly saw the lad's profile as he passed under the gas jet. He looked like Mirabella.

Mirabella?

Camden felt like a rock landed in the pit of his stomach as he watched the lad hurry through the doorway. He didn't know which hit him first, shock or denial.

"Mirabella?" Camden whispered. Why did the young man look like Mirabella?

"No." She wouldn't!

Fifteen

MIRABELLA HURRIED DOWN THE HALLWAY AS FAST AS her faux masculine stride would take her, frantically searching for a doorway that would take her out of the club.

Camden!

What was he doing at this club? And at this hour of the morning!

Merciful heavens! He must have recognized her. But how? She didn't recognize herself dressed as she was.

She ducked inside the taproom, refusing to look back, lest she see Camden on her heels and break out into a full run to escape him. She quickly scanned the room and saw Charles standing by the door leading outside. Her heart quickened. She was going to make it.

Suddenly a hand clamped around her upper arm and swung her around. Mirabella's hope spiraled down to her toes. She refused to look up. She didn't need to, in order to know it was Camden who held her. She knew his touch. Her heart beat so fast she thought she might faint. She took a deep breath to calm herself. She had to think fast.

"What's your hurry, young man? Let me buy you a drink before you leave."

Mirabella buried her chin so close to her chest she felt as if she were choking herself with her neckcloth. Her body froze with tension. Obviously he hadn't figured out who she was. Yet. She had to try to keep it that way. Her whole plan would be doomed if she did not get away before he recognized her.

"No, I have to go," she mumbled as low and raspy as she could. She tried to pull her arm out of his grasp, but his hand didn't budge.

"Nonsense. Every young man needs an older gentleman to show him around a club. A drink is what you came here for, isn't it? And maybe to step outside for a smoke? Perhaps you would like to try your hand at cards, too?"

"No, sir. I need to go." She shook her head as she spoke, but he paid no attention to her. He continued to usher her toward the back of the room. She was forced to follow him or create a scene.

"Come on. Just one drink. Let's sit over here in this corner."

Corner? She prayed it was a dark corner. Keeping her head low she walked with him to a table and blessedly it was dark. She took the chair farthest away from the light on the wall.

"Brandy for two," Camden said to someone that Mirabella couldn't see. "You look familiar. What is your name?"

"Adam Moore, sir," she said, using the name she had given the man at the door.

"Well, no wonder you look familiar. You must be a nephew of Sir Henry Moore from up near Lancaster?"

Mirabella had no idea who Henry Moore was, but she couldn't very well say that to Camden, so she simply kept her head low and nodded. She had to think of a way to get away from him before she did or said something that would make Camden realize who she was. Her disguise was good, but she knew Camden would not be fooled for long.

"Well, Moore, do you live in Town or are you visiting from the country?"

"Just here for the week, sir," she answered, not wanting to be trapped into stating an area.

"In that case, we'll try to see that you have a good time. Tell me, were you fortunate enough to attend any parties tonight?"

"The Windhams'," she answered, cleverly thinking to say a name where she knew a party had been held, but also one that she and Camden hadn't attended because she had pleaded the headache.

"I'm sure it was the toast of the evening. I had to miss that one. My fiancée became ill."

Her heart sounded like thunder in her throat and in her ears. Was he going to talk about her? What would she do?

Two glasses of a dark amber liquid were set on the table in front of them. Mirabella swallowed past a tight throat. She had had a glass of sherry from time to time and a glass or two of champagne at parties, but she had never had more than a sip of brandy. It was much too strong a taste for her.

Camden picked up a glass and extended it toward her. She quickly took hold of the glass from the bottom, wanting to make sure her fingers didn't touch his, or that he didn't have time to look too carefully at her hand.

"You've shown some courage in stepping out on your own, Moore, but you are too shy. Look up and let's toast to your week in Town."

Mirabella felt as if her throat had closed, but she had no choice if she were to remain incognito. She lifted her head only enough to see how to clink her glass on his.

"That's the way. Go on, drink up. It will make you relax. You seem a bit goosey."

A bit? She was frantic! Maybe she did need the drink to calm her. She needed to think of a rational way to get away from Camden, short of jerking off her wig and revealing she was Mirabella.

She put the glass to her lips and drank. It was far stronger than she remembered. She coughed a couple of times but managed to keep the burning liquid down. She took a stinging breath and quickly took another sip.

"There's only one thing that calms a man more than a brandy. Do you know what that is, Moore?"

Mirabella shook her head and took another drink.

"A woman in your bed."

Startled, Mirabella looked up and for the first time her eyes met Camden's. She quickly realized her mistake and lowered her gaze to the glass. She hadn't expected him to say anything like that, but she had to remember he thought he was talking to a young man.

"Oh, yes," he continued, "a woman in your bed can make you forget everything but the way she feels beneath you."

Mirabella drank more of the brandy, but did not look up again or speak. She knew her face was flaming red. Ladies enjoyed talking about gentlemen, too, but not in such intimate detail. There wasn't much brandy left in the glass. Maybe she could make her leave once the glass was empty.

"Perhaps a cigar would help make you more comfortable. You do smoke, don't you, Moore?"

"No, sir."

"I can see your uncle has been lacking in his duties of educating you in the ways of being a man. You must learn to smoke or take snuff. A young man learning his way around a club for the first time should try it all. We'll have to step outside to smoke, but I'll get one for you."

She was glad she appeared to be an inexperienced young man. Her disguise was working too well. It was like Camden to want to help. She remembered the first night they met. He would not leave her to find her way back to the party. Just as he would not leave Adam Moore on his own in the club. Why did he have to be such a gentleman at all the wrong times?

She raised her head a little more and looked at Camden. He rose and turned his back to her, but didn't leave the table. He spoke with one of the servers about bringing over a cigar. He didn't appear angry or shocked when he looked back at her. There didn't seem to be any recognition of her in his eyes.

Mirabella remembered her reflection in the mirror. She had astonished herself at how different she looked with her white powdered wig and face, and the dark, full eyebrows. She raised her head a little more. She was tempting fate. She had to get out of the club.

Camden sat back down. "So you were at the Windhams'. Lovely people. No doubt you had a partner for every dance."

Mirabella nodded and sipped the brandy again. Maybe the drink was making her more relaxed, but it was also making her hot. Heat seemed to rise up from her stomach and chest and settle in her neck and cheeks.

"Tell me, were you able to slip outside with any of the young ladies tonight?"

In shock, her gaze met his again, and she saw a wicked glint of light in his eyes. He was trying to jolt the young man he believed her to be.

"I beg your pardon, sir?" she managed to say.

"Well, surely your uncle told you that one of the things bachelors do at clubs is talk about the young ladies and interesting widows. Specifically the ones who are, should we say, free with their affections."

"Oh, yes, sir. I mean, no, sir. I didn't—"

"Are you telling me that you didn't persuade a single young lady to accompany you onto the patio, so that you might steal a kiss or get under her skirt?"

"No, sir," she mumbled and took her last sip of the brandy, although she felt as if her cheeks were on fire.

"Well, you are young and just learning the ways of a grown man. There's time for you to master all you need to know about seducing a lady."

"Yes, sir." This had to stop. Mirabella set the empty glass on the table. "I should be going home now. Thank you for the drink." She rose from her chair and a strong familiar hand clamped down on top of her shoulder.

She looked up at him and a grim smile touched his lips. "Not yet, Moore. Here comes the cigar. After a smoke you can try your hand at a card game. Come on, Charles will bring the cigar to us. I'll walk out with you."

Yes, if she could get outside the door she could get away from him. She walked beside him as they made their way out the door and into the night. She purposely walked over to the darker corner.

Mirabella's breath came thickly. Charles stepped outside behind them. She was trapped. She could do nothing but stand in stunned silence and watch Camden take a cigar and a long, thin piece of burning wood from the tray the server held. He put the cigar between his teeth and lit it with the flame. When smoke came out of the end, he blew out the flame on the stick and handed it back to Charles.

Camden took a comfortable draw on his cigar and blew the smoke out his mouth. "Why smoking this is considered more vulgar than snuff, I don't know. Here, you try it."

She looked at the smoke and at Camden. His eyes had turned dark and brooding. A deep-set frown marred his expression.

A quiver of doubt surged through her. Did she dare take it or should she take off running? Mirabella seldom ran from anything. Slowly she reached for the cigar and put it to her lips where Camden's had just been.

"Take a deep drawing breath, and then blow out the smoke." His voice had lost its friendliness.

Mirabella sucked in deeply on the cigar, but wasn't prepared for the rush of smoke into her mouth. In trying to expel it, she swallowed it. She started choking and coughing uncontrollably. She felt as if her lungs were on fire and she was strangling.

Camden took the cigar from her and handed it to Charles, then clapped her on the back. She tried to tell him she couldn't breathe, but couldn't speak as tears sprang to her eyes.

"He needs some fresh air," Camden told Charles. "He's not used to smoking. Bring some water outside for him."

Mirabella had never been more thankful to be out in the predawn air. She felt as if she needed a cold, wet blanket to bathe her throat and chest. She staggered away from Camden and flattened her hands against the wall to support herself. She coughed, feeling as if her insides were going to come up at any moment.

"Are you all right?" he asked, in a voice laced with concern.

"Yes," she finally managed to say—and didn't have to worry about trying to make her voice raspy. Her throat was raw and ached. Her stomach churned.

"You weren't supposed to swallow the smoke," he scolded her.

"I knew that and certainly hadn't planned to."

" 'Ere's the water. Do ye think 'e'll be all right?"

"He's fine, Charles. I'll handle this if you'll hail a hackney for me."

She felt Camden's warm touch on the back of her shoulder. And for a moment, she hated the reassuring feeling of comfort it gave her.

"Here, drink this," he said.

Mirabella grabbed the tin cup and downed the water quickly, keeping her back to Camden.

"I guess you're not ready to smoke."

"That's a remarkable statement of the obvious, sir."

"'Ere's yer coat and hat, Lord Stone'urst. The young man's, too."

"Thank you, Charles. I'll take him home."

She felt Camden's hand on her arm. She wanted to turn into his arms and pour out her heart to him, but she couldn't. "No, I'll walk."

"You'll ride with me." He took the cup from her, and started pulling her along. He handed the cup and a coin to Charles as they passed him.

"But no, you don't understand, I can't."

Mirabella was about to bolt when suddenly Camden forced her inside the carriage by grabbing her under the arms and lifting her into the coach. He stepped in after her.

"Drop us at the corner of Lowberry and Wiltshire," he said to the driver and slammed the door behind him as he took the seat beside her.

Mirabella gasped in outrage. Lowberry was her street. Had he seen through her disguise? The carriage started with a jerk. She squeezed her eyes shut for a moment, then opened them to stare through the darkness inside the coach into Camden's intense and smoldering brown eyes.

She froze. Her ploy was over.

"You know who I am," she whispered in resigned frustration.

"*Mr.* Mirabella Whittingham, I suppose."

With a tiny moan of protest she said, "Yes, my lord."

Camden grabbed her up close to him, held her tightly, but she felt no fear. She knew he was not going to harm her even though fury shook him.

"Did you think I wouldn't know you?"

His voice was so earnest it staggered her. She was incapable of speech.

"How could you think I wouldn't know those tempting lips, your beautiful green eyes, your slender neck? Not even this coat could disguise your softly rounded shoulders, nor could the trousers hide your walk. I know you, Mirabella."

At any other time his words would have thrilled her, but not now. She had been caught. "Wait." Suddenly she gasped. "Did you know it was me when you gave me the brandy and the cigar?"

His mouth tightened. "I knew you almost from the moment I saw you."

Her brow puckered into a frown of disbelief. "How could you be so cruel? My head is spinning from the strong liquor you made me drink, and I thought I was going to die, my throat and lungs burned so badly."

"You weren't supposed to swallow the smoke."

The tautness in her body increased. "I couldn't help it. You should be ashamed of yourself, Lord Stonehurst, for treating me so shabbily."

"Me? Ashamed?"

"Yes." She was so miffed she could hardly speak. "That was an irresponsible thing for you to do." She drew in her breath with a sharp gasp. "You—you talked intimately about things only men talk about."

"Yes, for a reason. I was trying to teach you a lesson that women don't belong in a gentlemen's club. It was either that or strangle you for putting yourself in jeopardy."

"Obviously I was only in peril from you."

"I saved you."

"From what? I was not in any danger until you came into the club. I can assure you I did not know you would be at this club tonight."

"Now who is stating the obvious?"

"I don't even know to which clubs you are a member."

He dropped his forehead to hers. "This is not the time to be mundane, Mirabella." He raised his head and his eyes searched hers. "You are dressed as a *man* in a *men's* club."

"You just tried to poison me with brandy and smoke."

"Do not try to change the subject, and do not try to be evasive."

"Evasive? I'm appalled."

His voice softened slightly. "Why is it that whenever you get in trouble I get blamed."

"Because my troubles are usually your fault."

It was too dark to see into his eyes clearly, but she felt rage in his hands that held her so tightly, even though he never raised his voice.

Suddenly anger left her. "No, that is not true. But you must believe that I have my reasons for being in the club dressed as I am dressed," she answered without a tremor in her tone. What she'd done had been necessary, and she wasn't sorry. Because of it, she had marked one more name off her list.

"No, Mirabella."

"Yes, very good reasons," she insisted.

"No reason could be good enough for this behavior."

Mirabella remained silent. The beating of her heart sounded far louder than the clanking of the carriage wheels and the clopping of the horses' hooves as the coach moved steadily along the street.

"Well?" he asked.

"Well, what, my lord?"

"Aren't you going to tell me what your very good reasons are?"

"Why should I? You just told me no reason would be good enough for you."

"You try my patience. Just because I said nothing would be a good enough reason for you to be in the club doesn't mean I don't want to hear what it is."

He was strongly appealing, but Mirabella slowly shook her head. Camden's fingers squeezed into the flesh of her upper arms, but she paid no mind to the pain he caused. "No," she whispered regretfully.

He uttered a shocked, "No?"

He let her go as if she'd suddenly turned into a hot poker. He laid his head on the back of the carriage seat and shoved his feet into the opposite seat.

Camden expelled an audible sigh. "You exasperate me to the point of madness, Mirabella. When I think I'm at the point of trusting you, you do something else to give me reason not to. What do you want to gain, to prove? Are you trying to see if you can cause a bigger scandal in my life than what Hortense did to me six years ago?"

She moved to the edge of the seat and looked at him. "No. No. Of course not! How could you think that?"

"What am I to think?"

"Half the *ton* saw your first fiancée in her lover's arms. No one but you and Uncle Archer has seen me in anyone's arms. And no one recognized me tonight."

"Correction. I recognized you tonight. And, no one has *admitted* to seeing you in anyone's arms or to being in your arms, because I threatened their lives if they dare utter a word against you."

"You didn't!" she exclaimed.

"Of course I did. That's how gossip is stopped."

Mirabella's mind was whirling. Had he really threatened someone's life? To save her?

"So it's true what was said in the *Society Daily* about you having a scuffle with two men."

"More or less, it's true."

She saw in his expression that he spoke the truth. Her heart swelled with love. *Love?* Yes. She loved him. This all-consuming need to be with him, to enjoy him, had to be love.

Oh, merciful heavens, could things get worse? When did she fall in love with Camden? What could she do about it? He could never love her. He could never forgive what she had done. Already he likened her to his first fiancée.

"Just when I think I might start understanding you, I catch you doing something completely unacceptable again. How many times am I going to have to save your reputation?"

"I don't know," she managed to say with a gasping breath.

"I do. This is the last."

Mirabella heard and saw the bewilderment he was feeling. She didn't mean to vex him so. Maybe she should tell him what she had been trying to accomplish and why. Would he believe her? Would he try to help her, or would he insist she stop her search immediately? She was so close to finding the man she sought.

"Tell me what you were doing in that club dressed like this. Albert Farebrother, the Earl of Glenbrighton, was in there tonight. He could have recognized you. Anyone could have."

"But only you did."

"That is not the point." He raked both hands through his hair, skimming it away from his forehead, and turned to look at her. "My patience is gone, Mirabella. I realize this ruse of an engagement was my idea, and I'm working hard to put my family's finances in order, but this stunt tonight is beyond the pale. The way I see it you have two choices. You can either tell me what you are doing dressed as you are, or when we get to your house we will march straight to your father's bedroom and you can tell both of us your very good reasons for being in that gentlemen's club."

"No. I—" She laid her hand on his chest. She felt him stiffen, and it broke her heart that he didn't want her to touch him. She removed her hand. "You must not disturb my father. There's no telling what it would do to his heart to be awakened before dawn and find me dressed in his clothes. I will do anything you want."

His expression softened, but his voice remained firm. "I don't want you to *do* anything, Mirabella. I want you to *tell* me the truth."

She leaned closer over his chest. Right now she could look for Sarah's seducer and be a part of

Camden's life. If she told him what she was doing there was the chance he would walk away and never see her again just as he was threatening right now.

"Don't make me. Telling you the truth frightens me."

For a moment she felt he had weakened and would relent, but he softly said, "What do you fear? Surely not me."

Still she hesitated.

"Mirabella, right now I'm thinking money be damned. My family's reputation will be ruined if my father's debts are made known on the streets, but I see no other answer. I will tell your father the truth. I'll explain that our engagement is broken, and that I cannot repay the dowry until I have sold my assets in America."

Once again she placed her hand over his heart and leaned close to him so that she could look directly into his eyes. "I won't do this again."

"That I believe, but what game will you come up with next? I can't carry this charade off any longer." His voice softened even more. He raked the backs of his fingers down her cheek. "You are successfully driving me insane."

Mirabella didn't know how, but she knew he was referring to more than just peace of mind. She felt the drain on her senses. In the darkness their eyes searched. Each waited for the other to speak.

The carriage stopped but neither moved. Mirabella heard the driver jump down. He popped open the door and stared at them for a moment. Suddenly she realized he saw two men sitting very close together with one man's arm on the other's chest. Camden must have realized how they must have looked to the driver at the moment she did for they both jumped up at the same time.

Camden stepped out and paid the driver while she climbed down. Thank goodness they were not right in front of her house.

As soon as Camden turned from the driver, he said, "Let's go."

He started walking. Was he really going to wake her father? His strides were long and purposeful, spurring Mirabella to action. She took off after him.

"No, wait," she murmured softly. Camden kept walking, nearing her house, nearing her front door. Anguish filled her. She started running. "No, Camden. Wait. Please, let us go to the back."

She took hold of his arm, and he allowed her to guide him through the iron gate to the back of the house where they stopped not far from the back steps. Under a shadowed sky with very little light, she stood close to Camden and felt the pull of her attraction to him.

She had no choice. She had to trust he would understand what she had done and why. She waited a long time before she said, "I had to get inside the club. I had to kiss the young gentlemen," she said in a whispered voice. "I'm trying to find a killer."

"A what?" He gave her a questioning look.

"A killer."

"Mirabella, are you in danger?" His tone became anxious.

"No, not me." She paused. "But other unsuspecting young ladies might be."

He stepped closer to her. "Tell me what you are talking about. I've read nothing in the papers about a killer on the loose."

A breeze raked across her face and cooled her heated skin. Now that she had started her story, she was desperate to tell him everything. "I'm trying to find the man responsible for Sarah's death."

"Your aunt's ward? I thought you told me she died in her sleep."

"She did, but a man with no honor caused her death."

Camden laid gentle hands on her shoulders. "Mirabella, I'm finding it difficult to follow you. Start at the beginning, not the end."

"It's a long, complicated story, my lord." Mirabella suddenly felt weary.

"Talk fast or condense your story. The servants will be up soon, and I'm still not convinced that I shouldn't speak to your father without delay."

Mirabella looked up at the sky. The first light of dawn was streaking across the darkness. "Everyone in the house thought Sarah had died in her sleep. A few days later, I found Sarah's diary."

"And you read the diary?"

"Yes. I was lonely for Sarah. I missed her, and I thought reading her writings might comfort me. I assumed there would be poetry and verse like I enjoy writing. Instead I read the most horrible story."

"What? Tell it to me."

Mirabella quickly told him the entire story of Sarah and her Prince Charming, ending it with how Sarah took an overdose of laudanum when she could see no honorable way out of her predicament.

"What did your father say when you told him this?" Camden asked.

"I never told him or the authorities. I was afraid they wouldn't do anything about it. And if they somehow let it slip that they were looking for a man with a scar it would give the vile man time to leave town and never be punished for what he did."

"What scar?"

"The scar on Prince Charming's neck. I told you it was complicated."

"I agree. Tell me, what has any of this to do with you allowing men to kiss you or posing as a man?"

"Shh." She put a finger to her lips. "You must not speak so loudly. I devised a plan to find Prince Charming myself. When I do, I will let it be known to certain ladies of the *ton* that he got Sarah with child and then wouldn't do the right thing and marry her. When they get through with him, he will not be welcomed in anyone's home again."

"It's true that most pushy mamas hide their daughters from known rakes and scoundrels. But how did you think you could begin to find the lecher?"

"I knew certain things from the diary. Sarah danced with him last Season. He is shorter than most men, and he has a wide raised scar on his neck, right about here." She pointed to the area just above her collarbone. "I made a list of suspects from her dance cards who fit that description."

"Mirabella, that must be half the eligible men in London."

"Of course not. You see, because Sarah wasn't very pretty, and she had a droopy eye. She only had a few opportunities. Occasionally some mama would feel sorry for her and force her son to ask Sarah to dance. So there weren't that many names on her cards."

"I'm still missing the part about how your schemes of kissing and dressing as a man fit into this story."

"I have to find the man with the scar."

"How the devil did you think you'd see that since it's under a man's clothes?"

"That, of course, was the problem. So I devised a plan to allow the gentlemen on my list to take me into the gardens and kiss me so that I might put my little finger down their neckcloths and search for the scar."

He shook his head in disbelief. "Mirabella."

"No, Camden. It was really quite simple once I learned how to do it quickly."

"Damnation! Simple indeed," he said harshly. "How many men did it take you to learn how?"

"Oh, I learned how to do it on my maid. I had her dress in a shirt and cravat so I could become skilled at it and do it quickly. I didn't want to spend too much time with the gentlemen."

Camden ran both his hands through his hair and expelled a loud sigh. "You overwhelm me, Mirabella. You let young men take you into gardens and kiss you just so you could feel their necks for a scar?"

"Yes, but I haven't done it since you returned."

He nodded. "So this is why you are dressed as a man tonight."

"Yes. It was really quite easy to see a man's neck when he's not wearing a collar or cravat. I didn't realize that so few of them relax enough to take them off. But tonight was much preferable to the kissing."

"What you did was madness." He turned away from her.

"No, Camden. I don't believe that." She took hold of his arm and forced him to look at her. "I want you to know I meant it when I told you that no other man's kisses made me feel the way yours do. And I found no pleasure in what I did tonight, either."

In the darkness he placed the tips of his fingers under her chin and moved his face closer to hers. "How many men have you kissed?"

His question wounded her, and she remained silent.

"Just tell me was it more than two? More than five? More than ten?"

No matter what she said, he could not think worse of her than he already did. "It was more than one."

"Which was more than enough to change our destiny." He took a deep breath and backed away from her one step. "Is that why you asked all those questions about my brother's birthmarks and scars?"

"Yes." -

She expected him to be more furious than he was. She wouldn't have blamed him. Mirabella reached up and untied her neckcloth and placed it in her jacket pocket.

"You suspected my brother had left a lover to take care of herself?"

"Truly, I have not suspected anyone specifically, and Hudson's name wasn't listed on Sarah's dance cards. But I noticed he had some kind of marking on his neck and naturally I was curious as to what it was and how it got there."

The anger seemed to have left his voice when he said, "Not a scar, a scratch. That is very recent, I might add."

"I was sure that would be the case."

"There are better ways to handle this."

"None that I could think of that wouldn't send the miscreant into hiding."

His gaze swept down her face and then back up to her eyes. "I'm relieved that you were not attracted to the gentlemen you kissed, but still you flaunt convention with reckless disregard."

Mirabella waited with hope that he might say more. She wanted to hear him say her story changed everything between them and that her past didn't matter, but he didn't.

"Sarah was unable to help herself. I don't know why she didn't confide in me, or why she thought my father would throw her out on the street. He wouldn't have. I know how high a price I have paid, and I am truly sorry for the trouble this has caused you. But I would do it again. I will continue until I find him."

"No, Mirabella." His tone was firm.

"Camden, I must, before he ruins some other young lady who has poor chances of making a match and is desperate for someone to love her."

"You should have just asked everyone to bare their shoulders and been done with it."

"Bare their shoulders?" An inspiration flashed through Mirabella's mind so quickly she gasped. "Bare their shoulders," she whispered again as the idea blossomed. "Yes. Oh my, Camden, I think you have something there."

"Mirabella, I don't know what you are thinking, but do not even think about doing it. You have done quite enough. Kissing men, dressing as a man was more than enough. I don't believe I want to know what else you have done."

Slightly embarrassed, she looked away from him.

He placed his fingertips under her chin and lightly pulled her face back to him. "What else *have* you done?"

"Nothing where anyone recognized me."

"You dressed as a man before tonight?"

"No. A maid."

"A servant! Blast it, Mirabella. I can see it's dangerous to leave you alone."

"I hated every moment of it and wouldn't think of doing it again. It was truly dreadful. But, Camden, your idea is a perfect way to find him. If only I had thought of it before now. I love it."

Mirabella threw her arms around his neck and kissed him on the lips. A long, hard kiss that took him only a second to return. His hands settled firmly on her waist and drew her close to him.

She was reluctant but finally broke away from the kiss and looked into his eyes. Shyly she said, "Thank you."

"That was very enthusiastic gratitude. I don't know what notion I put into your head, but don't even think about it. This must stop. Enough games."

"No, my lord. One more. This will do it. I know it. I'll give a masked ball and invite everyone I can think of. No one will be allowed inside unless they wear a toga with the right shoulder bare."

"A toga party? Mirabella, this is outrageous. I don't see how you can pull off a big party. Where will you hold such a large undertaking? Ladies plan all year for these lavish events."

"I don't know where or how. I only know I can do it. I'll pay for the Great Hall, or I'll hold it in Hyde Park if I have to. I will stand at the entrance and greet everyone who enters and send them away if they are not properly attired."

"I believe you would do just that."

"I will. Camden, I know it will work. Everyone in the *ton* loves a masked ball. If that young dandy is still in Town, I will find him."

She reached up and kissed him again. This time it was a slower, softer kiss that lingered, filling her with those wonderful sensations that only Camden could make her feel. She slid her arms around his neck and pulled him to her.

The kiss deepened and quickly turned desperate as he captured her lips with his and wouldn't let go. His tongue explored inside her mouth with accuracy, knowing just how to bring her the utmost pleasure.

"I have no willpower against you, Mirabella," he whispered against her lips.

"I have none against you, dear Camden. Do not resist me. No kisses have ever made me feel the way yours do. No touch has ever thrilled me like your touch."

"If you don't want this, Mirabella, you must stop me."

"Why would I not want this pleasure, my lord?"

"Why not indeed," he murmured hoarsely and pulled her into the dark shadows near the side of the house.

Camden's arms slid around her waist, his hands slid beneath her coat and up and down her back, caressing her as his lips moved hungrily over hers. He slipped his hands lower and flattened each wide palm on her buttocks and jammed her up against the bulge in his trousers. His pelvic area started a rhythmic motion against her softness. Mirabella thrilled to this new feeling and wanted to get closer to him, so she pressed into his movements.

There was an urgency inside her that she didn't understand. All she knew was that she didn't want him to stop. She matched him kiss for kiss, touch for touch and movement for movement.

To hell with the other men Mirabella had kissed. She wasn't just being a flirt or in love as he had heard was the case with Hortense. Mirabella was trying to avenge a friend and save other young ladies from Sarah's fate. That was an honorable thing for her to do.

He ran a hand down her breast and felt only flat rough material. He quickly unfastened the buttons of the waistcoat and slid his hand to the other side of her chest before realizing her breasts were bound tightly to conceal she was a woman.

He felt he would go mad if he didn't stroke her. He pulled the tail of her shirt out of her trousers and shoved his hands up her body, desperate to feel her bare skin in his hands. With frantic fingers, he struggled with the tight cloth until he yanked it down to her waist and freed her beautiful breasts to his touch.

Lingering kisses, loving touches or sweet words were all fine if you had the time. Camden knew they did not, and he was hurting to possess her. He had wanted her since the first night he saw her. He lifted her shirt and covered the nipple of her breast with his mouth.

A soft moan of pleasure wafted past his ear. Sucking gently, he savored the exquisite taste of her soft skin. He felt the weight of her full breast in his hand.

Mirabella moaned as he caressed her. "I don't know why you are the only man I desire."

Oh, she knew what to say to set him on fire.

"Let it always be so," he answered in a breathy voice. "Don't ever let anyone else touch you like this."

"Never," she answered.

His lips found hers again and his hand pressed down past her abdomen and found her soft womanly place. He caressed her there and heard his own soft sounds of desire. The trousers allowed him more freedom to touch her than he was expecting. It was like she had nothing on, and his craving shot toward the sky, making him harder, and hungrier.

He tasted the brandy on her lips and heard the uneven gasps of her breathing. She was as excited as he.

Suddenly a light came on in the window near them. Camden quickly shoved Mirabella against the wall of the house. He meant only to shield her and protect her from being seen, but pressed against her tightly as he was, he felt every inch of her body. He felt her ragged breath in his ear. He bowed his head and kissed her cheek and tasted her fear of being caught.

He was breathless. She was breathless, but he could not stop wanting her that quickly. He ached to possess her. He pressed her harder against the wall. He moaned silently to himself as he continued their pleasure. His hand continued to massage her breast. His lower body continued to press her with urgency.

Mirabella truly had no idea of the power she had over him, and he had to keep it that way.

Camden heard a window slide up. Still he pressed against her, unable to control his urgings.

"Miss Bella, is that you?" came a feminine voice.

Afraid she might answer, Camden clamped his hand over Mirabella's mouth. Still he crushed against her, glorying in the satisfying feel of her softness against him.

There was no other sound and after a few moments, Camden heard the window slide down. The light went out. He breathed an unsteady sigh of relief.

Mirabella dropped her forehead to his shoulder and took a deep breath. She kissed his neck. "That was close," she whispered.

Camden was angry at himself for wanting her so desperately that he snubbed caution and was prepared to take her without regret. With Mirabella, he seemed to lose all control. She had told him that she was a virgin, and he believed her.

"Too close," he whispered.

Camden pushed away from her. There was no way he could take her here and now as he desperately wanted.

In silence, Camden put his hands back under Mirabella's shirt and helped her pull the wrappings over her breasts. It was a shame to flatten and cover them. He then helped her shove the tail of the shirt back into her trousers. She had him on the edge. Thank God he didn't have to walk right now because he didn't think he could.

He pulled her neckcloth from the coat pocket and wrapped it around her neck, tying it in a simple bow.

"Mirabella, I want you to give up this idea of finding this Prince Charming."

"I started to tell you a few days ago. I wanted to, but I knew you would expect me to give up my search. Don't ask that of me. Surely you know that after all I have sacrificed, I will not."

"I must insist. You could be putting yourself in danger by continuing."

"Do what you must, my lord. I cannot stop searching for the man I seek."

She turned away and ran up the steps and into the house.

Sixteen

Dear Diary—

After all these years of wishing and praying for it to be so, I think I have finally met the man who will be my Prince Charming.

Dear Diary—

He noticed me again tonight. He told me how lovely I looked in my blue gown.

Dear Diary—

With all the beautiful young ladies seeking his attention, imagine how resplendent I felt tonight when Prince Charming took notice of me.

Dear Diary—

He asked me to meet him in the garden tonight. I asked him to call on me in the proper manner of a gentleman, but he said we need some time alone to get to know each other, so we must meet in secret. I trust he is right. I want to talk with Mirabella about him, but I know she will tell me not to meet him.

*I don't want to hear that, so I shall remain quiet,
but exceedingly happy about my Prince Charming.
He will let me know when the time is right to tell
others about us.*

Dear Diary—
   *He kissed me and touched me and did other
things too intimate to write on paper—even to you.
There was so much passion in him it frightened me.
He promised me it wouldn't hurt. After he finished,
I swore to him it didn't. I know now that he will
soon speak to my guardian. He must.*

MIRABELLA SLAMMED THE DIARY SHUT. WHAT WAS THE
use in reading Sarah's words again to see if she had
missed anything that might help identify Prince
Charming? She had searched the pages tirelessly for
clues before she began her quest. Nothing new was
going to appear.

"Oh, Sarah, how could you have given me so little
to go on?" Mirabella spoke quietly into the silence of
her bedroom. "I want to find this man and see him
appropriately shunned by Society. But as each day
passes that I don't find him, I fear he gets farther from
my reach rather than closer."

Oh, how she wanted to get her hands on that
reprobate. He shouldn't be allowed to roam freely
to call on innocents and to lure young girls into the
garden. He shouldn't be allowed to mix in Society as
if he had done nothing wrong.

Her Roman toga soiree had to produce the vile
seducer. Not only was she at the end of her tether, but

she feared Camden was, too. She was sure he would not accept another misstep on her part—no matter how good her reasons.

Leaving the diary on her bed, Mirabella walked to her window and pushed aside the drapery panel and looked down to the quiet street below.

An audible sigh slipped past her lips. *Camden.*

Simply thinking about him brought her exquisite pleasure. She loved dreaming about his kisses and caresses. She put her fingertips to her lips and dreamed. She could feel Camden's kiss. When she closed her eyes, she could taste him.

It had never entered her mind that she might actually fall in love with the man her father had chosen for her to marry even if he did return. What were the chances of that happening?

But she was sure of her feelings now. She was very much in love with Camden. It pained her to know he would never be able to love her. She didn't blame him for wanting an unblemished wife who hadn't been touched by another man. An unsoiled young lady was a titled gentleman's greatest pride. She understood why he thought her no better than his first fiancée. To Mirabella, there was a difference between the two of them. Mirabella had not wanted or desired any of the men she had kissed. She had heard that Camden's first fiancée had been besotted by her lover from the moment she saw him. Camden was the only man who had ever made Mirabella's heart soar with passion and long for his touch.

Camden was angry with her for going to the gentlemen's club, angry that she couldn't give up her search. She'd expected he might very well show up today and tell her father the whole story and be done with her once and for all. But she couldn't sit around waiting for that to happen.

What Mirabella had told Camden was true. She had sacrificed too much to give up without trying this one last opportunity. She had to continue with her plans to find Prince Charming.

There was no doubt Camden was attracted to her, and that he wanted to take her to his bed. She wanted that, too.

Mirabella dropped the window dressing. There was no use brooding any longer. She couldn't undo all the things she'd done wrong. Camden would never be hers. She had accepted that the night he caught her with Mr. Farthingdale. It was time to move on.

Her next step was to convince her father to let her give the party. She had to do that right now. Most ladies who put on parties as big as she intended usually started planning the Season before. Still, Mirabella had no doubt that she could do it.

She left her room and went to her father's door and knocked. "Papa? Are you awake?"

"Of course, come in."

Mirabella opened the door and saw her father impeccably dressed in a starched white shirt and dark red brocade jacket. He sat in a midnight-blue striped chair, holding his accounts book. She smiled at him. "Seeing you out of bed makes me feel better than drinking an entire bottle of tonic."

Her father closed his book and chuckled. "Silly girl. When have you ever had to take medicine? You've always been in perfect health."

"Well, I can imagine what a good invigorator must do to one. Aunt Helen swears by it. She says she wouldn't start the morning or end the evening without a dose or two of her special tonic."

"Indeed. The kind of elixir she takes is formulated with brandy."

"If so, only enough to keep her feeling restored."

Mirabella bent and gave him a kiss on the cheek. "I hope your accounts book shows that you have plenty of money in there."

"We have more than enough to see you properly married, if that is your worry."

"I've no fear about that, Papa." She hesitated. "But I do have another affair that I would like to talk to you about."

"What's that?"

"I want to give a party."

"Hmm." He pretended to ponder her words. He made a grand gesture of opening the book to no specific page, placed his forefinger on it and thumbed down as if he were looking it over carefully. "I think we can handle that. How many people do you want to invite to your dinner party? Six? Twelve?"

"Over two hundred."

He glanced up at her. "What kind of foolery is this?"

"Absolutely none, Papa."

He raked his hand down his neatly trimmed beard. "You look serious about this."

"I am."

"That number is preposterous. Only titled fools and the king himself give parties that grand."

"Nonsense. Look at it this way. Most people give a small party each Season. Because my fiancé has been away, we haven't entertained in the past. So we will give one big party, rather than several smaller ones."

"I don't know what to say. You've taken me completely by surprise."

Excitement at the prospect that it just might happen danced through her. "Say you'll let me give a masked ball and invite everyone we know and some we don't."

"Masked ball? Do you know what you're asking?"

"Oh, yes, of course, I know exactly what I want to do. I was awake last night planning the entire evening. I want everyone to dress in the same costume."

"The same? What kind of masked ball is that? Everyone will look alike."

"That's right. I want it to be a Roman toga party, Papa. Everyone will have to wear a toga baring their right shoulder or they will not be allowed entrance to the ball. No exceptions."

"Showing their shoulders? Whatever for?"

For me to see their necks.

"It's something I want to do. You know that masked balls are all the rage."

"Masked balls, yes. But baring one's shoulders sounds positively indecent."

"It will be perfectly acceptable if everyone does it."

"But why do you want to hold such a large, peculiar event? Your aunt isn't even here to help you. I'll be of no use to you. We'll have to rent a place to hold it, and I'm not even sure any place will be available at this late date. I could go on, but I don't think I need to."

Mirabella picked up the hem of her morning dress and dropped to her knees in front of him. "I'll take care of all of those things, Papa. The magnitude of this does not daunt me."

She took his warm hand in hers. She didn't like the concern etched in his pale features. His frail shoulders were rigid with disquiet. She disliked worrying him even for a moment, but she had to press him on this. There was no time left to be gentle and coaxing.

"I only worry about you."

"Don't." Mirabella smiled at him. "I can think of several ladies who will be delighted to help me pull this off. All I need is your permission to go ahead with my plans."

"There's hardly more than two weeks left of the Season. It's much too late to plan a party this big."

"That is why I plan to make it the first party of the post-Season. Everyone will stay in Town one extra day for it, Papa. I know they will. I'll make it sound so exclusive and sensational that no one would dare miss it."

He remained silent for a moment then shut his accounts book with a thud. "All right. No limits, Daughter. If you are going to do this bizarre party, make it the biggest London has seen in twenty years."

Relief soared through Mirabella. She rose and hugged her father generously. "I will, Papa. I promise I will. Now I must get busy. I don't have one moment to waste."

❧

Camden sat at his father's desk and sipped a strong cup of tea. He realized he felt less pressure now that his parents had left for the country. Even though he had assured them things were going to be fine in time, they still wore long faces when they thought no one was looking.

Too, their absence left him freer to handle their business dealings without his father's constant questions and intervention. Camden hoped to hear soon that his assets in America were sold and that his money would be available.

Regaining all the lands they had lost had been the first priority. Saving them had wiped out his savings.

His father wasn't the first man to gamble away the family fortune. There were still many smaller debts that had to be repaid, not the least of which was a handsome dowry, but the money wasn't available yet to do that. He would have to start making the rounds and assuring the debtors that the money would be forthcoming if they could wait a little longer. Right now, after he sent money with his father, he barely had enough for himself and Hudson to live on for the next couple of months.

Mirabella.

No matter what he had on his mind, his thoughts always came back to her. He wanted to court her properly. He wanted to give her gifts of expensive jewelry.

He chuckled ruefully to himself. He barely had enough money for flowers right now.

She had shocked the devil out of him last night. Dressed like a man! What courage.

What had stayed on his mind all night had been her admission about the young lady named Sarah. Mirabella hadn't allowed those young men to kiss her simply because she wanted to be kissed before resigning herself to spinsterhood. She wanted to avenge her friend's death.

Mirabella was obviously a fiercely loyal person. That was an admirable quality. Who else but Mirabella would have risked ruining her own reputation to help someone else? Who else would have thought of sticking her finger down a man's neckcloth in search of a scar? But didn't she know how dangerous that could be? Any one of those men could easily have forced more attention on her than she wanted.

Dressing as a man had been over the top. He chuckled again. It was a foolhardy thing to do, but she'd held her own—even when he had talked about getting under a woman's skirts. If she had been caught inside, Camden and her father would have been thrown out of the club and never allowed back in. Mirabella would never have been able to show her face in Town again no matter how many men Camden threatened.

He admired her, though. She was brave and tenacious. He liked those qualities.

She was devoted to her father and his well-being. She spoke kindly to her staff. Oh, damn, there were so many, too many things to find attractive about Mirabella Whittingham.

Now she wanted to give this harebrained toga party. He chuckled to himself just imagining a room full of people all in togas and masks. What madness. He didn't mind so much the thought of looking at the shoulders of beautiful women but the thoughts of looking at men baring their skin was too outrageous to contemplate. What a sight that would be.

One thing was certain, because of Mirabella, there hadn't been a dull moment since he had arrived back in Town. He didn't remember ever being this stimulated when he was courting Hortense. He craved Mirabella with a burning intensity that seemed to be unquenchable. When Hortense betrayed him, he had been certain he was through with love forever. Now he was beginning to wonder if that was so.

What would he do when their engagement ruse was over? He desired no lady other than Mirabella. What would Mirabella do? She could make a match with a baron or a wealthy merchant, or maybe an older titled gentleman wanting a young bride as Hortense had done.

Camden's gut twisted at his thoughts. If he didn't want her for his wife, why the devil did it bother him that some other man could have her? She had indicated she'd be his mistress. His lower body reacted differently from his head and his heart to that idea. Mirabella had been careless, but that didn't mean she deserved the secluded life of a mistress. No, if he didn't want her for a wife he would have to deny himself and leave her free to marry.

"My lord?"

Camden looked up and saw the maid standing in the doorway holding a silver tray. "Yes?"

"There have been two posts delivered to you this afternoon, sir. Shall I bring them in?"

"Yes, thank you." She walked over, and he picked up the envelopes.

"Would you like more hot tea?"

"Not now."

She smiled and left the room. Camden looked at the two envelopes. Each was written by a different hand. He smelled the scent of one. On it lingered a heavy rose perfume. Not bad but not breathtaking. He put the other to his nose and lightly breathed in. Mirabella. He knew her scent—fresh, clean, with a hint of spice.

He tore open her envelope and read.

> *My Dear Camden,*
>
> *I must beg your pardon a thousand times for I cannot possibly make our engagements tonight. My father has agreed that I may host the Masked Toga Ball, which we discussed last night. There is so much to be done. Please accept my heartfelt apologies, and know that I will join you for the Vanlandinghams' ball on Saturday evening. However, that is the only event I feel I can attend with you this week.*
>
> > *I am very truly yours,*
> > *Mirabella*

Did she expect him not to see her this entire week? He intended to see her, *wanted* to see her. What impertinence! He threw her note aside.

It was fine with him if that was what she wanted. He had plenty to do to occupy him. He would indulge in a game of cards or billiards at one of the clubs. He might enjoy an entire night at White's.

He ripped open the other envelope and immediately

looked at the signature. Lady Gwyneth. He scanned the note inviting him to call on her and her mother for afternoon tea. The chit had temerity. She was the beautiful young daughter of a wealthy duke, and no doubt she was used to getting what she wanted. She obviously had designs on Camden.

If he canceled his engagement to Mirabella and made a match with Lady Gwyneth, he would have more than enough money to pay off his family's debts. He crumpled the letter in his fist. And he'd be just like his father. God help him. He refused to give that idea a second thought.

He did not want to be like his father, or like his friend Albert Farebrother who was out each evening at the clubs or paying calls to his mistress. Camden wanted to be at home in the evenings with his wife. He wanted to find pleasure in her, not with a paid woman.

Camden leaned back in his chair and plopped his Hessian boots up on the desk. But he had to think about what kind of wife he wanted. Did he want a wife whom he and the *ton* deemed socially acceptable, or did he want a wife who set his very soul on fire? Did he want a wife who could match his intellect on long winter evenings while they sat by a fire, or a wife who was happy staying quiet with her needlework? Did he want a wife who would share his bed and the pleasures that lay waiting for them there, or did he want a wife who couldn't wait for him to leave her side and go to a mistress?

He knew most men kept a mistress. It was almost expected of a titled man to have at least one. But what need would he have of a mistress if he had Mirabella?

He couldn't see her sitting quietly and doing needle-work. No, she would be by his side enjoying conversation with him. Perhaps he could even convince her to read some of her poetry to him.

Camden slammed his feet down and rose from his chair. Just who did Mirabella think she was? They were supposed to attend the balls and parties and go for walks in the gardens and for rides in the park. He enjoyed dancing with her, talking to her, looking at her. He wanted to be with her.

"Wait until Saturday night, indeed," he mumbled into the empty room.

If Mirabella wouldn't come to him, he would go to her. He grabbed his coat and hat off the hall stand on his way out the door.

Less than fifteen minutes later he was standing in Mirabella's foyer waiting to be announced to her. He was sure his heart quickened when he followed Newton into the drawing room and saw Mirabella standing beside a desk. She wore a simple dress, the color of winter wheat. Her thick hair flowed over her shoulders and down her back. Surely it was an offense to always wrap such beautiful hair. He wanted nothing more than to take her in his arms and kiss her.

"Camden, I'm afraid you caught me at an inopportune time again."

"I do seem to have a habit of doing that, don't I?"

"Most certainly. As you can see, I'm not dressed for a social call."

"You look beautiful, comfortable. I feel fortunate to see your hair in such a becoming manner."

She reached up and shyly threw her hair over one

shoulder. "I believe it is quite inappropriate for me to receive you so informally."

"But nice." He smiled, knowing that his unexpected arrival did not bother her. There wasn't a hint of shame in her attitude or her expression. "I believe your reputation can withstand the gossip if anyone finds out I've seen you in your morning dress with your hair unbound, don't you?"

She returned his smile. "No doubt. I sent a message over to you. You must have missed it."

"No. I received it."

She gave him a curious look. "You did?"

He saw that she was confused. "Yes."

"Then you know I have to decline our evening engagements and daytime events, too. I was sure you wouldn't mind."

"Oh, but I do."

Her eyes grew wide with concern. "You do? Is there something wrong?"

"Most definitely." He stepped closer to her, but had to force his arms to stay by his side and not reach out to touch her face, her hair. "You have handled all this on your own for too long. I came here to tell you that I am going to help you."

She shook her head, but didn't take her eyes off his face. She smiled. "Really, Camden, how very sweet of you, but I can't ask you to help me plan this party. I will manage."

"I'm not talking about the party. I'm going to help you find that Prince Charming scoundrel."

Her expression gentled. "What?"

"That's right. Since you can't give up your search

for the miscreant, I have decided to join you. Between the two of us, we will find him if he is still in England."

Her lashes fluttered attractively. "Surely you trifle with me, my lord."

"No, miss, I don't."

"This is my concern, not yours. From the start, I never meant for this to affect you in any way."

"I believe that, but it has. And now it is affecting *us*. I intend to help you."

"You confound me, sir. I don't understand why you would help me."

I want to be a part of your life. All of it.

"I don't know what kind of scheme you might come up with next, so I'm going to assist you by taking on the indecent task of examining the necks of strangers at whatever avenue might be afforded me. I can only hope no one will realize what I am doing."

"You would do that for me? For Sarah?"

"For all of us."

A grateful smile lightened her beautiful face. "I don't know what to say or how to thank you, but I do wish I could put my arms around you right now and kiss you."

Camden cleared his throat to cover the rise in his lower body. "I want that, too. Perhaps we can find a private place and time for that later. Right now, I need to see the diary you mentioned."

"Sarah's?"

"She is the lady in question, yes."

"Oh, I don't know if I can do that. It has her private writings in it."

Loyal to a fault.

"Mirabella, the poor girl is dead. I don't think she'll be embarrassed by anything she's written in there. You've mentioned the clues that led to your list of suspects. Maybe you missed something of importance that I will catch."

"I don't think so. I was very thorough."

He could always count on her to challenge him. "That may be, but I still think it needs reading with a fresh eye. For example, did she come right out and say this man wasn't married?"

"No, but how could she expect a man who was already married to marry her?"

"It's been my experience that young women in love don't always use common sense."

"That's a beastly thing to say, sir. Sarah was not like that."

"Does her writing actually say he was young? Was there any mention of a title? Or is it possible you assumed some of these things? Is it conceivable one of her dance cards may have been lost?"

"I see your point. Perhaps I presumed a few things. All right. I'll let you read it."

Mirabella started to leave the room to go after Sarah's diary but turned back to Camden. "You know, when you arrived unannounced, I was sure you had come to break our engagement. I thought that after last night, you had decided I was too much trouble."

He smiled at her and saw her relax. "The word trouble was in my thoughts, but I was thinking more along the lines that the best way to keep you out of trouble is to help you find this man. And that is what we will do."

Seventeen

IT IS TIME TO BARE ALL

Everyone in town is talking about the suddenness of the Whittinghams' Masked Toga Ball. Hmm. It is no surprise that excitement is high. Whittingham hasn't been seen out in public in more than a year. No one knows if he will attend his own party. Mum seems to be the word.

Miss Whittingham and Lord Stonehurst haven't been seen at any of the parties in the past week and the viscount is spending most of his time at the clubs. Hmm. One has to wonder if love still blooms, or is it that the lady has been too busy planning her own party? And one has to wonder why a Roman Toga Ball? It's a perfectly scandalous idea for people to bare their shoulders in public! No doubt the Whittinghams wanted to make sure everyone would attend and, from what this writer has been hearing, everyone of the *ton* will!

How clever to make the ball the day after the Season ends. This writer will see you at the masked ball.

You shouldn't have any trouble recognizing me—hmm. I'll be dressed just as you are.

—Lord Truefitt, *Society's Daily Column*

THE BIG DAY ARRIVED AND EVERYTHING WAS IN PLACE for the party. Mirabella was surprised she didn't feel nervous as she walked down the stairs of her home dressed in her toga. She had planned well and was confident that she had done all she could to ensure a successful party.

Her dressmaker had done a superb job on her gown, but she felt a little strange without her evening corset and wearing so few underclothes beneath it.

Her toga was made of white silk with a neckline that swooped low under her right arm and lay on the outer edge of her left shoulder. The toga was held together on the left shoulder with a piece of uncut amethyst the size of a ripe plum.

She had taken great care in explaining how she wanted her mask made. She couldn't have her view obstructed by the lavender and white feathers. Her modiste had taken her ideas and had a craftsman fashion a petite mask that Mirabella thought perfect for the evening.

Her headdress of leaves and vine had been painted the same shade of dark, sparkling purple of the medallion on her shoulder. At the last moment, she added the teardrop amethyst earrings she'd been wearing the first night she met Camden.

Mirabella had been so busy with preparations for the party that she'd only managed to see Camden for a short time on two different occasions. He had stopped by to let her know he was making the rounds at White's and other gentlemen's clubs to which he belonged searching for a man with a scar. He'd promised to let her know immediately if he found such a man.

She hadn't allowed herself to consider the possibility of not finding Prince Charming tonight. He must be in attendance.

Miraculously the Great Hall had been available, which was the perfect place to hold the party. The ballroom of the stately building was already lined with fluted Corinthian columns. The woodwork was painted in gilt, and the walls were decorated with silks and brocades.

Mirabella had solicited the services of three other ladies and a host of temporary servants to help. They had worked tirelessly to see that the tall columns were draped with vines, leaves and tulle. Musicians had been hired and the food and decorations were all in place.

Mirabella walked into the parlor, gasped, smiled and then laughed. Her father sat in his favorite chair dressed in a toga. "Oh, Papa." She ran to him and hugged his frail frame. "I can't believe you are dressed for the party. Does this mean you are going with me?"

"You didn't think I'd miss the first soiree you planned, did you? Silly girl."

She stood up and looked at him. He seemed extremely pale dressed all in white. His bare shoulder was much too thin, and his arms looked no bigger than hers. His toga was pinned on the left shoulder with a piece of bronze and gray agate. On his head sat a crown

of leaves and vine that had been painted silver. Her heart
overflowed with love and appreciation for her father.

"I do want you to come, but I'm afraid you'll get too
cold dressed like that. You must put something else on."

"And not be allowed in my own daughter's party?
I think not."

"Oh, Papa, you know I never meant that."

He smiled reassuringly at her. "Nonsense. Everyone
knows you were emphatic about the costume. It's
been in the papers every day this week. Besides, I had
this made in wool. So I shall be fine. And I do have a
matching cloak."

"I don't know what to say. I never expected that
you would feel well enough to attend."

"I always planned to join you this evening. Last
week I told Archer not to plan to escort you tonight.
I will be doing that myself."

Love for her father made her eyes water. "I'm
overwhelmed with happiness."

"I know, but I don't want to see any tears even if
they are happy ones." He brushed her away from him.

"There will be no tears from me."

"Good. Now, I don't know how long I'll be able to
stay, but I'll be there for the beginning of the evening.
Newton is coming with me. I'll have him stay by me
so if I need to, I can have him get my carriage without
any fuss."

"Papa, you are so good to me. Is it a wonder that I
don't want to marry and leave you?"

He looked up at her and smiled. "Mirabella, my
greatest pleasure will be seeing you wed."

His words stole the breath from her lungs and

pierced her with pain. She had always known he wanted her to marry, but for some reason it hit her in the heart this time. Maybe it was that she knew she would never be the bride her father desired her to be. She had thrown that possibility away to become Sarah's avenger and to protect other innocent young women from Sarah's fate.

A heavy feeling of guilt threatened to consume her. Mirabella turned away from her father. Was it wrong of her to let him believe she would be married? She was deceiving him, but she had always looked at it as being what was best for him, for his health. Her father loved her dearly and only wanted to see her properly wed and cared for after he was gone.

"But," her father continued, "I agree that it wasn't a bad idea to give you time to get to know Lord Stonehurst, and to make sure that he intends to stay in Town and make this his home. I don't want you to be married to a man who plans to make his home in the Americas."

Mirabella suddenly realized what her father said could be an easy way out of the engagement for her and Camden. All he had to do was go back to America for a time, but the thought of him being so far away left her with a desolate and empty feeling.

She turned back to her father. "I don't think that will happen, but if it should, we'll deal with it at that time. For now, Camden seems happy here."

"Good."

"And you seem to be so much better since his return. I'm very happy about that."

"In some ways I am better. The viscount's return

has forced me to make efforts that seemed too meaningless to bother with before. There are days my heart feels strong, and I want to make the effort to be better for you, dear."

"Thank you, Papa."

"Tell me, have the earl and his wife come back for the party?"

"No. Camden said they had pressing business matters to attend to in Lockshaven."

"I see. No doubt the earl will want to transfer land or other holdings to Camden now that he is to be married. I hear the house at Lockshaven is large and more than comfortable. Maybe you'll want to visit there later this summer."

"Maybe," she answered, really only wanting to change the subject.

Mirabella's heart constricted. She didn't want to continue to lie to her father but what else was she to do? Would it be better if she told her father the whole story about Sarah? She knew it would end her relationship with Camden, but living this ruse was getting difficult. She would only grow to love him more and more as the days passed.

"I hope your aunt Helen will be able to travel by late summer," her father said. "It was such a surprise getting that note from her saying that she had twisted her ankle and was unable to walk."

"Yes, I hope it doesn't pain her too much. But as you can see, I was able to plan the party without her. I'm sure she'll show up as soon as she can travel."

"At the rate she is moving, you'll be married before she makes it back to Town. We can't count on her."

"Papa, she's your sister, of course we can count on her. She will be here soon, I'm sure."

"I hope it works tonight, Daughter."

Mirabella tensed. How could her father possibly know about Prince Charming? "What do you mean?"

"I want the party to be the best this city has seen in twenty years."

"Oh, Papa," she said, relieved. "That will be difficult. London has been host to parties they will be writing about in the history books. I don't think this shall be one of them."

"It will be all right with me if it's not remembered one hundred years from now, but I'd like the *ton* to still be talking about it a year from now."

She smiled at him and took a deep breath, feeling good about her decision to soon tell her father everything. He loved her and he would forgive her. She couldn't expect Camden to forgive her transgressions. Saying good-bye to him would be the most difficult thing she had ever had to do.

"That we may be able to accomplish."

"I'm very proud of you, dear, for planning this party. I never thought you would get everything done in time. I've received notes all week from friends and acquaintances I haven't heard from in more than a year, telling me they have postponed their journeys to their summer homes just so they can attend this ball. You have managed a coup d'etat, my dear."

She hoped so. She prayed this night would flush out Prince Charming. "Thank you, Papa. Now, I'll have Newton get your wrap. I must arrive before anyone else."

❦

Masked and in sandals, Mirabella walked to the entrance of the Great Hall, leaving her father seated in the coach until the guests started arriving. She didn't want him getting tired before the evening began. She stood at the doorway and looked inside the grand ballroom. The room was spectacularly decorated in the finery of a bygone era. The chandeliers were lit and the wall sconces glowed with soft light. Large pots of all white flowers and roses lined the steps.

At the far end of the room stood three long tables laden with silver and crystal dishes filled with such delicacies as chilled oysters, fowl baked in a fig and plum gravy, apples and pears cooked in a brandy sauce. The sparkling champagne glasses were lined up ready to be filled and handed to each guest who entered. The violinist, cellist and flutist were already playing a rousing tune.

The side doors were swung wide and a gentle breeze blew in just enough to flicker the candle flame. From the open doorways, she could see that the clouds had scattered across the spacious night sky and the darkness was beaded with twinkling stars.

She'd had a candle stand set up at the entry way where she would stand so that she would have no trouble seeing everyone's shoulder when they stopped to greet her. So far everything about the evening was in order.

Mirabella looked at the room and knew she really only wanted one thing to make the evening perfect—to find Prince Charming. She wouldn't allow herself to think about what she would do should she fail.

Mirabella didn't know how long she'd been standing there looking into the beautiful room when she heard the soft sound of sandals on marble. She looked behind her and saw a tall, masked man, dressed in a toga, walking toward her. She knew immediately it was Camden. She knew the tilt of his head, the swing of his shoulders, and the glide of his stride. Is that how he'd known her even when she was dressed as a man? Was he as aware of everything about her as she was him?

Mirabella had no doubts that she was in love with Camden. It was natural for her to know everything about him.

As he drew near, she saw that his neck and shoulder were the same golden shade of tan as his face. The exposed area of his chest and arms was thick and muscular.

Mirabella remembered that afternoon when she had touched his damp skin. Her lower abdomen contracted at the thought. It pained her to think that she might never touch him that way again.

His toga was made from heavy white muslin. The piece that held his gown together on his left shoulder was a large stone that was black and shiny as onyx. His fig leaf crown and small feather mask had been painted black to match his shoulder medallion.

When he stood before her, he said, "Miss, I'd like the first and the last dance on your dance card, and all the dances in between."

Her heart fluttered deliciously and her spirits lifted tremendously. Mirabella looked past his mask into his dark brown eyes. How could she find the courage to give him up when the time came to do so? She couldn't. She loved him with all her heart. Perhaps she should tell her father everything about Sarah and the ruse and be done with all the secrecy. But did she have the courage to do it knowing the truth would force Camden to walk away from her?

"What a brave man you are to limit yourself to one lady. Tonight the Whittinghams will play host to the most beautiful women in London. However, I will not bind you to your rash offer. I fear I won't be dancing tonight. I will be here at my post the entire evening watching everyone who arrives."

"Then I shall stay here by your side."

"That isn't necessary and I won't hear of it. I'm capable. You should enjoy the evening."

His gaze swept up and down her face. "I know how capable you are, and I will enjoy the evening right here watching over you. Now, tell me, Miss Whittingham, do you think your dressmaker could have cut your toga any lower? I fear the least bit of movement of your right arm will make you show more of your bosom than is proper."

"Sir, it's perfectly acceptable for a lady to show her bosom, but quite unacceptable for a man to make reference to it."

Camden chuckled softly. "A thousand pardons, my lady, but I have seen how beautiful your breasts are, and I don't want to share their beauty with others. I fear the material of your gown is frightfully thin."

Mirabella was sure she blushed crimson but was determined not to let his provocative words fluster her. "Nonsense. This material is very fashionable. My modiste swore to me she patterned this gown after one of Athena's gowns."

"Therein lies the problem, I fear. This is a Roman toga party, not Greek."

Mirabella realized he was teasing her. She relaxed and smiled easily at him. "Not to worry, my lord. I have no doubt I'll stay adequately covered the entire evening."

Camden stepped closer to her and said, "You are beautiful, Mirabella. You look like a very tempting goddess tonight."

"And you, my lord, look like an angel."

Camden burst out with a strong laugh. "An angel? I've been called many things, but never has it been said that I look like a heavenly creature. I suppose I could be considered an archangel since what I'm wearing is so white."

"It's not your attire that makes you look like an angel to me. It's because you have helped me in so many ways these past weeks. I am grateful."

"You are sounding much too serious."

"This is a very important evening for me."

"I know, but you must have enjoyment from the evening, too."

She smiled at him. "I will. I promise. I take it you saw no one with a scar in your nightly visits to the gentlemen's clubs."

"No. You must not be disheartened if you do not find the man you seek tonight, Mirabella."

Her body tensed and her throat tightened. "I refuse to think about the possibility of that happening."

"You know, I want very much to kiss your bare

shoulder right now. Your skin is lovely and inviting. Do you think anyone would notice if I just kissed your soft skin right about there?" He bent his head toward her.

"Camden, there are people everywhere. Don't you dare," Mirabella said with a smile and quickly stepped away. She would have loved nothing better than to feel Camden's warm lips on her bare skin. "My father is resting in the carriage waiting for our guests to start arriving before he enters."

"Your father is here?"

"Yes, God bless him, he is here tonight, even if only for a short time. Papa has said that Uncle Archer will see me home."

Camden frowned. "I wish Society would realize that chaperones are not needed for an engaged couple."

Mirabella heard voices behind her. She took a deep breath and gave Camden a hopeful look. "Here come the first guests."

"Good luck," he whispered softly.

The night began with a stream of people that had no end in sight. Everyone dressed as they had been instructed, baring their right shoulder. Each toga-clad person stopped briefly to greet Mirabella before entering the gala. She didn't look anyone in the eyes. She kept her focus on their necks.

Mirabella had no idea the neck, throat and shoulder area could look so different. She saw thin necks, fat shoulders, and bumpy-looking throats. She saw fair skin, dark skin, and spotted skin. She had even seen a couple of pock scars but no wide, raised blemishes or marks just above the collarbone on the left side of any of the necks.

Her father tired after only an hour or two and left. Camden brought her lemonade and some food, but she had very little appetite for the gorgeous dinner that had been prepared. She left her post to go to the ladies' retiring room only once and then only after Camden promised he wouldn't step away for anything, including a fire.

As the evening grew long, so did Mirabella's smile. She remained at her post, watching everyone who had entered earlier in the evening begin to leave.

The candles had burned down to dry puddles. Pale shades of dawn broke the deep purple clouds of night and split the sky between twilight and dawn. Camden stepped up beside Mirabella and said, "I've walked the grounds. I don't think any of the guests are still here."

She felt rigid and was trying her best not to sound that way. "There must be someone left, a few that you missed."

"No, Mirabella, only the staff."

She kept her shoulders erect, although she felt the weight of an unbelievable burden pressing them down. She faced the empty ballroom and declared, "I missed him. I'm sure he was here, but somehow I missed him."

"You couldn't have missed him. I searched everyone, too. He was not here."

"No," she whispered, refusing to look at Camden, refusing to admit defeat.

"There's one possibility I don't think you've thought of."

She turned to him in hope. "What?"

"Perhaps Sarah was delusional."

Mirabella gasped. She didn't know what she had expected Camden to say, but it certainly wasn't that. "What do you mean?"

"There's the possibility that she wanted to have a Prince Charming in her life so desperately that she made him up in her mind. Maybe there never was a man in her life."

Mirabella wished she felt like laughing, so ludicrous was Camden's suggestion. Sarah's mind was not weak. "That's the most preposterous thing I've ever heard. She wouldn't kill herself because of a figment of her imagination! A woman knows whether or not she is expecting a child."

Camden touched her arm affectionately. "I'm just saying that maybe in her mind all the things she wrote in her diary were real to her, but not true to life."

"No," Mirabella whispered earnestly. "No, Camden. There is no way I can believe she dreamed all this. If she lived in a make-believe world I would have known it."

"But she lived a life you didn't know about. A life with Prince Charming."

Mirabella's chest felt tight and heavy. Her eyes threatened to fill with tears. She had such an over-powering sense of loss, of desperation. "Sarah was afraid to tell anyone what had happened. What you're saying doesn't make sense. If she were immersed in an unreal life, she would have dreamed that they lived happily ever after. She wouldn't have ended her fairy tale saying Prince Charming wouldn't marry her when she told him she was carrying his child."

Camden gently took hold of Mirabella's shoulders

and looked deeply into her eyes. "I'm only trying to think of something that might help you accept the fact that you haven't found this man, and at this point, you're probably not going to find him."

Mirabella tried to pull out of his arms. "Trying to make me think Sarah had somehow gone mad won't do it."

"You would prefer to think he was here and you just missed him?"

She shook her head. "No."

"All right, do you want to believe he is out of Town, and that is why he didn't come?"

She tried to break free of him once again. "No."

"Then perhaps he's in Town but didn't attend because he knows you are looking for him?"

Mirabella felt she was at the breaking point. She looked up at him with pleading eyes. "Stop, Camden. I'm too weary for your logic. I'll find him. I know I will. I must."

"Mirabella."

"I must, Camden." She heard the pleading in her voice, but could do nothing about the weakness. "I gave up any chance of having a life with you to find this man. Don't you understand that failure to find him is too great a price to pay for what I gave up?"

"Come with me, Mirabella."

"No. I must find Uncle Archer. I haven't seen him tonight, and I need to find him and go home."

"I haven't seen him tonight, but I assure you there is no one here but you and I."

Confused, she shook her head. "He wouldn't have left me."

"I have walked the grounds twice already. I'm sure he must have misunderstood your father's plans for you. I will see you home."

Mirabella felt Camden's warm, strong hands on her arms. His gaze searched her face and a calm reasoning came over her. "I don't want to go home, Camden. I want to go with you somewhere we can be alone."

Eighteen

CAMDEN'S HEART THREATENED TO BEAT OUT OF HIS chest. What did she mean she didn't want to go home? Though she still wore her feathered mask, he searched her eyes, not wanting to misread what she had said. He wanted her. Desperately. He had wanted her from the first night he saw her when she was alone on the street, but had she meant what he was thinking?

His throat was thick and all he managed to say was, "Mirabella."

"I know it's not the thing a lady asks of a gentleman, especially one who has been as honorable as you."

"No. Do not make me noble, Mirabella. I am not."

"I know I shouldn't ask anything more of you, but I don't want to go home. I want you to take me to your bed and love me."

Camden's lower body reacted strongly to her words. He swallowed hard. What could he say? Could he deny her request because it was the right thing to do? Because Society expected that he not take a virgin to his bed, even if she was considered his fiancée, even if he loved her and wanted to marry—

Love her? Marry her? Where did those thoughts come from?
He wanted her, desired her, but did he love her?

If not, why else would he be willing to overlook her trysts with other men? If he didn't love her, the reason she kissed other men wouldn't matter, only that she had been ruined. But standing so close to her, looking into her eyes, feeling as he did, he realized he didn't care how many gentlemen she had kissed or why. He wanted to be with her. She belonged to him.

"If you won't take me away, will you hold me for a moment?"

She had misread him. "Oh, Mirabella." He opened his arms wide, and she rushed to his chest. He squeezed her tightly to him and whispered, "My silence didn't mean I don't want to be with you. I do. Desperately. But you aren't thinking rationally, so I have to."

She buried her lips into the corded muscles of his bare neck and asked, "Why is it not rational to want to be in your arms and in your bed? I know what I feel."

His arms stroked her back. He loved the feel of her soft breath against his cool skin. "You are overwrought and emotional right now. You've suffered a big loss tonight in not finding Sarah's Prince Charming. I don't want your desire for me to be a substitute for what didn't happen tonight."

She looked up and into his eyes and smiled at him. "You a substitute? Never, my lord. My devastation will be even harder to bear if you refuse me. I want you to show me how a woman pleases a man." She pushed aside the neckline of his toga and planted a warm kiss in the hollow of his throat.

Camden sensed her power over him, and suddenly felt as if he were standing steady on water. "You test me."

"Show me how to pleasure you," she whispered.

"Oh, Mirabella, you make my knees weak with your pleadings. I've dreamed of doing just that, but I must think of what is best for you."

"If you are worried that I will demand you marry me, I swear I won't."

Demand he marry her? He had just been thinking that he'd be a fool not to marry her.

"You have no need to force me to marry you, Mirabella. I don't want you to make a hasty decision tonight and regret it later."

"This has not been an impulsive determination, sir. I have thought a long time about this. Will you grant my wish and take me someplace where we can be together?"

Camden looked deeply into her eyes and whispered, "Yes, Mirabella. I will make you mine."

He took her hand and they fled the Great Hall, racing down the front steps together. Camden's mind whirled. Where could they go at this time of the early morning? He couldn't take her to an inn or any public housing where they might be recognized. With finances so tight, he had no place of his own. There were plenty of town houses he could have borrowed from friends, but those arrangements would have needed to have been made ahead of time.

The only place to go where there would be a reasonable amount of privacy was his parents' home. There would be no one at his house but Hudson. If Hudson should by chance see Mirabella there, he could trust his brother not to gossip, but he didn't like the thought of Hudson knowing anything about his intimate relationship with Mirabella. Camden would have to be very careful to make sure she wasn't seen.

Camden helped her inside his carriage and then climbed in beside her. She went immediately into his arms. He realized she was shivering. Reaching over to the opposite seat, he grabbed his great coat and wrapped it around her. He held her close to his chest and caressed her back and bare shoulder.

The carriage wheels clanked and the horses' hooves plopped along the silent street. His own heart pumped furiously at the thought that this woman he had wanted for weeks was going to be his.

Doubts struck Camden. Did she really know what she was doing? She had asked him to take her somewhere and make love to her. The thought made him tremble. "Mirabella, say the word and I will take you to your father's house."

"I want to be with you."

"It's dawn. Your father will be worried about you."

"My father will not be up for hours. Both he and Lily will assume the party has gone on through the morning, which is not unheard of, I believe."

"Certainly not, but I don't want to do anything to hurt you."

She raised her head and pushed her mask up her forehead so she could look into his eyes. "Then don't deny me this time with you."

Maybe she just needed to be held and reassured that it was not the end of the world just because she hadn't found Prince Charming. Maybe all she needed from him was comfort. Whatever she needed he wanted to provide it for her.

He wanted to tell her properly that he had fallen in love with her, and that he wanted to marry her. He wanted her to be his for a lifetime. But they could work out all those things later. Right now she wanted him and he wanted her and that was all that was important.

"I won't deny you anything you ask." He kissed the tip of her nose, and then pulled the mask back over her eyes. "Keep this on until we are safely inside. Should anyone see us going into my house, I wouldn't want them to recognize you."

She nodded.

The carriage stopped. The driver opened the door. Camden reached into the pocket of his great coat and brought out several coins. As he handed them to the driver, he said, "Forget you saw the lady."

"What lady, sir? I 'aven't even seen you tonight."

Mirabella stepped out, and she and Camden hurried in the front door. The house was quiet as Camden slowly, softly closed them inside. Though dawn was on the sky, it was dark in the house. Camden pulled off his mask, then hers and laid them on the foyer table. He reached down and gave her a hard, brief kiss. She smiled at him, and Camden had no doubts they were doing the right thing.

He took her hand and led her up the stairs. At the top of the landing, Camden paused. The house was quiet and dark.

He looked down the hallway to Hudson's room, which was opposite his. Camden tensed. Hudson's door was open. He motioned for Mirabella to stay at the top of the stairs. He walked to his brother's doorway and peeked inside. The room was empty. Hudson's bed was made up.

Camden relaxed. Obviously, Hudson had found somewhere else to spend the night.

"He's not here," Camden said. He walked back and took Mirabella's hand, and she willingly followed him into his room. He closed the door and threw the latch.

Camden reached for her, and she willingly went into his arms. Their lips met softly at first but the longing and the passion between them was too intense to go softly or slowly. He kissed her madly, and Mirabella matched his fierce hunger.

He shoved his hands between them and found her unbound breasts. He cupped, lifted and squeezed them firmly, feeding his passion. In a moment, her nipples hardened. Through the thin silky material, he found the tight buds and gently tugged on them. It aroused him as they grew harder under his touch.

The soft sweet sound of desire she whispered into his mouth elated him and quickened his own enjoyment.

"Does that pleasure you, Mirabella?" he mumbled against her lips, not wanting to stop kissing even to speak loving words.

"Oh, greatly, sir. Does it gratify you?"

"Exceedingly so."

He continued to massage her breasts. He loved the feel of the weight of them in his hands. Her breasts were not so large that they were too soft and not so small as to be too firm. She was the perfect size to build a burning heat in his loins and a longing in his heart to possess her.

"My sweet Mirabella. There is so much to teach you and so little time. Forgive me if I rush your pleasure today."

He grabbed hold of the large stone on her shoulder and pulled the toga down her arm, leaving the flimsy material to glide down her legs and puddle at her feet. He ran the palms of his hands and tips of his fingers over her naked shoulders and breasts and back up again as he caressed her beauty with his gaze.

Huskily he said, "I want your hair down."

"As you wish." Mirabella reached up and tore the crown of leaves off her head and threw it to the floor.

Camden slid his fingers into her hair and shook it free of the pins that held it up. He crushed its lush length into his palms before letting it tumble to her shoulders. It was so long it covered her beautiful breasts, so he quickly pushed her hair to her back.

His body ached and throbbed to possess her immediately, but he was determined to take their loving slower than his body wanted him to and please both of them this first time.

"You're so beautiful I don't want anything hiding your loveliness from me. I don't want to stop looking at you or touching you."

"I want to look at you, too." Mirabella reached up and placed her open hand on his bare shoulder. "I want to feel your skin against mine," she whispered as she pressed her lips to his.

Camden reached up and grabbed hold of the black stone that held his toga on his shoulder and jerked it, breaking the threads that held the toga together. The white muslin dropped like an unwanted garment to the floor and covered Mirabella's toga.

He reached around her and untied the strings at her back and her thin drawers fell to the floor. Mirabella stepped out of them. Camden pulled on the strings at the front of his undergarment and sent it the way of Mirabella's. They stood there unselfconsciously looking at each other for a moment.

She smiled at him. "You are magnificent. Your body looks just like paintings of Adonis."

Camden's lower body grew harder at her praise, but he humbly said, "You have always given me more credit than I deserve."

Mirabella lowered her gaze to view that part of him men were usually most proud of, and said, "This time it is truly deserving, my lord."

She reached out and let her fingertips glide softly, tantalizingly slowly over his chest. He trembled with need, willing her to abandon any thoughts of shyness and allow her hands to go lower and touch his hardness, feel its thickness and weight. Her fingertips tripped down his midriff, along his stomach, feeling like no more than a feather stroking his burning need.

Camden threw his head back in indulgence. His muscles contracted in sweet pain. His eyes closed with wanting. Her gossamer-light caress teased him and offered no mercy to the pure torment she inflicted on him.

She must have read his mind. Her hand closed around him and his breath stalled in his chest and his knees went weak. He knew he would be lost if he did not stop her soon.

"I did not expect it to be so thick and stiff, my lord."

He moaned softly. And she thought she did not know how to pleasure a man.

"You may not appreciate that at first, my lady, but I promise you, you will in due course."

With no thought of the pillows or coverlet, and before he was past his own endurance, he reached down, picked her up and laid her on top of the bed. He spread the length of his taut body on top of hers, and groaned from the sheer thrill of having her beneath him.

Camden wanted desperately to spread her legs immediately and enter her, but he couldn't move. If he did, he would surely spill his seed before he had given her what she wanted, what he promised. He had no desire to leave her wanting their first time together.

Pale morning light streamed in through a crack in the dark draperies, bathing the room in a soft glow. He looked down into her beautiful green eyes and smiled.

Mirabella returned the smile and asked, "Are we waiting for something to happen?"

"Right now, I'm trying to keep something from happening."

"What is that?"

She was too inquisitive. "I need to—rest a moment."

She questioned him. "Are you tired already? I am not. I very much enjoyed what has happened so far."

He smile at her. "So have I."

She fell silent, just searching his face.

"Keep talking, Mirabella. It calms me down."

She laughed softly and touched his cheek with her fingertips. "I do not want to talk. I want to touch you like this."

She slid her arm between them and found him again, running her hand the length of him. She squeezed him gently.

Camden gasped with ecstasy.

"I want to kiss you deeply, my lord. Can we not continue our pleasure now?"

"Oh, yes. We can. We have to."

He gently moved her hand up to his chest, promising himself that next time he wouldn't be so ready to spill himself.

"You don't like for me to touch you so?"

He swallowed hard. "I crave it, but now it's time to move on to other things."

"That will feel just as good?" she asked, placing her palm against the plane of his cheek.

He kissed the tip of her nose. "Most certainly."

"I would like that."

He bent his head and kissed that warm soft spot behind her ear. He inhaled the scent of freshly washed hair and feminine skin. With tenderness he slowly kissed his way down her neck, moving as if they had all the time in the world.

He brushed her moist lips with his, easing over them with the lightest contact. She opened her mouth and his tongue thrust in deeply as she had asked. With a loving hand, he raked his fingers down her breast, over her slim womanly hip and shapely inner thigh. He moved his hand back up and caressed the warm skin of her stomach before inching his hand lower until he found her softness. There, he cupped her gently for a moment before finding the center of her desire with his thumb. His movement was soft, circular.

She trembled beneath his touch, and Camden smiled. There was immense satisfaction in the way she responded to him.

"Oh, yes, my lord," she murmured, dragging her lips away from his. She kissed his chin, his neck and back up to his lips. "That is where it feels most pleasurable."

"For me too, my darling."

He didn't want her excitement to end too soon, so he stopped the stroking of her center and found her entry. He forced a finger inside. She was so tight. He feared she would not accept all of him the first time.

"I'm going to bring you to your peak, and just after that, I will enter you. It will hurt at first. Just lie still and it will be over soon."

"Oh, Camden, how can something this wonderful hurt?"

"That is a promise, Mirabella. It will."

He slid his fingers back to her center and relished the sensations touching her gave him. Within moments, she gasped in pleasure and arched toward him. He kissed her harder and drove his finger inside her. She tightened around him, and Camden almost lost control.

When her body started relaxing, he positioned himself at her opening and shoved into her with a quick thrust. She made a soft sound of discomfort but did not cry out. Her arms tightened on his back. He moved forward slowly, pushing in and out with long easy strokes.

"Stay with me, Mirabella, I swear it will not take long this time."

And it didn't. It was over almost before it began. She was so tight he knew it hurt her, but she didn't say a word of protest. He never had doubted she was a virgin, but still, there was a flash of immense satisfaction when he broke through her innocence and made her his.

His forever.

Camden rested his face in the crook of her neck. He breathed deeply, drinking in her warm, womanly scent. He kissed her skin softly. He would love her forever, desire her all his life, but he would never feel any more complete than he did right now. She had allowed him to make love to her in his room, in his father's house.

She had always told him that she didn't care what Society thought about her. He finally believed her, for surely no other young woman of quality would allow her fiancé such uninhibited freedom.

He was the one always worried about her reputation. He was the one who had threatened Stephenson and Farthingdale should they dare to talk ill of her again. He was the one who had fretted over her masculine disguise. She didn't have a problem with the unconventional. *He* did. And why? Because of Hortense? Because of a young woman who had made him the most talked about man in the *ton* for years.

Camden had vowed to deny himself love because Hortense had mocked his youthful love for her. She made him such a laughingstock in Town that he had left the country and had planned never to return to Society. He didn't know if he ever forgave Hortense, but he soon forgot about her. Mirabella was different. She had defied what was proper, acceptable and expected of her—and still he desired her.

The devil. He craved her.

He had returned to London thinking he only wanted a suitable wife to give him pleasure in bed and children to ride on his knee. Now he realized he wanted so much more from Mirabella than just being proper.

Lying with her, he realized he didn't give a damn if Society should think that Mirabella was unchaste because she had been kissed by other men. And he didn't give a damn how many gentlemen had kissed her. Not one damn. No one had possessed her but him and now she was totally and completely his forever.

Mirabella was right for him. And that was all that mattered.

Nineteen

MIRABELLA COULDN'T SLOW HER BREATHING. SHE didn't want to. She wanted to go on feeling the exquisite sensations that shuddered through her body and soul, making her want to moan with delight. She had never felt such wonderful fulfillment, such great contentment. What she had just experienced was so stunning she didn't want it to be over. It was unbelievable satisfaction and joyous completion.

But once this time with Camden was over, she would have to start learning to live without him in her life. Now, it was more important than ever that she dissolve this ruse with Camden. She had to do it now before he realized she had fallen in love with him, before she slipped up and stated what she felt in her heart. She could tell him of her love, but she feared it would fill him with guilt. It was better to keep what was in her heart to herself.

Last night, she realized she couldn't go on deceiving her father either, making him believe she would be married. Perhaps as Camden had suggested, Sarah had lived a lie, but Mirabella couldn't. She must tell her father everything and free Camden to go on with his life.

Camden lay quiet and still on top of her. His breathing was returning to normal. She stroked his back, loving the feel of his skin beneath her hands. He was heavy, but she didn't mind. She welcomed his weight upon her.

Oh, would this one time in his arms, in his bed, give her enough memories to last a lifetime?

Camden stirred.

"No, don't move," she whispered.

Let me enjoy this a few moments longer.

"I am afraid that I'm hurting you."

"The pain was only for a moment. Now it's gone. Does the pleasure have to end, too?"

"Only for a minute or two. Then I shall be ready to go again." He raised up on his elbows and looked down into her eyes. "Mirabella, I think I'm in love with you."

She gasped, not believing he had said to her the words she was too fearful to say to him. "No."

"Yes. Truly, it has shocked me as much as you, but I must be. I desire you as I never have any other woman. If I'm not with you, my mind is constantly filled with thoughts of you. When I'm away from you, I long to be with you. When I'm with you, I enjoy watching you, talking with you. I love the way you challenge me at every turn."

"But I betrayed your trust. I kissed those—"

He put a finger to her lips and silenced her. "It doesn't matter. I now know you didn't kiss any of them because you desired them."

"No, only you."

"Oh, Mirabella, my love, you make my heart soar." He kissed her lips softly as his hand lovingly caressed her shoulder and breast.

"And you, sir, make me happy," she said lovingly against his lips.

"That is a great compliment."

"When will you know for sure?" she asked.

He kissed her eyes, her nose and each cheek before giving her a questioning look. "What's that?"

"You said you *think* you love me. When will you know for sure that you love me?"

Camden laughed and hugged her tightly to him. "You constantly test me, Mirabella. I know for sure right now. It is here in my heart." He took her hand and placed it on his chest. "I love you, Mirabella, and I want to marry you and make you mine."

She tensed. It was one thing for him to love her, to accept her as a lover, but to offer marriage after she had behaved so scandalously?

"Marry you? Oh, Camden, do not tease me. Do you mean that?"

"Of course I do. These are not words I would use lightly."

Mirabella trembled with happiness. She felt like her heart would burst with the love she was feeling for him. After years of waiting for him to return and say those words, she was overcome with joy.

"And you truly want me for your bride?"

"Yes, my lovely and passionate lady. I want you for my bride."

"This is not a trick?"

"I am not a trickster. I don't want to wait until autumn is upon us, or next spring during the Season. I want to marry you as soon as possible."

Mirabella trembled with happiness. "Camden, I have known for a long time that I loved you."

"Then I am a lucky man."

"I never dreamed you would return my love."

"I have to admit that it took me by surprise. I vowed to never again fall in love. And what I have discovered is that I never loved Hortense the way I love you."

Mirabella raised on her elbows and kissed his neck, his shoulder, his nipples before raising her face to look into his eyes. "I was just lying here wondering how I was going to say good-bye to you."

"No good-byes for us, Mirabella. From now on, we will have only good nights and good mornings."

He moved inside her, and her lower body quickened in response. She lifted her hips to him. She wanted to show him just how much she loved and desired him. He handled her gently, in and out with long strokes. She matched his motion and met each thrust with eager anticipation.

"And we will not have separate bedrooms, Mirabella."

She liked the sound of the heightened sigh in his voice. "Never, my lord."

"I'll need you to be in my bed with me every night."

"And every morning."

Camden laughed but never stopped moving. "Mornings, too? I can see you are going to expect a lot from me."

"All you can give."

"Oh, yes, my dearest Mirabella."

Camden sank deeply into her with every plunge.

Mirabella lifted her face to his and claimed his lips in a kiss desperate to take more of him into her. Camden slid his hands under her back and cupped her tightly to his chest, making her one with him as he rode both of them to the climax of their pleasure.

Mirabella was out of breath again and still filled with wonder. She was overwhelmed with joy and contentment.

"You touch my soul, sweet, sweet Mirabella. I know you need to get home, but I must have more of you before you go."

"Do not send me home, my lover. I want to be here with you."

"I must give you up, but only until we can marry. I promise you, I will insist your father make the arrangements with all haste."

∽

Mirabella woke with a start. She lay on her back in Camden's bed. He was on his side facing her with one arm thrown over her breasts. She looked at him. He slept peacefully. Had he really told her he loved her and wanted to marry her? She smiled and then silently laughed. She was filled with immense joy. How blessed she was that Camden had overlooked her inappropriate behavior.

She turned to snuggle into his arms when she caught sight of the window. Daylight shone bright. She had to get home. Her father would be worried about her. She glanced back at Camden. There was no need to disturb him. No doubt he was tired from their lovemaking. She had no idea that it would be such an exhausting endeavor.

With care, she gently slipped out from under his arm and slid off the bed. She picked up her undergarments and toga and stepped into them. She searched the rug and found enough pins to twist her hair on top of her head and then replaced her headpiece. As an afterthought, she picked up Camden's great coat and stuffed her arms into the sleeves. She didn't want to be seen outside still dressed in her toga.

She silently threw the latch and eased out of the room without awakening Camden. At the top of the stairs, she stopped and listened. When she heard nothing from below, she hurried down.

On her way to the front door, she spotted her mask and knew that she should take it with her. She picked it up and tried to stick it in the pocket of Camden's coat, but some papers made it impossible. She placed the mask back on the table and pulled out the papers. When she went to lay them aside, she noticed the words *Mr. Brackley*. Who would address Camden so informally? No one should ever use his family name.

Mirabella unfolded the paper and immediately saw that the correspondence was from America. Of course, they wouldn't recognize his title over there. She didn't intend to read the letter, but her eyes just never left the paper.

Dear Mr. Brackley:
    I have received your urgent letter stating that you wish to sell your holdings in the Maryland Ship

Building Company with all haste. I understand your financial duress is immediate, but I can see no quick solution from this end as we are still awaiting final approval of our new steam engine.

I can only suggest that you make whatever arrangements you feel necessary in your own land to eliminate your current financial emergency. I shall be in touch as soon as it is appropriate to do so.

My best regards,
Thomas Peterson

Mirabella's heart went cold. She stared at the letter and read it again. *Make whatever arrangements you feel necessary... to eliminate your financial worries.* Marrying her without delay, as Camden had suggested, would certainly eliminate his immediate financial worries.

She shook off the offending thought. No, Camden wouldn't do that. It was a ridiculous thought. She had no idea why it entered her mind. Camden had never tried to hide from her that his family's financial status was in shambles.

What was wrong with her? She shouldn't be thinking that he suddenly wanted to marry her for her dowry. Why was she having these horrible doubts?

If Camden had only wanted to marry her for the remainder of the dowry, which was a considerable sum, he didn't have to tell her he loved her.

She had once told him she would ask her father to extend a promissory note to repay the dowry. She knew Camden's family's finances were in poor shape. Camden had admitted that more than once. But something else he had said suddenly struck her. He had told her she didn't need to *force* him to marry her. He *needed* to marry her.

She looked up the stairs toward Camden's room. Should she go back up and confront him? Would he deny it? She didn't know, but she was going to find out.

Mirabella turned to head back up the stairs when she heard a noise from the back of the house and froze. Someone was humming and heading her way. Hudson must have returned. She quickly stuffed the paper back into the pocket of the coat and hurried out the front door.

At the edge of the street she stopped. She couldn't talk to her father about this. As far as he was concerned love had nothing to do with marriage. She would go to Uncle Archer's house. Maybe he had some thoughts on what she should do about Camden.

She dug her hand into the other pocket and found several coins. She would hire a hack to take her to her uncle's town house.

❧

A knock on the door awoke Camden suddenly. He jerked upright in bed to find that Mirabella was not with him. He looked on the floor. Her clothes were gone. "Camden, it's Hudson. May I come in?"

"Just a minute." Camden hoped Mirabella had left the house before Hudson arrived. He jumped off the bed and went to his wardrobe and quickly pulled out a pair of trousers. He stepped into them as he walked to the door. He opened the door and immediately saw a worried expression on Hudson's face. Maybe he had seen Mirabella. Damnation, how had he slept through her getting out of bed? Why hadn't she awakened him to see her home?

"What's wrong?" Camden asked his brother.

Hudson walked in and closed the door behind him. "Nothing, I hope." He made a deliberate show of looking around the room, paying close attention to the bed and draperies.

Camden grabbed a shirt off a chair and pulled it on. Something was wrong. He asked his brother, "When did you get in?"

"Not long ago. You have guests downstairs. They arrived only minutes ago."

"Mirabella?"

"No, her father and his butler."

Blast it. "Mr. Whittingham?"

Hudson looked inside Camden's wardrobe, parting the clothes, but Camden remained quiet.

"One and the same," Hudson said. "And the old man doesn't look well."

"Did he say what he wants?" Camden sat down on his slipper chair to put on his shoes.

"His daughter."

Camden glanced up from his buckle and looked at Hudson. Their eyes held. "Mirabella?"

"Does he have another? For God's sake, don't be thick-witted, Camden. It appears he thinks she is here in our house. Is she?"

Camden had never known of Hudson using a reprimanding tone in his life, and his first instinct was to put his brother in his place. But Camden took it slow and finished buckling his shoe. Hudson obviously didn't know Mirabella had been there, and Camden intended to keep it that way. What happened between him and Mirabella was no one's business. Not even her father's. She was obviously making her own way home right now.

"Well? Have you disgraced your fiancée here in your own home?"

Hudson was dangerously close to being rammed against the wall, but Camden held his anger in check. "As you can see," Camden pointed to the wardrobe, "she's not here. If she's missing, I'll find her."

"I hope you know what you are doing, Brother. You are the last person who needs another scandal. And quite frankly, I'm not sure Mama could withstand another."

"You've said enough, Hudson." Camden prayed his brother heeded his warning.

Hudson backed down. "I'm going down to make the old man some tea. He looks as if he's on his last leg."

Camden grabbed a short length of black ribbon and tied back his hair without putting a comb to it. He then snatched a neckcloth off the dresser and tied it in a simple bow around his neck trying to make himself presentable.

He strode into the parlor with one thought on his mind. *Protect Mirabella.*

Camden had never cared what kind of shameful things had been said about Hortense. He remembered thinking she deserved whatever gossip made the rounds. But he couldn't bear the thought of Mirabella's reputation being ripped to shreds on damning tongues and scandal sheets. He would fight anyone who dared speak against her.

Bertram Whittingham sat rigidly on the settee.

Hudson hadn't exaggerated the man's condition. His face was as white as his shirt. His valet, Newton, stood behind the sofa.

"Dear God, it took you long enough to come down."

"I beg your pardon, I—What's this about Mirabella missing?"

"She hasn't come home from the party. I went to Archer's town house first, but no one was home. Is she here?"

The old curmudgeon got right to the point.

"No," Camden replied as calmly as he could.

"This was on your foyer table." Mr. Whittingham held up Mirabella's mask.

Camden kept his voice soft and his face free of expression. He deliberately looked into Mr. Whittingham's eyes. "It was in my coat pocket when I returned home this morning. Mirabella gave it to me to hold for her. The party continued until well after daylight. I left her not long ago."

"It is after noon."

Camden had no idea what time Mirabella left his home. It could have been five minutes ago or four hours. "We remained at the Hall talking about the evening's events. She hadn't eaten all night, so we ate a cold meal together. Perhaps you left just before she arrived, and she is now safe at home."

"That is a comforting thought. Why did Archer not see her home as he was supposed to? Did you relieve him of his duty?"

A strange feeling suddenly hit Camden in the stomach. "No. I don't recall seeing Mr. Hornbeck at all last night. When did you last see him? He certainly wasn't around just before dawn. Mirabella asked about him, and I searched the grounds thoroughly. More than once."

"Come to think of it, I didn't see him at the party last night, either. But, of course, I didn't stay long."

"Are you sure he knew he was to see Mirabella home?"

"Of course. We talked about it. He was clear on that."

Camden wasn't sure he liked where his thoughts were taking him. "Then perhaps he didn't make the party."

"That would be inconceivable considering he has been attending parties with Mirabella for two years now."

"Yes, that's just what I was thinking. So why is it no one saw him? Was he often a guest in your home?"

"Certainly. Often."

Unease settled over Camden, and he moved to the edge of his seat. "So it wouldn't be unusual to see Mr. Hornbeck at your house late at night or early in the mornings?"

"Of course not. He's quite welcome in my home at any time. What are you getting at?"

Hudson entered the room and said, "The tea should be ready soon."

"Hudson, did you see Mr. Hornbeck last evening at the ball?" Camden asked.

Hudson wrinkled his brow in thought. "No, not that I remember. But there were so many people there, I could have missed him. Why?"

"Newton," Mr. Whittingham said, "when you were with me, did you see him?"

"No, sir."

Camden put his random thoughts together and an idea started to fall in place. Mr. Hornbeck would have been well known to Sarah. He was shorter than most men, unmarried, and free to go and come from the Whittingham home without notice. His name had been on Sarah's dance card, but like Mirabella, Camden had overlooked him because he was her uncle. But not a blood-related uncle. A family friend. Someone who would never be suspected.

Camden stood up and looked down at Mirabella's father and asked, "Do you know if Mr. Hornbeck has any kind of distinguishing marks on his neck?"

Mr. Whittingham's eyes rounded slightly. "Why, yes, he does. When he was but a boy, his mama punished him for lying to her by sticking a hot poker to his neck. It's a rather nasty-looking scar about here." With a trembling finger, he pointed to his neck, just above the collarbone on his right shoulder. "You don't suppose he didn't go last night because he didn't want anyone seeing it, do you?"

"I suppose that could be." Camden rose. "I think I know where Mirabella might be. Don't worry. I'll find her and bring her home."

Twenty

MIRABELLA BANGED THE LION'S HEAD DOOR KNOCKER twice at Archer Hornbeck's door. "Oh, be home, Uncle, and for once offer some sound advice," she mumbled to herself as she stood on the landing wrapped in Camden's coat.

She wanted to believe Camden had forgiven her indiscretions with the other gentlemen, and that he truly loved her and wanted to marry her. Could he have touched her very soul if he didn't truly love her? Should she let that letter from America give her doubts about his love for her? She reached for the head of the lion as the door opened.

Archer's housekeeper showed Mirabella into the drawing room and at Mirabella's insistence went immediately to find her employer.

"Mirabella. Blue heavens, what are you doing here this time of morning?" Archer asked, tying the sash of his brown brocade robe. His thinning hair was mussed and a white scarf hung loosely about his neck and shoulders.

"I must speak to you. Do you mind?"

"No, certainly not, but I just arrived home and was changing. Come in."

She realized her head was pounding from lack of sleep. "I'm sorry for arriving unannounced, but I needed to talk to you."

"Come and sit down and tell me what this is all about. And what in God's name do you have on?"

Not bothering to sit down, Mirabella looked down at the coat. She felt warm and safe wrapped in Camden's great coat. "I have on Camden's coat. I haven't been home to change since the party ended."

Archer turned to face her. "That much is clear. You are positively bedraggled. What has happened to you?"

"Nothing," she said and prayed he wouldn't notice the blush she felt rising in her cheeks. "I wanted to talk with you about Camden, Uncle." She took an imploring step toward him. "I love him so much, and I'm so afraid of losing him, yet I'm not sure I have him to lose."

"That makes no sense, Mirabella. If he's done anything to harm you I'll speak to your father immediately. Now, sit down and start at the beginning."

"No, I'd rather stand. I assure you that Camden has done nothing to harm me." She put her hand to her forehead trying to hide the second blush to light her cheeks. There was no way her uncle could know she had just left Camden's bed.

"Then what is the problem?"

"It all started that evening you asked me if I had been free with my affections. Do you recall that evening?"

"Yes, yes. Go on," he said as if he were in a great hurry.

"I had allowed certain young gentlemen to kiss me, but—"

"Good heavens, Mirabella," he interrupted. "Don't admit such a thing out loud even in the privacy of my home. Is Lord Stonehurst making trouble about this? He saw you in the garden with Mr. Farthingdale. We can't very well do anything about that young buck, but we'll vehemently deny rumors of any other gentlemen."

"No, no. That is not the problem, Uncle." She folded her hands together and wistfully said, "I want to know how do I know if he is telling the truth when he says he loves me?"

Archer looked as if she had asked him to explain the wonders of the universe. "Mirabella, no young lady should worry whether her husband loves her. What madness. Love is fanciful notions for story-books and poetry. Lord Byron has ruined the acceptable order of things, I fear. What matters is that Lord Stonehurst should be good to you. He should give you fine homes, beautiful fashions, jewelry and, of course, children."

"But those are not the things I want from him. I want love, and I fear that he may only want to marry me for the dowry I bring."

"Mirabella, that is precisely the reason most men marry. Wives are picked for their beauty and their dowry. You are fortunate to have both. Lord Stonehurst knows this, and that is exactly why he has agreed to go ahead with the marriage even though you were most indecorous in allowing those young men liberties."

Her uncle was not making her feel any better. She was beginning to wish she hadn't come over to see him. "I had a good reason for allowing those kisses," she said, feeling a little irritated.

His eyes rounded, and he threw up his hands in a frustrated gesture. "What pray tell could that be?"

"I was looking for someone." Mirabella stopped and took a deep breath.

What was she doing here, trying to explain all this to her uncle? Plainly he knew less about love than she did. She could see now that the sensible thing to do was talk to Camden. She had to trust him to tell her the truth. Did he want to marry her because he loved her as he had said or were his words and his loving merely a ruse to get her to marry him so that he would have the money he needed to secure his family financially?

If, after talking to him, she didn't believe Camden truly loved her, she had two choices. One was to not marry him, break the engagement, and tell her father the entire story starting when she first read Sarah's diary. The other was to make her father and Camden happy by marrying him. There was always the hope that in time he would grow to love her. What she realized now was that she didn't need her uncle to sanction either choice. She was quite capable, and it would be her decision to make after she talked with Camden. She didn't even know why she felt the need to speak to her uncle. She should have gone straight home to rest, and she would have eventually figured this out by herself.

"Who have you been looking for?"

"Oh, never mind that, Uncle." She smiled pleasantly at him. "You've already helped me come to some conclusions and I'm feeling better already. I think I was just overtired from the party, and for a few minutes I wasn't thinking straight. But now I am. I must go home and sleep."

"Mirabella, wait." He grabbed her arm and swung her around to face him.

His robe parted at his chest and his scarf fell away from his neck. Mirabella stared at a wide, raised scar. At first she couldn't believe she was seeing it. She had wanted to see such a scar for so long that she thought she must be imagining it was there. Disbelief washed over her. Surely it couldn't be on her uncle's neck. She blinked but it wouldn't go away.

"Who were you looking for?" her uncle asked again, clearly puzzled by the way she was looking at him. "Perhaps I can help you."

Mirabella couldn't breathe. God help her, she couldn't move. She wanted to deny what was before her eyes, but she couldn't. Her head was pounding. She had never suspected her uncle. Even now, she couldn't believe he would be capable of seducing Sarah.

Her voice was no more than a whisper but she managed to say, "You? Uncle Archer? I've been searching for you."

"What in the saints' names are you saying, Mirabella? You've found me. Dear girl, you are overwrought. You've always known where to find me."

She tried to calm her breathing, and to think clearly. "You were supposed to take me home from my party last night, but you didn't come. Why?"

He cleared his throat. His eyes jerked nervously. "I was there, you must have missed me."

Tension and anger built slowly, heavily in her chest, sapping her strength, making her legs weak. "No. I would remember seeing you. You never arrived."

"Of course I did. There were so many people there, you don't remember."

"You are lying to me."

"Mirabella," he exclaimed, his eyes wide with indignation. "It's not like you to be so disrespectful."

"Do you want to know who I have been looking for these past weeks?" She advanced toward him with anger shaking her whole body. "I've been searching for a man with a wide, raised scar on the right side of his neck."

He straightened his shoulders and tugged on the front of his robe, then fumbled with his scarf in an attempt to wrap it around his neck and hide the scar. "That sounds positively rude."

"You must have somehow learned I was looking for a man with a scar, and you didn't come last night because you didn't want me to see your neck."

He straightened his shoulders and fumbled with his scarf again. "It's true I didn't want to bare my shoulder in public. That is an uncivilized thing to do, but I know nothing about you looking for a man with a scar. Whatever would you do something like that for?"

"For Sarah."

"What?" His eyes widened. His face flushed red. "Sarah? Clearly you are overwrought. I'm going to dress and take you home. You need a tonic. You're obviously not feeling well."

Mirabella's stomach knotted. "I don't feel well. I'm devastated that you are the man who defiled Sarah, left her with child and to make her own way in life. She chose death for her and her baby instead."

"What? You—you're going mad."

"No. I'm right." Her voice was surprisingly firm, and that renewed her courage. "Oh, Uncle, how could you do that to her? How could you make love to her and leave her with a child?"

"Mirabella, you don't know what you are saying! That's not true."

"Don't lie to me. Don't! What you did to Sarah was bad enough. You are a vile, contemptible man."

His shoulders reared back and the veins in his neck bulged. "How dare you say such things to me after I have treated you like a daughter?"

"But look how you treated Sarah. She was like a sister to me. You seduced her, and then abandoned her like a stray animal. You didn't even offer to marry her or try to help her."

"All right. Maybe I did have relations with her, but there was no force. She wanted me. She was very pleased with the attention I showed her."

Mirabella shook her head in amazement. She could hardly look at Archer Hornbeck. "I don't know why I couldn't see you for who you are. I don't know why Papa couldn't see what a vile creature you are."

"Sarah didn't think so. I made her happy. She enjoyed my touch. She enjoyed the things I did to her."

"No." Mirabella cringed at his words and backed away from him.

"I made her happy. It's not my fault she conceived. Women like her are supposed to know how to keep things like that from happening. No one else would have touched her, given the way she looked and no dowry to speak of. She enjoyed the small amount of love I gave her."

Mirabella shook with rage. *"Love?* How dare you use that word?"

"Yes. I told her what she wanted to hear. She wanted to be loved. She wanted affection, and I gave it to her."

"If you loved her why didn't you marry her?"

"I didn't say I loved her. Blue heavens! I didn't. I only said I did because she loved me, and she wanted to hear me say it. I had no desire to marry her. I have to marry a lady of wealth. My own fortune is low, and I have to make a worthy match. Sarah offered no money."

"You are despicable."

"No, Mirabella, I am a man. That's all. A man. She wanted affection, and I gave it to her. Love is the very reason you are here now. You want Lord Stonehurst to love you. Men know women want to hear those words, but for the life of me I can't understand why."

Revulsion mingled with hurt and anger inside Mirabella. "She would have been good to you. Loyal. She would have had your sons."

"What would I want with a son and a wife whom no other man could bear to look at? I need money."

"She called you Prince Charming in her diary, but you are a beast."

"You can't fault me on this, Mirabella. Sarah was not forced to accept my attentions, and during our time together she was happy. And I certainly have no idea what happened when she went to bed the night she died."

"Happy? She died with a broken heart because of you. She killed herself and her baby so she wouldn't bring shame on my father's house."

"No, I—"

"Don't pretend you don't know or at least suspect that she drank a tonic filled with laudanum."

His eyes blinked rapidly. "I—I had no idea."

Mirabella couldn't stand to look at him. She wanted to be done with him completely and forever. "You lie again. You are not fit to be a part of this Society. I want you to leave Town immediately, or I will let it be known what you did."

Sweat had popped out on his forehead. "You can't be serious."

"Oh, yes, I am. Dead serious. A few well-chosen words to Lady Portsmand, Duchess Bickerstaff, and Countess Vanlandingham should set in motion enough gossip to make the mamas keep their daughters away from you and make all the widows stay in hiding. They will help me see to it that you will never be welcome in anyone's home."

His eyes blazed and veins popped out on either side of his neck. "You wouldn't dare."

"I promise I will. You not only betrayed Sarah, you betrayed my father's trust. You either leave quietly and immediately, or I will not rest until you are ruined in Town."

"And what if I spread the gossip about *your* indiscretions?" He pointed a short finger at her. "Have you forgotten that your reputation has already been called into question in the scandal sheets?"

"I have always known that could happen. I am prepared for it. My father would be greatly disappointed and hurt, but I know he would not abandon me the way you deserted Sarah. I will be well cared for and loved."

"And what about Lord Stonehurst, this man you claim to love. I doubt he will want to marry you if he hears all I have heard about you."

"You cannot frighten me with that. Camden knows everything about me. I have not hidden anything from him."

Mirabella's confidence grew even stronger. Camden knew all her faults, and he still wanted to marry her. He had told her he loved her. Why had she doubted that? Camden was handsome, titled. He did not have to marry her for money. If he were just after money, there were a dozen young ladies who would gladly bear his name.

Archer picked up the tail of his scarf and nervously wiped the moisture from his face. "Now who is the one lying, my dear girl? Does he know that you have kissed more than a handful of beaux?"

"I have nothing to hide from him, and I will freely tell him anything about me that he wants to know. Now, I'll have your word that you will leave before this week ends, or I will begin my campaign immediately."

"No, you can't do this." Archer grabbed for her but Mirabella spun away from him.

"You dare to touch me, and my father will not rest until you are in prison. If you want to maintain any kind of acceptable lifestyle, leave now."

Archer hesitated for a moment but backed away. "Very well. I've had enough of London anyway. Perhaps Paris is more suited to my taste."

Mirabella didn't wait to hear more. She was shaking so badly she could hardly stand. She turned and walked out of the house and straight into the arms of Camden. He hugged her tight to him for a moment before setting her away from him.

"Mirabella, never leave our bed without waking me. I've been worried about you. You're trembling. Are you all right?"

She took a deep breath and looked into Camden's eyes. She saw the same concern she'd seen that first night they met and her heart warmed toward him. He had always worried about her reputation. Even now he wouldn't hold her in public for fear of causing a scandal.

"Yes, I am. I'm going to be fine now."

"Have you seen Mr. Hornbeck? Your father said he wasn't home earlier."

"Yes, I've seen him." She looked back at the house and asked, "How did you know I was here? When did you talk to my father?"

"He came to my house looking for you when you didn't come home this morning."

Apprehension gripped her. "You didn't tell him about us, did you?"

He smiled at her and slowly tucked a strand of loose hair behind her ear. "Of course not, but I did have a difficult time explaining what your mask was doing on my foyer table."

She breathed a sigh of relief. "Thank you. You saved my reputation once again."

"Mirabella, I know who has the scar. Your father told me Mr. Hornbeck has one on his neck. I believe he is the man you seek."

Mirabella moistened her lips and exhaled deeply. A carriage passed by, but she didn't bother to look at it. "You are right. Why did you tell Papa about Sarah?"

"Don't worry, I didn't betray your confidence in me, my love. I only asked about a scar when I realized we saw everyone last night but Hornbeck. Obviously you figured it out before I did."

She liked the sound of the praise and admiration she heard in his voice. "No, I saw the scar by accident. His neckcloth was hanging loose, and I saw it just now while I was talking to him."

"Please tell me you have not confronted him."

"I have."

"It was dangerous for you to come to face him with this by yourself."

"I didn't come to confront him about Sarah. I had something else on my mind, and I saw the scar by accident. I would have never thought of Uncle—Mr. Hornbeck."

Camden's brow furrowed. He took hold of her upper arms and pulled her close. She allowed herself to melt against him and enjoy a moment of his warmth before she backed away from him.

"Did he try to harm you?" Camden asked.

"No, nothing like that." Mirabella paused while a young lady and her companion walked past them on the street in front of the house. When they were a safe distance away, she continued, "All things considered, our conversation was civil. He's going to leave Town and go to Paris."

Camden's eyes brightened with approval. "Good. You took care of everything. I'm impressed by your fortitude."

"Thankfully, I had to say very little. He said he was tired of London anyway."

"Why did you come to see him before going home?"

Mirabella didn't want any more secrets between them. She reached into the pocket of his coat and said, "Because of this." She handed him the paper. "I thought I wanted to talk to Uncle—Mr. Hornbeck about it, but when I got here I realized I didn't. You are the only one who can explain this."

Camden looked down at the paper only long enough to see what it was. His eyes met Mirabella's and didn't waver. "You have always known my family is in need of money, and I am trying to raise cash to help them."

"I know, but until this morning we only talked of staying engaged, not marrying. I hate to admit to any weakness, but I think I was suddenly conflicted."

"About marrying me?"

She didn't hesitate to tell him the truth. "Thinking you only wanted to marry me to obtain money quickly."

"I don't need money from you, Mirabella. I have handled my parents' finances, and we will be fine until I receive the money from America. Didn't you believe me when I told you I loved you?"

"Yes, at the time. Then I saw this in your coat pocket, and I wondered if you only told me those things so that I would marry you immediately."

His eyes narrowed and searched her face. "After what we shared, did you really have so little faith in me?"

"Only for a short time. I do believe you love me as I am in love with you. I want to marry you, Camden, and be a good and devoted wife to you."

He stepped very close to her. "Hear me well, Mirabella. I love you today. I loved you yesterday, and I will love you tomorrow. I would never marry you for money. My family will have money as soon as my stake in the Maryland company is sold."

"Camden, I didn't want to doubt you. I must have been too tired and overwrought about the party and Prince Charming to think properly."

"And you still are. I see you are dead on your feet. Come, and let's get you home to rest and see your father. He's worried about you."

"Oh, I know I need to tell Papa everything."

"No. I don't think it's necessary to tell him any more than we must. Mirabella, I'm glad you found Prince Charming and have avenged Sarah by forcing Hornbeck to leave London. I've said it before, but I mean it more now. You are a woman of rare courage to take on the task you did."

"Thank you for all your help, Camden. I would not have found him without your help."

"Me?" He frowned. "I did nothing. And I arrived too late to help today."

"You believed in me. You didn't forsake me when

I went beyond the pale. I love you," she whispered with all the love in her heart.

He smiled at her. "You are my true love, Mirabella, and, as soon as I get you in the privacy of my carriage, I'm going to show you how much I love you."

Epilogue

MARRIAGE FOR THE VISCOUNT AND SCANDAL FOR THE EARL

Hmm. Where to begin? There was an elegant madness to the night. Delicious tales continue to trickle in from the masked ball of the year. Most assuredly nothing can top the fact that the very day after the toga ball, the hostess's father applied for a special license and Miss Mirabella Whittingham is now Viscountess Stonehurst. Hmm. One has to wonder what happened to cause their haste to wed, when both bride and groom had declared they would not marry before next spring. Could it be that her daringly low-cut toga slipped off her other shoulder? Hmm.

But the latest delicious morsel of a tale involves Albert Farebrother, the Earl of Glenbrighton. It seems his mistress took it upon herself to defy a strict unwritten protocol and attend the masked ball. No doubt she expected to go unnoticed. All was well until someone, we won't give away our secret sources, mentioned her presence to the Countess. The Countess

marched up to the paramour, who was talking to the
Earl at the time, and threw a glass of champagne into
the mistress's face. Having not a drop of champagne
left to fling at her husband, the quick thinking Countess quickly dipped her glass into a nearby birdbath
and splashed his face with the drink of birds. One has
to admire the Countess's aplomb during the unfortunate incident. But which one will be the first to show
their face in Society again? Hmm. One has to wonder
what was said in that house later that evening. Do tell
if you hear anything.

—Lord Truefitt, *Society's Daily Column*

"You are beautiful, Mirabella, but never more so
than by candlelight."

Mirabella looked up from the scandal sheet she
had been reading to see her husband walking into the
bedroom of the small town house they had rented. She
laid the newsprint on the table.

She smiled at him and said, "Good evening, my
lord husband."

"And to you, my lady. I'm sorry to be later than I
said I would, but I made a trip by Hornbeck's house.
It's been cleaned out. He's gone."

A sad relief washed over her. "It's for the best. I
didn't relish what I would have had to do to him."

"But I have no doubt you would have accom-
plished it. That's why I made sure he was gone."

"Thank you, Camden. I can finally put Sarah and
Archer Hornbeck behind me."

"I'm very happy about that. I see you are already

dressed for bed. How very nice." He pulled on the white ribbon that held the neckline of her night rail together and let the bodice fall open. He bent his head and kissed the swell of her breasts.

Mirabella wound her arms around his neck. "I'm glad you are home."

He smiled at her and said, "You are an eager wife."

"I have reason to be, my lord. You do know just how to please me."

He laughed against her skin. "I'm a fortunate man to have such a willing lady waiting at home for me."

He placed his hands to each side of her face and lowered his face to hers for a deep kiss. When he raised his head, he said, "Is that a wrinkle of worry I see on your brow?"

"I must have read that paper five times already. I can't help but concern myself about the countess. I've met her, and she seemed such a warm and caring person. This was an absolutely dreadful thing to happen to her."

He pulled Mirabella into his arms and held her tightly against him. "Don't worry about her. She and Albert might have a spot of trouble now, but all will be well by the time the new babe arrives. I would hope Albert would pick a more discreet mistress next time."

Mirabella raised her head and looked at her husband. "Camden, do you plan to employ a mistress? I realize it is all the rage and—"

He silenced her by placing his thumb over her lips. "Listen to me, my love. I have no need of a mistress in my life. I have a bride who is almost"—he stopped and smiled—"but thankfully not more woman than I can handle. You need have no fear in that direction." He kissed her sweetly on the mouth, and gently moved his lips down her neck and back to the crest of her breasts.

"Thank you, Camden." She ran her hands over his strong shoulders. "I have no wish to share you with another woman."

"Why don't you invite the Countess to tea?"

"Do you think she would come?"

He continued to graze her neck and chest with his lips, leaving little raindrop kisses on her skin. "You won't know unless you ask. But I'm thinking she probably needs a friend right now."

"I think I will. I can call on her tomorrow after my visit with Papa."

"How did your father look today when you saw him?"

"He's still quite tired from all that has gone on with the ball and the wedding, but I believe he had a little more color to his cheeks today."

"Good. And what did he say of Hornbeck leaving Town?"

"Only that he wished Mr. Hornbeck wasn't going. And perhaps he could find another friend to visit as often as Mr. Hornbeck had."

"Did your father mention grandchildren again?"

She laughed lightly and planted a quick kiss on the corner of his mouth. "What do you think, my lord?"

"I suspect he will mention them every day until you are with child."

She slid her hand down the front of his pantaloons and felt his hardness beneath the clothing. "We would not want to disappoint him, would we?"

"Absolutely not. Help me undress, my love."

"First, I have something for you." She left his arms and walked back over to the table and picked up a sheet of paper. She handed it to Camden.

He glanced at it and looked back to Mirabella. "What is this?"

"It is the list of suspects I made from Sarah's dance cards. You wanted to know how many men I had kissed." She took a deep breath. "They are there for you to count. The ones with an X by the names are the ones I allowed to kiss me."

His eyes searched hers, but he never looked back at the paper. "I do not need to see this. It no longer matters to me."

"Are you sure, my lord? It was once very important to you." He walked over to the candle and stuck the sheet into the flame. It caught fire with a swoosh. He watched it burn to only a small piece before throwing it into the fireplace to become ash..

"I don't know why I thought it was important. I think I was jealous that other men's lips had touched yours, and I didn't want to admit it. I didn't want you to know that I wanted you the moment I saw you standing on the street. I didn't know how to handle those feelings because I never wanted to fall in love."

"Camden, I found no joy in any of those kisses. You are the first and only man I have kissed because I wanted to. The night you were so angry with me and you kissed me, I felt I was on fire—and that flame has not gone out."

"I'll see it doesn't." He scooped her up and laid her

on the bed. He leaned over her and placed a hand on her breast over her heart. "Believe me when I say it does not matter how many men you have kissed. There is no reason to ever speak of it again. I love you."

Mirabella placed her fingertips to his lips and smiled gently at him. "And I love you with all my heart, my husband."

"You are my bride, my wife, and my lover."

She raised her eyebrows. "And if you should ever have need of a mistress?"

He laughed. "I know where to find you."

"Yes. I do not intend to share you."

"Have no fear, my darling. You are all I need in a woman, Mirabella. Wife, lover, and companion for all my life."

"I am so very happy, my lord."

"So am I."

Camden lowered his lips to hers, and Mirabella thrilled to his touch.

The End

Dear Reader,

I hope you enjoyed Mirabella and Camden's story as much as I enjoyed writing it. *Never a Bride* is a special book to me because it was my first book set in the Regency time period, and it started my love affair with sexy, titled gentlemen.

I'm currently putting the finishing touches on my ninth Regency Romance, titled *A Gentleman Never Tells,* which will be published in Spring of 2011. And if you haven't had the chance to pick up *A Duke to Die For, A Marquis to Marry,* or *An Earl to Enchant,* all three books are still available at your favorite local bookseller or any online bookstore.

I look forward to hearing from my readers so please visit me at ameliagrey.com or email me at ameliagrey@comcast.net.

Happy reading,
Amelia Grey

About the Author

Amelia Grey grew up in a small town in the Florida Panhandle. She has been happily married to her high school sweetheart for more than twenty-five years.

Amelia has won the Booksellers Best Award and Aspen Gold Award for writing as Amelia Grey. Writing as Gloria Dale Skinner, she has won the coveted Romantic Times Award for Love and Laughter, the Maggie Award, and the Affaire de Coeur Award. Her books have been sold in many countries in Europe, in Russia, and in China, and they have also been featured in Doubleday and Rhapsody Book Clubs.

Amelia loves flowers, candlelight, sweet smiles, gentle laughter, and sunshine.

Read on for the first in Amelia Grey's
Rogues' Dynasty series

A *Duke* TO
Die For

Now available from Sourcebooks Casablanca

One

My Dearest Grandson Lucien,

You would do well in life to heed Lord Chesterfield's wise words: "Never put off till tomorrow what you can do today."

Your loving Grandmother,
Lady Elder

LUCIEN TRENT BLAKEWELL, THE FIFTH DUKE OF Blakewell, strode through the front door of his town house, taking off his riding gloves.

"Your Grace, I'm glad you're home."

"Not now, Ashby," Blake said, tossing his gloves, hat, and cloak into the butler's hands without breaking his stride. "I don't have time." He'd stayed too long at the shooting match, and now he was running late.

One of his cousins was racing a new horse in Hyde Park at four o'clock, and the other had a high-stakes card game starting at six. Blake didn't plan on missing either event. But in order to make both, he had to finish reviewing at least one account book for his solicitor. The poor fellow had been begging for them for over a month.

From the corridor, Blake walked into his book room. Piled high on his desk was the stack of ledgers, numerous miscellaneous correspondence, and invitations he'd left unopened for weeks.

He shrugged out of his coat, loosened his neckcloth, and sat down at his desk with an impatient sigh. There were times when being a duke was downright hellish.

Grudgingly, he opened the top book, determined to make a dent in the work he had to do.

"I'm sorry to disturb you, Your Grace," Ashby said from the doorway.

Blake didn't bother to glance up from the ledger he was thumbing through, trying to find where he'd left off the last time he looked at it... which was too many days ago to remember. He still hadn't become completely used to hearing himself called 'Your Grace,' even though his father had been dead almost two years.

It was a time-consuming task, keeping up-to-date with all his holdings and property, not to mention the details of the various businesses in which his father had invested over the years. His solicitor constantly sent documents for him to sign or account books to check. And, last year when his grandmother had passed on, her estate had added more responsibilities to his already full desk of unattended paperwork.

His new role in life had certainly curtailed his once daily and quite enjoyable activities of riding, fencing, and late afternoon games of billiards and cards at White's or one of the other gentlemen's clubs he belonged to. He was not accustomed to being on anyone's schedule but his own.

The butler cleared his throat.

"Yes, Ashby, what is it?" Blake finally said when it was apparent the man wasn't going to leave him alone until he had his say.

"There's a young lady here to see you, sir."

That got Blake's attention. He glanced up at the tall, thin, and immaculately dressed butler, who wore his long graying hair held neatly away from his sharp face in a queue.

"A young lady, you say?"

"Yes, Your Grace."

"Who is she?"

"Miss Henrietta Tweed."

"Tweed," Blake said aloud as he thought about the name for a moment. He couldn't place it. "Who is with her?"

"Just her maid."

"No other chaperone?"

"None that I saw."

That was odd.

It was unusual for a young lady, or any gentleman, to call on him without making prior arrangements—and altogether inappropriate for a lady to do so without a suitable chaperone. Blake shrugged. On another afternoon he might have been intrigued by this strange request to see him, but not today. He didn't have time to entertain anyone.

"Just take her card and send her away."

Blake picked up his quill, dipped it in the ink jar

he'd just opened, and returned his attention to the numbers in front of him.

"I tried that, Your Grace. She says she doesn't have a card."

The quill stilled in his hand. That was most curious, too. A woman without an appropriate chaperone and without a proper calling card. For half a second he wondered if one of the ladies he'd met earlier in the day at Hyde Park had followed him home. And there were other possibilities. It was rare, but he knew that sometimes a lady of the evening would be bold enough to seek out a titled man in hopes of bettering her station in life by earning a few coins or becoming his latest mistress.

Blake's interest was piqued once again, though he had to admit almost anything could take his mind off accounts and ledgers.

He glanced back up at the butler. "What does she look like?" he asked, thinking that would help him determine if she warranted interrupting his work.

Ashby's chin lifted and his eyebrows rose slightly. "Like a young lady."

Sometimes Blake wished he hadn't kept his father's annoying butler. The old man could be downright impudent at times. But Ashby kept the household and the sizable staff running in near-perfect order. The butler's work was testimony to the care with which his father had trained the man. That, and that alone, was what kept the aging servant at his job.

"Did she say why she wanted to see me?"

"Not exactly, Your Grace."

In exasperation, Blake laid down the quill he had just picked up. "Ashby, what the hell did she say?"

Unflustered, the butler replied, "She said you were expecting her."

"Was I?" Blake asked. Since Blake had turned off his father's secretary a few months earlier, the butler had tried to help him keep up with his social calendar, but so far neither one of them was doing a good job.

"Not that I'm aware of, Your Grace. She also said that her trunks were on the front steps."

Blake made a noise in his throat that sounded like a mixture of a grunt and a laugh. He must have been in too big a hurry to notice her luggage when he came through the front door.

"What the devil?" Blake said. "I'm expecting no one, especially a young woman with baggage and no proper chaperone. She obviously has the wrong house." He rose from his chair. "Did you question her about who she is looking for?"

"Yes, Your Grace. She said the Duke of Blakewell was expecting her."

"That's not bloody likely when I have no recollection of knowing anyone by the name of Tweed."

"She also suggested that I should speak to you at once so that you could clear up what she called my obvious confusion."

That sounded rather impertinent coming from someone who was apparently befuddled herself. No doubt the quickest way to handle this situation was for him to take a moment or two to speak with her.

Blake looked down at his paper-cluttered desk. His eyes centered on the open book in front of him, and he swore softly to himself. Reviewing the latest entries would have to wait again.

"Show her to the front parlor and say I'll be in to see her."

"Right away, Your Grace." Ashby turned stiffly and walked out.

Blake marked his place in the ledger with a dry quill. He hastily retied his neckcloth and reached for his coat. No doubt the woman had him mixed up with someone else. The sooner he dealt with the waif and sent her on her way, the faster he could get back to checking the balances in the accounts book so he wouldn't miss the race or the card game. For the most part he got along quite well with his cousins, but they would be unforgiving if they felt he'd slighted them.

When Blake approached the doorway to the drawing room, he saw a short, rotund lady with her back to him warming herself in front of the low-burning fireplace. It took only a glance at the fabric of her cloak and bonnet to know that she was not a lady of means.

What was Ashby thinking to allow her entrance into the house?

"Miss Tweed," he said, striding into the room, determined to set her straight and then have a word with his errant butler.

The chit turned to face him and he immediately realized she had on a maid's frock. At the same time, from the corner of his eye, he saw a rather tall, slender, young lady rise from a side chair in the far corner and come toward him. When he looked at her, Blake felt his stomach do a slow roll. She moved with exquisite grace and an inner confidence lacking in most of the young ladies in Society.

Big, almond-shaped eyes—bluer than a midsummer

sky and fringed with long black lashes—pierced him with a wary look of impatience. Her lips were full, beautifully sculpted, and the shade of spring's first rose. The color of her skin was a sheer, pale ivory, and her complexion was flawless.

She was the loveliest creature he'd ever seen.

She wore an expensively tailored black cape that parted down the front as she walked, showing a blush-colored traveling dress. Her wide-brimmed bonnet with tightly woven trim matched her cape and gloves. He couldn't help but wonder what color of hair was hidden beneath her headpiece.

For some reason he found it exceedingly seductive the way the satin ribbon of her bonnet had been tied into a perfect bow under her chin. He had a sudden urge to reach up, pull on the end of the black ribbon, and untie it... despite the fact that every inch of her said "lady."

"Yes, I'm Henrietta Tweed." She inclined her head a little as if pondering whether to say more. "I'm waiting for the Duke of Blakewell."

Blake bowed and then said, "At your service, Miss Tweed. I am he."

Her eyes narrowed slightly. That was the only outward sign that she was confused for a moment. Quickly, she regained her air of confidence. She lowered her lashes as she curtsied in front of him.

"I apologize, Your Grace; I didn't recognize you."

A prickle of desire rushed through him and settled low in his groin as he watched her dutifully acknowledge his title. He found everything about her tremendously seductive.

"No harm done," he said.

Blake's gaze swept over her face once again. She appeared to be a self-assured, capable young lady who wasn't the least bit intimidated by his title. He also noticed she wasn't indifferent to his appearance as her gaze slowly swept down to his riding boots and then innocently crawled back up to his face. Her close observation of him sent a rush of heat like he hadn't felt in years searing through his loins.

Ashby cleared his throat. "Should I have Cook prepare tea, Your Grace?"

Despite all the work he had to do, not to mention contending with a cheeky butler, Blake found himself agreeing. Quite frankly, how could he say no to this intriguing lady?

"Yes, Ashby, and take the young lady's wrap. Have tea served in here after you show Miss Tweed's maid to the kitchen for refreshments."

"Yes, Your Grace."

Blake watched as his unexpected guest took off her gloves and then untied the bow beneath her chin. Her hands were lovely and without jewels. He'd never realized just how stimulating it could be to watch a lady take off her bonnet until he found himself experiencing another twinge of desire as the soft, fluttering ribbons slid along her shoulders.

She had lush, golden blonde hair arranged neatly on top of her head, and Blake had no doubt that it would be gorgeous hanging down her back. She handed her bonnet, cape, and gloves to her maid and softly told the woman she would be fine alone and to follow the butler to the kitchen.

Blake waited to speak until the maid and Ashby left the room. "I'm afraid I don't know of you, Miss Tweed. Who is your father?"

With ease and more self-confidence than anyone her age should have, she walked closer to him, keeping her gaze pinned on his. He liked the way her carriage was straight but not stiff. He liked the way she looked directly at him and didn't try to impress him with batting lashes, false smiles, or the unnatural soft voice some ladies used when talking to him.

Blake also liked the way she looked in her simple, high-waisted traveling dress. It was long-sleeved and quite modest for the current fashion. The fabric was of a fine quality, though not the best available. The neckline was high and trimmed in dainty pink lace that made her look absolutely fetching.

He was more curious than ever to know who she was.

"My father was Sir William Tweed. Considering your age, you probably never met him. I must assume your father knew him."

"And what makes you say that?"

"Because the Duke of Blakewell is the last name on my father's list."

What in the hell was she talking about? He became more intrigued with each word she spoke.

"What list is that, Miss Tweed?"

She clasped her lovely hands together in front of her, and once again she looked straight into his eyes. "If you don't know what I'm talking about, Your Grace, we have a problem."

"At last we agree on something. Those are the truest words you have spoken thus far."

A wrinkle of concern settled between her eyes, but it in no way detracted from her beauty.

"You were supposed to receive a letter and some rather important documents from a solicitor named Mr. Conrad Milton that would announce my arrival and explain everything about me."

Blake immediately thought of his desk. Not only was the blasted thing covered in account books that hadn't been reviewed, along with papers and documents that hadn't been signed, it was littered with all kinds of correspondence that hadn't been opened.

For the first time since becoming a duke, Blake wished he had taken his responsibilities as the Duke of Blakewell a little more seriously.

"I've been behind on mail recently. Just tell me why you are here."

"All right." She unclasped her hands and calmly let her arms fall comfortably to her sides. "I am your ward and your house is supposed to be my new home."

A Duke TO Die For

BY AMELIA GREY

THE RAKISH FIFTH DUKE OF BLAKEWELL'S UNEXPECTED AND shockingly lovely new ward has just arrived, claiming to carry a curse that has brought each of her previous guardians to an untimely end…

Praise for Amelia Grey's Regency romances:

"This beguiling romance steals your heart, lifts your spirits and lights up the pages with humor and passion." —Romantic Times

"Each new Amelia Grey tale is a diamond. Ms. Grey…is a master storyteller." —Affaire de Coeur

"Readers will be quickly drawn in by the lively pace, the appealing protagonists, and the sexual chemistry that almost visibly shimmers between." —Library Journal

978-1-4022-1767-8 • $6.99 U.S./$7.99 CAN

A *Marquis* TO *Marry*

BY AMELIA GREY

"A captivating mix of discreet intrigue
and potent passion." —*Booklist*

"A gripping plot, great love scenes, and well-drawn
characters make this book impossible to put down."
—*The Romance Studio*

The Marquis of Raceworth is shocked to find a young
and beautiful Duchess on his doorstep—especially when
she accuses him of stealing her family's priceless pearls!
Susannah, Duchess of Brookfield, refuses to be intimidated by
the Marquis's commanding presence and chiseled good looks.
And when the pearls disappear, Race and Susannah will have
to work together—and discover they can't live apart…

Praise for *A Duke to Die For:*

"A lusciously spicy romp." —*Library Journal*

"Deliciously sensual… storyteller extraordinaire Amelia Grey
grabs you by the heart, draws you in, and does not let go."
—*Romance Junkies*

"Intriguing danger, sharp humor, and plenty of simmering
sexual chemistry." —*Booklist*

978-1-4022-1760-9 • $6.99 U.S./$8.99 CAN

AN *Earl* TO *Enchant*

BY AMELIA GREY

HE'S DETERMINED NOT TO BE A HERO…

Lord Morgandale is as notorious as he is dashing, and he's determined no woman will tie him down. But from the moment Arianna Sweet appears on his doorstep, he cannot resist the lure of her fascinating personality, exotic wardrobe, and tempting green eyes…

Arianna never imagined the significance of her father's research until after his untimely death. Now she is in possession of his groundbreaking discovery, one that someone would kill for. She can't tell Lord Morgandale her secret, but she knows she needs his help, desperately…

Praise for Amelia Grey

"Bewitching, beguiling, and unbelievably funny."
—Fresh Fiction

"Witty dialogue and clever schemes…Grey's characters will charm readers." —Booklist

"A gripping plot, great love scenes, and well-drawn characters…impossible to put down."
—The Romance Studio

978-1-4022-1761-6 • $7.99 U.S/$9.99 CAN/£4.99 UK

My
UNFAIR
Lady

BY KATHRYNE KENNEDY

A WILD WEST BEAUTY TAKES
VICTORIAN LONDON BY STORM

The impoverished Duke of Monchester despises the rich Americans who flock to London, seeking to buy their way into the ranks of the British peerage. Frontier-bred Summer Wine Lee has no interest in winning over London society—it's the New York bluebloods and her future mother-in-law she's determined to impress. She knows the cost of smoothing her rough-and-tumble frontier edges will be high. But she never imagined it might cost her heart…

978-1-4022-2990-9 • $7.99 U.S./$9.99 CAN

Lessons in French

BY LAURA KINSALE
New York Times bestselling author

"An exquisite romance and an instant classic." —
Elizabeth Hoyt

HE'S EXACTLY THE KIND OF TROUBLE SHE CAN'T RESIST…

Trevelyan and Callie were childhood sweethearts with a taste for adventure. Until the fateful day her father drove Trevelyan away in disgrace. Nine long, lonely years later, Trevelyan returns, determined to sweep Callie into one last, fateful adventure, just for the two of them…

"Kinsale's delightful characters and delicious wit enliven this poignant tale…It will charm your heart!" —*Sabrina Jeffries*

"Laura Kinsale creates magic. Her characters live, breathe, charm, and seduce, and her writing is as delicious and perfectly served as wine in a crystal glass. When you're reading Kinsale, as with all great indulgences, it feels too good to stop." —*Lisa Kleypas*

978-1-4022-3701-0 • $7.99 U.S./$8.99 CAN

Uncertain Magic

LAURA KINSALE

A MAN DAMNED BY SUSPICION AND INNUENDO...

Dreadful rumors swirl around the impoverished Irish lord known as "The Devil Earl." But Faelan Savigar hides a dark secret, for even he doesn't know what dreadful deeds he may be capable of.

Roderica Delamore, cursed by the gift of sight, fears no man will ever want a wife who can read his every thought and emotion, until she encounters Faelan. As the two find their way to each other against all odds, Roddy becomes determined to save Faelen from his terrifying and mysterious ailment. But will their love end up saving him...or destroying her?

Praise for Laura Kinsale

"Laura Kinsale creates magic." —Lisa Kleypas, *New York Times* bestselling author of *Seduce Me at Sunrise*

"Magic and beauty flow from Laura Kinsale's pen."
—*Romantic Times*

978-1-4022-3702-7 • $9.99 U.S/$11.99 CAN

MIDSUMMER MOON

BY LAURA KINSALE
New York Times bestselling author

"The acknowledged master."
—*Albany Times-Union*

**IF HE REALLY LOVED HER,
WOULDN'T HE HELP HER REALIZE HER DREAM?**

When inventor Merlin Lambourne is endangered by Napoleon's advancing forces, Lord Ransom Falconer, in service of his government, comes to her rescue and falls under the spell of her beauty and absent-minded brilliance. But he is horrified by her dream of building a flying machine—and not only because he is determined to keep her safe.

"Laura Kinsale writes the kind of works that live in your heart." —Elizabeth Grayson

"A true storyteller, Laura Kinsale has managed to break all the rules of standard romance writing and come away shining."
—*San Diego Union-Tribune*

978-1-4022-4689-0 • $9.99 U.S./$11.99 CAN

THE
PRINCE
OF
MIDNIGHT

BY LAURA KINSALE
New York Times bestselling author

"Readers should be enchanted."
—*Publishers Weekly*

INTENT ON REVENGE, ALL SHE WANTS FROM
HIM IS TO LEARN HOW TO KILL

Lady Leigh Strachan has crossed all of France in search of S.T. Maitland, nobleman, highwayman, and legendary swordsman, once known as the Prince of Midnight. Now he's hiding out in a crumbling castle with a tame wolf as his only companion, trying to conceal his deafness and desperation. Leigh is terribly disappointed to find the man behind the legend doesn't meet her expectations. But when they're forced on a quest together, she discovers the dangerous and vital man behind the mask, and he finds a way to touch her ice cold heart.

"No one—repeat, no one—writes historical romance better." —Mary Jo Putney

978-1-4022-4686-9 • $9.99 U.S./$11.99 CAN

SEIZE THE FIRE

BY LAURA KINSALE
New York Times bestselling author

> "Magic and beauty flow from
> Laura Kinsale's pen." —*Romantic Times*

AN UNLIKELY PRINCESS SHIPWRECKED
WITH A WAR HERO WHO'S GOT HELL TO PAY

Her Serene Highness Olympia of Oriens—plump, demure,
and idealistic—longs to return to her tiny, embattled land
and lead her people to justice and freedom. Famous hero
Captain Sheridan Drake, destitute and tormented by night-
mares of the carnage he's seen, means only to rob and abandon her. What is Olympia to do with the tortured man
behind the hero's façade? And how will they cope when
their very survival depends on each other?

> "One of the best writers in the history of the
> romance genre." —*All About Romance*

978-1-4022-4683-8 • $9.99 U.S./$11.99 CAN

WHAT WOULD
JANE AUSTEN
DO?

BY LAURIE BROWN

Eleanor goes back in time to save a man's life, but could it be she's got the wrong villain?

Lord Shermont, renowned rake, feels an inexplicable bond to the mysterious woman with radical ideas who seems to know so much...but could she be a Napoleonic spy?

Thankfully, Jane Austen's sage advice prevents a fatal mistake...

At a country house party, Eleanor makes the acquaintance of Jane Austen, whose sharp wit can untangle the most complicated problem. With an international intrigue going on before her eyes, Eleanor must figure out which of two dueling gentlemen is the spy, and which is the man of her dreams.

978-1-4022-1831-6 • $6.99 U.S. / $7.99 CAN